THE CARDUCCI CONVERGENCE

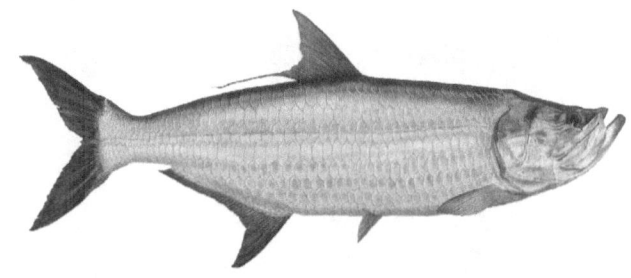

THE CARDUCCI
CONVERGENCE

Book One of the Trilogy
By Nicolas Olano

STORYARTSMEDIA

Published by Story Arts Media
PO Box 1230, Boulder, CO 80306
www.storyartsmedia.com

ISBN: 978-0-9863741-1-1
Library of Congress Control Number: 2014959997

Cover and Interior Design: Joseph Daniel, www.storyartsmedia.com
Illustration on Cover and Title Page © 2015 Flick Ford, www.flickford.com

POD Edition
Printed in the United States

For my love Lilita

Thanks to my publisher Joseph Daniel, editors
Elizabeth Darby Junkin-Shaw and Elizabeth Cameron,
and the editorial house of Story Arts Media
for taking a risk with me.

Beginning

*T*he massive, six-foot-long tarpon jumped nearly its length out of
the water, every inch of the spectacular fish alive with battle and
*fury. It would not be taken, not now, not ever. With strength that was
commensurate to its girth and weight the silver king stretched the
16-pound line-class tippet to its limit; but somehow it held. At the
other end, grasping the 9-foot, 12-weight fly rod and hanging on with
all he had, Uncle Sal was enthralled by the combativeness of the tarpon – a larger specimen typical of the Sarasota coast in western Florida, but not a record by far. Huge fish have been caught here and much
bigger ones have escaped heartbroken anglers who for few fleeting
seconds believed they were about to make saltwater fly-fishing history.*

*In a dramatic occurrence not unheard of by veteran saltwater an-
glers the tarpon jumped again, flying into the boat in a chaos of clat-
tering scales and copious slime, catching Uncle Sal and his guide totally by surprise. With one swipe of its powerful tail the fish broke
Sal's left femur and shards of the bone tore through his femoral artery,
opening it like a faucet and covering the bottom of the skiff in blood.
Within two minutes Salvatore di Dio Carducci was dead.*

*Semi-retired head of one of New York's most prominent Mafia
families, Sal had met his end in a battle of his choosing. The king of
fish had dealt the king of crime a fatal blow. The tarpon, quivering on*

the deck of the skiff, flopped itself back into the water, leaving its destruction to the mobster's guide/bodyguard whose desperate calls over the marine emergency frequency brought the Sarasota shore patrol and a Coast Guard boat that were nearby, but only to be witnesses to a pathetic scene: a grown man crying over the bloody body of his friend as he rocked back and forth, talking in Italian to the corpse whose head he cradled with filial concern.

No one knew it yet, but this death would send shock waves throughout organized crime around the world. Yet for now the only waves in motion were small ones that lapped against the skiff's hull replacing with their rhythmic thumping the now-silent heart of Uncle Sal.

* * *

Uncle Sal, as Salvatore di Dio Carducci was universally known, lay on the medical examiner's table while the physician filled out the papers that confirmed his death had come about by misfortune and that no foul play was contemplated. A terrified and bereaved bodyguard had told a story that had been confirmed by another angler who had witnessed the tragedy from another boat a couple of hundred feet away. The body, now washed clean of fish slime and blood, would be released to a local mortuary to prepare it for shipment via private jet to New York.

On the flight down in Sal's G5, Ernie Goldman, Sal's long time attorney and trusted friend, was talking to Marco Carducci, Salvatore's bereaved nephew and one of the two men who managed all of the Carducci family business. The other one, who by necessity stayed in New York, was Ian Carlo de la Rosa, Salvatore's other nephew.

The older man was deferential to Marco, a handsome man in his late thirties with a full head of brown hair that already had snow over the ears. He had soulful eyes that could go from soft to granite in a flash, and signs of an easy smile. The lawyer leaned forward in his seat and spoke in a low voice even though they were the only ones in the passenger cabin.

"We'll get him home by tonight. His wife understands what has to be done and is cooperating in every way. We'll talk about her later but for now we have to prepare a press release, because if they don't have something soon they'll make up all sorts of junk and we don't need that."

"I just have a couple of things that I believe should be included. Other than that I think someone from your office should prepare a statement and we'll look at it."

"Sure, what do you want said?"

"That Sal died doing something he truly loved. Fly fishing had become his passion and he died in his game. Then say something that indicates that Sal was retired so that people believe it's business as usual for the family and that Ian Carlo and I are at the helm. No need for somebody trying to take over what they might think is an empty seat."

"The first part for sure, but the part about you and Ian Carlo has already been communicated through the right channels and doesn't need to go into the press release."

"You're right. I'm not thinking straight. This really caught me off guard, Ernie…Let's get Sal home and then all three of us can sit down and talk this through."

They both leaned back in their chairs and became lost in their private memories of Uncle Sal. For Ernie Goldman it was a long flight back in time. Forty-some years ago he was fighting tooth and nail for the underprivileged and indefensible as a public defender in Rochester New York. For a Jew in those days it was a battle to get ahead in life if you didn't have a rabbi to whose coattails one could hitch his fortunes. Unfortunately Ernie, thin, short, and somewhat mousy looking with red hair, did not inspire much in the Jewish community of Rochester and thus lacked the opportunities others had. He was not considered a good catch for the wealthier girls of influential fathers, and his law degree was from a community college that did not bring with it influence or stature among peers. On the other hand, Ernie had a mind as sharp as a razor and read between the lines of the law, a quality that allowed him to win case after case without the need to mesmerize juries with presence and eloquence.

One such case was that of a young Salvatore, whose misfortune had brought him before the judge with a charge of aggravated assault upon another man from whom he was trying to collect on a bet. Research showed that the victim of the assault had been before the courts on exactly the same charge on more than one occasion and Ernie finagled for Sal a self-defense plea that stuck. Two weeks later he was called by a prestigious firm in New York City and offered a job he could not refuse. Soon after he established himself in the city, Ernie was invited to lunch with an important client. The client turned out to be Salvatore's father Giacomo, who, accompanied by his son, explained to Ernie that he would be working almost exclusively for their family. Ernie, who had no reason to be manacled by a moral compass, fell into the family with ease and became Sal's close advisor, teaching him how the law was written to accommodate the powerful, and how to avoid the pitfalls threatening anyone who wanted to operate marginal to that law.

When it was time to make his bones, Sal was thoroughly prepared and the day he shot and killed his father's main rival he did so with absolute *sangfroid* by walking up to the man as he got out of his limo and firing two bullets into him and two into his bodyguard. He dropped the gun from his gloved hand and walked twenty feet to the subway entrance where he disappeared into a panicked crowd. Later, witnesses contradicted themselves as to the size, color, demeanor, and posture of the assailant, as well as to his clothing. On the other hand, five witnesses, including Ernie, testified that Sal was at the other side of town at a charity function for the Benevolent Police and Firefighters Association, whose director backed the statement. Ernie never doubted for a second that his loyalty was with Salvatore di Dio Carducci and no one else. He had acted accordingly during forty years watching his friend's legal back and building a bulletproof corporate structure that kept Sal far away from the courts of law. Now he was on his way to say a last goodbye to his friend and mentor. Then it would be time to carry out the very explicit instructions as to the succession of Sal's empire, a daunting but necessary and, to a degree, satisfying task, because he would be rendering this one last service to his dear friend.

1

From the moment that he heard of Uncle Sal's death from Marco, Ian Carlo tightened the reins on the crews and the multiple operations that were beholden to the Carducci family in order to avoid confrontation with the law or, worse, from violent gangs that were always trying to capture turf. He made it known that the slightest disrespect during the mourning period would be taken as a personal offense and everyone knew what that meant. Ian Carlo made himself visible all over the place. He visited madams and loan sharks, underground betting establishments and rendering warehouses where stolen goods piled up for later sale and distribution. He made it a point to let competitors know that this was not the moment to pull a fast one...and then he went into a few hours of deep mourning for his beloved uncle. He sat quietly at the Church of the Transfiguration on Mulberry Street and wept for the father figure he had lost. The Chinese who are today's more frequent parishioners were politely told to come back later by several large men at the door.

It was late that night as the G5 cruised at 41,000 feet with five mourners and the simple casket that held the body of Salvatore di Dio Carducci. Patricia, his widow, sat next to the coffin while Marco and Ernie stayed up front, leaving her to her thoughts and private mourning. She was a mystery to both men. Sal had made a point of keeping her away from his nephews. They had only met her twice in ten years, once at a wedding and once at a funeral. They knew that Sal adored her and once when Ernie insinuated to Sal that she might be a gold digger he had smiled and then burst out laughing but made no further comment other than to tell Ernie to "forget about it."

Three days later the viewing began at Giovanni Morelia's funeral home. The undertaker had rendered a masterful job and Uncle Sal looked better than he had in years. Marco or Ian Carlo was always present with him, but rarely together; someone had to mind the business at all times. His widow, a beautiful woman from Peru, was well dressed in black and received the condolences with quiet politeness but deferred to Marco or Ian Carlo when it came to family protocol.

Salvatore's wake and funeral were a solemn affair. The families from New York, as well as the rest of the country, and some delegates from overseas sent their top people to honor the big man…and have a look at the heirs. Then there were the business associates of the legitimate world – lawyers, bankers, brokers, tailors, physicians, and last but not least, government personnel from three-letter agencies who, over the years, had tried and tried, and failed and failed, to pin something on Sal; not even the taxman had any luck.

The funeral was a parade. Twelve flower wagons followed the hearse and the limos with the principal mourners, one with the widow and her father Francisco Lujan, one with Ian Carlo, his wife, and his daughter, and one with Marco, Ernie, Ernie's wife Sara, and his son Samuel. Father Cellini talked about Salvatore's generosity and his gracious attitude towards all. He almost blew it lapsing into a soliloquy about Sal as the good thief until he saw faces in the pews scowling in disapproval. Visibly shaken over his indiscretion, he rapidly steered his oratory to safer ground

Salvatore was planted in style and after the interment most in attendance went to the house on Third Avenue, where caterers had set up a generous buffet and two well-appointed bars awaited the thirsty.

The widow, Patricia Lujan, a Latin beauty who had just turned forty and looked just thirty, was dressed in a very simple black Valentino and walked on Fratelli Rossetti shoes, also black but with a very slight gold rim. She played unconsciously with a strand of black pearls around her neck, which were large and fine enough to balance the budget of the small island nation from which they came. Her ring, a three-carat D class, was not a gift from Sal but rather had belonged to her mother. It split the scarce light that filtered through the veils and sent out flashes of dampened fire impossible to miss. Patricia and her father were engaged in conversation with the President of the Barbados Investment Bank, whom they appeared to know quite well. The man, who did significant business for the Carducci family, was respectful but very comfortable with Sal's widow. Marco, who together with Ian Carlo was observing her from a distance, made a mental note of this. It could be important down the line.

"What do you think of her?" murmured Marco.

"What would I know," shrugged Ian Carlo. "I've only seen her once or twice. Uncle Sal was pretty cagey when it came to Patricia. Once he told me she was his ticket to a better world, whatever that meant."

Ernie caught Ian Carlo's and Marco's eyes and signaled them towards Sal's old studio. Once inside he locked the door and activated an interference device just in case there were eavesdroppers using the windows as sounding boards to listen in. The room was constantly swept for bugs and was as safe as modern technology offered, but one could never be too careful. He got straight to the point.

"You two are going to have a lot on your plate for the next couple of weeks. Times change, people don't. Your right to keep Sal's businesses is going to be challenged. I believe that between the two of you any of these threats can be successfully dealt with, but you have to count on each other, depend on each other, and above all trust each other. After this is all sorted out you'll have other matters to confront, but for now we all have to be on our toes. There will be takeover attempts on all fronts and there will be renewed law enforcement efforts to seize properties if they can find any way to get RICO into the picture. I'll deal with the latter; you have to deal with the others. You can count on a week or ten days at most before someone makes a move." There was silence. They all knew what was coming; it was just a question of time. "Now let's get back to this wake, as you two have to be seen."

The day ended on a quiet note. Patricia and her father left for the Plaza Hotel where Ernie had secured them a suite. A few mourners that had sampled the bar's offerings once too frequently tended to linger but were politely escorted to waiting courtesy cars that would take them safely to wherever they were going. None were allowed to drive. Marco was the last to leave. He took a long look at the old familiar house where he had spent many days of his adolescence and young adulthood. He then said goodbye to the help and thanked them with a generous tip, and walked out.

* * *

The first goombah to try his luck at usurping more power and territory for himself was Tony Kisses. Tony ran scams out of JFK and Grand Central Terminal. His crew was mostly Jamaicans and a few Puerto Ricans with some paesano muscle to help with enforcement. Tony made a move on several pimps and some dealers in Jamaica, NY near JFK. Two days later Marco had most of Tony's vehicles impounded and ICE officers rounded up his crew. No blood, no news. Tony got the message and backed off. Problem solved.

Next up was Lorenzo Harvey Batista, a half-breed Irish-Italian who sold enforcement to several outfits. He was tough, quiet, and efficient – so he was appreciated for his services by most of the families. A.K.A. Lori Baba, he decided to visit Rochester and lay claim to Salvatore's action there. He made it known that his presence was a permanent feature and that Sal's people had to report to him. He underlined that claim by beating the pulp out of a couple of Sal's runners and a pimp who wanted confirmation from someone else. The pimp didn't make it. This case was taken up by Ian Carlo. Within 24 hours Lori Baba and his two main enforcers were buried in a landfill with enough witnesses present to get the word out. There was even a police lieutenant invited to the junkyard internment.

The word spread rapidly throughout the players and the law. Marco and Ian Carlo were working as one and the pressure was off for now. But everyone wondered how long that honeymoon could last. There has to be one boss, *il capo*, the man, and one of the two had to surface above the other. But who would it be. Both men were capable and proven ruthless. Marco and Ian Carlo had made their bones cleaning out a Russian mob that tried to muscle into the prostitution business bringing in some sweet from Estonia and peddling it to high rollers. The Russians were heavies who used their fists and guns but not their brains. Within a month the girls were integrated into friendly stables and all six bosses of that crew were dead. Ian Carlo was said to have strangled three of them with his bare hands in front of others who might follow suit. Marco just shot them. Uncle Sal was so proud of his two nephews that he gave each of them a brand-new Cadillac Escalade – just like his – to show that they were his main *capos*. Other people in the organization were encouraged not to use Escalades.

Takeover attempts came and went. Aggressive moves were countered and business eventually returned to its natural rhythm. Now it was time to deal with other matters. Marco called Ernie, Ernie called Ian Carlo, and the three met for dinner at Benjamin's Trattoria.

Marco started the conversation, not without certain doubts as to who should get the ball rolling. "The families are happy as things stand. Ernie's heard from all the locals and a few of the West Coast guys. Chicago hasn't said anything but they seem to be rolling with this," Marco opened. Then he hesitated, looking squarely at Ian Carlo. "Now I have to deal with some other things, business and personal issues of Uncle Sal's. Even though I will be working the banks and all the pertinent matters, I will be out of town for a couple of weeks."

Marco looked expectantly at Ernie and Ian Carlo, asking more with his expression than with words what he was to expect when he came back.

Ian Carlo smiled. "Take it easy, you'll find everything in order when you're back."

Marco assented with a sharp nod, but wondered what order meant to Ian Carlo.

Ernie looked at the table. "Okay, I'll address the elephant in the room. One of you two has to come out as the undisputed head of this family. There will never be loyalty from the crews or respect from the families until that happens. The problem is that both of you are capable and balanced individuals that can head the family if, and only if, you can count on the total cooperation and loyalty of the other. This said, I'm leaving you two to talk about this." He walked out of the Trattoria, leaving Marco and Ian Carlo in an uncomfortable silence.

These two men had worked together, or rather in parallel, managing the Carducci enterprises with great success; yet they had very little to do one with the other, probably by design. Sal had been a crafty old man and kept his eggs in different baskets. No, they had to come to terms. No alternative.

"I've only one question," Marco said with gut-wrenching anxiety to Ian Carlo, looking him straight in the eye. "Do I have to watch my back?"

"Not from me," shrugged Ian Carlo with total calm and obvious sincerity. "This is something you and I can bash out on top of the table. We got a good deal going here and I need you as much as you need me. There is no bullshit here. We'll always share power but we have to put a face to this; you or me, I don't care. Whichever is better for business."

"But that is precisely the question," pressed Marco. "Which of us is better for business? The way I look at it, and believe me, from a very selfish point of view, I know you should be the visible head of the family. You command a different kind of respect. One needed at a very primal level which is, after all, the one that keeps us going."

"So…are you saying that I should be the man? Just like that?" Ian Carlo was caught off guard by such directness, but deep down he knew Marco was right.

Marco had decided. It was a good business decision and he knew it.

"I will defer to you in public, and in all matters regarding our relations with the other families," stated Marco. "I expect you to respect my wishes when it comes to the management of our legitimate enterprise…and the way we control our money."

The two men held each other's gaze without defiance but expecting the other to continue, and it was Marco who finally continued, taking the matter for settled.

"I will distance myself from the obvious; I'll fade into the background, which puts you in a powerful but dangerous position as I said before. I want you to think about this. We don't have a lot of time before the crews and the other families get restless, so we have to act rather promptly."

"If you can live with this, so can I," said Ian Carlo without pause and with a sincerity coming to the surface in a man who rarely allowed anyone to perceive such emotion. "You should know that I always have and always will respect you as an equal. You know business better than I ever will; but do you realize how strange it is that we are becoming the two faces of a single entity? I will be in the light and you in the dark, yet it will be me who manages the darker side of who we are and you the presentable head of our legitimate operations."

If the old lawyer had anything to add, this was the time. Ernie was called back and quietly listened to the two cousins. He made no comment on their decision. He just said that he would make sure the families and the crews knew that Ian Carlo was now the head of the family. He shook hands with both men and, changing his mind about being aloof, added, "I think you chose wisely."

2

For the next few days Ian Carlo received delegation after delegation of mobsters, cops, politicians, and a bishop or two; all without exception presented themselves with puckered ass-kissing lips and extended greedy hands. There were petitioners, people with "great ideas," and more than one veiled threat. It was business as usual.

Marco stayed in the background, quietly dealing with the banks and shortening the leash on business managers of all the legit enterprises. This was no time to lower the guard. He needed to change the manager of the industrial laundry because old Mr. Burns was getting forgetful, no other reason. He received a great retirement package and handed the reins over to a woman who had grown up through the ranks. Natalia Lopez had started as a loader when Uncle Sal had bought the business more than fifteen years ago. She was now in her mid-thirties, smart, tough, and clean as a whistle. She was the first woman manager within all of the Carducci organization. Winds of change were blowing. Two or three more adjustments and a thorough audit done by Li Yu Wang & Associates brought every detail of every business up-to-date.

Two weeks into all of this Marco got a call from Uncle Sal's widow. Patricia wanted to know when he was coming to Florida. She wanted to meet him in a more personal way, she simply said. Marco promised to fly down as soon as possible but two more weeks went by before he was aboard his jet heading for Sarasota. The old Lear 35 was Marco's personal transport. He loved it with a passion and spent a fortune on its maintenance. He flew copilot as always. The left seat was occupied by Joe Strasso, a distant cousin who flew jets for the US Air Force before retiring after a bicycle accident disqualified him from high G-force flying. He found a home with the Lear and had a close friendship with Marco, whom he had taught to fly and who now held all the certification needed to fly the Lear as a private pilot.

At 48,000 feet tracking true south, the Lear was flying 10,000 feet higher than commercial airliners. The sky was bluer, darker, and more expansive. Joe was talking to air traffic Atlanta and was being passed on to Tallahassee control squawking 2250 on the transponder. Flight level and direction of the Lear was being monitored by at least three commercial air traffic facilities, and a few military ones as well.

Fifteen minutes later Joe indicated that Marco had the control and they began their descent at 3,000 fpm to flight level 280, at which point they would be under positive control by Tallahassee until they were transferred to Sarasota tower for final approach and landing. One half hour later the jet taxied to an FBO that offered a covered hangar. The door opened into welcome warmth and a bright sunny day, Florida at its best.

Two people were waiting for Marco: Uncle Sal's local driver/bodyguard and his personal valet/bodyguard. Both men were well known to Marco. Pete Morelli had been driving Sal for eight years and Luigi Di Tomaso had been taking care of the old man for nearly as long. Both men were in their mid-thirties, very fit, and very tan. Both wore Hawaiian shirts and were certainly well strapped. The signature Escalade was a few steps away and luggage was transferred rapidly. The only things missing were the ubiquitous golf bags.

That was what the FBI agent watching would report to his boss, who was sitting in his corner office a couple of hundred feet up in one of several federal buildings in New York City. He was head of a joint force delegated to investigate, pursue, and eventually prosecute orga- nized crime. His name was Joseph Delany Jr., Princeton and Harvard, MBA and Juris Doctor, both summa cum laude. Thirty-four years old and anxious to make his mark so that he could enter a political career that he felt was his birthright more than a calling. Son and grandson of senators, he could almost smell the rarefied air of the Senate Cham- ber. The death of Salvatore Carducci would be his chance at the brass ring...and he thought that he was ready. He believed that whoever in- herited the family business would have to contend with one or more interested parties, and where there is conflict, there is opportunity.

A little short of an hour later the SUV, with Marco on board, drove up the circular drive of a very contemporary, very large home. It had two different waterfronts – one to the Gulf of Mexico where deep blue water calmly shimmered only the width of a white sand beach away, and the other to the rear where a private marina for Uncle Sal's boats opened onto a wide canal that ran two hundred feet to the ocean.

A 183-foot Benetti luxury yacht with all the bells and whistles was shining white against the darker background of sea grape and red mangroves. A 28-foot Mako runabout rigged for blue-water fishing was moored beside an 18-foot Hell's Bay flats boat with double plat- form. This little skiff was powered by a 115 HP four-stroke and had a powerful electric trolling motor hinged to an automatic retrieve. Just enough to make any flats angler cry with envy. Both of the smaller boats could be hoisted aboard the Benetti into custom designed cradles for the ultimate in mother ship travel. The skiff, now washed clean, had witnessed Sal's last moments on this earth.

The front facade of the house was austere, almost forbidding. There were no windows above or to the sides of the large iron doors that opened from a semicircular porch. The heavy countenance was slight- ly softened by a few architectural details and the light yellow color of the walls. In sharp contrast, the fronts that looked onto the water were open and inviting. Ample terraces, balconies, huge windows, a semi- Olympic size infinity pool edged in black marble sparkled like a dia- mond on onyx. The pool's wet bar adjoined a large Tiki bar that highlighted the entertainment area. Wickerwork chairs and lounge chairs completed the feeling intended. The breeze brought the smell of brine and mangrove mixed with floral aromas and tanning oil from the not too distant beach.

Two sets of glass doors led to an industrial size kitchen and an indoor lounge, dining room and family rooms. Invisible was the entertainment lounge with its sixty-inch TV and two billiard tables, one French, the other pool. On the other side was an ample office and library equipped with all the latest electronic amenities of the day.

Upstairs was a single bedroom with two bathrooms, two "stroll-through" closets, and a private entertainment area with bar, TV and an audio system by California Sound Machine. At each end of the room there was a small office, Sal's dotted with fishing watercolors and two maps – one of greater New York, the other a world map. Each had flags with coded notes on them. Patricia's was much the same but starker. Curiously, it also had a world map with pin flags and codes.

Serious luxury without extravagance was the keynote. Every painting, vase, sculpture, tapestry, and rug spelled class and good taste. No thanks to Sal, the house was the palette of Patricia, well-raised, highly educated lady from Lima, Peru, who, for reasons unknown, had loved, married, and cared for a tough thug from Brooklyn.

Marco strolled through the estate in awe; he had never been there before. This had been Sal's private crib for the last ten years – ever since he had married Patricia Lujan – and no one in the family was ever invited there. Now, as he looked with amazement at every detail of this house, he actually wondered who Sal really was. Not the tough operator he knew, not the steel-eyed executioner, not the steady negotiator nor the clearheaded businessman who created a legal fortune many times that of the illegal gains that gave it birth. It wasn't the uncle that he had shared a life with.

Who was this man he could now picture with an arm around his wife looking from his balcony at the setting sun, waiting for that elusive flash of green that would sing requiem to the day. Who?

The rooms flowed into each other with grace, details making a unity, features differentiating the ambiance of one from the other. The bedroom was ample; two walls were fronted by floor-to-ceiling windows giving the impression of unlimited space, the large private terrace was landscaped with flower boxes, and a sunken spa pool tipped a cascade of water to the main pool underneath. Two wicker divans with a small cocktail table between them told a story of quiet mature love, hard to believe but evident. Noticeably, there was no trace of Patricia's personal things. No clothes of hers were in the closet, no personal items in the bathroom, no photos in frames of her and Sal, or of Patricia by herself or with others. A vacuum of personal items yet there was a lingering presence of her life with Sal that permeated the entire house. Patricia had moved to an apartment closer to town that she and Sal had bought in case anything happened to him. She had always known the house would go to Marco and Sal wanted her to have her own place.

Eventually, guided by Pete, Marco went back to the main floor and walked down a few steps to a garden-level semi-basement that occupied more than half of the house's floor plan. If he was confused before, now he was bewildered. Everything in this room was about fishing, specifically fly fishing. Dozens of fly rods were displayed along a wall in a beautiful wooden rack, a few of them with loaded reels, lines at ready, flies on tippets…taunt with anticipation. An antique railroad desk, handmade of fine mahogany, rolltop open, displayed a Renzetti vise rising from an explosion of feathers, fur, and synthetic dressings. The vise still held a half-tied fly, a bobbin of red thread dangling beneath – waiting for someone to finish the job. The desk had multiple drawers; some of them partially open, showing odds and ends of materials that they held. Marco carefully opened a few more and found expensive capes of different-colored hackle, all types of exotic furs, chenille, and Mylar flash, hooks of every type and size, threads of cotton and silk, beads of copper, gold and silver. In a house of understated order and modern efficiency, Sal's desk was a glaring yet homey exception. Even the floor beneath it was graffiti of peacock hurl, hare dubbing, epoxy drops, and bits of thread and flashaboo.

The walls of the den were covered with fishing paintings, watercolors of mangrove flats, idyllic trout streams and salmon rivers, anglers casting, fish jumping…shadowboxes full of flies, many tied by famous anglers, Chico Fernandez, Joan Wulff, Lefty Kreh and many more. A coffee table held a few early copies of *Wild on the Fly* magazine, one of them open to an article on fishing Russia's Kola Peninsula, which included a picture of Sal on the Ponoi River holding a nice Atlantic salmon by tail and belly. Big fish, big smile, big adventure, big bucks.

Marco took one more look around and headed back to meet up with Pete and Luigi. He had decided to stay in the guest cottage that was attached to the staff apartments. For some reason he felt that he would intrude on his uncle's privacy if he stayed in the main house. The guest cottage was well appointed and very comfortable. Luigi or Pete had unpacked and put away his clothes but his briefcase and computer bag were left unopened and set besides the bed on the side table.

What was more astonishing to him was that this house was now his with all its contents and accolades. Ernie had called Marco and Ian Carlo into his office and read them one simple testament. Everything they owned belonged to both of them in equal terms. The only exceptions were that Ian Carlo got the house on Third Avenue and Marco got the house in Sarasota. An annotation explained that Patricia had all she needed for now. Intriguing and even a little disturbing, but nobody commented on it.

Marco took a long shower, shaved, and dressed in tropical attire of blue chinos, a guayavera of fine linen that he had bought in Cartagena, and blue suede Topsiders. He found himself without much to do, so he opened his laptop and logged into his highly protected administrative site from where he could manage every aspect of the business. He made several transfers, cancelled out one account in Luxembourg and opened one in Tortola – routine stuff. By six thirty he was ready for a drink and went next door to look for Pete and Luigi so they could drive into Sarasota for refreshments and a meal. Instead he found Joe Strasso sitting in the living room watching a rerun of "How I Met Your Mother." Joe stood up and put the TV on pause.

"Pete and Luigi are at the marina, they asked me to call them when you were ready for dinner. They're getting some fresh fish from a local fisherman and Matilde, your cook, is making a salad and some tostones, maybe rice too."

"I didn't know we had a cook," Marco commented. "I was thinking we might all go to town for a steak and a couple of drinks…"

"Trust me, this cook knows what she is doing. Remember, I was here with the boss last May. The food is incredible and the bar is very well stocked…I imagine you've seen the wine cellar?"

"Wine cellar… what wine cellar?" asked Marco, suddenly on point.

"The one behind the bar, didn't you see the big metal door?"

"If I saw it I didn't give it a thought, too many things to get used to here."

"Come, I'll show you," Joe replied with a smile.

They walked to the main house and went first to the kitchen where Joe introduced Marco to Matilde, a plump fiftyish woman from Panama who warmed the place with a big bright smile that contrasted like a half moon against her dark skin. She greeted Marco effusively and immediately burst into tears and a staccato of Spanish about the Patron and Doña Patricia and God knows what. Instantly back to a smile she grabbed Marco by the shoulders and planted a kiss on each cheek and in a single motion headed back to her cooking.

"What was that all about?" Marco asked Joe, somewhat startled.

"She was welcoming you as the new patron," Joe replied. "She said how she lamented the boss' passing and how she adored Ms. Patricia, and then she said that you were going to love the grilled pompano."

"OK, back to the point. Let's see this wine thing…"

The wine cellar, as big as an average living room had two sections; one was for red wines that were kept at 67.5°F and a section for white wines that was kept at a frosty 42.5°F. The champagne was kept with the reds in a special case that rotated the bottles once a day; these would be chilled to 48°F or less just before serving. The labels of the red wines, Marco's preferred libation, were a veritable tour of the world, beginning with the Americas. Zinfandels, cabernets, and merlots from California, Oregon, Virginia, Washington, New York, and New Jersey represented the US. From Argentina; Malbec, syrah, pinot noir and bonarda; Chile had cabernets, particularly some well-aged Don Melchor that was worth a small fortune. Uruguay and Paraguay had some Tanat and to Marco's surprise a couple of Brazilian blends. Private vintages from Australia, New Zealand, Russia, Germany, Poland, South Africa, and Greece were also present, and, of course, a huge selection of French reds, followed by the best of Italy.

Again Marco thought of his uncle in a different light. While wine was always on the table at their homes, nobody ever asked what it was…because it was always red and always poured out of a gallon jug with no label. Now this incredibly sophisticated wine cellar was in the home of a man that Marco had always loved as a father but never thought of as a connoisseur of anything but the making of money.

Marco went to the chilled section of the cellar and chose a few bottles of pinot gris from Washington State's Russian River that he was sure would go well with the pompano. He walked back to the kitchen where Pete and Luigi had joined Matilde, who kept on cooking while chattering incessantly in Spanish with Luigi, who apparently understood what was going on. Matilde received the wine, smiled, and gave Luigi instructions in the tone of voice that Marco's grandmother used with him when she needed him to run an errand without argument. Luigi pulled two ice buckets out of a cabinet and filled them from a large icemaker that produced half-moons. In went the wine and it was taken to the table.

Marco, Pete and Joe sat down and were served by Matilde. Oven-broiled pompano, coconut rice, and grilled ripe tomatoes were on each plate. In a basket at the center of the table were fried green plantains that had been boiled, fried, stomped on, and then fried again. They were called tostones and were accompanied by large-grain sea salt and hogo, which was like a fried salsa. To complete the meal, a large bowl of fresh greens drizzled in homemade raspberry vinaigrette was passed around.

Luigi came back and joined them. "All's secure. The second shift reported all normal."

Marco tried not to sound too much like the fish out of water that he felt like. "What exactly do you mean?"

Pete answered without condescension "The house hired a primary security service from an outfit owned and operated by a retired special forces major who had no other mob connections and was loyal to his clients, and who was paid a fortune for his services. His loyalty's been tested several times and he's always succeeded in impressing us... with his abilities, the discipline of his people. He's also got the absolute discretion that men like Sal needed and appreciated.

"Furthermore," Pete concluded, "the house is covered from all angles and all fronts by CCTV, which generates a satellite feed at high resolution every three minutes. Help, if needed or anticipated, is only three minutes away – very capable and heavily armed help."

Marco had a general idea of this service because he had seen the bills from this operation and understood that a *capo* like his uncle could not afford to be without it.

The conversation shifted to other, more distracting themes, such as what was the story with all the fishing paraphernalia. Even though Marco knew that Sal was a fishing enthusiast, he never fathomed the depth of his uncle's commitment to the sport, and now both Luigi and Pete were enlightening him on the matter.

"For the last ten years two great passions dominated Sal's life," Pete explained. "Patricia and fly fishing, in that order. The boss picked up the sport early on in his relationship with Patricia. They were on a trip to Mendoza, Argentina, buying wine when the owner of one of the vineyards invited them to his "Estancia" near San Martin de los Andes in Argentina's Patagonia. There they were both enchanted by the marvelous landscape, the crystal lakes and rivers, but above all by the soul-seeking tug of a trout on the line."

"You get a little lyrical there, Pete, were you there?"

"Oh yeah, so was Luigi here, but at that time we were gofers, not the boss' backs."

"A few days of instruction with Martin Carranza, a famous Argentinean angler, got Sal and Patricia casting and fishing reasonably well,"

Luigi added, "Then they did a two-day float down the historic Chimehuin River, where they each caught dozens of fish. The experience left them hooked for life."

"That's for sure," Pete continued. "For the last ten years Sal and Patricia have been fly fishing all over the planet. But this home was their headquarters and their favorite getaway. As you may know, fishing, particularly fly fishing for tarpon, is world famous in these waters."

Another trip to the wine cellar, and a key lime pie later, and Marco was ready for bed. In a flash the two bodyguards did a security check and bid Marco a good night. Sleep came easy and dreamless.

He woke up early, feeling exceptionally refreshed. Coffee filled the air, bacon followed and then something sweet…maple syrup being warmed on the stove. Marco showered and skipped the shave, put on a pair of light shorts and a linen shirt, tan deck shoes, and he was down the stairs and out the door.

At the main house the dining room table was loaded with fresh pineapple, a bowl of assorted berries, sliced mango, and kiwi. There was a French press with coffee and a stack of waffles, butter and the maple syrup, agave and honey, a plate filled with crispy bacon and another with fluffy scrambled eggs. A bottle of Prosecco and a pitcher of orange juice completed the feast. A tone was being set for a lifestyle that Marco did not know. His idea of breakfast was a cup of black coffee and a stack of the night's banking reports.

Matilde stood proudly next to the table, awaiting the new patron's orders for whatever else he wanted. Her sunshine smile filled the room. Marco was looking at the spread with increasing appetite, soon bordering on ravenous hunger. He sat down and was promptly joined by Joe Strasso and Luigi. Pete had been out since early morning doing a security overview with a rep from the agency.

After breakfast Luigi and Joe sat down with Marco for an update on several things that were pending since Sal's passing. Luigi gave Marco two sealed envelopes. Predictably, both were addressed to Marco in Sal's handwriting, one read "Personal," the other "Business." Marco pocketed the personal envelope and opened the one that said business.

In the envelope Marco found a list of instructions and two keys that belonged to safety deposit boxes in Grand Cayman and Tortola, both with the same British Overseas Investment Bank logo embossed on them. Marco vaguely remembered that some ten or twelve years ago Sal had asked him to sign some cards from that bank, but then nothing more and he had forgotten about them. Now he wondered what these could be.

He also found a Black Titanium Charter member American Express card in the name of Marco Lorenzo Massimo, a US passport in the same name and a European Union passport also in that name. The photographs were recent and Marco remembered that he, Ian Carlo and Sal had these photos taken for an ID card for the New York's Italian American Athletic Club, a venue none of them had ever visited.

There was a very succinct note from Sal's own hand that simply read, "Go first to the Caymans." A second note read, "Take up fishing...Pete and Luigi can teach you. It's business, but you might find it enjoyable."

Marco put the passports and the Amex card back in the envelope and in his pocket. He looked at his men and realized that they knew what was in there and were waiting on his orders. "I guess we're flying to Grand Cayman. I've been there a few times but for business only, in and out trips...Joe, when can the Lear be ready?"

"Give me a couple of hours' notice and I'll file a flight plan."

"It'll be Monday morning at the earliest," Marco replied, "and before that I may want to go to New York for a day."

"Just say the word; it's an easy two hour hop from Sarasota," added Joe with some enthusiasm. The man was a flight junkie.

"Now one or both you guys can tell me why Uncle Sal wants me to go fishing for business and, questionably, enjoyment."

Luigi took the lead on this one. "The boss felt fishing is a perfect cover for doing business. Nobody questions a few anglers on a far off quest. Most countries welcome this type of tourist and your uncle was an artist at setting up his private business in outlandish places. He went trout fishing in Cuenca, Ecuador, just to meet quietly with a Bolivian politician and a Colombian businessman in order to get them to supply one of his companies with rare minerals destined for the electronics market in China. Naturally Sal's people became the go between at all stages, to the frustration and anger of a couple of multinationals."

Pete continued. "You know that doing legitimate business of large magnitude requires more cloak and dagger skills than most organized crime, and Sal was an artist at both. For example, that big Benetti yacht out there is an ideal meeting place. It's seaworthy and can cruise comfortably outside the legal jurisdiction of most countries. I've seen business personalities that grace the *Wall Street Journal* spend many hours on it; occasionally they even enjoyed some blue water fishing."

"Who's the crew?" Marco asked.

"I'm the captain," said Luigi. "Sal had me take a six-month course at the Boston Marine Academy, and I might add that I grew up on a ship. But on long trips we take a retired merchant marine first officer, a real sea dog if you like. The crew is provided by the security company; they play a double roll for which they have beenextensively trained. We also take a cook and a cabin steward. The whole crew is eleven including me."

"How long to set up a trip on this boat?"

"Not long, a couple of days maximum. It depends on how much time at sea and how far it's going."

Marco was just beginning to feel like he had a sense of his uncle's local infrastructure, and it was, to say the least, impressive. Now it was time to contact Sal's widow and see what "a better understanding" really meant.

3

Patricia answered on the second ring with a soft hello that offered a backstage sensuality to her front stage formality.

"It's Marco, Patricia. How are you doing?"

"Well, thank you. I was expecting your call..." She spoke like it was a foregone conclusion that he would do so.

"I thought we might have some lunch and go through some things Sal wanted me discuss with you."

"Lunch is fine Marco, but why don't you come by the apartment for a drink before we go out?"

"Suits me; see you around noon."

Marco asked Luigi to arrange the car to be ready with enough time to be at Patricia's by noon. Next he sat down at his computer for a couple of hours and called Ian Carlo to bring him current with some decisions and changes in banks that he had made. He, Sal, and Ian Carlo had a verbal code that would thoroughly confuse any eavesdroppers on their conversation. Ian Carlo brought Marco up to date on certain relationships that appeared to be a little awkward and should be looked into more carefully.

By the time he was finished and had changed into more formal attire, Luigi let him know that it was time to leave. A dark blue Lincoln town car was waiting, the back door open and a very large, serious looking driver stood by. Marco got in the back after acknowledging the driver and Luigi sat in the front passenger seat. It was obvious that both men were armed and he knew that under each seat there were additional weapons and that the trunk was well supplied with heavier hardware. This was part of being a Carducci. You never, ever, went without proper security.

It took twenty minutes to get to Patricia's condo. A valet indicated that Mr. Carducci was expected and that they could enter through the lower lobby adjacent to the parking. The driver dropped Marco at the elegant lower lobby door, and he went to elevator number six, which would take him directly to the penthouse apartment. As soon as Marco walked in, the doors closed and he was on his quiet ride to spend time with the mysterious Patricia.

She was at the door as the elevator opened to an ample foyer elegantly furnished with a table in front of a large mirror in a gilded frame that reflected a beautiful *ikebana* arrangement, very impressive.

Patricia kissed Marco lightly on the cheek and took him by the arm. "This way," she said, and guided him to a studio that had huge windows on the two fronts facing the gulf and the seventh green of a manicured golf course.

A large photo of Sal and Patricia dressed in waders holding fly rods, with a white capped mountain in the background that Marco would learn was the Lanin Volcano in Patagonia, occupied a privileged position on a large glass-top desk that also held an all-in-one ASUS computer and little else. No wire to be seen anywhere. There was a rolling bar with all the proper amenities and a variety of crystal decanters that held golden liquids of different tones and another two with shimmering clear liquids, surely vodka and gin, both on ice.

"What would you like?" asked Patricia.

Marco chose single malt straight. Patricia served herself a glass of Torrontes wine from Salta, Argentina. With libations in hand they sat in comfortable winged rattan chairs that faced each other angularly in front of a beautiful coffee table holding a few books on fly fishing and several photos in silver frames – some of Patricia and Sal and others of

Patricia and an older gentleman that Marco recognized as her father, Francisco Lujan. There was also a photo of her in what appeared to be an old Spanish setting.

Patricia saw Marco contemplating the image and said, "That's my mother a few days before she was killed."

"Killed how?" asked Marco.

"She was murdered by the Sendero Luminoso – Shining Path – guerrillas during a kidnapping attempt; I was only a few years old." A fleeting expression of loss and pain crossed her beautiful face.

Marco kept silent for a few moments, his own mind flying back to when his father had been killed on his own doorstep in front of him and his mother. A sniper from afar ended the life of an innocent man just for being Salvatore Carducci's younger brother. A crime many times avenged but never forgiven or forgotten, the pain of it lingering through the years and suddenly Marco felt closer to this woman who shared that feeling.

"I know you understand, Marco," said Patricia quietly. "Sal told me about your father. That is why I shared with you this intimate part of my life. I thought it might make it easier for us to talk sincerely about the many things that we must discuss."

Marco wanted to say something but found prudence in silence. He and Patricia finished their drinks and stood somewhat uncomfortably with each other. There was now a bond, but between total strangers.

Patricia decided on the restaurant, as Marco was a stranger to the area. They chose to go in Marco's car, taking advantage of the driver and the required security. Patricia gave the driver the name of the restaurant, the Epicure, expecting that he would know where it was. He nodded and they headed for downtown Sarasota. As they left the garage, a Mercedes S500 fell in behind the Lincoln.

Luigi turned to Patricia, "Are your people behind us?" Patricia nodded and raised an eyebrow; wasn't it obvious? Luigi turned back to looking forward. Marco said nothing but made a mental note to ask Luigi about the matter later.

Most of the good Sarasota restaurants are on Main Street nested between the "Fruit Streets" – Pineapple, Lemon, Orange, etc. The Epicure is no exception; an Italian trattoria with a large Florida accent.

Both Patricia and Marco had Caprese salads and shared a pizza capriciosa accompanied by a delicious bottle of Prosecco from Lago di Garda. Luigi and a Latino man sat at a discreet distance where they kept an eye on the couple and on passersby.

The conversation was kept light while an adjacent table was occupied by a young couple and two well-behaved children, but once they left Patricia changed the conversation instantly.

"Have you opened the two envelopes that Sally left you?"

This caught Marco off guard and he took a few seconds to look around as for eavesdroppers and then answered truthfully, "Only the one marked business, I thought of opening the other one tonight."

"Then there will be more to talk about later. For now, tell me, when do you plan to go to the Caymans?" asked Patricia, showing her intimacy with the matter.

Again Marco was caught off guard. Here was Patricia in a totally new light, as if she were a person who had crawled out of the one he knew, the discreet wife of a strutting businessman, now converted into a forceful entity of her own. Even her features, which until now had been slightly blurred as if in background, took on definition and clarity. She was truly beautiful he thought. Black hair cut in a pageboy, big dark-green eyes, a generous mouth, perfect nose, high cheekbones highlighted in soft tones of peach over very white skin that decried her Andean origin. Dressed in a white linen frock with little other adornment than a single emerald on a gold chain around her neck and matching earrings. He realized that her slim but well-proportioned body combined with that face gave her a regal look that didn't go unnoticed. He also realized that she aroused him. For a second, before he checked himself, he saw her naked in his mind. Then he forced himself back to the business at hand and answered her question.

"I don't know, probably Monday. I'm flying to New York after lunch but I'll be back early Monday and fly from here..." Marco hesitated before continuing. "I must say, Patricia, that you have me at a disadvantage. You obviously know more about me than I about you, and I'm guessing you know some things that I don't about Uncle Sal."

Patricia played with her napkin for a few seconds and then said, "Yes, it's true, there is a lot that you don't know about me and more than you can imagine that I know about you. Sally and I were truly married – body and soul, if you will. Sal loved you very much, Marco, but more importantly he had a great respect for you. There was nothing that you did that he didn't brag to me about. He was overjoyed with your achievements and suffered with your mistakes. Sally was particularly keen on your ability to control and enhance all aspects of his business and admired your total dedication to it."

Then she paused for a moment, as if searching for the right words. "...which brings me to one issue that intrigued him." Her soft voice took an intimate and almost maternal intonation. "You have never had a committed or even a stable relationship with a woman. We knew you were not gay, but never once did you bring a girl to your uncle's home. I found this particularly curious, as well. Not that you are celibate either; Sal was amused by your frequent use of Black Card Company Management."

This time Marco was outright flabbergasted. That his uncle knew about his particular preference of professionals over amateurs was unavoidable, but that he would share such with Patricia was unbelievable. He looked at her literally open-mouthed, as if he could not believe his ears. Black Card Company Management was the most private, most exclusive, and by far the most expensive escort service in the rarefied world of the very wealthy and very powerful. The escorts were educated, polished, worldly and amazingly beautiful. They only wore haute-couture garments and accessories; they didn't look impressed by any amount of luxury, whether it was a G6 or a luxury villa on Lake Cuomo, and they chose, without obligation or recrimination, to include or not include sex in the relationship. Marco had been using Black Card for over ten years without reason to complain. He could not imagine why Patricia should know about his very private life. Marco had never wanted a relationship by which he could be held hostage, no emotional entanglements that could be his downfall in a business in which a person he loved could be used against him in so many ways. His father's death had been just that; a way to hurt an untouchable man through a loved one. Marco was having none of that, no wife, no kids, not even a dog. Black Card gave him company when he needed it, sex when he wanted it, and time to forget it.

Patricia continued talking. "There is so much more that you must learn in just a few days. Sal was more, oh so much more than you or Ian Carlo knows. Ernie knows much but not everything and now you and I will have to learn even more. This is very big, Marco, more than you can ever imagine."

But at this instant when so much was about to be revealed, Marco perceived something out of sync in his peripheral vision and as he turned he saw a Latino man moving purposefully towards them, holding his arm rigid against his body. Instinct kicked in and he threw himself and Patricia to the ground as two suppressed pops were heard above the startled shouts of diners. Seconds later the man was dancing dead to a barrage of bullets fired by Luigi and José, Patricia's bodyguard. Yet before the bullets hit the assailant, a steak knife had buried itself deep into his throat stopping only when it hit bone. Patricia was on her knees with a hand extended in front of her. Like a cat she had grabbed the knife on the way down and before she hit the ground she had sent the deadly missile into the killer's larynx.

The whole thing took less than three seconds, but for the terrified patrons of The Epicure it seemed interminable. The assailant's body lay riddled with holes from which blood poured copiously, staining the white tablecloth of an overturned table and the powder-blue dress of an elderly matron upon whom he had fallen. The poor woman was in shock and could only open and close her mouth and move her arms in a fine imitation of a goldfish seeking freedom from its confinement. This pathetic scenario gave way to shouting, panicked screaming, and a rush to escape. And, since it was outside dining, exits were created by knocking over flowerpots, trellises ,and rope enclosures. In no time the place was empty, leaving only Marco, Patricia, and the two men whose guns had ended the life of the man on the floor…and the old lady in the blue dress who had opted to faint in place.

Luigi and José rushed directly to Marco and Patricia, who were both up from the ground and looking around at the place. They both stared at the dead assailant, in whose hand was a Taurus .22 caliber pistol with a black three-inch suppressor. Luigi had already called the driver with a 911 code and the Lincoln suddenly screeched to a stop right in front of them. They all got into the car and Marco ordered the driver to the airport as he called Joe Strasso to check on the status of the plane. Strasso confirmed it was ready and a flight plan had already been filed for Teterboro.

Sarasota's airport is located centrally, just minutes from downtown. The driver took them through quiet streets to the 441 North, which runs almost parallel to Runway 14 at Sarasota-Bradenton Internation-al. About halfway along, the entrance to Dolphin Aviation Services opened to them. They drove directly to the waiting Lear, which Joe had ready with engines on. Marco climbed into the copilot seat after send-ing Patricia into the cabin, and within two minutes they were taxiing to the runway under flight advisory, second for takeoff after an American Airlines commuter. The tower called their number and indicated that they were to roll into position and hold.

As Marco watched the American flight take off at a steep angle and veer right towards the Gulf, he heard "November-Charlie-Zebra-niner-niner-five, clear for takeoff" squawk in his headset. Joe pushed the two accelerators forward and in a breath they were moving down the runway. Less than fifteen seconds later they had positive flight con-ditions and a moment after that, with a slight pull on the yoke and the proper trim adjustment, the Lear lifted off the ground and rapidly gained altitude. A tight left turn indicated by the tower put them on a northeast heading. They would acquire Orlando flight control and from there climb toward the coast over Daytona and head north to New Jersey. November-Charlie-Zebra-niner-niner-five was authorized to ascend to flight level 290 with a heading of 010.

When the plane reached its altitude and Joe got involved with the controller, Marco went back to sit with Patricia in the passenger cabin. She had been quiet since the incident and had followed Marco's lead without comment. She never looked scared or distressed. She had reacted rapidly after the gunman was down and walked out to the car fast but without running. Marco had seen the knife sticking out of the man's throat but couldn't wrap his mind around the fact that it had been Patricia who put it there.

"So, what was all this about?" she asked Marco.

"Simple, someone tried to kill me or kill us, I don't know."

"Any idea who?"

"No, but there was one thing about this guy, he was not a pro," Marco answered. "He was full of tattoos and had jail scars under his eyes; just a gangbanger high on something following someone's orders. But that doesn't take the seriousness out of this attempt; these bangers often succeed even if they don't survive."

"So, have you talked to Ian Carlo?" Patricia continued. "He should know."

"Not yet, I'm waiting for Luigi to get off the phone with Pete. He's making sure the house is secure."

"I need to talk to my people also," Patricia said calmly.

"I think José may have done that already. As I came back he was talking on our secure line; our cell phones are not an option." Seconds later he was on the airplane's encrypted phone to Ian Carlo and rapidly in coded conversation, he gave him a short version of what had happened.

Ian Carlo made no comment about the assault; he knew better than that. "When you're an hour out change your flight-plan to MacArthur airport in Long Island. I'll have a chopper waiting for you."

Patricia asked for the phone and dialed a Peruvian number. She got a response on the first ring and fired off in such rapid Spanish that Marco could only surmise what was being said. She listened for a few seconds and sent off another few phrases and finished with a "Te quiero mucho, Papi" (I love you, Daddy). Then she looked up at Marco. "I'll call him back when we get to wherever we're going and he will be at a secure line; he also needs to know about this. Believe me, it could have been me this punk was after."

"Did you also tell him that you put a knife in this guy's throat?"

"Oh, Daddy would guess that something of the sort would have happened," Patricia replied with just the hint of a sad smile.

"My God, why on earth would he expect that from you?"

"Well, as you know, my mother was killed by guerrillas when I was a child. She died fighting the guy while trying to defend me. She went for his gun and got shot for her efforts. So from the time I was seven years old, my father had me take self-defense and martial arts lessons. I became fascinated with them when once in school I beat the living daylights out of the playground bully who was two years older than me and twice my size. Since that moment of total exhilaration I became very serious about martial arts and earned black belts in a few Japanese and Korean schools but most of all, I loved and became proficient in Krav Maga, the Israeli urban combat technique. That was because my father was very good friends with Israel's ambassador to Lima, who had one of his guards, whom I imagine was from their secret service, teach me. I was seventeen years old and Moshe taught me defense and attack moves every day for four years. He also became my first love and my first lover."

Marco took in the information, considering the mysterious Patricia. "Luigi practices Krav Maga, and some other martial arts. I don't know about Pete," Marco said, still trying to brain all this out.

"Pete's good, but not as good as Luigi or José," Patricia said, looking at them in the back of the airplane.

"Who's the best?" asked Marco.

"I am," said Patricia with the most innocent smile.

So much for pretty faces, thought Marco to himself. "And the knife trick?"

"Oh, that I learned from Gustavo Rueda; he works for Daddy. He used to be with the Colombian Special Forces. He taught me to throw practically anything with pretty lethal effect – a book, a bottle, a pen, but especially knives. It came in handy today, didn't it?"

Marco could not believe his eyes or his ears. He was sitting next to a beautiful woman, who appeared to be a sweet and delicate lady, only to find out she was a virtual maiming and killing machine. He was about to say something when Joe called him from the cockpit. Excusing himself he headed forward and slid into the right seat. He put on some headgear so that he could talk and listen to Joe.

"I changed the flight plan while we were over Charleston, and we are now heading for MacArthur in a somewhat roundabout way. We're flying out over the ocean and staying about twenty miles offshore. We will fly over Long Island Sound until we are under New York flight control who will then hand us over to MacArthur tower. It'll be a little over two hours to touchdown. Do you want to fly or are you going back to talk to Ms. Patricia?"

"I'll be in back. I want to talk to Luigi and José."

José was cleaning his 9mm Beretta with a gun kit that had appeared from somewhere on the plane. Luigi was prepping and checking three mini Uzis with 30-round magazines. There were also three additional magazines for each weapon. Marco knew that the plane was equipped with several weapons but had never needed to look into that matter too closely, now was a different situation and from what he could see the on-board arsenal consisted of the Uzis, plus two handguns and six stun grenades. Weapons all designed to defend and flee rather than attack. The compartment that held this entire armory was well hidden within the aft bench seat and a complex roll-back device in which under, if you opened the bench, you would find only flotation devises for six passengers.

"No such thing as too many guns," said José.

"Except when the other side has them," Luigi quipped.

"Tell me what you guys think about this situation," said Marco.

"Too many possibilities to guess," replied Luigi. "The only thing I know is that it probably wasn't from inside the family or anybody close to us. If that had been the case, they would have tried to neutralize me first. This guy didn't even look our way."

"He could also be shooting for Miss Patricia," said José.

"Why on earth would anybody want to hurt her?" Marco wondered out loud. "Sal isn't around anymore, which would have been the only reason I can imagine."

"Ask her, she might tell you." It was José speaking now as he looked toward the front where Patricia sat pensively looking out the window.

Marco made a note to do just that as soon as he was back in his seat, but for now he had to clear his mind and do some planning. Life was suddenly playing for keeps and he wasn't about to lose.

"I agree with you," said Marco to Luigi. "I have no reason to think anyone from inside our organization would make such a rash move with little to gain. The cards are on the table and Ian Carlo is the boss now. I have no direct hierarchical value to anyone and this would only be a setback for all interested parties. No, this came from way out in left field but I can't think of anyone, particularly if there is no all-out war on the family. If that was the case, we would know by now."

"Also, the shooter was out of whack," said Luigi. "He was either drugged, crazy, or both . . . probably both. My first shot hit him in a kidney and he didn't even flinch. It took the knife and three bullets to bring him down when any one of those should have been enough. I would give a pretty penny for the toxicology report on that 'putana.'"

Marco remembered that he had yet to call Pete at the house and get the lowdown on what was going on there. He dialed and Pete answered on the first ring.

"The major is here and he has men deployed all around the property." Pete sounded cool, as always; a real pro. "He's on the phone right now talking to a contact at Sarasota PD. I'll let you know about that as soon as he's finished. In the meantime you ought to know that I had the major secure Ms. Patricia's apartment as well. There are four men deployed there. One of her bodyguards is here and two are at her place. José is with you, I hear. Also, I got an update from New York. Apparently there has been no other incident anywhere within the organization but everyone is on high alert. Hold on a sec…" Pete spoke briefly to someone in the background. "Major Allen wants to talk to you."

Major Allen took his job seriously. Carducci, Lujan, Goldman, and others associated with them or referred by them signified most of his business and it was a very, very large business. His headquarters in Sarasota, Florida, was in a twelve-story building totally occupied by Allen Security. He employed several hundred people, of which the least number were administrative.

"Mr. Carducci, I'm sorry you had to live this experience. We are now in full defensive mode here and at Ms. Lujan's property, but this is not what I want to talk to you about. Sarasota PD is still at the incident site, which now has been dubbed a crime scene. My contact tells me that there are literally too many witnesses and every one of them has a different story. Nobody knows who the deceased was shooting at or really who shot him, and most mysterious of all, he had a steak knife deep in his throat and nobody knows where it came from. They're speculating that it just went into him as he fell on the table, or that maybe the lady he fell upon had it in her hand and involuntarily stabbed him with it. You have not been identified by anyone and only a waiter seems to recall having seen Ms. Lujan before but cannot identify her either. Sarasota PD is canvassing the area for video records of the incident but nothing has come up so far."

"Thank you, Major," said Marco. "Please keep me posted and if possible keep our names out of this matter. A bonus will be the outcome if this is handled to your usual high standards of discretion, of course. Please let me speak with Pete again..."

When Pete was back on the line Marco instructed him to secure his laptop and send it to the attention of the manager of the laundry via Fedex for next morning delivery. He stressed that the sender should be one of the security people, not from any of the household staff, and the origination address should be that of his or her home. One never knew if the Feds had a tag on the mail.

Marco decided to continue his conversation with Patricia and immediately felt exposed again. This woman had intimate knowledge of his life and she seemed to be comfortable discussing openly with him such private and personal details as his frequent use of high-end escorts. She was also very knowledgeable in all aspects of the family business, from what he had surmised from the short conversation before the attack.

As he made his way back to her, he remembered the second envelope that he had received from Sal, the one marked "Personal" that was still in his pocket. He excused himself from Patricia again and went back to the cockpit. With Joe wearing his earphones and talking to air control somewhere, he had some privacy. He opened the letter and read:

Well Marco, if you're reading this it is because I'm a goner. I know it's coming soon because I have an incurable bone marrow disease that will eventually create an embolism large enough to kill me. I hope I went while fishing or fucking, which are the only things worth dying for. Anyway, you will have read the other envelope with the bank instructions and that will be that. This, however, is a personal request. I need you to stick around Patricia; she is more than my wife, she is your partner. You need Patricia and she needs you so that things turn out right. You'll see what I mean. I imagine that by now you will have bucked off the family "leadership" on to Ian Carlo; smart move. You can trust him a hundred percent because he is terrified of dealing with big business in the real world, and he knows you thrive there. Also, I know that he can trust you for the same reason. Simple ain't it? So there it is; I need you to be totally open with Patricia about everything as she will be with you. It's gonna be a wild ride. Maybe I'll be seeing it from somewhere; hopefully from a mild climate! Goodbye Marco and good luck. I have always loved you as a son.

Sal

PS: Go fishing!

Marco headed back to the seat next to Patricia and she saw that he was holding the personal letter in his hand and tears were trying to leave his eyes.

"May I ask what that said?"

Marco handed her the letter without saying a word. She read it once and then again and handed it back to Marco. Her eyes, like his, were alight with imminent tears.

"I guess you inherited me," she said sadly, but with a warm smile. "And maybe I inherited you. I'm two years older than you so I'll be top dog."

Marco read both letters again a couple of times and then remembered the passports in the name of Massimo. He had put them and the credit card in his briefcase, so they would be in New York early the next day. He would need both, he thought.

An hour passed in relative silence with only some chatter between José and Luigi. Patricia was deep in thought, as was Marco. Both their minds were in the same place without each other knowing. Who was the other person that Sal had willed to each of them? Even though Patricia knew so much about Marco, she didn't know Marco. While for him, Patricia was a total enigma.

Joe came over the interphone to advise Marco that they were initiating the descent to MacArthur and Marco went forward to assist him with the delicate approach where JFK and LaGuardia-bound airliners would also be under the same control center. They would be descending in patterns within an upside-down-wedding-cake-shaped airspace until they were handed over to MacArthur tower for final approach and landing.

Twenty minutes later they touched down on Runway 6 and taxied to the General Aviation terminal. There they saw a Bell 525 idling with the doors lowered and Ian Carlo with two of his bodyguards waiting for them.

Marco mused that Ian Carlo did not look his part in life. He was five-foot-ten, athletic but not overly muscular, well shaved, black hair combed back. He was dressed in a slate black suit with off-white shirt and a toned-down copper tie; the perfect image of a Wall Street broker of the more successful kind – Andy Garcia, but not as handsome.

The crew was dressed in their standard uniform of loose-fitting blazers over gray pants and rubber soled shoes that lost in their effort to look formal. Two pilots were in the cockpit of the Bell 525, which can accommodate up to sixteen passengers depending on the configuration. Joe stayed with the Lear as all the others got into the chopper and were airborne in minutes.

Marco gave Ian Carlo a detailed account of what had happened at lunch and the subsequent conversation with the head of the security company. Little time was spent on niceties and Ian Carlo had acknowledged Patricia only with a nod, ignoring everyone else. Ian Carlo told Marco that he had scanned the whole country for information but no one seemed to know about an attempted hit and not even a side note had appeared in any major media. Only Tampa and Sarasota based news channels had given the incident some significance, but that was soon upstaged by an oil rig spill just off the coast. The evening news had said it was a Mexican drug cartel hit that went wrong and pointed to a Mexican waiter, who had conveniently disappeared, as the intended victim and suspect for the killing.

"I'm setting us up at the Roslyn place," said Ian Carlo, "because it's got better security than the NYC house and it attracts a hell of a lot less attention than the office. A couple of your people will be there if you need them."

While this was being said Patricia, who had been busy on her Galaxy smartphone interrupted them, saying, "Don't waste your time; this had nothing to do with you. I just got an email from my father, who is now in a safe house, telling me that this was an act of reprisal from a Tamaulipas, Mexico cartel called Los Locos. My father, at the request of interested governments, and because of their extreme violence, interdicted a supply of cocaine and heroin from Colombia to this cartel. What has him surprised is that they knew of my existence, let alone my location. I need to get rid of my cell phone and my clothes. A GPS might be embedded in either or they used the GPS on my phone as a locator. We have to do this before we get to wherever we are going. And Marco, please ask the security company to go over my cars to make sure they are not bugged."

Ian Carlo, who thrived on stressful situations, was cold as ice when he asked Patricia for her phone. He took out the SIM card, the battery, and unceremoniously threw it out the window and into the deep blue sea off the north coast of Long Island.

Marco got on the phone to Pete. "Get in touch with Major Allen and ask him to squeeze more information out of the cops. We need to know who the shooter was. That fucker's been in jail here and in Mexico from the tats on his neck. Do it now."

Under instructions from Ian Carlo, the chopper requested and got permission to land at St. Francis Hospital where a scrub Patricia's size was waiting for her. People who know people; that was the world in which they lived. In a few minutes the change of clothes was complete and they were on their way. It was decided still prudent to retire to the Carducci Estate at Roslyn.

The estate spread over several acres not far from the Vanderbilt museum in Suffolk County. The Bell landed lightly in the stone yard next to an ample side entrance to the home. All of them, with the exception of the pilots and Patricia's bodyguard, had suites in this home. Ian Carlo had not taken over Sal's quarters, so Patricia went there and found all the clothes that she needed for what was to be a short stay.

By now it was dark and everyone was starving. Ian Carlo arranged for the staff's accommodation and meals, then he, Patricia and Marco sat down to roast rack of lamb, medium rare, spinach and dandelion salad with orange pekoe vinaigrette; a loaf of ciabatta bread and a good chianti rounded it off. As they were finishing the last bottle, Ernie Goldman showed up. He was the only person other than Marco who could enter unannounced. He kissed Patricia, gave her a new phone, and hugged both Marco and Ian Carlo.

"I just finished talking to Francisco, Patricia, and I'm comfortable to say that this incident has nothing to do with our organization here." he said looking at them gravely. "But it has everything to do with some of our most lucrative international business abroad. On both sides of the tracks, may I add."

* * *

Francisco Jose Lujan y Cordoba sat in a comfortable but basic office just outside of Lima looking at a long list of transactions that scrolled past his eyes. The monitor was huge by any standards and all of the navigation was touch screen or voice commands. He had spent hours at this and was weary of the effort. At sixty-six years he was in fine condition, but age forgives no one and he could not put in the hours he had even just a few years back. He let the monitor go to sleep and as he rose from his chair, the computer automatically went into shutdown protocol and would not come to life again until his voice and an optical recognition of his retina brought it back. He moved to a small lounge with a large window overlooking the darkened sea where only chips of light confirmed its existence in what otherwise was a black void.

He poured himself a generous glass of a fine Malbec and replayed in his mind the events of the day as he sipped the wine. It had been a peaceful morning until the panic button on Patricia's phone had sent him into action. Following her whereabouts with very sophisticated GPS tracking software furnished by the CIA, Francisco knew the exact location of her cell phone and was able to listen to what was going on around it, as well as see through its camera lens if the situation allowed. He was immediately aware that she was unharmed and in the company of trusted people. He called his contact at the FBI and was soon talking to a very deferent agent in Sarasota who would promptly assess the situation without creating unnecessary lines of inquiry.

Within an hour Francisco was totally apprised of the attempt in every detail. He was satisfied that Patricia was in no way connected to it by the local authorities, and proceeded to determine its origin. He called his offices in Bogotá and gave specific directions to the head of that operation, which, under the guise of a call center, administered an immense amount of data that was filtered and prioritized originating from every cell phone, computer, and tablet in the hands of known illegal drug merchants, terrorists, arms dealers, and pirates throughout the world. This chatter would come in from clones on every government spyware and eavesdropping system on earth, from PRISM to LECTOR. From Canada to Patagonia, DC to Beijing, the software would milk the satellites and databases with the same sophistication that Google tracked every website. As if on cue, the intelligent software traced an unusual pattern between a cell phone in Matamoros in the State of Tamaulipas, Mexico, and two cell phones in Sarasota, one of which was found in the perpetrator's pocket; all of them were burn phones but the traffic pattern did not evade the spyware.

Within minutes the team was almost certain that the originating phone belonged to a small but vicious cartel called Los Locos who were famous for their ability to smuggle goods into Texas and their propensity for violence. The area where they operated belonged in principal to the New Gulf Cartel but was constantly disputed by Los Zetas. "El Chusma" Camacho, the head of Los Locos, managed to maintain tempered relations with both cartels – mainly because his ability to smuggle and his willingness to kill were mutually appreciated. With this confirmation Francisco knew that this was a retaliation taken against him for having "quarantined" Los Locos. Mexico and the US had been putting pressure on everybody since Los Locos had butchered a couple of ICE agents and four Federales who had raided one of their tunnels at the wrong moment. What puzzled and alarmed him was that they even knew who he was, and who Patricia was – and where she was.

This revelation was now Bogotá's priority. To keep his head straight while they crunched data, Francisco had immersed himself in the multibillion dollar transactions that moved the world – which he constantly monitored for the patterns and evident algorithms that would guide his own very significant actions on the world financial stage.

Finally he thought about his conversation with Ernie Goldman, a man whom he had learned to trust and appreciate through the years. He was an alter ego to Salvatore Carducci and now was the man to talk to while Marco and Ian Carlo fledged. They had reached the conclusion that the shooting was not part of a takeover attempt within the Carducci operation; both agreed that the most important matter at hand was to determine who was really behind this action. After all, Los Locos was small potatoes and didn't have the know-how or clout to pull a stunt like this, particularly because Patricia had been the target and her role was known only by a handful of people. This spelled problems at the highest level.

4

After dinner at the Roslyn mansion everybody retired to their suites and slept easily knowing that the security of the house and grounds was in the hands of professionals. Patricia went to the main suite while Marco and Ian Carlo went to their respective quarters, rooms that they had known since their early teens when Sal had bought the place from a prominent New York stage actress who had fallen on hard times. Each suite had a private bathroom, walk-in closet, kitchenette, and all the necessary amenities that assured privacy when it was needed. Ernie went to a guest suite that he had used for the past twenty years, yet it held no imprint of the lawyer's life. He pulled out his tablet and perused emails in several accounts sending the significant, urgent, and important to a folder and delegating the rest to his secretary in NYC who would distribute them among several attorneys and paralegals for action or information.

Ernie then opened the folder that held only six emails that he had chosen as worthy of his personal attention. One beckoned for immediate attention. It was from MI6 and disclosed that a Saudi national who had been detained at Heathrow for improper documentation had been found carrying photographs of Marco Carducci. The photos were attached to a sheet of paper with addresses and telephone numbers as well as recent whereabouts for Marco. The final destination of said individual was New York City. The MI6 network had a flag for Marco Carducci and indications that Ernie Goldman was to be contacted in regards to anything related to this name. Furthermore, the individual had been identified as Ali Hussein Waked, a low-echelon thug with ties to several terrorist groups who was listed on Interpol's no-fly list. Relieved of his false documents, cell phone, and tablet, Waked was promptly sent back to Riyadh to face Saudi authorities, a one-way ticket to hell.

The burn phone carried by Waked only contained one number in the memory and that corresponded to a line that was no longer in service, but Ernie noted that it was the same as one of the phones in Florida that had been called by Los Locos just before the attack on Marco and Patricia. This was a definitive indication that the attempt had been on both Patricia and Marco, which had grievous implications.

* * *

Alfredo "El Chusma" Camacho was relaxing at his favorite whorehouse just outside Matamoros. He was drinking pulque and beer, a lethal combination, while he enjoyed the company of a sixteen-year-old puta called "Gingercita" because her mother was named Ginger. Five of his men were with him and another five sat outside in their SUVs keeping guard. At 9:00 p.m. three RPGs entered the establishment's door and two windows while another two immediately followed, taking out the two SUVs and their occupants. The only surviving member of the party was a soldier who had been taking a piss behind an abandoned cement mixer, but he couldn't say a word because both his eardrums had been ruptured by the explosions. Los Locos had been permanently decommissioned.

The commandos who executed the mission quietly confirmed the effectiveness of the interdiction and returned to a chopper that would fly out into the Gulf of Mexico and deposit the team on an oil rig from where they would be flown to their operational headquarters in New Orleans under the guise of oil workers. An encrypted and highly circumvented email went out to Lausanne saying only "All is quiet on the

Western Front." The recipient, a Saudi prince in his early thirties then sent confirmation to a man known only as "M&M" – a moniker used by the people who worked for him or were in any way associated with his operations.

* * *

Early Saturday morning Patricia, Ian Carlo and Marco were having breakfast when Ernie walked into the room to join them, still talking on the cell. Usually very private with his phone habits, Ernie's one-sided exposure caused the group to quiet for news written already on Ernie's face, which had morphed into a thin, cynical smile that had no mirth.

"I just received confirmation that Los Locos is no longer a factor but that both Marco and Patricia were the targets of this attempt," Ernie announced, taking a seat. "While we know that they had the motivation, we're sure that they didn't have the ability to know where you were with such precision and timing. It implies a far more sophisticated operation and a highly-placed and dangerous opponent. And, while Ian Carlo has apparently not been targeted, it would be prudent to maintain a high level of security until every detail of this attempt has been clarified."

Ian Carlo and Marco looked at Ernie with questioning eyes. This didn't make sense. Ian Carlo was the one exposed to danger, not Marco. it was clear that the latter was being targeted, which was confusing. On the other hand Patricia was obviously accepting of these facts and did not look flustered by what was being said.

Marco took the business letter from Sal out of his pocket, held it in his hands for a few seconds, and showed it to Ian Carlo and Ernie. He kept the personal letter to himself for the time being.

Ian Carlo pulled out a similar letter, two passports, and a credit card that he had received from Ernie in an envelope addressed to him by Sal. The letter congratulated Ian Carlo on his becoming head of the family...apparently Sal had anticipated the outcome. But it also reminded Ian Carlo that Marco was indispensable to him and that

Patricia would be playing a very significant role in both of their lives. He said nothing about fishing but explained that he had left the Sarasota home to Marco for personal reasons that had nothing to do with the equal love he felt for Ian Carlo and his family to whom he had bequeathed the Third Avenue townhouse. He said that Marco, once having completed some instructions, would advise him of what was, in reality, their business and their patrimony.

The one outstanding point was the underlined importance of Patricia in all their futures and that Sal still pulled some strings from the other side. Ian Carlo and Marco, but not Ernie, looked at her in unison with the same expression of puzzlement and expectation.

Acknowledging the time had come for a significant explanation, Patricia rose to the occasion. "My father Francisco and my husband Sal became very close friends over the years, and eventually business associates," she began. "Together, with others, they pooled their international interests and created a fund, as they put it. These interests did not consider national or international borders, cultural boundaries, or even laws as impediments. They surmised that the world had dynamics that no particular nation, organization, or man could alter significantly, but that anyone in tune with these dynamics could exploit them for the acquisition of immense wealth and eventually, immense power. They anticipated that the Arab Spring was inevitable and they profited greatly from that happening. They forecasted with precision the investment market's revitalization, gaining billions on futures. When diametrically opposed forces took root in Venezuela and Colombia, they divested in the first and bought mining and oil rights in the second. In five years they quintuplicated their investment and expected yet another five years of growth at an accelerated pace."

Patricia paused for a few seconds while she poured herself a cup of coffee, an action that she used to put her thoughts in order before she continued.

"More to the point as to why I'm… or rather we… are here, is that these are, and were older men who wanted to ensure that their creation would live on even after they died. The first to go was Sal – and per their agreement, when the first of them passed a new generation would be brought into The Board, which, by the way, is the only name by which the organization is known to its insiders. As I am the daughter of one board member and was married to another, I was inducted early on and participated through my father and Sal in many decisions that apparently have created enmity enough to have someone want me or us dead. Now your family, represented by Marco and advised by Ernie, will be on The Board. And by what Ernie just told us, Marco too was targeted by whoever wants the demise of our organization."

Patricia paused, for a moment shaken by the reality of what she had just said and what she was about to reveal. Marco and Ian Carlo had not moved since she had begun talking, but sat in rapt attention as she continued.

"Among the possible enemies that would take this sort of action, and who have the necessary capabilities to act, would be a group of Middle East billionaires who have an organization similar to The Board. After years of economic dominance this group has lost clout within the international political community, opening opportunities of which we took advantage. These include the Chinese, who really don't like anyone with enough power to put a kink in their vacuum as they suck up the natural resources of the world, and a faction of the US Congress, puppets of more powerful individuals, whom we see appear and disappear with impunity in manipulation of war throughout the world. This last is by far the most dangerous as it is very diffuse and hard to pin down to a specific agenda or even know all the players. Besides that, they wield tremendous power within military establishments at home and abroad, particularly within Great Britain where some lords of the realm with mighty influence over British armed forces need the constant activation of war to maintain their wealth and influence. These are wars that we have sometimes thwarted for economic gains or upstaged our opponents when the conflict is unavoidable. In both cases it has cost them billions of dollars.

"Until now our greatest strength has been anonymity and fluidity. The Board does not have a headquarters or any geographic address. It has no visible governance and a profile that is indistinguishable from that of myriad organizations, countries and individuals whose interests coincide with ours at any particular moment. Utilizing the cat's paw has always been a standard procedure for The Board."

Once again Marco, and now Ian Carlo, were flabbergasted by the dimension of what Patricia had just presented. Their man-dominated world was coming to a not totally dislikable end.

* * *

Thousands of miles and several time zones away M&M considered his options. He was deciding on which side of the board he would make his next move. He could ally with Lujan, he could go with the Yankees, or he could just lie low and watch what would happen... maybe even see if the ragheads were willing to do some business. M&M was the ultimate service broker who had no real loyalties but appeared so to those who could pay, in one way or another, for his very expensive services. He had organized on very short notice the elimination of Los Locos for two opposing parties, Lujan and the Yank. M&M always thought of Senator Joseph W. Delany as "the Yank." Why both wanted Los Locos dead or decommissioned was not clear but it presented an interesting conundrum, one for the price of two... how profitable!

* * *

At his large estate in Maryland, Senator Delany was entertaining Cardinal Jean Dupree from the Vatican Bank, Congresswoman Tatiana Wells from California, Sub-Secretary of the Treasury Tomas Maldonado, and senior Senator Archie Mason; they were also expecting Lord Sir Humphrey Haughton of Her Majesty's Exchequer. All were Catholics, except the Anglican Brit, of extreme right political affiliations. The conversation of the day centered on the latest capitalization of war efforts in the Middle East by all the parties concerned and the net benefit to the arms industry where billions of dollars represented by that group had been invested since 9/11. More to the point, Syria was the main focus of their attention. Barriers had been lifted on sales to the rebels, which simply made the deals that they were already doing a lot easier. Once they had discussed all of the advantages, moneys that were to be invested, profits that were to be distributed, and payments that were due, only one point was reported by Senator Delany that was somewhat disquieting to those present and consequentially to all those whom they represented:

"The sanction on the heirs to The Board, the Lujan woman and Marco Carducci, was not successful. I think the choice of the Mexicans proved, in hindsight, not an advantageous one. We used them because they had complained to one of our associates about Lujan's interference with their business and that made me think that it would deter any suspicion of our participation. We gave them all the information about the targets and their location through a sterile intermediary and after their failure I have sanitized traces of our involvement by eliminating Los Locos through the proven but highly expensive services of M&M. I see no consequences of significance from this setback, but we must continue to interfere with the integration of Carducci into The Board. All our information indicates that he could become a formidable asset to them and an equally significant obstruction to our activities. Francisco Lujan's daughter is the induction point of Carducci into The Board and therefore she too must be eliminated – but all in due time." He looked at the quietly concerned faces in the room around him, absorbing his disappointing report. "Ahh, here is Lord Humphrey and it's time to enjoy this fine evening. I'll bring him up to date later as he is staying overnight." They all entered the elegant dining room and joined other guests that had been entertained by Mrs. Delany while the senator concluded his meeting.

The senator, his wife, and Ms. Wells did not survive the night. Even though they were rushed to Georgetown Memorial, they all died of a paralyzing shellfish poisoning before dawn. It all started about half-an-hour after the party had been served Chesapeake oysters as starter. Mrs. Delany felt her lips and fingers go numb and a high she hadn't experienced since her days at a sorority at St. Maria Immaculata. Soon the senator collapsed, followed by Ms. Wells and the cardinal. Within minutes the mansion was illuminated by the red and blue flashing lights of police and rescue vehicles. The hospital staff did everything possible for the VIPs but by 4:00 a.m. three were dead and the cardinal was in intensive care, yet now expected to survive. A few more of the guests had presented with symptoms but were already recovering without significant consequences.

Upon confirmation of the deaths, Sir Humphrey made two calls and went back to Ronald Reagan International where his G550 Gulfstream jet was ready for departure. The State Department made sure that no reference was made of Lord Humphrey's presence at the fatal dinner. Only Tomas Maldonado was to brief the other five senators of the conclave on the events of the evening. No possible connection could now be made with them and the failed attempt on The Board. The cardinal needed to report to no one.

Special Agent Joseph Delany learned about the death of his parents on Sunday morning, as he and his wife were getting ready for Mass at St. Patrick's Cathedral. Senator Delany's chief of staff called him with the news just after she herself had been notified by the Maryland state police. Devastated by the news and obliged to personally take care of all pertinent arrangements he asked for and immediately received a compassionate leave of absence, which by coincidence delayed the ongoing investigation into the Carducci family and subsequently his path to political glory. Climbing the political ladder on the clout provided by his father's powerful position had just been curtailed by his untimely demise.

The cause of death in the autopsy results for all of the deceased victims had been a rare but powerful form of saxitoxin, which is common in mussels but rare in oysters. It eventually paralyzes all neurotransmitters and brings death by heart failure. What could have been interesting if somebody was looking was that all the non-fatal cases with the other guests were from a totally different factor...but nobody really looked.

Next morning Marta Escobar, a kitchen maid at the Delany residence, flew back to Venezuela and bought a small but well-located house in Maracaibo where she moved with her aging parents and four parrots.

* * *

Marco and the others were unaware of the deaths in Maryland that night and proceeded with their planning, completely oblivious of the continued sanction on their lives. Marco was particularly in the dark as to the importance the enemies of The Board had placed on his and Patricia's life.

"At this point," Ian Carlo concluded, "we must follow Sal's instructions and Marco should go to the Caymans and on to Tortola. Then maybe we can all learn how this plays out."

They all agreed and plans were made to fly back to Sarasota on Tuesday, which would give Marco and Ian Carlo time to tighten the strings on all their businesses and secure the management of all in capable and loyal hands. Marco and Patricia spent Sunday together, relaxing in the security of the Roslyn estate, taking time to talk about their lives. Marco was especially curious of the period of time Patricia had been involved with her father's business, but she warned him that it was a long story that would have to be told in one stretch so it made sense.

"OK, so here we are and as far as I know we have nowhere to go or anything else to do. You have my full attention."

Patricia smiled willingly and started her narrative,

"I always thought that my father's business was wine. He has extensive viniculture in Argentina and Chile, and some partnerships all over the world. You have seen some of his wines at the house in Sarasota. Most of them come from vintners associated with him or from wholly owned vineyards. He is fascinated with wine, its history, its making, and above all in creating perfection, which is unobtainable. He taught me about wine since I was twelve and he allowed me to sip and then spit wines of all types, harvests, and origins."

"When I was twenty he sent me to Davis University in California where there is more information about wine than anywhere in the world, but it's technical knowledge, which will never replace a good palate. One can educate a palate to some degree and be proficient enough when needed, but a real wine palate is born. It's a gift of nature and a rare one at that. A good taster can demand six figures for the evaluation and classification of a flight. My father believes that those who have the best olfactory levels are those best suited for wine testing, as the whole experience will depend as much on the olfactory sense as it does on the tongue if not more. Anyway, I spent a couple of years learning about wines and then went home to help my father with his business. That was what I did until I met Sal. He was an investor looking to buy into some vineyards in Argentina and ended up being my father's partner in Salta where the unique and fantastic Torrontes is grown, and also some of the world's most exquisite cabernet."

Marco leaned back into his chair, but found he didn't want to take his eyes off Patricia as she continued.

"Over the next few years the partnership grew and extended to several other parts of the world. In the meantime I was away at school getting an MBA and getting my fill of New York. One night I was out with my roommate at a small Italian restaurant and someone sent us a bottle of the best Chianti I have ever tasted. It was from Sal. He recognized me and treated us to the wine. Sara, my friend, and I invited him to the table and spent hours talking with him about wine, New York, Peru, Argentina, my mother, his wife who had passed, and the fun he was having being my father's partner in the world of oenology. The next day when I came back from school I found a huge basket of roses and a case of the Chianti waiting for me. Sal had gone all out to impress me, and he had. The man had a crude worldliness that I found fascinating, but most of all he had an indomitable joy for life."

Marco, who had only known the serious side of Uncle Sal, was astonished by these revelations. Patricia saw his expression but continued her story.

"Sal had made my father aware of our budding but chaste relationship, as I had also done, and on my father's next visit to New York he sat me down after dinner and explained to me who Sal was and what he did. I did not shrink from him and the next time we went out to dinner I asked him about his business and about his life. The first thing he did was point out the men that followed him around. I already knew his driver as Sal never drove himself, and sometimes there was another man in the car with us who Sal said was his personal assistant, but beyond that I had never noticed the discreet entourage that followed us everywhere. He also pointed out that he and my father had agreed that I should be protected and that I have an entourage of my own; two bodyguards day and night.

"That night I went with Sal to Roslyn where he had just remodeled the house. We spent every weekend there until I had to go back to Peru to help my father with several large vineyard acquisitions. Sal and I didn't see each other for a few months although we talked on the phone almost every day. He then started visiting us every two or three weeks, flying in on Friday and flying back to New York on Mondays. Sometimes I flew back with him and sometimes my father and I had to travel to New York on business and I would stay a couple of days extra. In those days he had a G3, which became the venue for most of our romance before he proposed, first to my father and then to me. During all that time, he made a point of not introducing me to you or Ian Carlo for reasons that are not all too clear, but he never stopped talking about both of you. He was up front about his business but never discussed details of the darker aspects of it and told me that that was in the hands of others...."

She paused again for a few seconds, lost in memory, and then continued.

"We got married in Cartagena on a Thursday evening with only my father, Ernie, and Sara in attendance. It was grand; a handful of locals were in the church and for some reason spread the word to others and by the time the ceremony and mass were finished there was a crowd of well-wishers with rice and flowers that rained on us as we left the church. We stayed there for our honeymoon and did nothing special. We just kind of blended into the old city, had great food, danced every night, went sailing to the Rosario Islands and lay by the pool at the hotel drinking rum with passion fruit juice. Time flew by and we eventually went to New York because Sal was getting anxious about the business. I stayed in Roslyn for the first week while Sal got back into things. That weekend he said that he wanted to change his lifestyle. He wanted more time with me in a different life. He also said that you were better at business than he was and that Ian Carlo was tougher, while Ernie was Ernie and no flak would come from there."

Marco gently interrupted, remembering that moment. "I talked about that with Ian Carlo – suddenly we were in charge without much warning. Uncle Sal simply told us that we were responsible of our part of the business and that he would be following up now and then and to rely on Ernie for whatever we needed. The next thing we knew he was off to God knows where."

"Yes, at that time we started traveling and he accompanied me to Argentina to buy some wine for my father. That was when we met Antonio Arquiza, an exceptional vintner and a fantastic fly fisher. He invited us to his estancia in Patagonia, which was crossed by a section of the Rio Malleo, one of the best dry fly trout streams in the world. We watched him fishing one morning and I found it to be oh so graceful. It was a dance, rhythmic, elastic, full of longing yet patient. I was fascinated and when Antonio had finished and brought with him some lovely trout for breakfast I asked if I could try to fly-fish. He responded with great enthusiasm and immediately arranged for a good friend of his to teach me. After lunch we met with Martin Carranza who brought along several rods, reels and gear. Martin began by teaching me how to thread the rod by looping the line as I took it through the guides so that if I let go it would not snake out again. Then he taught me how to tie a leader to the line with a loop. Soon Martin had two pupils, as Sal was asking questions and seemed to be genuinely interested, so he repeated the exercise with him and in no time we were set up to cast.

"Antonio took us to a lago, a small pond, not far from the house where we were free of obstructions so that the lesson could take place without tangling our lines in the many willow trees that were thick all around the river. For our first casts Martin tied on a fly that he had clipped off the hook so that we wouldn't stick ourselves. I stepped up first and Martin stood behind me and took my wrist in his hand and, letting out only the rod's length of line, started to demonstrate the arch of the cast. In two hours of instruction we had achieved a modicum of skill being able to cast thirty feet of line without snapping off the fly or imbedding it in our ear. At this point Martin and Antonio decided that it was time to fish for real in the Malleo."

Patricia became soulful in her narrative.

"That afternoon was a dream. We both caught fish under the tutelage of Martin and Antonio and we shared such an experience – it was deep and peaceful, not void of excitement yet it soothed the soul in the arms of nature. As evening came and with it the end of the hatch, we broke down our rods and walked silently back to the estancia, each in a meditative mood – teachers and pupils all happy with the results of their efforts. That evening Martin stayed for dinner and was joined by his wife and sons, a lively bunch of intelligent, vivacious people. We dined in the quincho room, which is the equivalent of an open hearth where metal spears held to the embers a splayed baby lamb, short ribs locally called asado de tira, blood pudding, and a variety of sausages, all to be drizzled in chimichurri sauce. A communal carrot and tomato salad was constructed and a huge loaf of bread was baked in a breadbox directly in the quincho. Bottles of fantastic Malbec rounded out this meal that lasted deep into the night. We were in great company, enjoying great food and wine at the end of one of the best days of our lives!

"We fished together for another three days, a non-stop angling tutorial that included an exciting float down the Rio Chimehuin. Each day our fly fishing skills improved and we caught increasing numbers of trout. On the final night we camped under the stars near the confluence of the Rio Aluminé, both of us intoxicated by the sudden richness of our life together.

"The next morning we returned sadly to the estancia, packed our belongings and said our goodbyes, and drove south to San Martin de los Andes where the G3 was waiting for us. We flew to Bogotá where my father was busy setting up a communications center and a call center to service a big deal contract with a German multinational that was growing in Spanish speaking countries. By this time I was aware that my father's business interests extended far beyond wine, and Sal participated in them with growing commitment. Both my father and Sal shared with me total access to the details of their enterprise, which was admittedly startling in its sheer size and complexity. The source of the investment money was a very lucrative intermediation in the distribution of cocaine and in the subsequent legalization of the funds generated. Sal had access to distribution organizations throughout the US, Canada and Italy, which covered all the European market. My father had created associations with the greedier banks of the world, from Switzerland to tiny island nations whose only real source of money is the laundering of it."

Marco listened with growing astonishment by revelations present and predictable. His uncle was a player exponentially greater than he dreamed the man could be. Now he understood Patricia's comments just before the attack at the restaurant. Sal's New York persona was gruff, direct, ruthless and private, yet Patricia was telling him that Sal was a financial giant living in a parallel universe of sophisticated culture and travel. Even though Marco managed millions for the Carducci family, he realized that it was a mere pittance compared to what he was now learning. He was riveted to Patricia's words.

"As time went by, my father and Sal grew their financial activities and decided that Ernie Goldman should be informed of all their business, as Sal had blind trust in his loyalty and acumen. Ernie was not the least surprised and they had many strategy meetings, which little by little included other key players particularly from Wall Street, and later a few predominant political figures from the US, Italy and the UK all of whom were retired but held immense power over those in the limelight of the day. As their business developed they realized that laundering money was far more lucrative and held far greater growth potential, while being far lower in risk than any other illegal activity.

"The truly big money, they realized, came from graft, political and corporate corruption, and other underworld businesses ranging from human trafficking to extortion. Trillions of dollars needed to be laundered every year. Of almost every government budget in the world at least a ten percent was siphoned off in kickbacks, nepotistic assignments, false business fronts, futile consultant contracts and so on – money that the politicians needed laundered efficiently. In some third world countries a hundred percent of some public works money disappeared into black holes of greed. The arms dealers of the world had billions to launder for their military clients and the many churches that fleeced their believers brought huge sums of money to the table. Biblically it was money that begot money that begot money in a never ending parade of human greed and immorality; millions became billions and these became trillions, and as money goes it returns to the source through the financial institutions of the world and to the coffers of the state through taxes, fines and fees. If you are the intermediary of these activities you are not only unlimitedly rich, you are also immensely powerful. That power became The Board."

Patricia stopped. It was hard to fathom and she knew a few moments would be needed to consider all she had said. She refilled her glass and sat back.

After the enormity of Patricia's recital had sunk in, it was Marco's turn for disclosure, albeit now seemingly insignificant, financially speaking. He briefly explained to Patricia how the Carducci family's businesses operated, emphasizing the high yield of some of the legitimate enterprises, particularly casino and partnership arbitrage. Then he explained the family's "contentious" enterprises, as he preferred to call the Carducci's role in the American mafia operations.

As one of the top families, the Carducci had become facilitators and intermediaries of the activities of others, holding territorial rights that were enforced by Ian Carlo's people but without direct participation in any of them. The family charged a fixed rate and never extorted more than what was agreed. That rule of Sal's had allowed them to grow and acquire the wide respect the Carducci enjoyed. The other was brutal retaliation upon anyone who broke the contract to such a level that nobody dared cross that line. In the last ten years only one such action was necessary when the Russians had tried to muscle in on the prostitution trade of one organization that was under the family's protection.

Over the years that Marco had worked with Sal, he had created, together with Ernie Goldman and his associates, an almost perfect laundering system. Now he understood that much of that was thanks to The Board. The one dicey area was the payoff process that funneled millions of dollars a month to the powers that be. US Senators down to street cops had to be compensated to avoid interference with the operations. Unfortunately some politicians were very greedy and unstable people who would turn around and demand more than the agreed numbers and then try to blackmail. The handling of these cases was fraught with danger but unavoidable. Ian Carlo and Ernie managed this. If reason did not prevail, records of the individuals were carefully kept and used to leverage a reasonable solution; otherwise, a final sanction would invariably be applied, an action that was rare and far apart, but that did happen occasionally. There were professionals in the world who, for a price, took care of this in such a way that nothing could be traced to the hiring party and in most cases these deaths appeared to be accidental or of natural causes, except when a message was to be sent out; then things were up front and bloody, gruesome deaths that made the point.

Marco and Patricia talked until late in the evening that Sunday, having settled for light fare at lunch and dinner that was shared with only Ian Carlo and the bodyguards. They agreed that Ian Carlo would head back to New York City early Monday morning and meet with Ernie and some key people of the organization in order to secure new lines of communication and elevate everyone's awareness.

Marco had to meet several executives of various business enterprises that required attention. He had them come to Roslyn and met them one by one during the day until late evening. This included Natalia Lopez ,who brought with her Marco's briefcase and laptop. They were still in the FedEx box, confirming the well-placed trust that Marco had in Natalia. The last person Marco met with was Leon Goddard, Natalia's boss. He was an alter ego to Marco in the management of the hundreds of franchises and several other companies under the umbrella of Carducci Enterprises. He spent several hours with him and they traced a good sustaining strategy that could hold up other businesses if they ran into problems. At nine he went to his room and packed for his trip the next day.

Patricia was on the phone most of the day with her father and then several wine executives and vintners who needed updating on decisions and changes. She also finished late, packed, and was ready to leave. She and Marco met at ten for a glass of wine and final coordination. Ian Carlo called and suggested some changes. Marco should not use the Lear; instead he would have the use of Sal's, now Ian Carlo's, G550 so that if there was a tag on the Lear it would be for naught. They would take a chopper to Teterboro in New Jersey and then fly directly to Sarasota. Marco reviewed his Massimo passports and other documents and asked Patricia if she had alternative documents.

"I do, of course. They are in my apartment. I'll get them when we stop in Sarasota."

* * *

In Washington DC Special Agent Delany watched his world crumble as he keenly observed the slight but significant change in his bosses and his father's friends and colleagues. The condolences were sincere but conveyed a distancing that told him his brilliant future was no longer guaranteed. He buried himself in the business of preparing his parent's funeral with all the rigmarole and protocol that his father's position demanded. After this he had to regroup and look at his options. He would talk to Senator Mason, his father's closest friend and colleague and ask for advice. But that had to wait until after the funeral.

* * *

Across the Atlantic, M&M watched with concern the developments in Washington. He did not buy for a second that the demise of Senator Delany, his wife, and Ms. Wells was accidental. He should have known something in advance; after all this was his business. He was the world's best fixer. Delany was his client, or, better yet, represented a very powerful group that was his client, so how could he not have known? He had put in motion every resource and pulled every string but to no avail. The word was that it was an accident. He kept on looking.

5

The luxurious G550 private jet belonging to one of the family's businesses flew at 48,000 feet heading south-southwest. The plane had been used by Sal to accommodate his ever-increasing travel lust. The crew provided by the security service in Sarasota were ex-Air Force pilots and vetted service personnel. Patricia knew them well but they were strangers to Marco, who always flew his Lear. This princely indulgence had full accommodations for four passengers with lounge, seats, and ample berthing for them and three crew members. Two full crews were necessary on flights longer than six hours by Sal's own rules. Tired pilots make mistakes and pilot mistakes cost lives.

"We have about an hour and a half before we get to Sarasota," Marco pointed out looking at the receding landscape under them. "Pete and your people will be waiting for us at the airport. I'll send the G550 back to NY from Cayman. Ian Carlo may have to do some traveling of his own."

"I think we should send some security people to Tortola and have them get a feeling for the place. I imagine we are bringing some people with us?" Patricia sounded preoccupied for the first time.

"Yes." Marco tried hard not to show the concern he felt. "Luigi and Pete are coming with us and you should bring whomever you feel comfortable with. The plane can accommodate them all for the short flight. Later on they can travel commercial or we will see what's needed."

* * *

The funeral took place in Wellington, Delaware with the attendance of the Vice President of the United States, at least half of the sitting senators, and many more public, private, and ecclesiastical figures. Senator Delany and his wife were laid to rest in the family mausoleum. It was a grand funeral, but all things considered Salvatore Carducci had a better and more sincere send-off than did the senator. Special Agent Joseph Delany, his wife, and daughter stood together with his sister Marla and her husband through all the ceremony and then went to the senator's family home, just outside of Wilmington, where much fewer people than expected went to pay the family a last gesture of support.

"I hope you're not surprised, Joe. Washington is a fickle community and rarely offers more than it expects," said Senator Mason to Joseph Delany Jr. who looked almost as dejected as he felt.

Joseph Jr. did not know the senator had been among the last to see his father alive, or of his involvement – or of his father's – in their work to neutralize The Board. "What am I supposed to do now, Uncle Archie? Even my boss and the director were avoiding me like the plague at the funeral. It's as if I had contracted a social disease or something."

"Be realistic, Joe," said the senator, assessing the reception. Most of the people that came after the funeral stood around in small groups talking quietly, looking uncomfortable and snatching glances at their watches. Soon there was barely a soul left and most of the food that had been laid out was going to waste. "You were flying high on your father's coattail, which was fine, but now people are going to see how you land before they decide where they stand in regards to you. It's simple math; the doors are still open to you, but you're going to have to show some greatness of your own before they become your allies. For one thing, do your job. Do it well and far beyond what is expected and then come to me and I'll make sure that you get the proper political juice out of it."

Mason leaned back and took a sip of scotch and then nonchalantly went on, "Where do you stand with the Carducci? Now that Salvatore is gone, they should be an easier target. Ian Carlo is not a brain surgeon and he will make mistakes."

"I'm not too sure about that," Delany grumbled. "So far he has kept everybody in line and my people haven't found the least flaw where we can get a grip. I have the IRS sleeping with them and not one dime seems to be out of place. We have undercover agents in every racket; confidential informants in every corner, but when it gets close to the Carducci all lines vanish. We haven't been able to justify one search warrant and every judge becomes bookish and legalistic when it comes to them."

People continued to leave and only a few lushes taking advantage of the free alcohol were left. Even they stood as far away from Joseph as the room permitted.

The two men looked around to make sure no other ears were listening; Carducci had friends everywhere in Washington. Delany grimaced at the nearly empty room; he hadn't realized his father was so unpopular. "On the other hand," he continued, "we have been served on a platter every startup gang that thinks New York is an open table. We get Russians, Colombians, Jamaicans, and some Middle Eastern wannabes every week. NYPD has all the business it needs to keep up the statistics and to be fair, they share it all with us. Our record is good, but definitively not great."

"Well, Joe, it's time to make it great or you'll lose credibility." Mason stood up, a sign that the meeting was over. "You won't be getting a free ride anymore. We'll have to see what we can do."

Joe felt the void: the once ever-present greatness that followed his father vanished from his life. It was time to do or die.

* * *

M&M got a break. A contract on a maid that disappeared from the Delany home a day after the deaths of the senator and his wife was going around Washington without resolution. She had disappeared into thin air. It was easy to find that the contract was put out by a crack dealer from Georgetown. Now it was time to find out who really wanted the maid silenced for good, and why.

* * *

Back in Florida, Marco sat in the kitchen finalizing the plans with his men. Luigi and Pete would come with Marco. Patricia was bringing José and Cucho, her two bodyguards. The major was also at the meeting. He would man Marco's house and Patricia's apartment. No one from NY was necessary. Shuttered apartments and homes were common sights in Florida. Wealthy people used them during the season and during short periods throughout the year, but the rest of the time they were closed, locked up, and manned by minimum staff. Their trip to Caymans and Tortola to see the safety deposit boxes whose keys had been left to Marco was open ended. They couldn't forecast with precision when they would be back and the necessary preparations had to be made,.

"I need the yacht fully manned, fueled and with enough food and water for its maximum range. The crew must be totally reliable and high seas worthy. In a couple of days I'll call you with a port of destination. We will need full armory for your men, mine, Patricia and me; defensive mode only, which includes whatever you consider necessary to prevent a boarding by hostile forces. I'm transferring two million dollars to your escrow account and will replenish that fund when and if you need it. This is apart from your fees, which I will cover as billed. Also I would like the flats boat loaded on the yacht, together with whatever fishing gear Luigi considers we should carry with us if a cover be necessary."

Marco pulled a flash drive from his briefcase. "Furthermore, here is a code protocol. If you receive any communication from us that does not conform to this protocol, disregard whatever it says and prepare a team for a possible rescue mission."

"Then you are expecting more trouble, Mr. Carducci?"

"Yes, Major Allen, we are."

Three hours later Marco, Patricia and company were on their way to Georgetown, Grand Cayman. The G550 flying almost directly south at 44,000 feet over the island of Cuba. Marco was in a pensive mood as he headed for an unclear future. He was aware that whoever tried to kill him was not giving up so easily so that his sense of awareness was high but as such was taxing on his energy. He had his PA in NYC book him and all his people in a private villa just outside of Georgetown. The house had been vetted by Major Allen and determined to be safe and the staff had been in service for over ten years without a hint of wrongdoing. Four SUVs had been rented in the name of a Chilean corporation and waited at the airport for Messieurs Massimo and company.

Patricia had been on the phone to her father for almost an hour and they agreed to meet as soon as possible; The Board had to get together with this new and significant member. Such a meeting would be tentatively set for Tortola, in the British Virgin Islands at as short of notice as security measures permitted. Those details were now in the hands of Major Allen who at this precise moment was talking with an associate of his who rendered security services for mining operations, protecting those who had to work in very dangerous countries. A contingent of 24 men and women from regions as diverse as Israel, Colombia, Kashmir, and South Africa were to be assembled under the orders of a retired British SAS captain and two lieutenants, a young woman from Colombia, and a man from Iraq. In the two weeks of service that they expected to serve in this operation they would make more money than the average sales executive in the US could make in a year. Loyalty had been bought and vetted more than once and confidence in the team was high.

Cayman immigration and customs people are trained to be efficient, courteous, and welcoming. The islands live off financial business and tourism, so upon arrival Marco's party was processed in minutes, luggage passed without an inspection, and a catering cart was taken from the airplane for cleaning. The cart was loaded onto a waiting panel truck and left for the villa where it would be unloaded of sufficient defensive weapons to outfit everyone in Mr. Massimo's entourage.

* * *

At Teterboro, Joe Strasso prepared and filed an IFR flight plan with destination Isla Grande airport in San Juan, PR. When Marco, following Ian Carlo's suggestion, decided to take the G550 instead of the Lear he told Joe Strasso to fly to Puerto Rico and stand by for further instructions. He would need him in Tortola or elsewhere depending of the circumstances. Joe was to take the Lear along the US coast until Vero Beach, Florida to refuel and fly directly to San Juan. He departed according to schedule at 12:30 p.m. One hour later when it reached a cruising altitude of 43,500 feet it exploded so violently that what rained down into the deep Atlantic off the coast of North Carolina was hardly detectable on the most sophisticated radar. Nobody saw the explosion of November-Charlie-Zebra-niner-niner-five because of the cloud cover. The distant boom of the explosion was heard by a few a minute or so later, but nobody knew what it was and cared even less. Only the flight control center was automatically notified when the signal for Private 995 disappeared from the radar. Several calls went unanswered and a general all points on the flight plan were notified of the possible loss of P995. A military flight control with different capabilities noted the explosion and tracked the event to coincide with the trajectory of P995. They notified the civilian air controls on the flight route that already had the advisory and NTSB officials received the proper notifications.

Aboard P995, the flight plan stated, were Pilot-in-Command Joseph Angelo Strasso, Laura Dima Strasso who had been listed as copilot, and four unnamed passengers. All six were presumed dead. A perfunctory search by the Coast Guard yielded no results, but a fishing vessel out of Charleston, SC reported finding a piece of what appeared to be part of an aircraft, which later was confirmed as a section of the right-side elevator of a Lear 35 registered under number November-Charlie-Zebra-niner-niner-five.

Ernie Goldman was notified of the disaster by an official of the NTSB shortly before 5:00 p.m., as he was the person registered as agent for the Tri-State Industrial Laundry Service Corporation, owners of the Lear.

Ernie hung up and sat quietly at his desk for a few minutes. The news was disastrous. He knew that Marco and Patricia were not aboard the Lear and that they were safely ensconced in the villa in Cayman, but the brutal aggressiveness of the attack indicated an all-out war on The Board. Ernie decided to first call Ian Carlo and then Francisco Lujan. Ian Carlo was silent for a few seconds, and he simply told Ernie that he would apprise Marco of the event and secure a jet from NetJets and have it available for him. The call to Francisco Lujan was more difficult. Francisco was aware of the danger his daughter was in and this new attempt increased that awareness hundredfold, a mind taxing situation that a man in Francisco's position did not need.

They agreed that the meeting of The Board was to take place as soon as possible taking into consideration that Marco had work to do in Cayman that was of paramount importance.

Major Allen responded professionally and proceeded to outline several contingency plans for the safest possible travel of the members of The Board to Tortola and suggested that the *Toscana*, as the Benetti Yacht was called, be deployed off Tortola at a resort in Virgin Gorda, an island a few miles from Tortola that had world-class facilities with able berthing for the yacht. Under orders from Marco, the ship was fully channelled and manned, ready to go to whichever destination Marco assigned, but under the circumstances the *Toscana* would sail for Virgin Gorda under Ernie's authority unless Marco had different plans.

Ian Carlo called Marco and told him about the Lear and the loss of Joe and his wife. At this moment they didn't know who the other passengers were and as it was not an international flight, it didn't have a passenger manifest. Fortunately they had no children to orphan, though someone had to tell his parents, who lived in Sicilia.

Marco took the news very hard. Joe was his close friend; he had taught Marco how to fly and had gone with him everywhere. Marco had spent several Thanksgivings at the Strasso home and loved both of them dearly. And, while the sense of loss was great, the fury he felt overshadowed any other feeling. He kept to himself for over an hour while he channeled that fury into focus and prepared mentally for what was to be a war.

The others took the news with equal degrees of loss, sorrow and outrage. Joe was part of a close team that had shared the prosperity of the Carducci and had committed themselves totally to the family. Patricia knew Joe and had met his wife a few months back when she came down to Florida with him in the Lear while the G550 was in maintenance. He had flown Sal and Patricia down to Sarasota and then had taken them to Cartagena for a weekend to celebrate their anniversary. Pete and Luigi had also come on that trip and enjoyed the stay as a group while Major Allen's Colombian team took care of security. Laura had proved to be a fun-loving girl with an uncanny sense of rhythm who danced to cumbias and porros like a local. Patricia felt that she had lost a dear friend even though she had not seen her since.

Francisco Lujan was stoic as ever. He understood what was happening, and that it was happening faster than he anticipated. He understood that Patricia's life was in danger and that all he could do was trust in the Carducci security, which was also Patricia's armor at this time. He had to find out who the engine behind these acts really was. He could narrow it down to two groups: The US Senate contingent or the Middle Easterners, as he did not see a Chinese hand in this. There was always the chance that someone else was the author of the attempts but he doubted it. He got to work. First he gave instructions to the Bogotá operation to sweep for chatter in the known circles of the senators and the Arabs, but most of all the senators as he thought the Arabs had far too much on their plate right now to be expending resources attacking The Board.

He was not wrong. Senator Mason received the report of the Lear's demise and the NTBS preliminary report with satisfaction but not joy. He was a fervent Catholic and despised the necessary violence. It indicated without confirmation that aside from the crew, Marco Carducci, Patricia Lujan, and a couple of bodyguards were the victims. He sent off short advisories to colleagues here in DC and to Rome, London, and Luxembourg. The sanction appeared to have been successful. Cardinal Jean Dupree from the Vatican Bank said a prayer for those whose deaths had been necessary to the greater good as he saw it. In his London office Lord Humphrey Houghton received the news early next morning with little emotion though he missed the enthusiasm that Delany used when communicating these things. He ordered the second part of the payment due sent to the hit man who had accepted the mission as ordered by Cardinal Dupree.

* * *

Sitting in his office within a trailer just outside of JFK, Tony Kisses saw the bank confirmation of the five hundred thousand dollars that had arrived from Luxembourg. He not only had his vengeance on that Carducci asshole, he had half a million to celebrate with. A buddy in the Liguria family out of Vegas had asked him if he knew of anyone willing to do the hit knowing perfectly well that there was no love lost between Tony Kisses and the Carducci. Tony had taken the job without thinking when the figure mentioned was more than he was worth. One hundred thousand down and five hundred thousand when the job was done. Rigging the Lear was no big deal; he had an airplane mechanic who worked for him at JFK go to Teterboro where the Lear was and rig it to explode when the interior cabin pressure reached the equivalent of 8,000 feet, which was about 38,000 to 40,000 feet in real altitude. When Joe had gone home for the night, the mechanic had nonchalantly gone to the Lear and planted the four kilos of C4 deep inside the landing gear well. Nobody looked twice at a mechanic doing his job where others like him were doing the same.

* * *

On Wednesday morning Marco went to the bank with Patricia, having sent Pete and Luigi ahead to check out the area and keep him posted. All was well; they entered the bank and headed directly towards the assistant manager. He presented himself as Marco Lorenzo Massimo showing his Italian passport and presenting the key to the safety deposit box. The assistant manager welcomed them to the bank and asked them to follow him.

The vault was huge. It was located underground and reached by an ample elevator that went down a few seconds before it opened to the high ceilinged room. The door to the vault was an ASMEC of gargantuan proportions that opened to a code, a handprint and a retina scan. Marco and Patricia were escorted to a room with a sturdy table, two chairs, and little else. Seconds later an electric cart, unmanned, guided only by its robot brain brought a metal box the size of a milk crate next to the table. The manager inserted one very high-tech looking key and bowed out of the room, telling them that they could press the button on the box when they were ready to leave. They had all the time they wanted until 5:00 p.m., when the bank closed and the automatic locks would go into place until the next day. Marco inserted his key and the box emitted a green light and the top slid back more than halfway. Inside were several manila envelopes, and a large stack of US dollars and another of euros, several hundred thousand judging by the denominations of €500 and $100.

There were also two UK passports for Marco and Patricia, both under the last name MacKenzie. The instructions indicated that the security box in Tortola was under these names. In an envelope there were valid drivers' licenses, club memberships to a posh London club, and several credit cards all in the same names. They put every-thing in two bags that the bank provided and closed the box, touch-ing the button on the robot's console, and it shut the top and rolled out as it had come. Seconds later a clerk came and asked if the bank could do anything else for Mr. Massimo. Next they were escorted to the bank lobby where Marco called for the car. It came followed by two others and the small caravan set off for the villa.

With the news of the Lear and its crew also came a sense of iso-lation and, you might say, island fever. Marco was accustomed to leave at very short notice from practically any location and the lack of that option weighed on him, particularly because of the immi-nent threat upon their lives. He was already making contingency plans on his way to the villa when Ian Carlo called to tell him that a NetJets G3 was on its way to await orders from Marco. The call came from one of twenty burner phones that Marco and Ian Carlo each had acquired for communications during the next week or so. Ian Carlo also told him that two additional bodyguards from Al-len Security were on the way to Grand Cayman from Miami and would contact Marco upon arrival. They were a man and a wom-an who traveled as spouses so that they did not attract attention. Both needed to be armed locally but the G3 carried some additional equipment.

"We went to the bank," Marco told Ian Carlo. "There was some cash and some envelopes that I haven't opened yet but that I will look at as soon as we get to the villa."

Marco asked if there was any further information on what hap-pened to Joe.

"No, it's too early to know anything in concrete. All we know is that the plane blew up and there is little left to tell a tale. But I have some ideas and I'll tell you what comes from that when we talk next time. By the way, did the Lear go anywhere after you landed?"

"To Teterboro. I asked Joe to have a mechanic go through the plane for a safety check and then to wait for orders. As far as I know he did that, left the Lear locked and secured at the FBO at

Teterboro, and went home. Why he took his wife to PR and who the passengers were and why they were aboard, I don't know."

This said, they disconnected as the SUV reached the entrance to the villa. Pete and one of Patricia's men got out of the first car and did a rapid check of the perimeter even though all appeared normal and the smiling butler, actually named James, was at the door to greet them. Marco and Patricia headed for the dining room and placed the bags on the table and proceeded to empty them of their contents. The cash was stacked on the side and the envelopes, three in total, were opened.

The first contained other envelopes with addresses and keys to safe houses in several major cities: London, Luxembourg, Rome, Buenos Aires, Bogotá, Los Angeles, and Hong Kong. Each was maintained and serviced by an international real estate management company that belonged to one of the members of The Board and were considered highly secure, consistently swept for bugs, and located strategically for all possible advantages. The second envelope contained the biographies of men that The Board considered dangerous opponents, their present positions and, where possible, relations of one with others. Such was the case with Senator Joseph Delany, Senator Archibald Mason III, Lord Humphrey Houghton, and Cardinal Jean Dupree. About twenty more biographies were included and a list of names and general locations of several dozen more, but without much detail. One such was referred to only as M&M and had a Post-It note that said "Neutral?" The third envelope contained only a sheet of paper with a link that, when Marco typed it into the address line of his computer, sent him to a database of thousands of individuals, their location's, how to reach them and the reason they were reliable in certain unique ways and why they could be compelled to cooperate with The Board. From all over the world and in different walks of life they all held special abilities, capabilities, and/or positions that could render them very valuable in the right circumstances, a database of human assets, a private Angie's List if you like.

Marco called in the people on his team, starting with Luigi and gave each of them $5,000 dollars and €5,000 Euro and told them this was money that they were to use instead of their company issued or personal credit cards. No paper trace was to be left behind. All major bills would be paid directly by an asset management company in Barbados. He emphasized the prohibition of using the credit cards unless specifically told to do this. Patricia's men received the same cash and she underlined the order in very stern Spanish that made even Marco want to throw away his cards even though he hardly understood what she said. Now plans had to be made for the trip to Tortola, hopefully without leaving a footprint.

In New York, Ian Carlo was applying his greatest personal asset to the problem: his capacity to focus and cut through the bullshit. Somebody, he thought, put the bomb on the Lear sometime between the time Joe went home the night after his mechanic had done a thorough check of the airplane and the time Joe got back to Teterboro, which was nine the next morning. During that time somebody saw something, even if they didn't know it. He was going to find out who and what. Ian Carlo called two cousins on his mother's side, one of whom worked as a homicide detective with NYPD, and his kid brother, who was an enforcer for one of Ian Carlo's operations. He gave them a clear picture of the situation and what he expected from them. Within an hour both were on leave from their jobs and headed for Teterboro and the FBO that serviced the Lear. After hours of very professional and surprisingly courteous interrogation, they learned about a mechanic who worked mostly at night and who was changing the main fan on the engine of a Embraer right next to the Lear. They went over to the man's home and caught him leaving for the shops. Yes, he remembered the mechanic who had spent about an hour with the Lear that night and, no he didn't know the man personally, but yes he did remember that he was wearing the overalls of a maintenance company at JFK and yes he could give a description of the man including his nametag on the overall, "Andy."

The cousins called Ian Carlo with the information. He decided to take care of this personally and asked the two brothers to locate the man and bring him to a warehouse in Brooklyn.

Andy Pasco was returning from lunch when a NYPD detective asked him to please answer some questions. They took him to a car that was later described as a "cop car" and left the area. Andy was nervous and jittery but seconds later a pinch in his thigh rendered him unconscious until he woke up hanging upside down looking at the inverted face of Ian Carlo Carducci. The realization of where he was and who was in front of him sent distress signals to the sphincters of his lower body and as he uncontrollably urinated over himself the piss flowed down his neck and onto his face. Ian Carlo just stared for about a minute with a deadpan face that revealed nothing – yet promised the worst – driving the utter fear of God into Andy. Diarrhea overcame him and added streams of shit to his misery.

"I only have one question for you," Ian Carlo said in a low voice that did not betray the fury that he felt. "Why did you put a bomb on the Lear?"

Andy was no standup guy and much less for a fuck-wad like Tony Kisses. He told Ian Carlo everything with detail down to the night he spent with a couple of hookers using the five grand that Tony had paid for the job. Drained of all he knew he fainted and mercifully missed the nod from Ian Carlo that was followed by a brutal smash to the back of his head, so vicious that his worthless brains joined the shit and piss on the cement floor. Ian Carlo then dismissed the two brothers with a fat envelope for each. It would be several days before the stench of the hanging carcass attracted a security guard who, after vomiting, called it in to the NYPD.

* * *

Far away M&M had managed to find out who and where the maid was wholeft the Delanys' so soon after their death. And he planned to find out a lot more.

* * *

Tony Kisses was walking down Jamaica Avenue towards his favorite diner when he was unceremoniously shoved into a van together with his two bodyguards who were unconscious on the floor, trembling from massive doses of stun gun juice. Tony on the other hand was well aware of what was happening to him as an entire team of enforcers from the Carducci family were his silent and sullen companions. The two bodyguards were dumped in an alley behind a K-Mart as they were not part of Tony's betrayal. A half hour later Tony was being expertly waterboarded in an abandoned YMCA in Queens. The tender ministrations were being applied by an ex-CIA thug who had learned and practiced the technique in a Polish jail where several dozen Al-Qaida members from Saudi Arabia were interrogated for months before being returned to the more intense and devastating attentions of the Saudi secret service.

Tony was not given a chance to say much; every few minutes he would be given time to recuperate and before he could say much the process would begin again, over and over. Several hours later Tony's vital signs became erratic and his blood pressure was going through the roof. A nurse who was monitoring him advised Ian Carlo that further waterboarding would kill him. He was then tied to a chair and fed two bottles of Five Hour Energy, a glass of orange juice, and a cup of very strong coffee. Two minutes later he was hyped up to an unbelievable level with his heart racing at 130 beats per minute yet his blood pressure had tanked. There was a lot of anxiety but no disorientation; Tony knew where he was and what was happening to him. Before anyone asked him a single question Tony told everything he had done, who had hired him, how much was in his bank, what his mistress' address was, where his mother lived and anything else he thought might save him from further hell.

What surprised Ian Carlo was that the contract had come from Las Vegas. The Liguria did business with the Carducci and if the hit was sanctioned by the family, there was going to be a lot of retaliation; it was something Ian Carlo did not want but would not back away from, though he seriously doubted that was what had transpired. Tommy Liguria had been a friend of Ian Carlo since they were in their teens and had always come across as a straight player. He doubted Tommy would sanction a hit on a Carducci *capo*. Tony Kisses 'fessed up the name Jerry Birko, but it rang no bells in Ian Carlo's mind or in that of any of the guys present. This had to be settled directly with Tommy Lee, as Tomaso Liguria was known among friends.

6

Special Agent Delany was still buried in paperwork, meetings with his father's attorneys, and deciding some property issues with his sister and her asshole husband who thought that by being a junior congressman, the sun shined out of his ass. Finally, there were issues regarding a special election for the now empty Senate seat in the very important and influential state of Delaware. One must remember that an obscene number of the country's major corporations were seated there. Time was going by and he was not able to get back to his post and strive for the greatness needed to be positively acknowledged in the public eye.

* * *

M&M was following threads at his usual efficient rate. He now had people "interviewing" Marta Escobar about the fatal night at the Delany's. Her interrogator, a local police major, had chosen a paternalistic approach and now had Marta giving him all the details of how the cardinal's assistant, the handsome Monsignor had offered to help her family in Venezuela by giving her a small house that coincidentally had been left to the church by a pious nun who passed on to her heavenly reward. He had exacted two promises from her, the first was that he be permitted to privately bless the food that was to be served that night and second that she must go home soon and follow God's wishes that she take personal care of her parents. He gave her an envelope with $5,000 dollars and his special blessing. She planned to go at the end of the month, but the deaths of the Delanys told her it was better to get out of town in a hurry. Unfortunately when she got to Maracaibo, the address of the house was an empty lot but with a $3,000 down payment she had bought a very small house which she now shared with her parents. Some savings and a job cooking at a local café should keep them in food and shelter.

M&M now knew that Cardinal Dupree and his associates had killed the Delanys and Ms. Wells, but he didn't know why. He wondered if anything to do with the Tamaulipas cleanup of the Los Locos cartel precipitated this assassination since it had been Senator Delany who had contracted the hit. M&M had to keep looking and he knew exactly where to start.

* * *

Cardinal Dupree considered the situation now that Marco Carducci and the Lujan woman were out of the way. In the United States, Senator Mason was taking lead of the others and he himself was in full control of associates in Europe and Asia; maybe Humphreys was a bit of a loose cannon being the only non-Catholic, but he seemed to be keeping his ducks in line. After all, being Anglican was being Catholic, just that they didn't know it yet...but all in due time. Dupree was the only one of the group who knew with total clarity what he wanted and there was nothing that he would not do in order to achieve it.

The Catholic Church, God's only foothold in this world, used to be the most powerful entity in it and he, Cardinal Dupree, was going to bring it back to that position with or without the help of the pope and his curia. He knew that in order to do that he needed unlimited funds and power over the powerful of this world. His sense of destiny overcame any moral or ethical concern, which he didn't have anyway. Jean Dupree was born a sociopath to a mother obsessed with religion. He was fed Catholicism from his mother's breast onwards and saw no other destiny for himself other than joining the church at an early age. He grew in "sanctity" in the eyes of a church that rewarded dedication and selflessness. Asexual by nature, he despised the promiscuity of the seminary and the one time that a priest had made an advance on him was the last time that pervert made an advance on anyone. A few days later he was found hanging from a rafter having left a typed note confessing his sins and begging the Lord for mercy on his wretched soul. Young Jean had killed him without remorse or satisfaction. It was the disposal of trash.

Soon he understood how to progress in an organization that was seniority-oriented but had several escalators that bypassed such stupidity. Dupree became proficient at using them so that before he was thirty he found himself in a comfortable position at the Vatican, away from the Marseille that had been his home since birth. A polyglot and mathematician with an eidetic memory promptly earned a position of trust in the place he wanted to be, the Vatican Bank. He understood from an early age that money and not prayer achieved worldly power and thus the only way he saw for "his" church to be great was to have a great amount of money, and who else better to manage it than himself. The salvation of immortal souls was left to those whose work was fueled by his money. That money also fueled the brilliant careers of politicians the world over who, in Dupree's psychotic view, would be a power for a "good" that only he could conceive. To achieve his goals he tapped on the most profitable activity that would always be available: laundering money. Unfortunately there was competition.

* * *

On this clear day the Virgin Islands were seen from the cockpit of the G5 like cookie crumbs on a blue mantel. They were named Virgins by Christopher Columbus on his second trip to the West in order to honor St. Ursula and the 11,000 martyred virgins. Most of these islands became British around the end of the sixteenth century when privateers wrestled them from the Dutch. They were slave-powered sugar plantations until the liberation of slaves almost 200 years later. They rose from the Caribbean adjacent to the US Virgin Islands, which were taken from the Danish and then from the Spaniards.

Terrance B. Lettsome International Airport at Tortola is not really on Tortola. It's on Beef Island, where it occupies most of it except for a tiny town and a couple of white crescent beaches. Beef Island is joined to Tortola by the Queen Elizabeth Bridge and is the only commercial airport in the B.V.I. The landing is fascinating – you approach over water until a thin strip of beach separates the runway and water. Tourists love to lie on this beach and experience the incoming jets flying by only feet from their noses giving them an adrenaline rush from the sheer size of the huge metal birds overhead.

The G3 made a perfect touchdown and taxied after a "follow me" truck that took it to a parking spot a hundred feet down from the main building. The arriving party was loud, pompous, and flashy. They made sure everybody noticed the arrival of Mr. & Mrs. MacKenzie, rich, fun-loving, and ready to take on the islands. They and their entourage were escorted to a villa situated on the slopes of Mount Healthy overlooking Brewer's Bay. At just £3,000 a night it was considered a bargain. Seven bedrooms with en-suite bathrooms, two pools and a waterslide that went from one to the other made this as unique a playground as one can find. A staff of ten served, cooked, cleaned, and gardened. All were locals who had been with the villa for years.

Separately, another Mr. and Mrs. MacKenzie arrived from Puerto Rico on a small island-hopper airline. A middle class British couple that spoke little, bargained much, and chose to stay at a reasonable hotel right outside of Road Town. They were rapidly dismissed by the observer as the typical low-budget tourists that did not deserve a second look. They rented a moped and went off into the sightseeing wonder that is the botanical garden and Mount Healthy. They came back in the evening and nobody noticed that those who left and those who returned were not the same people.

Marco and Patricia went to their rooms at the villa to shower and change after making a roundabout trip in economy class, changing planes in Miami and Puerto Rico and now anxious to cleanse the grime of that last flight. They later met for an early dinner with all the staff before the substitute MacKenzies went back to the hotel dressed in clothes identical to those that Marco and Patricia had donned when leaving in the moped.

"We need to be totally aware of our surroundings, here and anywhere we go. There are people trying to kill us and they mean business," Patricia told all their staff. "That includes everyone here; as you know, sadly, in the attempt to kill Marco and me our enemies did not hesitate in destroying a plane with its crew and all on board."

Plans were made for the next day so that Marco and Patricia could go to the bank. The bodyguards who would go to the hotel posing as the other MacKenzies would walk around Road Town and survey the area to see if anyone looked or acted out of place, but it would be Marco and Patricia, dressed in a similar attire who would later enter the bank and open the box registered to Marcus MacKenzie of Avon-upon-Thames, Stratford, UK. The rest of the party would spread through town and act spoiled rich so that attention could be diverted from the main event.

After dinner everyone retired to rest for what could be an eventful day.

* * *

The bank in Road Town was on Main Street just off Rite Way. It was in an old building and only had a small sign with the name on a metal placard and a bell with a speaker. Seconds after Patricia rang the bell, a polite British accented voice inquired the visitor's name and business. "Marcus MacKenzie to visit my safety deposit box," answered Marco in what he thought was a somewhat English accent. The buzzer opened the door to a long corridor that led to an interior patio, but before reaching it there was a sign that indicated the British Overseas Investment Bank was to the right.

The bank was a far cry from the one in Georgetown but was elegant and subdued. A gentleman of many mixed races, dressed in a white linen suit and white shoes but with no tie, received them.

"I am Ian Locklear," he said, shaking hands with both of them. "If I can see your passport, Mr. MacKenzie, we can proceed to our vault room."

He took the passport, went to a scanner, and scanned the page where the signature was. Satisfied, he returned the passport to Marco. He led them to an adjacent room that was behind a secure looking door followed by a vault door. It was the usual arrangement seen in banks all over the world. A room full of small doors with two locks in each, one for the bank and one for the client. Ian went to Box 260 and opened his lock. Marco unlocked his and the small door opened to reveal a metal box that the bank manager withdrew and placed on a table that was in the middle of the room. He bowed out and told Marcus to take his time. Marco and Patricia looked into the box and found only a small white envelope. They took it without opening it, aware that cameras would be on them. They left the box and called for Ian to open the gate so that they could leave. On the way out Marco returned the key to Box 260 and said he would not be using it anymore. Ian asked if Mr. MacKenzie would continue with the account at the bank. Marco, who didn't know anything about an account there, asked for a latest statement.

The investments held by Marcus MacKenzie were all money market and reached nearly 115 million British pounds; the activity was mirrored to that of the bank's own investments and had proved to be very profitable, having paid in taxes to Her Majesty's Exchequer the princely sum of nearly nine million pounds in the last year alone. Marco held a straight face, or as straight as he could manage. He said to Ian that he was satisfied with the performance and would continue with the account. Ian asked if the conditions should remain the same, being that the order was not to send statements except when requested by coded fax. Marco said yes to everything except that he wanted to change the code to an algorithm that would change it every six hours. This done, they departed with the envelope in Patricia's purse.

* * *

Marcello Mastroianni Mascerano, better known as "M&M," was pondering the information he had. Obviously the Vatican banker had killed a close associate, a powerful senator of the United States, and apparently got away with it. What was not clear was why. Jean Dupree was a very young cardinal and held the second post within the Vatican Bank, yet he moved in very rare circles. Since the Yank, as he called Senator Delany, had called the hit on the Mexicans coincidentally at the same time as Francisco Lujan, and as M&M did not believe in coincidences, he now knew that the killing of the senator, the attempt on Patricia Lujan, and probably the American who was with her were all related. What made his ears prick up was when he noticed the name of the American, Marco Carducci. He knew Salvatore and this was one of the heirs apparent even though it was a man called Ian Carlo de la Rosa who had assumed the head of that family when Salvatore died. This was getting better and better. If he chose well whom to cast his lot with there could be many millions in the making. "Think, M&M, think," he said to himself out loud.

* * *

Francisco Lujan didn't own a jet but he always had one when he needed it. In Lima, Bogotá, and Miami, which were his most frequent residencies, he had charter companies that would give him priority over anybody. He never had used a weapon, but he was a very protected and lethal person. He was the chairman of The Board. He had more power than most presidents of large nations with the exception of the G8, but then, they could always be persuaded to share some of that power with him. Today he was at his Bogotá office at the top of a big building on Avenida Chile, which is the city's financial center. Shortly he had an early breakfast appointment with the president and his Natural Resource minister. It would be in the same building as the Bankers Club, just a floor above. The food was good, the view exceptional and privacy guaranteed. The meeting was about royalties on a couple of mining licenses that had turned out to be far more productive than any geological study predicted. Thus the minister had recruited the president to negotiate a better deal with the owners of the enterprise, represented by Francisco Lujan. But before that he had to review again the events of the last few days. His only daughter had been targeted as well as the heir of his partner and close friend Salvatore Carducci. Things like that did not go unanswered in Francisco's world. There would be consequences, first the ones that affected business and then the personal response to such an affront.

Directly after breakfast he headed for Tortola flying non-stop from Bogotá in a jet that belonged to a bank he dealt with and was chartered through Privé. For this flight he was using a Citation that was more than enough for the trip. The only inconvenience was the hellish traffic from his office to El Dorado International Airport, and that had been avoided by the generous use of the private helicopter of a very rich and very corrupt ex-president whose money The Board administrated or, better said, dry cleaned and pressed to impeccable standards. Simultaneously, another jet had departed for Lima ostensibly having him on board, and so it would appear in immigration records both in Bogotá as well as Lima. The jet that flew to Tortola was carrying Telluride Bosch, a rich businessman from Luxembourg, and so the records showed.

* * *

Ian Carlo disposed of Tony Kisses in such a manner that not a trace of him would ever be found. A blast furnace that melted titanium eventually vaporized the bastard leaving nothing but assorted gasses that flew out of a cooling tower. Unfortunately for Tony the feeding belt to the furnace was very slow and he roasted alive for what must have seemed like eternity before his blood finally boiled him dead.

In the Limo on the way back to NYC Ian Carlo called Tommy Lee.

"'sup, Gucci," said Tommy. He had always called Ian Carlo "Gucci" because since they were young, Ian Carlo always dressed in impeccable suits and handmade shoes.

"Tommy, long time. Why such a stranger? Isn't New York good enough for a transplanted Brooklyn Heights spaghetti pusher or you just don't bother to call?"

"Hell Gucci, if I was in NYC the first goober I would call was you. You know that the business keeps me here on a short leash. You're planning on a Vegas weekend or what?"

"Tommy, I need to know something, who's a guy called Birko? Does he work for you?

"Yeah man, he's a minor associate, why?"

"I need to ask him some hard questions. Do you have a problem with that?" Ian Carlo held his breath. The answer would tell him where Tommy stood on this shit.

"Gucci, you call it, I'll play it. How do you want to do this?"

Ian Carlo breathed out.

"Keep him under your thumb and I'll get someone to bring him here."

"Better yet, I'll ask him to come with me to NY and you can take it from there."

"I'll have a jet for you at McCarran tomorrow morning. Bring along whomever you like and we'll have some goo with the wife after we have our chat with Birko."

Tommy Lee knew better than to fuck with Ian Carlo. He ran the toughest outfit in the New York area and he also meant security for a lot of Tommy's family who still lived in the area. Besides that, he was a friend. Birko was expendable if it came down to that. He was not a made man and Tommy had always suspected he served more than one master. Anyway, he called his girlfriend Tatiana, a respectable girl from Phoenix who managed a Chico store in Vegas, and asked her to call in sick for a couple of days. Then Tommy called his first lieutenant Joe Tellez and told him to get a couple of guys to come with him to New York to watch his six. He knew Joe would include Birko and that would also confirm something he suspected; Joe was AC/DC and Birko was for sure a little faggot that spent all his time dressing saints at Guardian Angel Cathedral.

Next morning Tommy, Tatiana, Joe Tellez, a Mexican trouble shooter named Esteban Torres, and Jerry Birko boarded the NetJets Falcon at a private terminal at McCarran International airport and departed for MacArthur on Long Island at 8:05 a.m. local time. It would be well into the afternoon when they got there.

* * *

When Marco and Patricia arrived at the villa they opened the small envelope that had a 64GB memory card in it. A note said simply, "Patricia has the password." Marco popped the card into the slot in his laptop and promptly the tile for the drive appeared on the action bar of the screen. He double-clicked it and several icons appeared. The first and largest was a .mov file – obviously a video of some kind. He clicked on that and a request for a password appeared. Patricia thought for a few seconds and typed in "BoneFish2009." Nothing happened and the request appeared again. This time she typed "Tarpon2012." Bingo! The screen showed the traditional black square and an arrow triangle indicating readiness. Marco made it full screen and hit the arrow. The amused face of Salvatore di Dio Carducci appeared, looking straight at them.

* * *

When Tommy Lee and his people arrived at MacArthur there were two SUVs waiting at the airport. He sent Tatiana with Joe to a hotel in Glen Cove and told Jerry Birko and Esteban to come with him in the other. They would meet in a couple of hours at the hotel.

The SUV headed west and then north. The conversation in the car was short and to the point.

"I'm meeting with some possible associates from around here. The meeting is on a boat and I want you guys to stay close to the stern and pay attention to what's going on," Tommy told his men. It was standard procedure for a *capo* and his bodyguards. Neither of them thought twice about it. The orders were clear enough.

* * *

Marco and Patricia were watching for only a few seconds when they were advised that Francisco Lujan had just landed at Beef Island. They closed down the laptop and went to pick him up in the SUV in the company of Luigi and José who, since the Sarasota incident, seemed to work well together. Within half an hour they had Francisco in the car sitting next to Patricia, who could not hide the joy of being with her father. It was the first time they were together since Sal's funeral. They talked in Spanish for a few minutes before Francisco apologized to Marco.

"I'm sorry, Marco; it's been so long that I forgot my manners. Patricia was just asking me about some of the staff in Lima whom she has known all her life and I was inquiring about her, but it's obvious that she is her usual self." Francisco directed himself to Marco but still held his daughter in a warm embrace.

"How are you? I know how close you were to Sal and now the loss of your dear friend José Strasso; I can't imagine how difficult this must be. Now I guess that you are up to date with everything?"

Marco could hardly believe that he was feeling jealous of Patricia's father; he wanted to be the one holding her.

"Not everything. Patricia and I were about to look at a video that Sal left us in a safety deposit box here. We will all see it when we get to the villa. By the way, accommodations are available at the villa for your people. Patricia tells me they are coming from Lima via Puerto Rico. When they arrive Luigi and José will pick them up."

"That's fine. It's only my personal assistant and a security person who has been with me for many years."

When they got to the villa Patricia escorted her father to his room and suggested he take a rest. "*Descanza un poco y siquieres tomate un baño antes de seguir.*" But by the time he was ready it was time for lunch. A grand buffet of Caribbean delectables was served under a large awning in the patio next to the pool. Lobsters split in half, steamed then grilled and sprinkled with paprika and butter, cold peeled shrimp, conch salad, Russian salad, fried bone-fish, curry rice and a couple of coconut pies filled the table. Large belly bottles of ice tea and lemonade together with a bucket full of iced Heineken and another with a good New Zealand Sauvignon Blanc completed the fare. Not a crumb would be wasted.

After lunch they sat at the table where Marco's laptop waited. He had taken the memory card with him so he put it back in the computer and went through the protocol until again there was the smiling face of Salvatore Carducci. He clicked the mouse and the figure came to life.

"Hello Marco, I believe you are with Patricia or you would not be seeing this." His head turned slightly as if looking for her and said, "My love, if I'm still anywhere in the universe, I'm missing you, of that you can be sure. But now is a different time and you must continue with your wonderful life, with the magic of being you."

Patricia looked away for a moment, her eyes softly closed.

The image of Sal shifted his eyes back to the center of the screen and said:

"Marco, there are many things that you have learned about me in the last few days and there are many more that you will learn now and in the days to come. You must realize that in the last ten years I have evolved slowly and almost imperceptibly into a some-what different person. Part of that is Patricia's doing, but most of all it has to do with how Francisco Lujan and I came across businesses that we didn't even know existed and organizations that control the lives of almost everyone on earth and rarely for the betterment of humanity. The first culprits are not the most obvious. The world in general despises those that govern them in democracy or dictatorship; civil, military or religious are equally loathed. Then there are the transnational powers, basically circumscribed to multinational corporations and religions. There are billions of people in each religion. Christianity dominates the Western World, Islam the Middle East and great parts of Asia and Africa, Buddhism and Hinduism a big chunk of Asia. Then of course there is Judaism, which has a fingerhold everywhere in the world. Among these is where we found the footprints of those who truly have power and comprehended the mechanics of the machinery that controls the world."

Sal stopped to drink some water and then continued his narrative. Marco and Patricia were eager to get on, but Francisco just sat there relaxed, feeling the presence of his partner even from beyond the grave.

"Since ancient Rome we see men dominating nations with powers far greater than of those elected to govern. The Fabian and the Cato ruled throughout the Republic and far into the Empire, bending the will of emperors and generals, priests and popes, and even though their names diluted and changed they were there, profiting from every war and every conquest and extending their power throughout the Roman Empire and beyond. The descendants of William the Conqueror dominated Europe for centuries, and Peter the Great's half-brother left a brood of powerful men and women that permeated even the Soviet Union of Stalin. While at the time the difficulties of travel and communication curtailed the power of men, now when such obstacles have been overcome, a single individual or a dedicated group of individuals can control the destinies of billions.

"Money, Marco, is a powerful engine but belief is so much more so. Repeat something enough times and, no matter how absurd, it will become the accepted truth. Millions of lives have been sacrificed to propaganda spewed through the mindless mouth of elected officials whose election was just another fraud. Believe me when I tell you that it's not the ignorant masses that are mesmerized by the spin doctors. An example at a smaller scale was the Madoff case. He fooled brilliant people who had made fortunes. Top executives of employee funds and charities that invested billions bought his story, and yet looking back one can hardly understand how a puerile scheme like that fooled government regulators as well as investors. He didn't generate a penny...ever. All he did was tell everyone just how brilliant he was and they believed him and handed over their money. On a grander scale Adolf Hitler convinced a downtrodden people still reeling from defeat that they were the dominant race that was owed fealty by the rest of the world. He needed the money the Jews had, and even though he had Jewish blood in him, he convinced a nation to exterminate them like rats. Don't be fooled into thinking that there was an adult German that didn't know what was being done to the Jews; they were drummed into believing that it was the right thing to do by one of the greatest flaks of his day, Joseph Goebbels. Then a nation of disciplined, hardworking individuals such as the Japanese were led to believe that a timid little man with thick glasses was God on earth and they committed suicide in his name, yet he was nothing but the hostage of a military class that had dominated Japan for centuries. This control is being exercised today at a more subtle but much greater scale by a few people. And, by the way, that includes us.

"I'm tired and will take a rest. Patricia and I are going to the opera tonight and I need a nap. I'll continue this tomorrow."

When Marco looked at Patricia tears were flowing freely from her eyes.

"I remember that night so clearly," she said quietly. "Sal had been in his study for hours and that night we went to see Mozart's *Magic Flute* and then to dinner at Le Cirque. It was a wonderful evening."

Marco had the impulse to hug her but didn't; Francisco felt the same and did.

The video continued. Sal appeared again in different attire and the background was now Sal's Sarasota home studio next to the bedroom.

"Well, it's been a few days but let's continue. I was saying that the world is being manipulated by a few people, and I do mean few. Francisco and I found traces of huge transactions that affected the monetary value of some currencies or created financial crisis of unimaginable dimensions. The 2008 world crisis is the latest example of incredibly brash manipulation by which the middle classes of the world were stripped of their wealth and then were taxed to "salvage" the same institutions that had ripped them off.

"To illustrate what happened I'm going to use a story that economists use to explain how money works: A man arrives at a small town and goes to the local B&B. He pays the owner $100 for a room under the condition that if he doesn't like it he will get his money back. As soon as the man goes to his room, the owner of the B&B runs to the butcher to pay his outstanding bill. The butcher then goes to the bar to pay $100 toward his tab, the barman pays the local hooker the $100 for commissions owed to her and she runs to the B&B and pays $100 for a room she had used. The man comes back to the owner and says he doesn't like the room and gets his $100 back. In other words, money functions while it circulates. If the B&B owner had put the $100 in a drawer he would still have given it back to the traveler but none of the debts would have been paid.

"In 2007 the banks simply said they didn't have money using a simple formula. They didn't circulate the cash they had and using an accepted accounting practice they declared illiquidity and forced governments (a.k.a. the people) to bail them out – talk about having your cake and eating it too! If there is no liquidity (cash) the value of everything takes a dive – real estate, stocks, real property of all types, everything. Simply the law of offer and demand collapses the value of all goods, because there is no demand and no demand because there is no credit, no credit because the banks, etc. Then it takes only a tiny spark to blow the whole thing to smithereens. In 2007 it was the French bank Paribas that refused credits of some hedge funds. Had it not been that, it would have been something else because those who were manipulating the crisis had a plethora of options."

Sal paused a few seconds, drank some water, and then continued. Franciso smiled; this was his dear friend preparing to share his wisdom – insight hard-fought for on streets and halls of power.

"Anyway, I think you know this better than I do, but I'm not a wizard in these things and I have to tell this story at my own pace. On the other hand by now you see that I'm not an ignorant goon – that's just for show. When Francisco and I found ourselves with a very good cash position we saw the opportunities for great earnings, but so did others... those who had created the situation in the first place. Discreet purchases of huge tracts of land were being made all over the world, particularly land with freshwater access. We were looking at some of these and noticed that we were being thwarted by fathom interests that appeared and vanished with amazing speed. They bought, split, sold, bought again and so forth. All traces of a deliberate monopolization of undervalued land diluted beyond recognition...except for some guarantees and positions that were worded in such manner that our computers found a common denominator. It led back to three origins, one in Luxembourg, one in Jersey, and one in Rome."

Obviously Sal had no way of knowing that Francisco would be present when Marco and Patricia saw the video, so he referred to him occasionally and then Francisco just nodded knowingly and let the narrative go on.

Sal continued. "None of these were depository banks but held huge investment portfolios for others that were, as well as those of insurance companies and employee funds from all over. The only thing that they had in common was an unusually high number of exchanges through the Institute for Works of Religion (IOR), better known as the Vatican Bank. Here we were faced with a very difficult problem. The Vatican Bank is the most secretive, impenetrable and slippery financial institution in the world. Every regulator like

FAFT and MONEYVAL has been trying for years to pin it to money laundering, illegal arbitrage and tax evasion, to no avail. Part of the problem is how the Vatican Bank works. It is run by a president that theoretically comes from outside church interests, but under him are five cardinals, two of whom hold very close to the seat of St. Peter. Three of these cardinals rotate faster than the regulators can catch up and with them disappear all traces of wrongdoing. They are protected under the laws of Italy and many other countries and never are brought to render testimony."

Sal took a pause to bring a beer from the fridge and continued with his story. His three viewers each smiled, seeing the Sal they each loved in their own way, enjoying a beer again, albeit seemingly from the grave.

"By then we had joined a group of people that we met through, believe it or not, the wine business. Wine is a cult among the very rich and very powerful and over time we had entered in several business transactions at which both Francisco and I were most adept. Between the two of us we distributed and laundered the proceeds of Colombian and Peruvian cocaine for ourselves and others using third parties to do the physical work – the Mexican cartels are particularly useful. But the real asset, as you might have guessed, is our ability to launder money. Everybody that we met along the way needed to "legitimize" substantial amounts of money, either for themselves or entities to which they belonged. And in so doing and with the aid of technology, we came across the faint traces left behind by the mega money launderers. From Wall Street to Hong Kong and Rio de Janeiro to Johannesburg and deep into the country residences of peers of the realm in the UK we found that a few players held the reins to this lucrative business. Men and women whose financial strength exceeded the concepts of value held by the regular individual; they governed unimaginable wealth and wielded silent power that is by far superior to that of known world leaders who, in reality, are only their puppets and messengers.

"Here you can see the absurdity of the system. They who are

supposed to regulate and control the sanity of money are controlled by those that "sanitize" it by use of loopholes and wormholes intentionally built into the laws for the safeguard of those who make them. In short, Francisco, I and several other people who you will shortly meet dedicated our wits and worth to becoming major players in the worldwide conversion of questionable money into unquestionable assets. This small group of people we call The Board is now one of the strongest players in this rarefied environment where the rules are different, money is secondary to power and the significance of these two are subject to no moral standard. This video you are seeing is your induction – welcome to The Board."

Sal drained the last of his beer.

"By now you are aware of the account in the Tortola Bank. At present it's about £100 million or just under $150 million USD. Well, don't be impressed by that. In another section of this card there are the numbers and access codes of several more which constitute the gross of my money, which is now yours. The Carducci family net worth as you knew it before is a pittance. You will have to find someone to help Ian Carlo in the position you have held until now, because if you join The Board it will take most of your time and all of your ability."

Sal brought his hands together, crossing his fingers. He bowed his head over as if in prayer and then looked up and said:

"This is a very serious and challenging endeavor…and a dangerous one. As a matter of fact I might be dead because of it, but that I don't know. As I said before, hopefully I died fishing or making love. Anyway what I want to convey to you is that you now have so much money, several billion dollars, that it doesn't really matter."

Marco sat in shock, unable to move or even blink. The numbers mentioned blew his mind but more significant was the sheer brutality with which his uncle dropped all this on him. He continued to watch and listen.

"While I said that there is no moral restraint to the actions of The Board, Francisco and I have committed enough sins and broken enough laws to render us poor judges of the actions of others. But the fostering of war for no other reason than monetary profit and the methodical destruction of the middle classes sacrificed on an altar of sheer greed does revolt us and the others on The Board. Both of these acts seem to be the mainstay of our competitors or if you wish…opponents. While war has been a business since man was man, it still had some vestiges of altruism and philanthropy where a great number of people benefited in liberty. Now this has been abandoned and wars like Iraq and Afghanistan leave nothing but corpses, devastation, misery, and a few pockets lined with unimaginable profits.

"Then there is the methodical destruction of the middle class, which until recently constituted the engine of progress. Since just after the Second World War brought productivity and human welfare to unexpected heights converting the technology of war into the vehicle for prosperity, the middle classes surged. Since then, no war has produced any benefit to humanity. Korea, Vietnam, Iraq, and Afghanistan have been to the deterioration of millions for the benefit of few. Not to mention the thousands of regional and local skirmishes that keep the weapons manufactures in business. The bottom line is that the wealth of the world's middle class is under water. It owes far more that it owns. The value of the currency that supports its remaining assets is fallacious and can collapse at any time at the will of few. Since no form of substitute value is possible, the primitive requirements of mankind, food, water, and shelter will prevail and precipitate wars so devastating and senseless that humanity may not survive. It will be religious and racial mayhem where national boundaries become irrelevant and their currencies with them."

Sal looked straight into Marco's eyes and he felt the strength of the man even through the inanimate media at which he was looking. The substance of Sal's statements was stratospheric compared to the highest macro-economic contemplations he'd ever had, even in the highly charged liberalism of his days at Kellogg. Patricia seemed to be as astonished as he and only the calm countenance of Francisco Lujan anchored the naivete of their thoughts. Marco looked at Francisco with questions in his eyes but the man just signaled towards the monitor, indicating that he should continue listening to what Sal had to say.

"As you may have surmised by now, money means very little to us as an element of value in itself and we have acquired in time a great amount of influence over the outcome of much, but, so have our opponents and they have a simple agenda: dominate the world's food source and dictate to its population not only how they should act but how they should think and feel. Better yet if that population has been disseminated by war and reduced to a more controllable number. Without pretending a moral stance our objectives, or if you wish, our agenda, is to fortify and expand the middle class everywhere as we believe this will create stability minimizing the strength of racial and religious tensions and allowing trade to flourish – trade that we hope to control to a substantial degree. Note that I say we, as I expect to continue this quest through you. I love you both."

And the video stopped.

7

The *Toscana* had been navigating for three days and was approaching the Virgin Islands. The order was to dock at Little Dix Bay but the captain who was appointed by Allen Security did not feel comfortable in that situation and decided to anchor offshore. He stopped first off Tortola and had a refueling barge fill the almost depleted tanks and then cruised to Virgin Gorda and weighed anchor just outside Spanish Town around the corner from Little Dix Bay. He deployed the tender and waited for further instructions.

* * *

On another boat just off the north coast of Long Island, Tommy Lee called Jerry Birko into the lounge of the trawler. When he walked in and saw who the other person was he blanched and turned to flee. Strong arms and a gun in his face stopped him in his tracks. The two *capos* were comfortably seated in ample chairs, looking nonplussed, and staring at the panicked Birko who was now on the verge of tears.

A few seconds passed until Tommy said to him, "Tell us all about it, Jerry. Leave nothing out."

Birko was stupid enough to say he didn't know what Tommy was talking about. A flat hand slap to his right ear sent pain shooting through his head and made him dizzy and nauseous.

"Do I have to ask you again?" said Tommy.

Birko was silent for half a minute not daring to look at either man in the eye. Then he asked in a low voice, "Is this about Carducci?"

"What do you think, asshole? Yes, it's about you trying to kill someone in whose shadow you cannot stand and it's Mr. Carducci to you," said Tommy. Now answer Mr. De la Rosa's questions and don't make me get off this seat or you will live to regret it."

"I was doing God's work," said Birko, puffing himself up with borrowed righteousness. "Monsignor told me that Mr. Carducci was trying to destroy the Church and that it was my duty to help him get rid of an enemy of God. I did nothing wrong. It's God's will. He told me that God would show me the way and soon I heard about Tony Kisses' problem with Mr. Carducci. I knew it was God telling me what to do. I told Monsignor about Tony and he asked me if Tony was a believer. I checked him out and as it turned out Tony is a heathen who loves only money. So I told Monsignor about that and he told me to offer Tony a hundred grand to listen and five hundred grand if he did the job. He thinks it was the Liguria who was paying him."

Ian Carlo did not bother correcting Birko about Tony's status among the no longer breathing.

"Who are you talking about? What monsignor is this?"

"He told me his name was Gabriel Angelo and that he came from Rome. He had the purple hat and everything. I met him at the Cathedral when I was working in the sacristy. He said that he had come from Rome just to meet with me. He blessed me and told me all about Mr. Carducci trying to kill the pope and destroy the church."

Ian Carlo stood up suddenly and shouted in Birko's face:

"You fucking idiot, don't you have enough brains to know that the name he gave you was that of an archangel?"

"Yes, yes it was him," shouted Birko as if enlightened. "It was the Archangel Gabriel who came to me. Can't you see that I had to do God's will? I am blessed among men for I have heard the voice of God!" Then he knelt and started shouting hosannas and praising God and all his angels. All those present realized they were in the presence of an irredeemable idiot. Ian Carlo looked at Tommy who raised his shoulders like saying "what can we do? The guy's a moron." There was little more that they could get from him. Ian Carlo had planned a dramatic demise for the little prick but knew that it would not be a morale booster to his men if he made him suffer. At a signal to one of his enforcers they grabbed Birko, took him outside, and unceremoniously threw him overboard.

Ian Carlo and Tommy returned to shore, picked up the ladies and went to dinner at La Bussolla, a nice Italian restaurant that served an unbelievable osso buco. On the way Ian Carlo asked Tommy to see what he could find out about the visiting monsignor. He also spent another burner phone for a few minutes putting Marco up to date. Surprisingly Marco told him that he was pretty sure he knew who had sent the impersonating archangel.

Marco said he would be away for some time but that he was up to date on all business matters and that he wanted to know if Ian Carlo would agree to give Leon Goddard a more significant role in the running of the legitimate side of the business. Ian Carlo didn't hesitate to agree as he was confident of Marco's judgment in that area. Also Marco enigmatically told him that their businesses should expect a substantial capital investment from overseas.

Leon Goddard was Marco's classmate from the Kellogg Business School of Northwestern University in Chicago. Before getting his MBA he had worked for Lever Brothers, Johnson & Johnson, and Ciba, doing five-year stints at each. He had been general manager or managing director in several overseas posts and finally a VP of International Business. He then decided that he needed more credentials before he could aspire to the big money. At Kellogg he met Marco Carducci and a friendship accompanied by better money than he could ever get in the corporate world had put him at the head of Carducci Enterprises Inc. Now with a wife and two children, he could afford to live in a penthouse apartment overlooking Central Park East. His daughters were in Christ Church Elementary and his wife shopped on Fifth Avenue. He was frequently wined and dined by the business elite of NYC, the operating managers of the city government, and several reporters who consulted him. Leon had a 24-K work ethic, no mistress, and a fierce sense of loyalty toward Marco. His police record showed one traffic violation in 1999 that had been dismissed with a warning. That was it. Even though he was aware that Salvatore Carducci had been investigated for alleged racketeering, nothing had been proven and that was enough for Leon. His business was to manage legitimate enterprises of unimpeachable record without ever having to cut corners or sacrifice his views or criteria to anybody's whims.

Today was a hard day for Leon. He was going to the memorial service of a close friend. Joe Strasso and he had been members of the Long Island Soaring Association where they shared their passion for flying gliders. They owned together a Falcon developed by Advanced Soaring Concepts on which they had enjoyed the freedom of powerless flight in a high performance machine. At today's service he would be representing the company and Marco, who was out of the country and could not return for the memorial. Ian Carlo would not show up. He didn't want to taint one business with the other. Hundreds of employees from the Carducci companies had been given a few hours off so they could attend the service which had been the wish of both Marco and Leon, even though most of them had never met Joe or in many cases had never even heard of him. He was referred to in the obituary as Vice President of Transportation and Logistics. Joe's aging parents who lived in Sicilia couldn't make it either because his father was too ill to travel and his mother would never leave her husband's side. Thus Joe was memorialized by one close friend, several acquaintances, many strangers... but no family. His and his wife's mortal remains rested forever adrift in the deep Atlantic.

* * *

By now it was known that Marco Carducci had not been on the Lear when it exploded but the other four passengers who were presumed dead in the accident were not yet identified. This news had people in Rome, Washington, London, Dubai, and Cape Town seriously worried. The assumption of Marco Carducci's demise had precipitated decisions that were now considered rash for they showed a hand that was not yet to be played.

In Rome Jean Dupree, Cardinal of the Roman Catholic Church, Dean of the Vatican Bank, was concerned but not worried. He was never worried. He didn't have the emotional capacity to be worried, but he was concerned. Failure was not a common occurrence in his experience and the survival of Carducci from a well-planned attempt was not an expected occurrence. What was worse was that his whereabouts and that of the Lujan woman were not known. He also knew that with time he would be located. Nobody can hide too long and if Carducci was going to be a player he would have to show his hand. But this cardinal was proactive and called in his "sword" as he called Monsignor Enrico Testa and briefed him on the situation and the need to complete the mission at which he had failed.

"Carducci is potentially a problem. He is of no significance at this moment but once he becomes active on The Board he can interfere in our mission and that is not a risk I'm willing to take. He will acquire knowledge of our operations soon if he has not already done so. So find him and kill him – and the Lujan woman too. I think she already knows too much. Use the Luxembourg account for your expenses. There is no fund restriction on this one. Just go out and do it. And Enrico, don't fail us this time. God be with you."

Testa knelt down to receive the cardinal's blessing and left without another word. He went back to his apartment in Via Capucci and packed his suitcase with ecclesiastical and lay garments together with two pairs of black cargo pants and black long sleeve T-shirts. The only weapons he packed were a garrote well camouflaged in the piping of his suitcase and an insulin kit for diabetes in which he carried two types of very lethal poisons. The injector was a powerful blowgun that could accurately deliver a small dart with the poison up to twenty feet from the victim. A missal that included the New Testament was the only non-practical item in his luggage. The three passports that he carried were real: a US passport to which he was entitled, as he was born in Milwaukee to an Italian father and a Polish mother; a Vatican passport issued by the Holy See as per his operational post; and an EU passport that he had right to by his father's Italian birth. Two more full sets of documentation were waiting for him in New York, his next port of call: a false but very credible US passport with driver's license and credit cards that corresponded to the address of a safe house that he used as a general base of operations when in the US The other was a Brazilian passport issued to Joao Pernambuco whose address in Rio de Janeiro was also legitimate. That evening he took an Alitalia flight to JFK using an untraceable American Express to buy a business class ticket. The last time he had been in the United States he was in Washington DC in the company of "his" cardinal. On that occasion he had managed to access the kitchen at the Delaney residence and assure that the right plates with the toxin went to the right people. It all went perfect except for the maid that disappeared before he could eliminate that loose end.

* * *

That loose end had already provided M&M with enough information about the monsignor that he was able to determine which of Dupree's several assistants the assassin had been. He was looking at the dossier his people had prepared on Enrico Testa. The thirty-six year old ex-Seal and ex-NSA agent had lost faith in the institutions of his country as they secretly acted to compromise the people in futile police actions and distract them with sexual scandals and minutia of the glitterati, keeping them blind to the reality of their diminishing liberties. He quit his job and drifted for some time taking odd jobs on cargo ships until once in Naples he had killed a man who was trying to rape a young girl in an alley next to a bar. He had used only a fast openhand to the man's nose that sent bone into his brain and busted one of his eyeballs. His bad luck was that the police passed by as the girl ran away screaming and he was caught red handed, to be blunt. He was sent to jail and left to rot because the dead man was the brother of a local magistrate. The case reached the curia because the prisoner, an American, spent most of his time on his knees praying. Other inmates had soon learned not to bother or much less attack him. Several broken limbs and two blind inmates were sorry witnesses to the man's prowess. His constant praying had caught the attention of the prison's chaplain who reported the case to his bishop and so on until it reached the desk of the then-head of the disciplinary office of the Holy See, Monsignor Dupree, who was now on the short list to become Cardinal. Dupree had gone to visit this man in prison several times. Eventually, and through the services of lawyers and some financial aid to the family of the magistrate, Enrico was released into the custody of the Catholic Church.

Soon Enrico Testa was an intern in a quiet monastery just outside of Siena where he was thoroughly indoctrinated in the tenets of Roman Catholicism. A year later he was ordained and two years after that he was elevated to Monsignor. The background in the Navy and the NSA read like the training manual of a covert operator. All the boxes checked; multilingual, proficient in hand to hand combat, holding the highest black belt in Gu Yu Riu and other lesser schools of karate. He was trained and highly effective with handguns of all types, but he preferred the Glock 17 9mm. He had a full explosives training and several missions applying all those skills deep in Kandahar.

What the dossier didn't say was that Testa had been since he was a child a religious fanatic of reborn Christian parents who dragged him from revival to revival showing him off because he could enter into "Divine Trances" at every opportunity and used him to milk the cash cow of imbecility. He enlisted in the Navy the day he left high school and was rapidly accepted as a candidate for Seal. He excelled at this new "religion" and graduated first in his class. He served honorably and bravely as he defended and fought to the death for his teammates but never made a close friend. A loner by nature, he did not participate in off-duty activities but spent innumerable hours in the dojo sparring with whoever was available. He became a sniper and learned about explosives including IEDs, at which he became the team's expert. He did three tours until a psych evaluation caught the attention of an NSA deputy director who made him an offer he couldn't refuse. His job there is a secret as secrets can be in the dark files of the darkest agency of the USA. That man was now "the Sword" that Dupree used as God's enforcer; but that part was obvious to M&M.

Testa was in the right place at the right time. He was doing the only thing he thought was right...whatever Cardinal Dupree told him to do. After all Dupree had been God's answer to his prayers. Now M&M had the who and the how; all that he needed was the why. Delany had been a very powerful US senator who was indubitably a valuable ally to Dupree, yet the cardinal, most surely with the concurrence of others in that conclave, had eliminated him and his wife. M&M wanted the bigger picture and to that effort he set his well-oiled machinery to work.

* * *

Special Agent Joe Delaney was back in New York feeling a loss of power. Many calls went unanswered, others barely acknowledged, and his quest with the Carducci investigation was going nowhere. De la Rosa was keeping a low profile and Marco Carducci apparently was down and out. His informers said that he had been shunned from the business and was living somewhere in Florida. He needed a break.

* * *

Francisco, Patricia and Marco were sitting in the main lounge of the *Toscana*. Their luggage was being brought in later by the tender under the supervision of Luigi and Jose. Pete was to stay in the villa. The security in the *Toscana* was as good as materially possible. The decoy establishment at the villa continued and the "MacKenzies" were in residence. Now it was time to get The Board together and plan for action. Ernie Goldman was on his way to St. Thomas from La Guardia and would immediately be transferred to the *Toscana*. Cornelia Papadakos was already in St. Bartholomew with her fifth husband and she alone would join them later that evening. Erick Williams, a flame-red Welshman, and Esteban Espinoza, a banker from Spain, were flying in directly to Tortola on the G500 of an obscure Lebanese electric engineer by the name of Hakim Abilshair, whose enterprises were constructing dams all over the world, including China. The last two members of The Board were Airi Takahashi and Sun E, two women who were partners in the second largest silicon and germanium semiconductor factory in the world, were now in Puerto Rico visiting one of their manufacturing facilities and would be aboard the *Toscana* by early evening. The fellow board members called them Sunny and Airy in a bad westernization of their names. The safety of these people was in the hands of Major Allen.

Major Allen also belonged to an informal association of security enterprises that had learned to act in tandem when needed and held strictly to the same standards and ethical behavior so that each knew that they could extend their reach throughout the world without risk of compromising the interest of their clients. Thus a small army of highly qualified PSCs were locating into the BVI and the USVI forming a coordinated perimeter along the navigation route of the *Toscana* that would be circling around these waters for a couple of days. These men and women had quietly been supplied from an American trawler with an assortment of weapons that went from Glock 9mm pistols and mini-Uzi for each to Ferfrans HVLAR, or High Volume Light Automatic Rifle, for a few of the operators.

Similar hardware was aboard the *Toscana* with the addition of several RPGs and two 50-caliber machine guns. Two fast twenty-foot jet boats armed to the teeth would maintain a 2,000-foot perimeter around the *Toscana*. A Schweitzer 333 light helicopter adapted with two rocket launchers and two 30mm machine guns was at readiness on a barge that followed the *Toscana* at a distance.

Defense of the *Toscana* included the ship's high-resolution radars plus the feeds leached off the US Coast Guard and the British Navy radars located high on the island's mountains. To this add two satellite feeds that alternated every two minutes. Bogotá's array of sophisticated listening software was attentive to any chatter that could compromise the safety of The Board.

It was not enough.

* * *

While the members of The Board converged on the highly fortified boat, Enrico Testa had been able to trace the only thing that was missing from the picture and that was precisely the *Toscana*. Once he noticed that the house in Florida, though well guarded, lacked the urgency of a siege; he saw the empty docks and realized that the *Toscana* had to be the clue to Marco Carducci's whereabouts. From there it was simple to follow the tracks of the megayacht to the waters off Tortola. Dupree had used Senator Mason's access to US satellites and radar to complete the picture. Within a few hours Testa had a plan and began its implementation. He needed a team of six experienced operatives preferably ex-Navy Seals or HMSS Boat Services with great expertise but low moral values. Fortunately there were plenty to choose from. Then he needed the proper equipment and the delivery of the same to a location in Aguadilla, Puerto Rico where he had found a dive trawler with ideal specifications.

He found the operatives through the Mercenary Contractor, an online service that provided "proactive" security personnel. Of the twenty five submitted he chose four men and two women. He made the travel arrangements and proper documentation for the operatives and ordered them to fly to Dominican Republic and from there to Aguadilla. They were posing as an underwater exploration team for the National Geographic going to sea on the *Abnegated*, a 72-foot trawler with all the necessary support for a team of divers.

* * *

Dupree was on a conference call through secure lines with Senator Mason and Lord Humphrey, discussing the latest impasse to their progress that they blamed on The Board. One of their enterprises, a huge agricultural conglomerate that was privately owned by the Meredith family, a member of their group, had been accused of accumulating enormous tracts of land in Colombia, Brazil, Argentina, and Uruguay. These purchases were done by a diversity of companies but the land authorities of these countries, and most unfortunately the press, had received detail of the transactions and how they all traced back to the same owners. The investigations were now of public domain and the reversal of many months of hard work was imminent. In all of these countries there were anti-trust laws precisely against "Latifundistas," a word that means great landowners, and now the Meredith family was caught with their pants down and their dirty underwear for all to see. Expropriation, fines, conspiracy, incarceration, disbarment of counsel, and many other such expressions were rampant among the corridors of the justice departments of these countries and Meredith was spending hundreds of millions in legal defense fees.

All thanks to The Board.

"This is just the latest of their interference in our endeavor," said Mason who was the most directly affected other than the Merediths, as they were the biggest supporters of his political career. "We cannot sit still and not retaliate. Meredith expects me to do something and even though I have the State Department working this through our embassies in these countries, they want more than that. They want blood. I've had Edward Meredith in my office twice this week and the man is adamant. He wants to know how the information got to the press and who is responsible. He may lose billions on this deal and he wants, as he put it, 'The help I paid for,' though I think it's Ana, his mother, who is the person we should worry about."

"I second that," said Cardinal Dupree. "Half the dioceses in the Mid-west depend on the Merediths for most of their charitable work and they also support the Church in all the countries you mentioned. And if Ana gets pissed off at us much of that money may evaporate."

"This is nonsense," Humphrey Houghton countered. "We have too much at stake here. Land purchase in South Africa, Namibia, Kenya, and a few other countries has been going on without obstacle, but this is a big warning that things can go south if The Board gets wind of it. In the meantime we have been wasting time and money chasing this Carducci character and the Lujan girl. I just don't see why they are so important. I understood that old Joseph Delany had to go because he sold out to the Saudis and that would have put us at too much risk...but Carducci is a nobody. I mean, who is he...I don't think he has or will ever have the caliber of Sal Carducci and even he never posed that much of a threat."

"You are wrong, Lord Houghton," said Dupree with some impatience in his voice. "It's not what he is or what he was. Marco Carducci wrote his master's degree dissertation on the economic recuperation of the Western Hemisphere. I sent you all a copy of this document. If you read it, and you understand it, Marco Carducci as part of The Board can use the resources available to them in ways that would really impede our common and individual goals. For the time being you must know that every penny spent on getting rid of him is well spent. And in that respect I hope to give you positive news is the near future. God's will be done."

"Amen," said the others.

8

Major Allen was looking at a chart that indicated the location of the *Toscana* which was updated every three minutes. It also gave the location of all vessels and aircraft up to twenty five miles from it. Most of them were identified by their radio calls, transponders or power signatures. It showed which ones were moving and which were static and graded them by size as well as by proximity to the *Toscana*. This lovely piece of software had been "borrowed" from the US Navy and allowed him to evaluate possible threats. He did not like the congestion of the waters where the *Toscana* was and gave it orders to head east into deep water and away from the traffic of small recreational boats. He gave orders for the speedboats to pick up some of the assets from both Virgin Gorda and Tortola and to maximize fuel so that they could be of support to the *Toscana* away from land. Finally he ordered that the landing platform of the *Toscana* be deployed and the helicopter to land on it after refueling on land. Satisfied with these measures he continued to monitor the progress of the yacht as it headed out to the Atlantic at 25 knots.

Inside the *Toscana*, dinner was being served for members of The Board. As it was custom, the meal was simple and only nonalcoholic beverages were available. Francisco had welcomed each of the arrivals and sent them to their stateroom cabins to get ready for the evening meal and meeting. There were no previous meetings scheduled and everyone other than the crew was encouraged to stay inside until advised by the captain.

Marco had spent all his time aboard getting through a lot of information that was on other sections of the same memory card. The accounts with banks, hedge funds, investment funds and a few portfolio managers in known financial havens added up to over eleven billion dollars. His uncle was right. The Carducci fortune was a pittance and so was that of any individual crime family in the US that he knew of. Maybe all together they would be in the same league; but not individually. The legal manipulation of other people's money and other people's trust was where the real money was and that is what the big boys and girls were doing. The other documents pertained exactly to what The Board was doing and what the opposition was up to. There was a lot of detail about subverted land purchasing by an American firm, a British-French enterprise and a retired Italian politician. That land had a book value of at least one hundred and fifty billion dollars. Now his money was a dime in the piggybank compared to the figures being played by these folks. Furthermore, the assets held by The Board were a third of a trillion dollars. He had to stop and try to equate micro-economic assessment to macro-economic figures. This was about as much as the total wealth of Chile yet it was at the disposal of so few.

A light knock at the door and Francisco Lujan came in, accompanied by Ernie Goldman.

"Have you seen the figures?" asked Francisco.

"Yes, broadly. It's just very hard to comprehend."

"Maybe I can help you with that." He was silent for a few seconds, concentrated, thinking, and then he said, "The money you have and the money that we manage belongs to us as much as the stars in the sky or the salt in the sea. Man has had stewardship of the wealth of this earth since self-consciousness appeared, yet the inescapable reality of our own mortality negates the strength of that hold. The more we hold in that stewardship the less dominion we have over it. We are no exception, nor is our opposition. The vast amount of wealth held by each of us has its own mass inertia and is all but impossible to derail or change its direction. This is where we believe you will become a great asset to this group. We read and re-read your thesis at Kellogg and we are convinced of its wisdom. If I were to put your whole dissertation in a nutshell, you believe that there has to be reforms in four fundamental economic factors or the world's socioeconomic structure which, as it now stands, will implode."

"Yes," said Marco, "depolitization of the lendable capital allowing for bank reform without loopholes; land reform by geographic consumption which gives midsize farming operations a business opportunity; and recapitalization of the middle class by tax and social service reform. Finally, a rationalization of our energy and transportation resources, which is symbiotically linked."

"OK, let's leave this conversation for later when we're all together," said Ernie. "I think The Board needs to hear more of it.

"By the way, I just received an updated report from Allen Security. All protective assets are in place, but the major feels that the waters around the Virgin Islands are by far too congested to maintain a good level of security, so he has ordered the ship east into deeper water and less traffic. Given the events of the last ten weeks, we have to assume that there is an active pursuit of you and Patricia, which means that this applies to all aboard the *Toscana*. As a precaution we are keeping everyone on board just for the meeting and then we are headed back closer to land and we will disembark several of us via helicopter and others via speed boat. Now, let's enjoy dinner and continue with our agenda with The Board."

Marco stayed for a moment alone while Ernie went to greet the other guests. Had it really only been ten weeks since Sal's death? It felt a lifetime away now, with so much at stake, not the least his life and that of Patricia's, which, he realized, he suddenly cared greatly about. How close he had become to that mysterious woman and her father.

Once dinner was over the dishes were taken away; the table was now all business. Francisco Lujan stood up and addressed the group.

"As sad as it is to meet without Salvatore Carducci, our partner, our friend, and husband to my daughter, I formally present to you Marco Carducci. You all know him through the documentation that was submitted to you days ago and some of you might have met him personally before dinner. It is now my duty and honor to formally submit his name for full membership of The Board."

One by one they all voted "aye" and Marco stood up, accepted, and thanked everyone individually, going around the table and shaking hands. He then returned to his seat and said, "I have been told by Francisco that you have bestowed this honor on me more because you believe in a thesis I wrote over fifteen years ago than because it was Uncle Sal's wish that I do so. This I find extremely flattering and I find myself humbled by your trust in what I've held dear over the years but did not have the means to implement in any way. I have given this much thought and I think I understand your motivation.

"Most of you are highly invested in the consumer. You need disposable income in the hands of many so that your businesses truly succeed. The other or others, on this I'm not clear, appear to desire centralization of wealth and redistribution of benefits to a subservient society. A society without the capacity to consume what you have to offer would convert you to the service of a single client. Not a pretty picture. Also I see you compete with the opposition for the business of asset conversion throughout the world and so far I can see that in the last year or so, you are succeeding brilliantly. This has to have caused stress among them.

"I also believe that they are aware of me and Patricia and probably know about Francisco, and obviously knew about Sal; but, from all I can gather, the rest of you continue to be quite anonymous as far as this association is concerned."

"And we fervently wish that it stay in such manner," said Sunny. "It would make us extremely vulnerable to those whose interests you have so succinctly put. But as we are mostly unknown to them, so are they to us. The picture is always blurred, there are so many fronts, so many transactions, so many people involved, that it is hard to see through the fog of business."

"Mostly true but not entirely," said Francisco. "Ernie and I have implemented software that recognizes legalise in several languages and this has cleared the picture to some degree. We know for a fact that the Vatican Bank is a major player but we don't know their motivation. They have been under tremendous scrutiny by regulators everywhere and all their transactions are now vetted by a team of international auditors that reports to the IMF, yet time and again we find the hand of the IOR, the Vatican Bank, deep into the pockets of national wealth of several financially disrupted countries."

"And a group of US Senators show their hand far too frequently influencing the outcome of land purchases by an agricultural conglomerate owned by the Meredith family," said Ernie. "This has been particularly obvious because of the lobby by diplomatic personnel in several countries in Latin America."

"Also a couple of earls who own a bank in Jersey that owns a bank in Canada which owns a bank in Caymans and so forth," said Patricia. "They show up in as many transactions as the Vatican bank in tandem or sequentially."

A discreet knock on the door interrupted their discussion and Francisco answered the door ready to give a piece of his mind to the person who, in spite strict orders for privacy, had violated the rule, but it was the captain in person who handed Francisco a note, saluted, and retired. Francisco read it twice and thought for a few seconds before he continued.

"I'm going to read this aloud as it is by coincidence, or not, very pertinent to our present discussion. It was sent to me via Bogotá by a person whose services we have used to great advantage in several occasions but whom I don't trust at all, as he is for sale to the best bidder."

He read the note in his hands: "The person who is trying to take out Marco Carducci is Cardinal Jean Dupree. He also had Senator Delany and his wife killed. He uses an ex-Navy Seal who works for him. His name is Enrico Testa and he is beyond dangerous. Do what you deem pertinent, but you owe me big. Signed M&M."

Silence prevailed during a few seconds and then excited chatter broke out among the present. It was interrupted by Marco.

"At least now we have a name to this threat. Ian Carlo de la Rosa had told me that it was a monsignor passing himself as God's messenger who had duped a fanatic bagman with the Liguria's to set up the destruction of the Lear, believing that we would be on it."

"We have a lot more than a name," said Francisco gravely, "we have an extensive dossier on His Eminence Cardinal Jean Dupree. He is one of the 'super cardinals' of the Catholic Church. A strict disciplinarian, he headed the purification process that tried to eliminate the pedophile invasion of the rank and file and particularly prosecuted the bishops that covered up the actions of these degenerates. He gained the trust of the pope and practically asked to be placed in the IOR supposedly to do the same for that institution, which was fraught with corruption. He has been there three years and while playing ball with the regulators who think he is impeccable, we have reason to believe he heads the operations and manages the associates of the capital centralization effort that we oppose. Now we have a smoking gun, if you can excuse the venality of the example. Dupree is adamant about the Catholic Church's adhering to its fundamental principles and truly believes that it is mankind's only path to earthly salvation.

"We fear that he's Machiavellian in his pursuits and will stop at nothing to achieve the recuperation of power, prestige and wealth of the Roman Catholic Church. What makes him a very formidable foe is that he has no personal agenda. No secret life of his own, no desire of personal wealth, and no romantic attachments of any kind. He lives in a one-bedroom apartment with no elevator to his fourth floor lodgings. He exercises by walking up and down the stairs and to and from his office at the bank or the one he keeps at the Holy See. He says Mass every day at 5:45 a.m. at St. Giuseppe della Montagna, a very quiet convent on Via de Vaticano, and then has breakfast at a small café nearby, generally with Testa or another of his adjutants. The rest of the day he spends at his office except when the pope calls him in, which is about once a week."

"All good to know, but why in the world does he want Marco killed?" asked Esteban Espinoza, the Spanish banker. "And why on earth would he have Senator Delany killed?"

"Both good questions," Ernie answered. "I would say that Senator Delany was getting too cozy with the Saudis. Since he was Ambassador there, he has lobbied shamelessly for extended relationship and uncensored sales of armament and sensitive equipment to the kingdom. This had caused some asperity between him and another Catholic, Senator Archibald Mason, who is very close to Dupree. I cannot see the cardinal looking kindly upon resources and support going to active enemies of the Catholic Church."

"OK, so now that we know what we know; what are we going to do about it?" asked Erick Williams, who was Protestant enough to abhor a man like Dupree.

* * *

Miles away, chugging at eight knots an hour, the *Abnegated* was just leaving the Puerto Rican coast and headed for St. Croix on her way to intercept the *Toscana*. On board, Testa was testing and re-testing the capabilities of his small team. He had staged several hand to hand combats between them, not distinguishing age or sex until he had a clear idea of who was the best and who was the least. Then he had the two best train the others time and time again. He also did target practice with hand guns and small automatic weapons; he threw colored light bulbs into the water and expected hits with no more than two shots. He personally trained them showing how to anticipate the position of the target more by feeling than by thinking about it. One's brain works much better at geometrical calculations without the interference of deliberate thought, after which good hand-eye coordination kicks in.

They had stopped once to do an invasion of a private club so they could practice with the re-breather, the OTC communicators and the underwater scooters. They went in at night, in the hours before dawn and ripped off the golf shop just for the hell of it. They also immobilized two security guards and a couple of German shepherds for practice. The mission was successful and they flew one of the security guard's pants from the flagpole. Testa barely put up with the prank but thought better of saying anything. He let it go for a few minutes and then had them restore the US flag of the ship's registration.

* * *

In New York, Special Agent Delany was deep in thought and disappointment. His request for a warrant to search the Carducci residences had been rejected by several judges, not without the admonition from a couple of them about probable cause. A month ago his name alone would have given pause to any of these puffed up cretins before rejecting a request by Joseph Delaney Jr. His mood got blacker when a secretary entered, without knocking, and dropped an envelope on his desk, turned around and left without a word. Oh how the mighty fall!

He looked at the white standard envelope that bore his typed name on it, without title, just Joseph Delany Jr. Period. He looked at it for a few seconds and then opened it. Blood rushed to his head and his jaw clenched with utter fury. He read it again: "Your father's death was not an accident. Your parents were deliberately killed by a group of people that include your esteemed Senator Uncle Archibald Mason. Think very carefully about what you will do with this information. I will keep in touch. Signed, a friend."

Agent Delany knew instinctively that what the note said was the truth. He had lingering feelings about Mason's continuous distancing from him and his family. He had not shown up at the memorial Mass itself and he failed to return his calls, and when he did, he was distant and always in a hurry. Now he knew why. His training and instincts took over and he sat back in his chair totally calm. It was time to think.

* * *

Ian Carlo hung up the phone after talking to Tommy Liguria. The monsignor who had hired Tony Kisses through Birko was an envoy from Rome who had been in Las Vegas discussing several real estate investments for which the Vatican Bank held notes in trust for the Archdiocese of San Francisco, who in turn had inherited them from a repatriated Italian who died in Maratea, a small town in Calabria. He had spent a few days talking to lawyers and following probate. Then he had returned to Rome via New York. Why on earth, he asked himself, would a priest from Rome want Marco dead? Was Birko a coincidence or was he a target? Ian Carlo didn't believe in coincidences. He called Tommy back and asked him about Birko's background. Tommy told him that a couple of years ago one of his lieutenants, Joe Tellez, had vouched for him. He had a suspicion that they were kind of sweet on each other, but no proof. The thing is that Tellez was loyal as hell and Tommy trusted him so he had given Jerry Birko the job of collecting some skim from some of the downtown bookies. Proof of his loyalty was that Joe had never said a word about Birko and proved to be as efficient as ever, but Tommy would talk to him and find out more about Birko.

* * *

Aboard the *Toscana* the meeting was deep into its detail. The organization of The Board was fractal; in mathematical terms, it was an equation that repeated itself unto infinity with slight variations in dimension until every possibility was realized. Each one of the members of this board headed another board similar to it and those other boards and so on. Knowledge of the higher board was known to only one member. Thus The Board had knowledge of all the subsequent boards and their activities and could share with them assets of all types and gave The Board an immense world-wide reach without compromising its existence. Loose guidelines helped all members in exploiting opportunities and developing relations at all levels with those government or private individuals who needed to clean their assets, whether they be cash or properties. If it was big money that had to be cleaned, The Board would "buy" a financially distressed country. Then it could funnel literally tons of cash through its banks and financial institutions and before any regulator could do anything, banks closed, managers disappeared, and then the cry for help from the nation that had lent itself to the deal was seen as a much greater priority than a few busted banks. The world's money would flow in to "keep them afloat" and avoid an invasion of immigrants into the wealthier countries. What a racket! The Board would charge a very reasonable 33-percent of all transactions and at the end of the deal a hefty five-percent to eight-percent went to the pockets of its members. The rest paid off government officials, bankers, NGOs, brokers, currency exchange houses, and all other intermediaries who lubricate the process with the sweat of their greed. Obviously the competition was great but there was enough for all – considering that about ten-percent of the world's gross product needing to be laundered – nearly seven trillion dollars!

Laundering systems vary, but the "silent partner" deal is a classic. Mom and pop operations are set up in which the innocent partners are capitalized by a convenient loan and the "silent partner" provides an operational software and accounting system. The till has a five-percent to ten-percent phantom sales that correspond to purchases from one or two key purveyors whose books match the corresponding purchase of goods supposedly sold. They buy from the manufacturers and float the surplus goods into the grey market. They use shrinkage along the line and one with the other the laundering is complete. The surplus cash is deposited into second or third accounts to which the active partners have no access. With several hundred thousand audits needed to expose the laundering, the IRS would spend more in doing that than it could ever hope to collect. On a larger scale, if a government official has to launder $100,000; he hands over the cash to one of the boards in the organization, maybe his wife will get a consulting contract from an NGO in a far off country which pays her $5,000 a month, which she dutifully reports in her tax return. The cash goes through one of the cleansing mills and everybody's happy. Except the taxman, that is.

* * *

Across the Atlantic, M&M was thinking that as he had now stirred the waters with his notes to Francisco Lujan and Agent Delany, he could sit back and see what surfaced. He knew that it would always be profitable to him, because in this case and in whatever he did, he had much to gain and nothing to lose. He sat at his tying desk, put a #14 trout hook in the vise and started tying his favorite fly – the Purple Haze, a modern variation of the classic parachute Adams. As he tied he thought of Salvatore Carducci. He was a good fly fisherman and the few times they had fished together was what had inclined him to help out Marco and Patricia, not that he doubted that it would be better money than siding with the crazy priest. Patricia was a better fly-caster than Sal or himself, but lacked a sense of fishiness that is so much a part of success. Patricia was an extraordinary woman, beautiful, smart, and rich. Too bad he didn't like women.

9

The *Abnegated* reached the *Toscana's* vicinity about 2:00 a.m. under a moonless night. Testa's team had slept since early evening and he had taken his usual four hours of sleep and now was wide-awake and fully attentive to every detail. He ordered the *Abnegated* captain to cruise parallel to the *Toscana* at a distance of two kilometers. He would wait until about 3:30 a.m. to send in his team. That was called Dead Man's Hour because it was the lowest ebb in human vitality; the hour in which most terminally sick people die; the hour when sentries lower their guard and are killed. He had everyone check out their equipment, particularly the underwater scooters, making sure that the lithium batteries were at their maximum charge, that the re-breathers were working properly, and the communications equipment functioning correctly.

Across the water the two sentries walked in tandem around the *Toscana*, one always on opposite sides of the other. Only the distant navigating lights of a single ship could be seen on the horizon.

At the operations room of Allen Security, Dave Whitaker, a senior VP and experienced military strategist, was looking at the screen that showed the *Toscana* and about five miles of radius from where she was. The crew had reported on schedule and nothing other than one ship that was traveling parallel to her for about an hour was on the scope. The ship had been checked twice and corresponded to a deep sea recovery trawler hired by a team from National Geographic. There would be no way of confirming this till morning but it didn't look like a threat as it kept a significant distance from the *Toscana*. The infrared satellite images of both ships showed brightly on the monitor, leaving long trails of bright water behind them as each power plant's exchange water from the cooling systems on board created a visible signature in contrast to the cooler waters of the sea. There had been little or no radio communication from either vessel but both had transponders that blinked their exact position at all times. That they were out in international waters did not mean that the US Coast Guard and Her Majesty's Navy dropped the ball on any ship that was anywhere near one of their precious islands. They too saw the ships cruising leisurely at six knots in a flat sea that reflected the stars of the ink black night.

* * *

It was about 2:30 a.m. in New York when the chime of a text message brought Joseph Delany out of a nervous sleep. He had been dreaming of his mother. She was sitting on a beach chair waving at him but he couldn't see her face because the sun, a big bright sun, was behind her. But he knew it was his mother. He wanted to talk to her but no sound came out of his mouth. He wanted to wave but his arm wouldn't move. Then as he was getting anxious, the loud chime had rescued him. He saw the screen alight and picked up the phone. The message was from an unknown sender. He swiped it and the message appeared:

"The people that killed your parents are also trying to kill Marco Carducci and a woman named Patricia Lujan. The enemy of my enemy...you know how it goes. Think carefully."

So much for sleep; the chime had woken up his wife and he waited till she went back to sleep before he left the room quietly and went to his studio. He opened the FBI search page, put in his code, confirmed it with a second code and entered the query "Who is Patricia Lujan?" The answer came back quickly; there were half-a-dozen Patricia Lujans in the system but he knew promptly which one was his objective; the one that showed an "Access Denied" when he clicked on her.

* * *

Patricia woke up feeling that something was wrong. She looked at the bedside clock and saw it turn from 2:59 a.m. to 3:00 a.m. Some of her senses wanted to go back to sleep while the ones that won took her out into the hall and up the short staircase to the lounge and galley. She saw the pod coffee machine, chose a Jamaican Blue, and put it in the contraption. She took a mug and put it under the spout and pressed the button. Seconds later steaming coffee streamed into the cup, infusing the air with a rich aroma. She took a shallow sip against the heat and then walked out onto the stern of the boat and looked into the night. The strong beverage made her feel better but didn't totally shake the feeling of foreboding.

At 3:30 a.m. Testa's team left the *Abnegated* through the dive port and each went with his or her assigned underwater scooter to a depth of 25 feet. They collected at the stern of the boat and followed the lead scooter that had a GPS with a fix on the *Toscana*. A half an hour earlier the trawler had accelerated the pace to eight knots and moved in at a shallow angle towards the *Toscana* so when the scooters headed out they were less than 1,200 meters from the Toscana and at least 1,000 meters ahead. This would allow them to converge on its path.

The change of direction was not noted by Dave Whitaker until about 3:15 a.m. This didn't register as an aggression until he noted the variation in speed. He decided to advise the crew of the *Toscana* of the event and talked to the first officer who was at the helm. By 3:30 the other boat was again parallel to the *Toscana* and had diminished speed. Odd but not alarming per se; he kept his attention focused on the monitors.

Even at only six knots the *Toscana* was faster than the scooters could possibly be. Their maximum speed was 4.5 knots and at that speed they depleted the batteries fast. So two of the scooters converged on the path of the *Toscana* and released from their bags hundreds of neutral-buoyancy, very sticky "worms" that were absorbed by the intakes of the turbines and within seconds expanded to several times their size and tangled every moving part that they came in contact with. In less than a minute the *Toscana* was doing barely three knots and within reach of Testa and his mercenaries.

The change of speed alarmed the first officer, who immediately called the captain to the bridge. He also shot the alarm to Sarasota and within a couple of minutes Major Allen joined Dave Whitaker in the operations room. Major Allen made two decisions that proved crucial; he ordered general quarters and had the second officer engage the sonar with active pinging. General quarters were called on the personal communicators of the whole crew and not by a klaxon or loud bell. Yachts are not designed to panic rich and powerful guests. Unfortunately the call did not include Luigi or José who went on sleeping. Within a couple of minutes all the security personnel, twelve in total, were at their posts. Urgent calls were sent to the speed boats but one was out of commission and the other was of little help, now several kilometers from the *Toscana*.

Patricia whose sense was uncommonly good went to Marco's and her father's state rooms and made sure they were aware of a potentially dangerous situation without alarming the others. So far there was no absolute indication of danger other than the abrupt loss of speed. But the events of the past few days required precaution if not outright paranoia.

Testa had planned the boarding to take place as soon as the *Toscana* was disabled and stopped in the water, and he was now only a few hundred feet away from the boat. Three of his crew were right behind him and the two that had deployed the worms were converging on the stern of the yacht. That was the moment that the loud sonar ping hit them all and he knew there would be no surprise.

On board and on one of the monitors at Allen Security six distinct points were about two hundred feet from the *Toscana* and closing. The captain reported that the engines were overheated and had stopped. The *Toscana* was adrift with an attack imminent.

Patricia and Marco armed themselves with handguns and Francisco, who did not handle weapons, retreated to the bridge where he could monitor communications to and from Allen Security. He did not say a word and found himself a non-obstructive position. He always let the professionals do their work and it had always paid off.

Testa ordered all his people to starboard on the opposite side from where the *Abnegated* now loomed near and menacing. This would force the defense to spread out and he could concentrate his attack without having to engage all the guards. Accelerating, the attackers surfaced and ejected their respirators, tethering them to the buoyant scooters. Each prepared a flash bang grenade and slung their automatics over their wetsuits. The action was seconds away.

Patricia and Marco were on the starboard side of the stern deck when the scooters surfaced. They had stirred plankton, which emitted a green fluorescent light disclosing the location of each machine before it reached the surface. Patricia shouted to the guard nearest to her and told her to advise the bridge of this. It was too late. Several flash-bang grenades went off on both decks and the stern on the starboard side, and even though the security personnel were trained in a simulation of this kind of situation it was a far cry from the heat and confusion of the real thing. The noise woke up Luigi and José who sprang into action.

The attackers were climbing the short space to the first deck using grappling hooks and carbon fiber ropes. The flash-bang grenades had done a good job of disorienting the hands on deck and two guards fell to short bursts of 9mm fire from the Taurus MX9s. One of the attackers shot the pilot of the helicopter, who was trying to climb the ladder to the chopper, and was in turn shot by a guard who appeared on deck. Testa gained access to the lower deck and was confronted by a guard who appeared out of nowhere and leveled a gun on him. His reaction was instantaneous and a fast kick sent the weapon overboard and a punch to the neck rendered the guard unconscious. Other guards were disabled or killed by the attackers as two of their team fell to defensive gunfire, one to a guard and one to Luigi who was wearing only a frown and a gun. Time was running out for the attackers. The Coast Guard would be here in less than half an hour in response to the SOS that the *Toscana* had sent as soon as the attack commenced. Now Enrico and two mercs were alone on the starboard lower deck. Defenders would be coming in seconds but they had the advantage. It was time to complete the mission and get out of there. Testa headed for the stern deck looking for an entrance to the staterooms while his people defended the position. He had not finished turning the corner when he came face to face with his target. Marco Carducci was four feet from him. He raised his Taurus and touched the trigger to discharge a five round burst towards him but at that same instant a hard kick to the side of his knee made him miss and the deadly hollow points ripped harmlessly into the Atlantic. José had pump-kicked him through a porthole. The pain that shot up his leg was brutal but his training did not fail him and he regained his stance only to be bear hugged by Marco, causing his gun to fly useless to the deck. He reached to the scabbard on his leg, pulled out his British combat knife and plunged it into Marco; but it struck his shoulder bone and was defected from vital organs.

Marco shuddered from the impact of the knife that hit him with such brutal force it sent the hot pain of Hell's lightning coursing through his upper body. He instantly felt nauseous and puked all over Testa, who was raising his arm to complete the kill, which gave Patricia enough of an opening to fly-kick him fully on the chest. In spite of his great agility and resilience the cannonball hit his sternum and sent him over the rails and into the water, where his only option was to dive before fire from the *Toscana* terminated him. He swam deep and came up behind the scooter that he had tethered to the hull with a vacuum cup. He cut the rope and headed towards the shore. His sole companion was a pain worthy of penitents in Hell.

At about 500 feet he ran out of power and he activated a beacon that brought a black shell boat to him in less than a minute. One more beacon was about a hundred feet away and they picked up a woman who was a few seconds from death with an open chest wound. Testa threw her back in the water and they headed off. There were no more beacons. Five of the six assailants were dead or dying as searchlights from the upper deck and bridge of the *Toscana* scanned the surface, hunting with desperation for more enemies. Testa sat looking at his watch and counted the seconds, eight, seven, six, five, four, three, two, one...then one of the three charges that they had attached to the hull with time detonators lit up the sky and the water around the *Toscana*, and engulfed the yacht in flames. But it wasn't the charges that had been placed to blow up the yacht's fuel tanks. It was the one at the bow that was to sink the remains rapidly when the other charges and the tanks had blown. Apparently the other two charges had dislodged and sunk because seconds later plumes of water shot up indicating that the charges had detonated far underneath the surface. Yet another failure.

The *Abnegated* headed out to sea, distancing itself from the *Toscana*. The Captain knew that he would probably be intercepted by the Coast Guard, but the further away it got the better. Right now his two mates were sanitizing the ship from anything that could possibly show the presence of the mercenaries. He had been paid in full and would not say a word about the National Geographic team. He would say that he was supposed to meet up with the team in Anegada where he was headed. The story was plausible and, being in international waters with no inculpating evidence aboard, he felt confident that no consequences would come from this deal. He opened a beer and sipped, it enjoying the bitter brew.

Aboard the *Toscana*, fire from the charge that had exploded on the hull intensified amidships. Those members of the crew who had survived the attack now focused on distilling order from chaos. All the guests were taken to the stern deck and lowered into lifeboats. Only Sun E was missing as her stateroom had been close to where the explosive charge had gone off. Several of the Board were wounded but none critically. The worst was Marco, who was suffering tremendous pain from the damage that the blade had done to his shoulder bone. Fortunately the first officer had appeared with a morphine syringe from the emergency kit and soon Marco was out of pain and in a drug-induced slumber. Several cuts, bruises, and burns were administered to as the four lifeboats, with all aboard but the fatalities among the crew and Sun E, headed away from the burning ship. Luigi and José both had minor wounds but ignored them and created a barrier of will and guts around their charges. Luigi was burnt when he was helping Patricia get Marco to the lifeboat and José had a through-shot bullet wound in his left pectoral muscle.

When they were about 200 feet from the *Toscana*, intense heat from the conflagration onboard ignited her fuel tanks and a ball of fire rose into the sky so large it was seen from Virgin Gorda, Anegada, and other neighboring islands. The sound wave hit the survivors with repulsive violence; then a large real wave tossed the lifeboats threatening to capsize them, and then... nothing. No fire, no noise, no *Toscana*. There was just the buzz of the electric engines that distanced the lifeboats from the nightmare that had lasted less than ten minutes. Shocked, the survivors were in silence. Francisco Lujan and Ernie Goldman were in the same lifeboat as the captain of the yacht and after a few minutes Francisco asked how this happened so far out at sea. The captain said it was a team of pirates out of a trawler that had been navigating about a mile from them.

"We know they came in on under-water scooters because some of the crew saw the fluorescent signature of their propellers moments before we were boarded. I don't know what they were after but they were set on destroying the *Toscana*. Did you see the huge waterspouts that shot up next to us? Those were charges that must have fallen off because had they detonated on or against the *Toscana* we would not be here to talk about it. They meant to destroy the ship with all souls on board. What I don't understand is why they boarded us at all."

"We know," said Francisco, "and we know who. The problem is we can't do much about it for now."

Patricia was holding Marco close to her. He seemed peaceful and the blood from his shoulder had stopped flowing with the pressure she had been applying. Apparently no major artery had been compromised. As she was accommodating herself to hold Marco's head up the boat hit something and a loud moan was heard. The crewman who at the helm of the lifeboat stopped and the first officer shone a light around the boat. There was a person floating a few feet away. They could see it was a young woman and they edged towards her. They dragged her onboard where they were able to see her clearly. She was one of the assailants. She wore a black wetsuit with Velcro patches that had probably held weapons and maybe explosives. She was barely conscious and delirious. A gunshot wound in her thigh bled slowly but constantly. The first officer applied a tourniquet and made her drink Gatorade from the supply bag. This seemed to stabilize her but she drifted out of conciousness.

"What are we going to do with her?" asked Airy.

"We'll hand her over to the Coast Guard when they get here. There isn't much else we can do."

"We can toss her overboard," said the crewman at the helm with a grimace of disgust.

"Nah," said the first officer. "I bet she's got a story to tell. Major Allen will get it out of her. I sent him a last SOS and he should be on his way."

"I much doubt it," said Patricia, "she's a mercenary and they get well paid to keep their mouth shut."

"Yes, and once the Coast Guard has her, it will be impossible to interrogate her," said the crew member.

"Don't bet your lunch money on that," said the first officer who had been with Allen Security for over five years and knew that his boss rarely took no for an answer.

He leaned over and took a small box that was attached to the wetsuit. It appeared to be some sort of communications device because it had an antenna, a toggle on and off switch. He flipped the toggle and a small blue LED light started blinking.

Now miles away the signal reached the shell boat as it headed for Road Town, Tortola. It was ignored because it was too late to do anything about it.

"I think this is a locator beacon," said Luigi. "I've seen those before. They are used by divers to signal their location when they surface far from the dive boat. The receiver will indicate the direction and distance to the signal or in some cases exact coordinates."

Victor Martins, the first officer, shut off the device.

"Yeah, but I don't think we need to tell these sons of bitches where we are."

It was almost 4:30 a.m. when everyone in the lifeboats heard the thumping of an approaching helicopter. Soon it was hovering over them with searchlights ablaze. Through the loudspeaker they were told that two Coast Guard vessels were minutes away and that they would maintain their position over the lifeboats, which were now converging upon each other aided by the lights, until rescue arrived.

Five minutes later a US Coast Guard rescue boat shortly followed by one of Her Majesty's Navy cutters were pulling the survivors from the lifeboats. The wounded received provisional medical assistance with IV and blood substitute that was applicable to all types while their wounds were cleaned, disinfected, and dressed. Antibiotics were added to the IV solutions and ID bracelets placed on everyone's wrist.

The captains of both Coast Guard units received the report from the captain of the *Toscana* and deemed it necessary to place the wounded assailant under guard and transfer her by helicopter to Puerto Rico. A US cutter would pursue the trawler *Abnegated* and escort her back to Road Town, where the survivors indicated that they needed to return to a villa on Tortola where they had personal belongings of importance and a private airplane that would eventually take them to the US. Most of the people on board were from nationalities other than the US so it was decided that the British territory was the best destination for all. Most personal identification had been lost in the catastrophe but replacement documents would be obtained. Necessary interviews and paperwork would be conducted by the British with copies sent to US authorities.

10

Leon Goddard and Ian Carlo de la Rosa sat together in the sauna of a very private golf club in Manhasset. Neither man was comfortable with the other but a lot of things had happened in the last 24 hours. It was necessary to discuss these and their consequences. Ian Carlo had called the meeting so he opened the conversation.

"Marco has been wounded in another attempt on his life."

"Another?"

"Yes, the third in less than two weeks. And now you gotta belly up to the bar 'cause in that side of the business I got nobody else. Marco trusts you so that means that I trust you."

"So…"

"You will have another meeting this evening with an attorney of ours, Mr. Ernie Goldman. He's gonna give you access and power of attorney over a lot more than you know about."

"Mr. de la Rosa…"

"Ian Carlo…call me Ian Carlo,"

"OK Ian Carlo; is this something that can get me into problems with the law?"

"No, this is all on the up and up; but you know what I do and so that we don't bullshit ourselves, much of that money that is nice and rosy wasn't when we made it. OK?"

"I didn't need to know that," said Leon.

"Yes, you did. I need you with eyes wide open. People might come at us through the businesses that you will be managing and you have to be ready for anything. These are not nice people. They tried to kill Marco in Florida, and again by bombing his plane; and now they've stabbed him and blown up the yacht he was on."

"Hold it a second. Are you telling me that Joe Strasso's death wasn't an accident?"

"No. It was fucking murder is what I'm telling you."

Leon was silent for a few seconds and then looked Ian Carlo in the eye.

"I have a family, a wife and two kids, but Joe was like a brother to me...just tell me that my family is not at risk and I'll do whatever you need."

"I don't see why your family could be at risk because you will not be doing anything different than what you do now. It's just going to be bigger; a lot bigger. But I will have security added to your home and your kids will be protected when they go to school and when they are not with you. That's a given for a man of your income level."

"My income level?"

"Yes, as of now you make fifty million a year plus bonus. You get paid any way you want. Set yourself up."

Leon left the meeting in a daze. Things were happening that he did not understand but he soon would. He knew that Mrs. Goddard didn't raise an idiot. But for now he needed to talk to a friend, so he headed for the Long Island Flying Club and had the tow take him up to 5,000 feet. When the Aeronca that was pulling him bucked its wings and took a slow turn to the right and down, he disengaged, dipped his left wing and pulled lightly on the joystick. The air was smooth and the sky was clear. There was not much chance of a thermal but he did slow "Ss" looking for rising air. Within a few minutes he was down to 3,500 feet when he felt the pressure on his butt that indicated rising air. He tightened the turn and pulled on the stick. The altimeter started going up...3,800...4,000...4,200 until he was at almost 8,000 feet. There the thermal petered out but sustained him at that altitude.

"Well, Joe," he said out loud, "this is going to get interesting. I've been offered...or better yet, I've been told that I'm going to make more money than I ever thought I'd make in ten lifetimes. I'm going to do this job. I don't know why, but I guess in some way you have something to do with it. Rest easy my friend. Your family in Palermo is going to get enough to live in luxury for the rest of their lives and leave enough for whatever relatives you have for them to live well."

This was his real goodbye to Joe. Up where they both believed that God was. Leon soared for an hour going in and out of the thermal. Then he put the nose down and gained speed until the airspeed indicator showed 100 mph. He pulled the stick and did two consecutive loops, and then he let the glider rise straight up until his speed was about 40 mph and he kicked the rudder and did a perfect wing over. He repeated the maneuver but this time he let the plane stall and buck over completing a hammerhead.

When he landed he was a man with a brighter soul.

* * *

Joe Delany was trying to locate Marco Carducci without raising flags all over the place. He had learned by now that the Carducci clan was better connected than a leech to a beaver's ass and he couldn't afford to get sideswiped by one of the big guys. He had lost the trail in Sarasota but now it was pretty obvious that he wasn't at the house and the agent that had done the visual inspection of the place failed to notice that the docks were empty. It had been a week of looking and he had nothing. He was about to despair of the hunt when a flag came to his attention. A yacht called the *Toscana* that in the past had been in some way linked with Salvatore Carducci had been destroyed by an act of piracy in international waters east of the Virgin Islands. He went to work finding the provenance of the yacht that had a Bahamas registry and was owned by an overseas corporation that after a little digging showed Salvatore and now Marco Carducci as "permanent consultants" to the board of a Canadian corporation that owned the Bahamian one.

Bingo.

He asked for and received the Coast Guard report on the incident and copies of the interviews with the survivors. There were no passports or other IDs as all was lost in the wreckage, but a dutiful British investigator had included a detailed description of each of the survivors, their age, name, place of birth and residence. He also made a point of referencing the request for new passports for the British personnel. He requested copies of those through the State Department and set to wait for them to come back. State Departments are notoriously slow so he armed himself with patience and addressed other matters in his workload. He especially spent some time planning how to get back at Uncle Archie.

* * *

The captain of the *Abnegated* and his two shipmates were celebrating the end of this job. They had been happy to help out the Coast Guard in any way they could. No, they had not seen the explosion as two of them were asleep and the other sheepishly confessed that he had his earphones on and was listening to a great concert of Guns 'n' Roses. No, they didn't have anyone on board other than themselves. Yes, the Coast Guard and whoever else could inspect the boat. That was the end of that. Now they were pretty drunk and full of lobster, shrimp, clams, and conch, all cooked in beer and accompanied with coconut rice – a specialty of one of the fish shacks on Tortola. Too bad that later that night they all died of the same toxin that had killed the US Senator a few weeks ago. What a plague! Earlier the bearded long haired hippie who had sat quietly at a table paid for his meal and limped back to his small sailboat using a makeshift crutch and sailed west into the sunset.

* * *

Cardinal Dupree was again concerned. If one could venture a leap of faith one could say that His Eminence was pissed off. He had no confirmation of the death of Carducci. He was not listed as a survivor but then he was not among those aboard as declared in the investigation. There were several wounded and several dead but no confirmation of the death even though Testa said that he had put a knife in the man himself. What he did get were the names of people that were obviously collaborating with Carducci. But those names would take him nowhere. Nobody traveled under their real names except for the crew.

* * *

Ernie landed in NY and called Leon Goddard. They agreed to meet as soon as Ernie got to the city. For a man of almost seventy years of age he was fit and vital, but the past two days had taken a lot out of him. He felt exhausted and deeply saddened by so many dead. A total of nine people were lost on the *Toscana*, not counting those of the opposition. He felt a great loss in Sun E's death. They had only met a few times but she and Ernie had hit it off famously, both of them having a love for the Blues. They exchanged music over the years and lately had joined ThisIsMyJam.com and shared with many their magnificent collections of the most unique voices that the United States had offered the world: Billie Holiday, Ella Fitzgerald, Nina Simone, and so many more. As the limousine headed in from LGA towards Manhattan Ernie took out a flash drive that he was going to give to Leon Goddard. It contained a lot more than Ernie was comfortable sharing but there was no alternative. Marco was going to be out of commission for a week at least and then would have to lie low until he, Francisco, and probably Ian Carlo could decide on a path of action, because the evidence was that the cardinal was not going to give up trying to kill Marco and Patricia. And now that Francisco and he were probably in the fucking priest's sights they would have to have contingency plans for their own safety. This was getting out of hand. He would have to talk to Ian Carlo. The man knew how to deal with this shit.

Leon was waiting in the reception when Ernie arrived. Hellos were short and they went directly to Ernie's office. He went right to the point.

"I know Ian Carlo talked to you and you are more or less up to date on what happened in the last couple of days. Marco wants you to take over most of the responsibilities that have been his until now. He has new ones and has to dedicate some time to understand them and make decisions that will be required. This flash drive has all you need to know and the way to access whatever else you want to know. My office is preparing directives and the corresponding powers of attorney that will allow you to take your place in the boards of a number of corporations here in the US and abroad. You will need help. Promote from within or hire outside the people that you trust. The operational profit and loss statements of each venture should be sufficient of a guideline for salary structures. In other words, at Marco's specific instructions you have a free hand with this. Go through everything and when you have questions, which you will, we can have all the time you need and if Marco is available at that time, he will join us."

"Not much I can say at this moment," said Leon, "I have to trust Marco's judgment. I have since we were in school and I don't see a reason to change."

"Even after what Ian Carlo told you?"

"Yes, even after that. But I suspect that a lot of my questions are going to end up right there."

"Fair enough, I did not totally agree with your involvement but Marco was adamant about it and Ian Carlo agreed so, that's that"

"Then until I have my questions. Do you have a copy of this drive?"

"Yes, so does Marco and there are another two copies at safety deposit boxes. Just guard yours."

* * *

Marco was at the villa in Tortola and while the wound was not life threatening it was extremely painful because the carbon steel blade had scraped a long way down the bone. A top trauma and orthopedic specialist had been flown in from Miami to complement the excellent job that a British Navy MD had originally done and now it was only time and physiotherapy that would bring what was expected to be a total recovery. Jeremy Allen was also at the villa with a group of 24 security people. The villa and all its access points were sealed off and guarded 24/7. There was not going to be another attack on his watch. A complex communications system with a private satellite access had been deployed and the return of all of The Board member's to their bases was being monitored. Francisco, Ernie, and Marco believed that The Board's members had been collateral damage and not the objective of the attack.

During the following weeks, Marco spent his time reading all the documents that had come to him from Sal in the envelopes and the flash drives. He had spoken several times with Ernie, Ian Carlo, and Leon Goddard and was beginning to feel comfortable in his new role. Patricia and he had also had several conversations with Francisco and some changes were being implemented into the fundamentals of the investments.

Marco believed that instead of confronting and competing with the other groups head on, he could do a MacArthur on them. He would go to the source of their money rather than confront them on grounds where they were strong. He was also sending hundreds of emails giving instructions to all the banks, brokers and funds creating a much more agile financial structure. He had also "bought" several of the Carducci operations from overseas and had capitalized them with over two billion dollars, and gave Leon Goddard the management of those assets through extensive powers of attorney. They leveraged the holdings to the hilt and at the end of the day they held over seven billion dollars in multimodal transportation assets that were key to his plans. The initial moves were in place and he and Patricia decided that it was pertinent to disappear for a time in order to avoid another attack and plan counter-measures rather than retribution. After all it was only business.

The Lear and the *Toscana* were lost but they understood that those were the assets by which the opposition had located them. Now they were planning to move using NetJet and other similar facilities but discarded commercial flight for the moment.

* * *

M&M saw that Joseph Delany was still handicapped by the loss of his father on whose influence he had so relied. The kid needed a kick in the ass and he knew exactly what to do. He sent him another note.

Dear Special Agent Delany, on the island of Tortola there is a gentleman by the name of Marcus MacKenzie who can give you precise details as to the whereabouts of Mr. Carducci. Act promptly because he may not be there for long. By the way, he's a British citizen so don't try to play the heavy.

* * *

Enrico Testa was in a hospital in Dominican Republic. He had undergone surgery for a torn ligament in his knee and would require several weeks of therapy and rest. He had no alternative. The son of a bitch had really winged him. He also had two ribs detached from the sternum. A little more and the woman would have killed him. His stay at Casa de Campo was pleasant and he used the time to pray and read. Then he would find them both and finish the job. This time it was personal.

* * *

Major Allen returned to Sarasota and left a highly qualified lieutenant in charge of the security of the villa. There had been no threats and he had to be at the helm of his operations. Most of them were for The Board, even though he didn't know it.

* * *

Ian Carlo was in high gear consolidating his turf. He could not allow that any distraction take him away from his business for too long. Not in his line of work. There was always somebody sniffing around for the opportunity to move in on something. Wind of the FBI intentions of investigating his operation in depth had reached him as did the good work that "friends" in the New York Attorney General's Office and other branches of the judiciary had done to frustrate this. Big bonuses were sent out to the key players and the armor of bureaucracy tightened around him.

* * *

Ernie was hard at work with the management of Wall Street. While it was Marco and Leon who actually managed the money, it was Ernie that located and used the loopholes that were so necessary to keep the banks happy. His relationship with these and with some key people in the Securities Exchange Commission guaranteed that nobody was doing anything "illegal" while they laundered hundreds of millions of dollars every month. Good politicians always leave a back door open so that they can clean the graft.

* * *

Francisco was in Bogotá dealing with a particularly interesting situation – Colombia was no longer the major coca producer in the world. That honor had shifted to Peru. While the Colombian coca plantations had been reduced by 25% the better quality Peruvian and Bolivian plantations had grown proportionately, but the processing labs continued to be nomads in no-man-land. They drifted between Colombia, Ecuador, Venezuela and Peru. Now there were some in Paraguay and Bolivia. Net cocaine demand was up because of the avid consumption in emerging countries; but the US, believe it or not, had managed to reduce consumption and tightened the Mexican border to the point that the price of cocaine in the street was increasing. Europe was the opposite. Lack of cash in the 18 to

25 age group, because of rampant unemployment, had reduced the demand so the price tanked. This presented a problem of cash flow among the distributors and could precipitate even more brutal gang wars battling for territory on both sides of the Atlantic. This violence was bad for business so Francisco and now Ian Carlo had to do a review of all procedures and an evaluation of means. Assets were not a problem. So, they decided to meet in Miami.

* * *

The Biltmore Hotel in Coral Gables is a throwback to the '20s except that it has been remodeled at great expense and with exquisite taste. It was designed by Schultz and Weaver and was built in 1926 by John MacEntee Bowman and George Merrick (the creator of Coral Gables) as part of a hotel chain. It served as a hospital during WW2 and as a Veterans Hospital and then a campus of the University of Miami Medical School until 1968. It became a hotel again in 1987. There is a story that claims Al Capone killed Thomas Walsh by bashing his brains in and then throwing him off the Biltmore tower. Some think the ghost of the man still haunts the place. Also, it boasts a pool that for many years was the largest in the world and had luminaries like Johnny Weissmuller and Esther Williams spend time there.

It was at the Biltmore that Francisco Lujan and Ian Carlo de la Rosa had their meeting. Each had a suite on different floors and their meetings looked casual and public. Guests and tourists crowded the public areas and attendees to the always-present events and conventions occupied salons, restaurants and recreation facilities. On Sundays, brunch at La Fontana Restaurant was by reservation only and you still had to wait for your table. So Francisco and Ian Carlo chose to sit in the small café that services the golf course. Their ubiquitous security people mixed in well with golfers and their golf bags.

Having ordered the club sandwich and a Shark beer each, they waited for a foursome to go by noisily discussing, bragging, and bitching. Then Francisco gave Ian Carlo a detailed and rather graphic account of the attack on the *Toscana* and the days of interrogation, declarations, and explanations that the Coast Guard extracted.

"So how bad was his wound really?" Ian Carlo asked.

"Bad enough to put him out of commission for a week or ten days more and a few months of therapy and exercise to be at a hundred percent, but very fortunately no permanent damage is expected. He's learning to do everything with his left hand and arm, even though he still signs with his right which apparently hurts a lot. He's got a full time nurse and Patricia is there with him."

"Oh," said Ian Carlo without further comment, but his thoughts were on point.

"How is Goddard doing?" asked Francisco, changing the subject.

"Much better than I expected. The guy is the most incisive deconstructor of complex management organizations that I have ever met. He can see how the whole operation works as if he was looking at a clock in a glass casing. I can say that in just a couple of weeks he has improved some of the overseas corporations to become far more efficient with fewer resources, which has liberated both human and monetary capital. Or so Marco tells me because I don't know shit about it," said Ian Carlo.

"Well, our conversations now are more in our field of expertise and between the two of us, we can come up with solutions to some problems that are beginning to develop that I'd like to head off before they bite our collective asses."

"What's on your mind, still the border crossing problems?

"Yes, but more than that. Let's accept that the market is changing and we have to change with it. I think several factors are making marijuana a much more attractive recreational drug than before. If you pay attention you see that the people have decriminalized marijuana in their minds. The whole social attitude has changed in the media, the entertainment business, and even in law enforcement.

On the other hand I don't see open marijuana crops adorning the countryside quite yet. The Federal Government still has a bug up their ass about it."

"I see where you're going with this, Francisco. The problem is more than ever the border crossing of Mexican and South American weed into the US. Far more so than C or H and they are becoming more difficult every day. Between the gangs snitching on each other and the increase of border patrol agents, the Mexican border is not the sift it used to be. Also the Federales or at least some of them have become efficient and far less corruptible than before."

"True and things will get tighter as the US efforts to improve Mexican economy show results. There has been an increase in middle class population in Mexico while in the United States it has taken a beating. This creation of employment in Mexico will drain the human resources of the cartels and the turf wars will increase. That makes life difficult for us; so Sal and I came up with a plan a few years ago and now it's about to take place."

"You mean the pipeline, I'm guessing."

"Yes, I see you have done your homework; but it's a lot more than just a pipeline. It's a virtual highway. In 2009 we bid and won three contracts to increase the natural gas pipelines between three points in the US and five points in Mexico. These contracts allowed us to dig and lay pipe crossing the US/Mexican border under the watchful but blind eye of the law on both sides. Any pipeline is really a bunch of pipelines. The transport line itself requires power lines, pump stations, maintenance lines, etc. We added one unobtrusive line to this complex. It has the advantage that it produces no detectable underground signature like a tunnel does and can transport a ton of C in a few minutes over several hundred miles. The vacuum and pressure pumps are off sight from the gas facilities and are disguised in legitimate industrial sights. A fifty-kilo package in a capsule can travel at a thousand miles per hour. That means that if there is only one capsule in the tube at a time and the stations are 200 miles apart you could send five capsules an hour which would be two hundred and fifty kilos in an hour, or six tons a day. Multiply that by three and you have eighteen tons a day. Cut that in half for delays, maintenance, and other factors and you are still passing nearly ten tons a day, practically undetectable.

In the near future we can make the stations a thousand miles or more from each other and then the speed goes up to four thousand miles per hour and the logistics become simple for us and practically impossible for the law to catch on. Evacuated tube transport systems are the future in all types of transportation. They are extremely energy efficient as the impulse to the pod is given by the attraction and rejection of magnets but only at the point where the pod is, so it's only for a fraction of a second at each point. Those same magnets levitate the pod so that there is no friction and thus the high speeds are obtained. Exclusion valves at each end maintain the integrity of the vacuum and allow for the loading and unloading of the pods."

"I thought all this stuff was just theoretical. That it was, excuse the pun, a pipe dream."

"Yes, it still is for human transport, but small object vacuum transportation has existed for quite some time. Now with the new magnetic-impulse systems and perfected energy recuperation this is, for us at least, a very economic transport system. And, it is not labor intensive like the handling of these goods has been in the past. There is less chance of snitches, plants, rip-offs, and all the bribes that plague our business."

"So the point is? Apart from the obvious I mean…"

"We go back into the marijuana business because it's going to bloom!"

11

Agent Delany was still dressed in his standard FBI attire of dark suit, white shirt, and reasonable tie as he walked down the stairs of the American Airlines plane that brought him to Tortola from Miami. He looked like a fish out of water and a fly in the milk all rolled in one. He was wasp white with a buzz haircut and a look of disconcert that would tempt the most honest taxi driver to rip him off. He went through customs and to a HM Coast Guard Range Rover whose driver was leaning against it holding a card that said only DELANY. As it turned out it was Chief Inspector Buchwald, his local contact, who was there to receive him. They shook hands and went into Road Town to a small but very nice hotel that the inspector had reserved for Joseph Delany.

"I reserved it for two days if that suits you."

"That will be fine," said Delany, and went straight to the point. "You said that the MacKenzies are still here, is that right?"

"Yes, they are up at their villa, a real posh and well-guarded place. You can't get in there unless you have an appointment and from what I hear nobody gets an appointment. The vicar from the local Anglican Church went up there to offer his support and was flatly turned down by the guard. Shopping is done by the housekeeper with two nasty looking bodyguards keeping her company and so far I'm the only official that has gone up there because the pirate attack on the yacht is my case. Major Wills, the Navy MD, goes up every day but he keeps his mouth shut about his patients.

"Patients...more than one?" asked Delany

"Oh yes, several of the crew of the *Toscana*, that was the name of the yacht, were wounded and they are being cared for at the villa. Very decent of the misses, if I might say; she does the rounds with the doctor and keeps them all in high style."

"Can you get me in to see Mr. MacKenzie? I have information about the attack that may be of interest to him."

"First you ought to tell me, as I'm the bloke in charge of the investigation, aren't I?"

"Well, the survivor of the assailants is now in our custody. She is an independent contractor hired by an Internet security firm. What we found interesting was that her fingerprints rang a loud bell in an Interpol search that says she is a Spaniard by the name of Dionisia Iragorri of ETA fame. I would like to know if Mr. MacKenzie has any connection with that group."

"Wouldn't we all mate? Let me make a call. In the meantime get out of that suit. You're making me hot. Ufff!"

Twenty minutes later Special Agent Delany and Inspector David Buchwald met in the lobby. Delany was now wearing light cotton pants, a Hawaiian shirt and Dockers, yet he managed to look just as uncomfortable and out of place. Maybe it was the briefcase or the redness of his neck that a few minutes in the sun had stamped there.

"Himself will see us at noon and the misses. has invited us for a light lunch. High times for us working blokes isn't it. In the meantime I'll give you the tuppence tour of the island."

"I'd rather see the wreckage of the yacht if that's OK?"

"There is no wreckage. All that we got was a few suitcases with clothes, most of them badly burnt, and a few odds and ends. The fire and the current after the explosions left little."

"What about dead bodies? I understand about ten people died."

"Not a one so far. Like I said, fire, current, and I suppose sharks might have taken anyone left in the water. Our mates and the Yanks…sorry, the US Coast Guard, spent a day looking for survivors or casualties but found nothing."

They got in the open Ranger and headed towards the center of Road Town. There they saw the daily ritual of the tourists and the vendors. While Tortola is not the destination of many cruise ships it gets several ferries a day from the other islands and keeps busy. They left the town behind and started climbing along the winding road to Brewers Bay, only a mile or so from there but the road does a weird circumvention and it took almost half an hour. The villa was on the slopes of Mount Healthy overlooking the bay and it was reached by a private road that was well kept and surrounded by a magnificent garden of palms, bougainvillea, ginger, birds of paradise and many other tropical species. The guards were expecting them and they were directed to the main entrance from where they were escorted to an ample terrace with a pool and bar. The villa itself was an old plantation house that had been modernized and appointed with all the facilities of a retreat in paradise. The place spelled power and money enough to impress the son of a man who had everything and had spent lavishly on himself and his family.

Coming out of the house was an impressive woman; tall, slender, blond, dressed in a one piece summer outfit that could only come from the design table of one of the great coutures of our time. She extended her hand towards the inspector, who barely resisted the temptation to kiss it but who did bow deeply to the lady.

"Inspector, a bit early but always welcome," she said, now turning her attention towards Joseph.

"May I introduce Special Agent Joseph Delany with the FBI?"

"My goodness, what serious title for such a young man," she said smiling and shaking hands. "Marc will be coming out in a few moments. He is just finishing a physiotherapy session with the nurse. In the meantime, tell me what can we offer you? There is lemonade, iced tea, a grand beer that is my preference, and then anything stronger if you like."

They both accepted a beer seeing that the lady had one herself. Besides it was what the soul craved in this setting. That, or a long, long, Long Island tea. But that would not be advisable.

As they were served by a uniformed waiter, the door opened and a man about six-foot-three with snow on his temples and a sprinkling of the same on a full beard walked onto the terrace. He wore a light blue linen shirt over beige linen trousers and canvas slippers. His right arm was in a sling and he was obviously bandaged over his shoulder and around his chest and back. He had dark Costa del Mar sunglasses that didn't let the eyes be seen but the crinkles at the edges hinted of the smile that he wore naturally. Joe guessed he was in his late thirties or early forties and appeared to be about eight to ten years older than his wife.

"Gentlemen, welcome. Before we discuss the business that brought you here let me get one of those beers that look to be just what the doctor ordered." He received the beer that appeared almost miraculously and indicated that they should go under the awning where a table was set for four.

Other than the guards at the entrance from the road Joe hadn't seen any other security but was sure that it was there. He participated in the small talk for a few minutes while lunch was brought in. A side table was set up and a roast beef tenderloin in pepper sauce was placed together with abundant half lobsters, a big salad of fresh greens, and a bowl of tropical fruit. The lady was served first, then the guests, and finally Marc MacKenzie was helped by his wife who carefully de-shelled a lobster and cut it to manageable pieces and did the same with a couple of slices of beef. She put some salad and small fresh potatoes on his dish and then drank some beer. As if this were a sign, the waiter disappeared and they were alone. Or so it appeared. They ate quietly for a few minutes and then the conversation went to the point.

"The inspector tells us that you have some information about our assailants special agent. What, pray, may that be?" asked Celia MacKenzie.

"I have more questions than answers, but I'll tell you what we know. The wounded mercenary that is now under our care in Puerto Rico is a wanted ETA member who has committed a bombing and a murder in Bilbao and Santiago. She refused to say a word but the threat of extradition to Spain shook her up enough to tell us that she was hired through an agency that operates on the Internet and that she was paid $30,000 from an account in Luxembourg that we traced to a Swedish corporation that denies knowledge of such payment and has sued the bank in that respect. She told us that the leader of their group, which she thinks was not a hired gun, had an American accent but used Italian terms when he got mad or excited. By his physical description and his abilities we have narrowed it down to a few hundred Navy Seals. She described a tattoo of an eagle, an anchor, and a trident that the man had on his right shoulder blade and that he tried to keep out of sight but she saw by chance. That's a common tattoo among members of that elite group and of whom only a couple of hundred are believed to be working as soldiers for hire. But then she kind of insists that the man did not appear to be a mercenary. He was out of character for that. He spent all the time that he was not training the group locked in his cabin, but one of the others had seen him on his knees praying in there. That is all we have."

"Thank you, Agent Delany, I can see that this may be of help to the inspector but I fail to see where we can be of any service in this matter," said Marcus MacKenzie.

"Well, Mr. MacKenzie, this was, I confess a bit of a ruse to meet you. The truth is that I'm trying to get in touch with a man called Marco Carducci and I have reason to believe that the owners of the *Toscana* or you may know where I can find him."

The one who answered, surprisingly, was Mrs. MacKenzie.

"And the reason for this is..." she asked?

"I believe that the attempt on the *Toscana* had nothing to do with you or your group of friends. We have determined that the *Toscana* had been at dock for some time in a house in Sarasota,

Florida that was owned by Salvatore di Dio Carducci who passed recently and we believe that Marco Carducci could have been on that boat because the other possible heir is Ian Carlo de la Rosa, and he is in NYC as we speak and was there when the *Toscana* was destroyed. So that leaves me with few alternatives. The last we saw of Mr. Carducci was in Florida a few weeks ago."

Joe Delany put his briefcase on his lap and pulled out a tablet, turned it on and hit a few icons. Satisfied, he showed a photo of Marco Carducci as he got off the Lear in Sarasota what now seemed to Marco a lifetime ago. He looked at the man in the photo and realized how different he looked now. He was twenty pounds lighter, had a beard, his hair was now long, lighter and combed by Patricia in a very European style. He was pale compared to his deep tan at present and the clothes he wore then were such a far cry from what he was wearing today. This, plus the well-documented persona of Marcus MacKenzie, rich businessman from Wales, made it impossible to think they were one and the same.

"There is one more thing. It is very private and personal and I must speak this only with Mr. Carducci himself. As a matter of fact his life may well depend upon what I have to tell him."

"Well, Agent Delany, as much as I would like to help you, our trip on the *Toscana* was improvised and we chartered the boat through an agency in London. Our stay here at the villa is by courtesy of some friends, the Parkers, who looked kindly upon our circumstances. We can give you all the details if you like, but I doubt they could help you. But now I suggest we enjoy this dessert that my wife created. It's homemade coconut ice cream with starfruit slices and Chantilly cream. It's my favorite and you cannot leave without trying it."

A most elegant dismissal if there ever was one.

On the trip back Delany was telling the inspector what a delightful couple the MacKenzies were and how much he would have loved to meet them under different circumstances. He asked how long did the inspector think they were going to be there.

"They have the villa booked till Sunday week and at the price they pay for that place I doubt they would leave before."

"Well, I cannot thank you enough for your help and even though I'm booked for the night, I'm going to Puerto Rico because I want a crack at the survivor from the assault group before she's transferred to Florida, which has the jurisdiction on this case."

By five that afternoon Delany was on a flight to San Juan and had arranged a meeting with a local agent to see Dionisia Iragorri at Veterans Hospital in San Juan. When he got there he was surprised at how young the girl was, barely out of her teens, yet he knew she was an international terrorist. After two hours of questioning he got little more than what he already knew. The mission was to allow for their leader time to terminate one or two targets and then destroy the vessel. They were to activate their beacons when back in the water and run as far as the scooters would take them with what battery was left and wait for a shell boat to pick them up. She would not say a word as to where they came from.

* * *

Dupree received Ana Meredith and her son at his Holy See office that had the trappings of the Vatican, which was not the case with his office at the bank that was spartan and functional. Here the proximity of the Holy Father always impressed and intimidated powerful visitors.

"God be with you," Dupree greeted his visitors.

"And with your spirit," they answered in unison.

He indicated that they should take a seat in the small but elegant sitting room attached to his office and asked if they would like something to drink. Getting the negative, he went straight to the point.

"Other than the nominal ownership of land by monarchs, I believe you now own more land than any single individual or corporation in the world. Am I right?"

"One point two billion acres at last count," said Ana. "Not that anyone knows that except for a couple of people, you included."

"Well, let it be for the greater glory of God," answered the cardinal. "I'm aware that a good portion of that is in dispute right now?"

"About a third of it; almost everything we own in South America and that we owe to very poor management of our assets by your banks," said Edward Meredith with a huff of disgust.

"Not a time to point fingers... yet," said his mother who turned to the cardinal and said, "I believe His Eminence is doing all that is possible to secure our holdings, we would just want some reassurance."

"And you have it, my dear Ana. Every diocese in the region is working hard to appease the conscience of some politicians, who edged on by the liberal, godless press acted hastily. We know that apart from a lot of noise, nothing will happen in Colombia, Brazil, or Uruguay. We are working hard in Argentina but they have a conflict of interest as the president does not want to show preference for the Church for obvious reasons. But rest assured that God's will be done."

"In that case our support of your work in that region will continue," said Ana with the implied threat that those words carried.

"And God will bless you for it," said the cardinal, "and how is your effort in Africa and Russia progressing?" He asked knowing full well that the Merediths had just bought about 400,000 acres in Russia through a local billionaire who needed to hold money outside of the country. He trusted Putin only as far as he could throw him, though they were fishing and hunting buddies.

Once finished with the formalities of the blessing and a private audience with the pope the Merediths departed for their villa in Tuscany and a meeting with someone special, as they were not going to wait for the cardinal to pull his blessed finger out of his most holy ass. The sheik would be there soon and they needed to be sure that nothing in the house would offend his Muslim sensibilities. It was time to negotiate with the Arabs because the cardinal was showing signs of incapacity. Delany had managed a good deal with the Saudis; why couldn't they get an even better one from the Emirates?

* * *

M&M was getting ready to leave for three days of tarpon fishing in Los Jardines de la Reina off the southern coast of Cuba where the abundance and wildness of the fish were legendary. He had packed two four-piece Loomis 12-weight fly rods with Able reels, the only ones in his opinion that could take the beating a large tarpon can hand out; two Sage rods, one 11-weight and one 9-weight, also with Able reels; a dozen extra lines and some extra backing; about four dozen tarpon flies of his own creation, half of them already tied to 100-pound hard mono shock tippets connected with a slim beauty knot to 16-pound class leaders complete with Bimini twist butts; and thirty more pounds of paraphernalia needed or better yet, wanted, for this adventure. He was knotting the last of his leaders when his very private line buzzed for his attention. He listened for a couple of minutes, thanked the caller, and leaned back in his chair to think about what shenanigans the Merediths were up to. The caller, his friend the prince, would surely fill him in as soon as the sheik was back from Italy. This thing got better and better every day. Before he finished packing he sent Francisco Lujan a short heads up. He would appreciate it.

* * *

The Meredith organization exported and imported grain, soy, fertilizer, salt, nitrate, pork, beef from several countries, and now lamb, wool, and lanolin from Australia, New Zealand, and Argentina. They had ships and trains and trucks to move their multibillion dollar business, but not enough. They also depended on multimodal companies to do their growing trade with China and Russia, Brazil, and Argentina. With such a huge business the Merediths had a communications center rivaling the CIA...or Francisco Lujan's Bogotá operation. By coincidence, that very day Francisco Lujan's people had managed to break down the last firewall of Meredith's mainframe and had started leaching out information that, for over half a century, had remained secret. A six-month effort by one of the world's greatest hackers had paid off. The young Indian girl was going to be rich for life and her family would be able to move out of India. They would like Bogotá. It was crowded and crazy like Bombay but had a much better climate.

* * *

Marco and Patricia decided that it was time to leave Tortola behind and head for New York. He and Ian Carlo had much to discuss and Patricia wanted to stick around to be part of the plan to take on the cardinal. In her mind she thought that it was the logical thing to do. In her heart it was also the thing she wanted to do. She did not want to be away from Marco, but she didn't really know why or maybe she didn't want to know why. Not just yet anyway.

All the security personnel that had been on the *Toscana* got a cash bonus of $10,000; those on land got $5,000 as did the staff at the villa. This was a way to say thank you but mostly to say, "Keep your mouth shut." The MacKenzies would stay on till Friday to quench local curiosity. The inspector was summoned to the villa and was given all the information he needed to contact the MacKenzies at a recuperation clinic in Barbados and then at their home in Wales. He was discreetly given a week at the villa, all expenses paid by the MacKenzies, who were so very grateful for his help in such terrible circumstances. He ran back to ask for his vacation days. Oh, wouldn't Betty just love this and so would the kids.

They all took a speedboat to St. Tomas where they passed through US Customs & Immigration and met their chartered G3 to fly them directly to New York. Only Luigi, Pete, and José went with them. The flight was uncomfortable for Marco who still suffered a lot of pain but did not touch painkillers except at night when he needed to sleep. He was not going to get hooked on that shit.

They landed in Teterboro and limoed into Manhattan directly to the Third Avenue house. Ian Carlo was there to meet him and as of that moment, life accelerated. Ian Carlo and Tommy Lee had traced the introduction of Birko into the Liguria family via a recommendation from a small *capo* of the Esposito family from San Francisco. Upon further research it was obvious that the placement of Birko had been intentional but he doubted that it was about Marco. That had been a convenient coincidence. The truth was that the church had come into a large inheritance from an Italian American who had interests in Las Vegas and surroundings. Joe Tellez and Mario Esposito had met in Vegas and had hit it off. Esposito had asked Joe if he had a job for a friend of his who had a pulmonary problem and needed to move to a very dry place; thus Birko in Vegas. The coincidence was that the dead Italian-American who left the church all that dough was old man Esposito; and the family wanted it back so they placed someone in Vegas who could connect with the local Catholic Church and see what could be done. It backfired though because Birko was a wacko and became part of the problem. The Espositos were about to whack him when Tommy Lee took him to New York. The use of Birko by Testa had been just dumb luck.

But that was not all. A couple of days ago every local news broadcast led with the story of a man who had been found by fishermen somewhere near Montauk Point floating in a slick of garbage holding on to an empty Costco brand five gallon detergent bottle. He was dehydrated, hypothermic and starving but had miraculously survived for several days. The man had a story to tell. Satan, in the body of a Mafia *capo* who had died several weeks back, had thrown him into the ocean and he was alive only because every morning and every evening he was visited by the Archangel Gabriel who brought him food and water. The man was taken to Bellevue where he praised God nonstop and told whoever listened that he was now an angel of God and was here to save the pope. Thorazine was administered in ample doses and now he lived in happy la-la land. End of story. It was the first time in weeks that Ian Carlo, Marco and Patricia had had a good laugh.

Now it was time for business. After updating each other, they decided that a meeting with Ernie, Francisco, and Leon Goddard was necessary because they were setting in action a plan that would put a lot of pressure on the opposition. They also decided that it was convenient that Marco have a face-to-face talk with Special Agent Delany; there was nothing to lose and much to learn.

Francisco Lujan left Bogotá for New York making a short stop in Miami to meet with a Russian Diplomat. He arrived in Teterboro, and boarded a chopper into downtown. Ernie was at the heliport to meet him. Francisco's security people had stayed in Miami because in NYC he was in the very capable hands of the Carducci. The two had been notified by Airy that a substitute for Sun E had been chosen by their board and would be inducted and then introduced at the next meeting. They both felt the loss of a good friend but life and the show must always go on.

Marco and Ian Carlo were sitting in the library of the old house talking about Leon Goddard.

"I've gotta tell you that this guy is solid gold," said Ian Carlo as he poured more coffee into his cup. "I see things going as well or better than before and there is no amount of work that he won't take on. You really know how to pick them!"

"Leon was better at most things in school. He has the best analytical mind that I have ever met and has great imagination that makes him creative. This is a combination that few people have. Thank goodness he's not entrepreneurial, otherwise we wouldn't have him."

"We had the talk by the way" said Ian Carlo, "even though he doesn't see my side of the business now he knows where the seed money to all those kosher businesses came from. So far he hasn't gone squeamish on us, which is good."

"I hope not. That's an area that worried me to some degree. He's always been a straight arrow, which is why I hired him. I never expected all this shit to happen and having to put him in this position."

"What position would that be?" asked Leon Goddard as he entered the room in the company of Patricia. He saw the faces of the two men and added, "I am expected, right?"

"Oh, yes you are, Leon, take a seat," Marco said as they all shook hands, "and you are most welcome. Now as to what I was saying, is that too many unexpected things have occurred in the last few weeks that have placed you in what might be an uncomfortable position...."

"You hear me complaining? I've never had so much fun in my life and on top of which you're paying me a shit load of money to do it," laughed Leon. "This is like a good chess game. You wanted me to block every move that the Merediths do and that's just what we're doing. By now Ana must be really pissed, which means she must be giving hell to poor Edward."

"Ana...Edward?" asked Ian Carlo surprised.

"Oh yes, I've known them for years. They offered me a job when we finished school. I even spent a weekend at their place, but after seeing how that old lady treats her son, I ran. That's about when you offered me a job and here I am," said Leon affably.

The five turned their discussion to the plan that they had come up with, each of them contributing with details and different points of view. It became a plan both strategic and tactical, and decisions were made to put it all into effect.

* * *

Earlier, Ana Meredith, her son Edward, Lord Humphrey, and Sheik Faruk Al-Enezi were looking at Senator Archibald Mason pour himself a large whiskey. The others, with the exception of the Arab, were drinking the fine Chianti from the villa's winery.

"So you think that all our transactions managed through the network set up by His Eminence have led our opponents to compromise our efforts. Correct me if I'm wrong," said Mason without turning around. "And furthermore, you think the sheik here is going to offer us a better deal and not be exposed to the beady little eyes of Lujan and company?"

"In sum, yes. That is the gist of it," said Edward Meredith. "I'm tired of the bullshit. Yesterday Dupree told my mother and me that things had been solved in Colombia and that it would only be political posturing. Well, today the Attorney General indicted our manager in Colombia and put a government lien on all our properties acquired after the first of January of last year. That's more than half our holdings there."

"And," said Ana, boiling inside, "the significant part is that other governments are watching and this could become a landslide. If we cannot transact in secrecy most of our business would deteriorate."

"I concur," said Humphrey, "too much is at stake here and Dupree doesn't keep that crazy priest of his on a short enough leash."

"What priest?" asked the sheik.

Nobody answered.

* * *

Across the ocean and in the few seconds before the edge of the sun began to dim the stars, M&M sat in a skiff off a small key south of Cuba. His boatman and guide was a rail-thin man of undeterminable age who wore a dirty old straw hat and a shirt washed so many times you could never guess what color it had been. The skiff was as old as the shirt, made of wood with planks for seats and an old but serviceable cooler that stored the drinks and served as a casting platform. The engine was a Johnson 20 HP that probably powered Washington across the Potomac. M&M was particular about his guides and Vicente was by his judgment the best tarpon guide in all the Caribbean. As they sat quietly for the day to break both sipped on Cuban coffee, strong and sweet like most of the people of that island. The ever-present cigar went to and left from Vicente's lips, lighting up his wrinkled face as he sucked in the velvet smoke. When there was enough light to see the silver-blue water of the flat, Vicente stood on the cooler and looked north, toward land, toward Cuba. He stood there in perfect stillness as if to see who upon that land was looking back. Time passed slowly, like the clouds that drifted west, fleeing the rising sun. An hour passed and Vicente never moved. His cigar clenched between his teeth had probably died by now.

Suddenly he said only one word "Vienen!" – "They're coming" – and got off the cooler. M&M got on and stripped line from the reel until about sixty feet lay loosely coiled on the floor of the boat. Then he made a couple of slow casts, leaving about thirty feet of line out the tip of the rod and laying in the water in front of him, and looked at where Vicente was pointing. There in the clear water, over the uneven sand, long shadows that looked almost like torpedos move quickly toward him. About twenty feet to the east of the shadows he saw the fish, a line of six large tarpon.

They were suddenly only about a hundred feet away and he would have time for just one cast. Holding the loose line in his left hand he raised the rod up and back with his right arm and gave the line a strong but steady pull, loading the rod off the tension of the water into an energy-ladened backcast. At the point when the line was nearly fully extended in the air behind him he pulled down hard on the line in his left hand to increase his line speed and reversed direction with the rod, driving the cast forward on the haul and letting the energy release through the entire length of the rod into the fat belly of the line. It shot forward in a powerful, tight loop, feeding its length from the excess line on the floor of the boat and unfurling into a straight seventy-foot extension of flyline, leader, tippet, and fly, all touching the water at the same time with barely perceptible disturbance. It was a perfect cast and M&M smiled in satisfaction as he felt the few remaining joules of energy from the effort stop at the reel with a solid jerk. He dropped the rod tip to the surface of the water and made sure he was tight to the line, letting the fly at the other end sink for a few seconds to reach the same depth as the approaching tarpon. He then began a slow, steady retrieve, drawing the fly – a pattern tied to imitate a small shrimp or other crustacean – into visual range of the lead fish, which instantly surged forward and engulfed the tiny offering into its dinner-plate sized maw.

As the tarpon turned back into the line of fish M&M struck. Keeping his rod low and parallel to the water he grasped the line just in front of the reel and in several violent strip strikes yanked it away from the fish as hard as he could, driving the razor-sharp 1/0 tempered steel hook of the fly into the tough, bony mouth of the tarpon. Instantly the silver king erupted, going airborne in a trademark explosion of water and scales, its huge gaping mouth trying to swallow the sun while light fractured off his frantically shaking body tossing rainbows in all directions.

M&M bowed to the King. He extended his arm forward and bent from the waist to lessen the tension on the line in anticipation of the huge fish landing back on the leader and snapping the thin 16-pound line class tippet. His experience and skill paid off and the still tethered tarpon took off like a freight train bound for Chattanooga, scattering the other tarpon and causing M&M's reel to resonate with the high-pitched wail so beloved by big fish anglers everywhere. The tarpon's frenzied retreat was punctuated by several more leaps and each time, with trained humility, M&M bowed and bowed again, rendering upon this king of fish the honor that it deserved.

M&M used the strong butt of the rod to dominate the beast, knowing that if the battle did not end quickly and decisively the tarpon would begin to gulp air at the surface and would slowly regain its strength, resulting in a battle that could go on for literally hours. Every time the tarpon ran to the right M&M pulled to the left, and visa versa, never letting the leviathan lift its head. Fifteen minutes later he felt the fish finally give up against his pressure and roll in the direction he pulled. He knew the contest was over.

He reeled in as quickly as possible, steering the tarpon to the boat where it lay docile on its side in exhausted silver splendor, its large eye the only part of its magnificent body still denying the defeat. As Vincent grabbed the fish by its huge lower jaw and popped the insignificant fly from the armored mouth, M&M and the tarpon fixed each other in a stare reminiscent of knights in the jousting arena. Then the fish quivered, righted itself, and with slow kicks of its tail swam away from the boat. The fish gone, M&M sighed and looked up at the horizon. It was going to be a great day.

* * *

The meeting in Italy was going well.

"I don't want to pry into your affairs unless they may be of significance to our transactions," said the sheik.

"No problem," answered Mason curtly, "our current banker has some eccentric associates that we rather not comment on."

"Then to our business. I understand that you will be making substantial land purchases and investing in mining, oil, and pharmaceutical research and that you want that investment to be untraceable to your group. Is that a correct statement?"

"Yes, very precise indeed. Obviously the most important detail is missing. All the deposits your bank will receive will be in cash, and those must appear as normal business transactions within your banks."

"Yes, naturally; and I'm sure you are aware of the fees entailed. Am I correct?"

"A fifth of the cash and it becomes immaculate," said Ana, with her usual directness.

"We understand each other very well," said the sheik.

"Yes, but are you sure your banks can handle all that cash? We are talking of container loads of dollars and euros," said Ana brashly.

"I will explain this once to set your mind at ease. Our banks, all based in the Middle East, are not interfered with by Western regulators. The West has few friends in the Middle East and they do not want to aggravate the few they have. You should know this to be a fact, Lord Houghton."

"That is why we're here," answered Humphrey, raising his glass.

"Your shipments of so many items to one or more of our nations will no doubt be laced with the cash and it will be instantly credited to your accounts, less our fee, naturally. What you want us to do with that money is entirely up to you and other than making it untraceable, we hold no further responsibility. The accounts can be managed by one point of contact and will be coded and encrypted to your satisfaction. The banks are spread out from Lebanon to Tunisia, but you can operate as a single account and we will do the juggling." The sheik looked briefly toward the sky. "Now I must retire to privacy as it is time for prayer. Discuss this among yourselves and I will return later."

* * *

Vicente released a second tarpon of the day and M&M was feeling light as a kite and relishing every moment when his sat-phone buzzed his attention away from the fish. He picked up and grunted a hello; he listened for about three minutes, said thank you in Farsi, and hung up.

"Que día más bueno, Vicente!" ("What a good day, Vicente!") said M&M with a bright smile. The prince had just given him an update of the meeting the sheik had with Ana Meredith and her group. It was time to collect on his good deeds. Later that day he would get in touch with Francisco Lujan, but right now he was going to jump another tarpon.

12

Special Agent Delany shivered with the thought of what he was about to do. Was he betraying his sworn duty? This meeting with Marco Carducci was not going to be according to FBI protocol. He did not tell his superior, he did not take backup; he was winging this, but he needed to know more about his father's murder and apparently Carducci could tell him something. He entered the lobby of the Ambassador Hotel and headed for the quiet lobby bar. There in one of the booths was Marcus MacKenzie and his wife. What were they doing here? From behind, a voice called "Joseph" and he turned to see an older man, about five-foot-six dressed in a dark blue pinstripe suit, white shirt, school tie, and very polished burgundy wingtips. He put out his hand.

"I'm Ernest Goldman. I'm an attorney for Mr. Marco Carducci and it was I who arranged this meeting. Why don't we join Marco and we can get on with it."

"Sure but where is he?"

"Right here," said Ernie pointing.

"No, that's...Oh, I see," said Delany. He wasn't always the brightest star in his family, he thought disappointedly, sitting down.

Marco stood up politely.

"Hello Special Agent. I'm Marco Carducci and this is Ms. Patricia Lujan. I'm sorry about the small deception. We borrowed the personas of some dear friends because we were concerned for our safety. There have been three attempts on our life including the one on the *Toscana* and we had no way of knowing who you really were."

"I came to talk about those attempts," said Delany with only a nod to Patricia. "My parents were murdered recently and I was told by an informed source that it may be the same person who has tried to kill you."

"That source told you something else, Agent Delany. He told you that a close friend of your father was involved in the murder." This was Patricia talking.

"How did you know that?"

"Probably the same informed source. He is an international fix-er of the very highest caliber. If he said it, you can count on it. He trades in information and as far as we know, never tells a falsehood; it would destroy his credibility."

"Why did he tell me this? I have nothing to offer him."

"That may be now, but he trades long term. Maybe you are an investment. Rest assured that he did not do it out of altruism and that sooner or later he will collect."

"Mr. Carducci, you are aware that until recently I was the head of an investigation focused on organized crime and that the Car-ducci family has been a significant target of that investigation?"

"That is of no concern to Mr. Carducci, as he is nothing more than a legitimate and very successful businessman," interrupted Er-nie Goldman. "He is here with you to help solve murders and at-tempted murders of which you and he have been victims, but if you have any legitimate questions and not intimidations, I'm sure Mr. Carducci will be glad to answer in my presence."

"No, I've been re-assigned and that is not my case anymore."

"I'm surprised, what happened?"

"My father died, that's what happened. It appears that his ab-sence affected my status within the agency. And since it appears that

Uncle Archie...I mean Senator Mason, had something to do with it, my influence in Washington not only vanished but has turned against me."

"Why would that be?"

"I don't really know."

"Well, here is where we can join forces," said Patricia. "We know about Mason, Meredith, Dupree and some priest that's his henchman, but we know little else. There are people in the US government that are involved in this and others in Europe and maybe the Middle East, but we have yet to pinpoint whom. We know that they are trying to centralize wealth and corner fundamental natural resources. We know that they are doing all this under subterfuge and if they succeed we will see a dreadful combination of the Third Reich, Stalin's Russia, and Victorian Britain dominating most of the world."

Patricia waited for her words to soak in to the young agent. She was skewing his previous worldview and she knew it. "We saw what they can do in 2008 and that was just a test. Think what a total collapse of the world's monetary system would mean when just a few can control water and food for most of the western world. Look at Detroit, for example. At this moment Merediths or another conglomerate can walk in and buy 100,000 properties for practically nothing. This can become pervasive if somebody doesn't stop these people – and don't count on the government. They owe their positions, their income, and their lives to those who are building this trap. These are the same people who killed your father and your mother."

Delany was silent for a few seconds. Finally he whispered, "How can I help? What can I do? I feel so impotent. Most of my clout at the agency is gone and my new job is a dead end."

"What's your new job?" Marco asked.

"Information distribution for the East Coast."

"Oh! Now that's interesting..." said Marco.

* * *

Monsignor Testa was testing his leg. He had been walking a few miles a day for the last few days and now he was running along the beach heading west, parallel to the little landing strip and the seventh hole of the golf course. He was taking it easy; just an accelerated walk really, but he felt his muscles come to life. In a few minutes he was sweating copiously and he felt it was cleansing him, taking out the bitterness and the fury. His chest was also feeling much better and his lungs were filling with air, life giving fresh air. Dupree had been sending him coded messages pressing him back to Rome but he was not ready yet. He needed at least a week of controlled exercise before he was going back. And that was that. He was leaving a week from today and not a minute earlier. He jogged for an hour and then swam for a few minutes in the lukewarm sea. He returned to his room, stood because he could not kneel yet, and started the routine of his daily prayer.

* * *

Not too far from Hispaniola, at La Havana International Airport, M&M was taking his first class seat on a flight directly to Madrid and from there a short flight to Milano. His chauffeured car would be there waiting for him and in no time he would be home. Home to M&M was a beautiful Mediterranean villa overlooking Lago di Lugano in the Ticino, the most southern canton of Switzerland. The city of Lugano was a short ride away and Lake Como was minutes by car. He worked from his home or from ample offices in Lugano where he had a staff of twenty working his pool of clients and sources that were many and widely spread around the planet. As soon as he got home he would get in touch with Francisco Lujan and maybe, just maybe, he would start communicating directly with Marco Carducci. He leaned back in his seat and watched Cuba recede below his wings.

* * *

Just south of McAllen, Texas, a vacuum-forming plant that had recently been inaugurated to the fanfare of a local high school band and a speech by the usual dignitaries was working at full blast. Its business was assured by several clients related to The Board. It would be working twenty-four-seven. The first capsule arrived with a WHOOMP and a release of air pressure. It carried a compressed package of high-quality marijuana and three kilos of Colombian cocaine. This would happen ten times today. The value of the merchandise had multiplied by five from the moment it left a plastic bottle factory in Mexico to the moment it arrived in McAllen. Tomorrow morning it would leave in a container that carried vacuum formed trays for a medical instruments manufacturer in Minneapolis. Now it was time to return the capsule loaded with fifty kilograms of hundred dollar bills or about five million dollars, which had arrived in drums marked Polyethylene and Polystyrene; and if someone opened one of the barrels, that is what he would find… for the first twelve inches or so. Those dollar bills would then be packed tight into a container that would leave from Veracruz for Greece, where arrangements had been made to disperse the funds to a dozen or so banks, where it would be sanitized and transferred to hundreds of accounts around the world. All of this managed efficiently by The Board's computers and protected by the powers that be for which the deal was done.

* * *

When Francisco got off the phone with M&M he saw his opportunity to move in on that association of bandits. Driving a wedge between the cardinal and his cohorts would be a pleasure. He and M&M both knew the sheik's network and could make it hobble the Vatican Bank without The Board ever showing their hand. Now Francisco had the upper hand and M&M could afford another thousand trips to Cuba and have a fortune left over. He would talk to Ernie, Marco and Patricia before the day was over and taper this new development into the plan they had…but he had to make a lot of arrangements before that. He had his lunch brought down from the Club de Banqueros on the top floor and asked them to include a bottle of Alto de las Hormigas Reserva Malbec, a delectable wine that he enjoyed. It was time to move some money.

* * *

Joseph Delany walked into his office with a smile for the first time in weeks. Somehow he felt liberated. Free from the obligatory deference to this cadre of assholes that were his "superiors" and from that little ass kissing dork that was his brother-in-law who, since his father's death, had been trying to act as the *pater* of the family because Archie Mason had been favoring him on the hill and his star was rapidly rising.

Joseph sat at his desk and for the first time in a long time he felt purpose to his life. He powered the computer, put in his password and scanned his index finger on the machine that came to life with the seal of the Federal Bureau of Investigations. Each symbol and color in the FBI seal has special significance. The dominant blue field of the seal and the scales on the shield represent justice. The endless circle of thirteen stars denotes unity of purpose as exemplified by the original thirteen states. The laurel leaf has, since early civilization, symbolized academic honors, distinction, and fame. There are exactly 46 leaves in the two branches, since there were 46 states in the Union when the FBI was founded in 1908. The significance of the red and white parallel stripes lies in their colors. Red traditionally stands for courage, valor, strength, while white conveys cleanliness, light, truth, and peace. As in the American flag, the red bars exceed the white by one. The motto "Fidelity, Bravery, Integrity," succinctly describes the motivating force behind the men and women of the FBI. The peaked beveled edge that circumscribes the seal symbolizes the severe challenges confronting the FBI and the ruggedness of the organization. The gold color in the seal conveys its overall value.

Bullshit, he thought. He himself had followed the directives of politicians pursuing goals that had nothing to do with justice. He did recognize in most agents the "Fidelity, Bravery and Integrity" of the agency's motto, but the farther up the ladder these blurred and vanished being replaced by political kowtowing, because unfortunately their careers depend on the elected representatives of the people, who in reality did not represent any people. He remembered Dr. Evil – of pinky to the mouth fame – saying "Freedom failed"… and then his Cyclops #2 said, "There is no world anymore…only corporations." He went to the query bar and typed in "Sheik Faruk Al-Enezi."

* * *

Marco and Patricia had gone to the Third Avenue residence for the night but were reluctant to part one from the other and so spent long hours talking about their lives and how they were brought into their present strife. They found comfort in their stories where privilege and wealth had been mired by deep personal loss. Marco realized that he had used the excuse of vulnerability to shun love and personal commitment. This warm and beautiful woman had found an emotional refuge in an older man who, far from his apparent persona, had offered her unconditional love without any interest in her wealth or her father's position. Sal was a man unto himself and that was a treasure to be valued. She had lost the pale morality of Catholicism at an early age and did not shy from Salvatore's role as a *capo* mafioso, because after all, that was what her father was. The hours passed unperceived and accompanied by the warm glow of a bottle of exquisite Barolo from the cellar. It was 2:30 a.m. when finally Marco hit the sheets, only to fall into an erotic dream where Patricia was bathing luxuriously, soaping herself intimately while he watched. Her movements were slow and deliberate and when finally she stood from the bath and he was about to see her in desired nakedness he awoke to a violent ejaculation and the vision erased slowly from his mind. He went to the bathroom shed his boxers, put on some pajama pants, and went back to a dreamless sleep.

In her master suite Patricia was awake with desire for this younger man, a desire that made her feel wanton because of their relationship, because of her recent widowhood, because of the way she thought she should act. But desire and arousal always triumph and she held her hand between her legs, tightening and releasing until a surprisingly strong but deeply welcome orgasm arched her body in waves of pleasure. Spent, she drifted off to sleep.

* * *

In the days following the visit of Ana and her son, Dupree noticed the drain of funds from several accounts that the bank held for the senators and the Merediths. He also noticed the call for funding that came from several dioceses in the US and sub-Saharan Africa. He immediately placed a call to Ana Meredith but was told that she was in a spiritual retreat and could not be reached; her son Edward was not available either. Then he called Humphrey with the same results; his Lordship was in Ireland fishing and could not be reached. Money was draining rapidly from Spain, Portugal, Paraguay, Latvia, Estonia, and not one major cash deposit had come into these or other banks in his network. The banks in Jersey, Barbados, Bahamas, Canada, Australia, and India were rejecting credits issued by his banks. So far over twelve billion dollars had left His purview. Mason was in the Senate in session and would return his Eminence's call as soon as possible. No, his assistant did not know when this would be. He called the bishops of several key cities and asked them to personally contact his quarries but later negatives were received from all over. No one was available. He called Enrico Testa; the time for nice was over.

Enrico Testa was packing his bag and preparing to leave for Rome via Miami when the call from Dupree came. He listened for a minute or two and answered with the humble "Yes, Your Eminence, God's will be done," that had been his mantra for years at the service of the Holy See. He opened his bag again and changed passports. For this trip he would be Joao Pernambuco. He then cancelled the reservations for Enrico Testa and bought a ticket for a direct flight to Atlanta. He reserved a full sized car at National and made reservations for hotels in several cities. He would buy new clothes in Atlanta. Then he went to the shop in the hotel lobby and bought dye for his hair. The sun of Santo Domingo, his hours of running on the beach and the breeze from the sea had given him a deep tan. He put on dark contact lenses and once finished the man who looked back at him from the mirror matched Joao's passport photo.

* * *

As the G5 flew west Ian Carlo's thoughts were on Marco; he was getting the feeling that Marco was falling for Patricia. Odd, was what he thought. It was almost like falling for his stepmother, but there were odder things. It was about time that Marco settled down; nobody can live off bread alone, much less off hookers only, no matter how beautiful they were. Ian Carlo knew that Marco had not made use of the service because Lucrecia Ovechkin, the manager, had called him to find out if anything was wrong with Marco. Well, Ian Carlo thought, I wonder if he's getting any. Now Ian Carlo set his mind on business. He was on his way to meet with Tommy Liguria. Tommy had proved to be a true blood and it was particularly convenient because Ian Carlo was going over to show him some big money. Tommy was no slouch; he had grown his family's business in Vegas in the years he had been helping his old man who these days spent more time playing bocce than paying attention to the business. Years ago the Liguria had been big in the casino business but now that was corporate stuff. Ian Carlo was sure they still had a hand in it but like the Carducci everything was handled via multi-layered international corporations and little if any hanky-panky happened there anymore. The Liguria had their corner of the drugs, the call girls, the off-strip betting, and the unions. They sold protection and they collected for third parties and skimmed off everything. Now, Ian Carlo thought, it's time for Tommy to join the big boys.

* * *

Marco and Leon Goddard had spent two full days discussing business. Leon presented his overall plan showing Marco a very ambitious growth based on acquisitions and expansion of present business by intense promotion that would slow the earnings, which at the time was convenient, and would assure a deeper relationship with the clients and consumers. Everything was mid-to-long term but the cash-heavy corporations needed to invest now to grow later. It was a plan that would generate close to fifty thousand new jobs over the next five years and if successful could quadruple that number over the decade. The hold Carducci Enterprises had on multimodal transportation was being verticalized and a top man had been hired to head that division. Marco had plans for that. Leon also wanted to turn Carducci enterprises into a public company with an IPO planned for eighteen months in the future. That part was something that Marco had to really think about. Leon's arguments were good and addressed the need of transparency, security, and anchoring of the existing assets. In the future other corporations could be created to, as Leon put it, "manage the alternative funds." On the other hand,, Marco was not comfortable with more government regulators. With a general agreement to all things planned except the IPO that was to be decided later Marco approved and told Leon to limit his reports to once every fortnight.

* * *

On the airplane to Atlanta with only 45 minutes to spare, Testa went into the bathroom and took out a fingertip kit and carefully stuck a film to each. Then he applied a protein and lanolin based lotion to his hands that would make the fingertips register as natural to the sensors on the screen at immigration. Now the fingerprints would correspond to those in the database for Joao Pernambuco but the makeup would not last more than a couple of hours and time was critical or the deception would literally peel right off.

Fortunately it was a slow day at Hartsfield-Jackson International Airport and he was walking to his connecting commuter flight to Kansas City within the hour. He had plenty of time to get on the train that took him to his terminal and for a light lunch at one of the sit-down restaurants. He reviewed carefully his "insulin kit" to make sure it was in working order. He changed the CO2 capsule that propelled the tiny darts and adjusted the pressure to minimum for the time being. Nobody needed an accident. He put the injector in his shirt pocket and the kit in his briefcase.

* * *

Marco and Patricia crossed in the air with Testa as they flew in a NetJet Falcon to Sarasota. A new Bombardier 6,000 transcontinental Jet would be delivered to one of the off shore corporations based in Barbados but it was still a couple of weeks away. They had bought it by recommendation of Ian Carlo and Ernie who thought it would be essential in the near future. They had lucked on it as the plane had been booked by a Venezuelan billionaire who had fallen in disgrace with Maduro and had to cancel the order and lose his ten million dollar deposit. Now the jet was being re-fitted to Patricia's specs because the design chosen by the Venezuelan was tacky as hell. As much as Marco loved the Lear he did not want to have the constant memory of the previous one's sad demise. The other advantage was that the Bombardier is Canadian manufacture and fitted particularly well with the structure of the company that bought it.

They landed in Sarasota and as the door opened inside the hangar, they felt the hot breath of Florida, fruit laced with ocean and a touch of what...coffee? Luigi and José would take care of the luggage and Pete would drive them directly to the house. Two Allen Security SUVs accompanied them. It was no time to take risks. When they arrived at the house, Major Allen was there to review with Marco the security procedures that he had established, but it turned out that it was Patricia who asked the questions and made suggestions. Major Allen thought to himself, "So, we're back to the way things were …" and looked at Marco and Patricia as a couple. It was probably the first time that happened.

Patricia said she wanted to take a swim and left to change into a bikini she bought in Tortola but hadn't worn. Marco went to make himself a drink but Matilde beat him to the bar and asked what he wanted. He watched her fix a mojito with fine Cuban rum, he saw her muddle the fresh mint, mash the lime and instead of sugar she added raw cane syrup; then he had a sip of the ice cold drink and turned to look towards the pool only to be stricken by the sight of Patricia. In Tortola she had used the pool a couple of times but wore one-piece bathing suits. Marco had not been around either time and this was the first time he saw her body almost entirely. He tried to look nonplussed but Matilde burst out laughing and let go with a lot of gibberish in Spanish that made Patricia blush and dive into the water. Marco turned towards the bar and again got an earful from Matilde while she prepared Patricia's favorite drink, a Sazerac. It calls for rye whiskey, bitters, absinthe and a twist of lemon. She took it to her and they engaged in a short conversation and both looked back at Marco and laughed. Patricia swam back and got out of the pool, wrapped herself in a kind of sari and walked over to Marco while Matilde brought her drink to the bar.

"Sorry about that, Marco, it's just that Matilde has some crazy ideas occur to her."

"Like…?"

"She has decided that as you are the new patron, that entitles you to me."

"What?" Marco raised his eyebrows and his eyes kind of bulged.

"Don't worry, Matilde is half Kuna Indian and that is their custom. If a woman becomes a widow she belongs to her husband's brother or closest relative. In our case that means you." Patricia spoke with a mischievous smile.

Marco was still recovering from the sight of this magnificent woman; slender but firm and with curves in the right places. Her breasts were high and needed little help from the top as was her well rounded and perked butt that stretched the fabric of the panty in oh, such a wonderful way! He had to turn well into the bar to hide the bulge in his trousers and was at a loss for words like he had never been before. All he managed to say was, "Oh my God it's hot out here," and took to the mojito like an orphan to a wet nurse's breast.

Patricia noticed his arousal. It was impossible not to see. Now she understood why Matilde was so excited about the "patron" being horny like a dog. Against her own will she found that she was flattered since the man provoked in her reciprocal feelings. It had been so little time since Sal's death and yet it felt like a lifetime ago. So many things had happened. Things that were transcendental to her life and Marco had been with her almost every waking minute since the day they were attacked in Sarasota. Events had not allowed them to be aware of each other but with a few days respite they had been warming to one another's presence; but the warming was turning to hot and that required some soul-searching.

13

The insurance company had not paid yet while they investigated the circumstances of the events that led to the loss of the *Toscana;* on the other hand they had paid, to a different claim, the loss of the Lear, whose value was a shade of what the new Bombardier 6000 had cost. The *Toscana* pushed well beyond a quarter of a billion dollars and that would give any insurer pause. Marco had discussed with Ernie and Ian Carlo and now Patricia the wisdom of getting another yacht but the issue was still up in the air. The ease with which the *Toscana* had been located and disabled by the enemy was something to think about. While it offered a great offshore meeting place, its vulnerability had been exposed. Neither Marco nor Ian Carlo thought it worth the money, not that it counted, or the inconvenience of having a crew around when decisions such as theirs were taking place. Patricia who had really enjoyed the *Toscana* thought differently but supported whatever decision Marco and Ian Carlo took on this. Anyway, one can charter a mega yacht anytime.

What she really missed was the flats boat. She would go out with Sal to fish early in the mornings, enjoying the solitude of the water, or in the evenings to watch the sun dip slowly into the gulf. She had mentioned that by way of conversation with Marco some time when they were talking up in New York and to her surprise a brand new Hell's Bay Neptune was rolled up to the house that morning.

It was a 19-foot beauty, custom fitted to the instructions of Luigi and Pete who were the knowledgeable ones in this matter. It had all the gizmos of the one lost on the *Toscana*, plus an incredible electronics package. The trolling motor was new technology that eliminated the hum that disturbed the fish and now would run so silently they could ambush a dolphin. The electric pole had more extension and the double platforms had reclining rails; but most important, the engine could take the skiff to fifty miles an hour in a few seconds; a tactical detail that had nothing to do with fishing but everything to do with safety. That afternoon, after Luigi and then Pete had played with all the gadgets and tested the skiff to their hearts satisfaction, Patricia said she couldn't wait to try the boat herself. She insisted that Marco come along and with Pete at the helm and an Allen Security speedboat following at a discreet distance, they headed for the flats in search of redfish.

They reached Manatee River and slowed down to a stop when they were in just a couple of feet of water in an out-going tide. The grass flat was slightly murky but still showed well to the trained eye. Pete poled slowly pushing into the receding tide and keeping his eyes focused on the grassy shore. Soon he saw the telltale bending of the reeds as a fish fed along the edge looking for crabs and shrimp that came out on the tide. He pointed towards the redfish as they pushed water and told Patricia to get onto the forward platform. She took an 8-weight rod loaded with a floating triangle taper line that was armed with a sparkly shrimp pattern that Sal had tied so long ago.

Pete pushed ahead of the fish and turned the boat to give Patricia a better cast. She did a few false casts in a different direction so the line would not disturb the fish, then she turned the cast midair and double-hauled about fifty feet of line, which took the fly to within ten feet in front of the feeding fish. She let the fly sink to the bottom and, putting the tip of the rod near the surface of the water started stripping, pulsating the fly across and ahead of the feeding fish. No action. The fish had stopped to feed on something else. She repeated the cast and this time waited, watching the reeds until she expected the fish to be within sight of the fly. One strip, two strips, three strips, BANG! A fish sucked in the fly and before it could spit it out Patricia had set the hook and the fight was on. The redfish shook its head as it ran for the grass and then turned on itself and headed for the boat. Patricia was stripping like mad to keep up with the fish but again it changed directions and headed away at full speed, evaporating line off the reel in a circular spray of water and accelerating screech from the gear. Then it circled wide around the boat, carrying the line with it. The drag soon tired it and Patricia reeled in the exhausted creature, which surrendered to the net. It was a perfect slab of copper with two black and gold spots near its tail. About ten pounds, estimated Pete. Since it was getting late and Patricia wanted to give Marco a taste of really fresh redfish they decided to go in for the day. Patricia was radiant in the waning light, her hair messed and a smile stamped on her face. Marco was simply mesmerized, which was a state now familiar to him. Maybe one of these days he would try his hand at this fishing thing, he thought, and like reading his mind Patricia told him that he would learn to cast tomorrow. Mind you, she didn't ask him; she told him. But it wouldn't happen; at his first attempt at simply waving the rod back and forth Marco yelped with pain as his wound acted up.

That evening the redfish was served Caribbean style, gutted, scaled, washed thoroughly, salted, spiced with paprika and cayenne pepper, and fried in peanut oil, dusted again with a mix of corn and wheat flour, spiced, salted, and again fried lightly in oil and butter. This process assures a moist, tender fish. Squeeze some fresh lime and rain finely chopped cilantro, and serve with deep fried yuca sticks and ratatouille. The wine that evening was Patricia's favorite, the exquisite, aromatic, fruity Torrontes from the edges of the Atacama Desert near Salta, Argentina. A passionfruit flan with crème

Anglaise closed the meal. With a comforting cup of chamomile tea in her hand Patricia started to reminisce about her first fishing experience with Sal.

"The day we fished the Rio Malleo with Sal on our first fly-fishing experience – I can still feel the excitement of that first trout. When it took the fly and jumped out of the water I screamed with excitement, and although Martin had taught me to set the fly lightly by simply raising the rod, the excitement took over and I struck way too hard, launching my trout out of the water and breaking the delicate tippet. I stood there looking at my line, now flaccid in the current, flyless and lifeless. Downstream, action caught my eye – Sal stood mid-river with water up to his waist, rod held high above his head, fighting a trout that kept taking spectacular jumps into the air, sending flashes in the waning light of the evening. I couldn't see his face but could guess that look of determination that was so much part of him."

Marco wondered why this had come up just now. Last time she talked about that day she had skipped the detail and went on to describe the dinner they had enjoyed that night. He listened on.

"Martin quickly tied another fly on my line, dressed it and I was ready to try again. This time we waded a few steps further up river and again waited for all to settle. The rising trout returned, more avidly than before indicating the impending end of the hatch and the anxiety of fish trying to get filled. I cast again to the feeding line and managed a good presentation on my first attempt. Before my fly had floated more than a few inches, an avid trout once again slurped it under. This time I set the hook properly and the fight was on. This fish did not take to the air and Martin said it was a bigger trout and indicated how to give and take line as the fish fought for its life. Minutes passed in eternity. Each time the fish ran my heart seemed to run with it. Time stopped and the sun stood still letting the light settle upon the micro drama of my first fly fishing experience, something that was to become a passion for Sal and I, and which brought us together until the very end.

"Finally the trout tired and Martin scooped it into his net and out of the water in one swift movement. It was a spectacular wild brown trout, a twenty-inch bar of shimmering gold with blue, red, and black jewels along its side. Antonio and Sal, who had seen the fight from downriver, came up to admire the fish. Both men were highly excited to see that my first trout was such a beautiful animal in full maturity; a male beginning to show an extension of its lower jaw as it prepared to battle others for primacy. Martin expertly revived the big brown by holding it gently, head towards the current, flushing oxygen-rich water through its gills and allowing it to regain its strength. About a minute later, and with a dignified swish of its tail, it swam slowly back towards deeper water, giving us a full display of his disdain."

Marco understood that Patricia was bringing the past to the present so she could deal with the future. Yes, he understood her internal battle, the same he was having... about the same man.

* * *

Ana Meredith woke up at her usual time after a long siesta that she needed more and more every day. She took off her sleeping mask but the room was very dark from the blackout curtains that let little light in. Through the haze she saw something out of place. She had been sleeping in this room for over seventy years since she came here as a young bride and little had changed since then. Maybe she was suffering from the effect of the half pill of Ambien that she had taken with her lunch. It happens, she thought, but the rationalization did not help because the tall dark bulk remained there. Then she heard the low authoritative voice that said, "May God be with you."

"And with your spirit," she answered by reflex.

"Why have you deserted him? Has he not given you enough?"

A chill ran through Ana, her palms became sweaty and her voice broke. "What do you mean? What do you want?"

"You and others that call yourselves Catholic have confabulated against him and his prince, allying yourselves with an enemy of the Lord, with a heathen."

"Who are you?"

"I am Gabriel Angelo, a servant of the Lord and of his church."

Ana knew now that she was hallucinating. Visitations by angels were not part of her belief, no matter how many times she heard the stories in church. So she decided to get up, take a short shower and get the drug out of her system.

"Stay where you are," said the hallucination. "We are not finished here," it said, pushing her back lightly into the bed.

Ana screamed at the top of her lungs and tried to reach a panic button near her bed but was again restrained by soft but firm hand. The scream would not be heard. The room had been soundproofed again recently because of her insomnia. The vision waited patiently until she stopped screaming, now short of breath.

"Why did you stop funding God's church? Why did you drain his coffers?"

"What are you talking about?" she asked desperately.

"You and the others have taken funds away from the church. Why have you done that?" asked the now more human looking apparition.

Ana, with her wits back, knew perfectly well what he was talking about and that made her mad and made her bold.

"That's none of your business. I do with my money whatever I want and you can tell Dupree just that. I know who you are, Monsignor, and I'm too old to be afraid of you."

"Fear me not woman! Fear the Lord thy God that has your immortal soul in his hands and to whom you owe what you call yours and the light you see and the air you breathe," said Testa, raising his voice with the indignation of those who believe themselves enlightened.

Again Ana tried to get up but this time was restrained in a less than gentle manner. Testa put his hand heavily against her dried up chest and pressed the "insulin injector" to her neck. He delivered two tiny darts into her jugular and held her still while he looked into the old but brilliant eyes drilling him with contempt. In a minute her eyes glazed a bit and her body relaxed and fell further into the pillows. She was awake, and aware of what was happening, but her limbs did not obey and she couldn't breathe as deeply as she wished. After another minute or two her body did not respond at all. She was virtually paralyzed.

"It is time to pray," said Testa and took Ana's will-less hands into his.

"Our Father who art in heaven, hallowed be Thy name..."

Ana tried to follow but her voice did not come. She heard the other voice..."Thy kingdom come, Thy will be done"...she felt tears rolling down along the crevices of her old cheeks and leave her forever as they fell on the pillow... "and forgive us our trespasses as we forgive those"...yes, forgive me Lord, forgive me... and those were the last human words that crossed Ana Meredith's mind at the end of her ninety years of life.

Raymond the butler noticed that Mrs. Meredith had not come down from her room at the usual time and was in fact an hour late for her "office stint," as she called the time spent in her studio attending to the many communications received that invariably required her approval or comment. He sent Nadia, the Lithuanian maid, to see why. Minutes later the chilling scream of the maid propelled him up the stairs and into his mistress' room. Literally hanging from the rafters was the body of Ana Meredith; the sleeping gown soiled and a puddle of disgusting liquids pooled underneath her. Apparently she had taken her own life and tied the curtain rope while standing on the bed and had jumped off. She had a rosary in one hand and a note in the other.

When the police came the cop was convinced that it was suicide but the medical examiner later pointed to the one odd thing in the room. The crucifix that had hung over Ana's bed for decades was on her pillow. While it was something she might have done in an altered state of mind it was out of place enough for the inquiry to be done more thoroughly. And so happened that homicide detective Amiable Manning, yes, that is his name, looked carefully at the scene and concluded that the length of the rope did not correspond to the suicide scenario simply because it was too long. She could not have jumped from the bed because if that was the case and the rope had been long enough to reach the beam from the bed, her feet would have hit the floor before the rope stretched her neck and here there was at least a foot between the floor and the tip of Ana's feet. Conclusion…murder!

Soon the Kansas City crime scene unit was crawling all over the place. Detectives were interviewing the butler and the maid since apparently there was no one else in the house at the time of death. The kitchen was never used except to make breakfast, as all other meals were catered in from a variety of health food restaurants so there was no kitchen staff.

"Oh boy," thought Amiable, finally after twelve years on the force and five in homicide, he had a case where he could raise his voice and pompously point his finger and say "The butler did it!"

There were no fingerprints other than those of Ana, her son Edward who was away on business, the butler, the maid, and Ana's massage therapist who came once a week on Mondays. The maid was too small to lift Ana and the butler was a stretch but barely possible, so…"The butler did it!"

As the investigation progressed and neighbors were interviewed, a new possibility presented itself. The gardeners from an adjacent property had seen a Latino man of average height leave by the front gate and depart in a silver or gray car. This was about the time at which Ana Meredith had breathed her last. Maybe…"the butler didn't."

By 5:00 p.m. the world knew. The governor, the mayor, the police commissioner, the two senators from Kansas, two from Missouri, and about seven congressmen were demanding action. Roadblocks were up, airports furled, trains delayed, news networks looking for talking heads that could say something, anything at all about the murder of the richest woman in two states. The cardinal, the bishop, the parish priest, a cadre of nuns were all demanding to be present with the body of the most Catholic of their now to be impoverished domains. Ana's son Edward was flying in from Chicago with Senator Archibald Mason, a close friend of the deceased.

The medical examiner was ordered by all who mattered to do an immediate autopsy, but the results of the thorough job that was needed would not be available for at least 24 hours. By then every tabloid in the country would have their own conclusions. Those would range from government plots to aliens punishing the head of a multinational that was raping the earth.

That night, Senator Mason and Edward Meredith drank their Irish whiskey and discussed in low voices what they knew as soon as they received a description of the crime scene. Dupree had done this...and they knew why. They had called Lord Humphrey and several more of their alliance and all were coming in to meet and pay last respects to their matriarch. Among them was Terry Taylor, congressman for the seventh electoral district of Texas, and married to the daughter of the late Joseph Delany and his also departed wife. Absent from this conclave and who had interests in its outcome would be Sheik Faruk Al-Enezi.

Computers in Bogotá, Lugano, and New York picked up on the news and promptly Francisco Lujan, M&M, and Special Agent Joseph Delany Jr. were digging through all possible information on the matter and all of them picked up on one particular mail from Edward Meredith to Lord Humphrey: "The cardinal killed my mother. Come ASAP, Edward."

Promptly Marco and Patricia were informed by Francisco and Ernie. The opportunity to act had come without notice and a plan was beginning to form in Marco's mind. It could be the time to truly defeat or at least seriously debilitate their opponents when obviously there was a deep rift between them.

* * *

Ian Carlo and Tommy Lee were discussing their business at Ruth's Chris Steak House in Vegas. The place had practically been invaded by them and their security details and their booth had been isolated so that they could converse without being overheard.

"Gucci, are you telling me that I can have ten tons of prime Mexican weed at eighty percent of what the market is today?"

"That is exactly what I'm telling you. I can also include a few kilos of top quality snow with about ninety five percent purity."

"To what do I owe this generosity." asked Tommy who never took anything without expecting to pay its price, one way or the other. Life had taught him that much.

"It's no gift, Tommy; I'm just giving you a few weeks advance on what the price is going to be."

"What are you telling me, Gucci? Are we gonna have a flood a weed or what?"

"Things always change. You make money when you're ahead of the curve. That's all I'm giving you."

"What are the logistics on this, Ian Carlo?" He only called him Ian Carlo when things got very businesslike.

"You get four GPS points with one hour notice. You send trucks to all four points. Only one will pay off."

"Okay, what about payment? COD or what?"

"No, Tommy, I'm giving you credit for the first shipment. I trust you. You get a shipment every few days. You pay in cash before the second delivery and so forth. I carry you for one full shipment. I'll give you precise instructions for each payment. Pick up will always be the same; four points, one hour."

Ian Carlo passed Tommy a flash drive. "Feed this into a clean lap top. No desktop and no computer that has wi-fi or is online in any way or at any time. It will erase after the first download so just throw it out or whatever, I don't care. That gadget carries an algorithm that will decode the message that I send you to your email, which you will download in another computer and then port it to the laptop on a flash drive. That message has the details for pickup;

use it once and that is all. You will get new drives for every deal. The same goes for payment, one drive, one set of instructions, and that's it. We never talk about this again unless it's face to face and I call the meeting. If you don't show up for a pickup or a payment, the deal ends. Capische?"

"This is a lot of shit to move Ian Carlo, where am I allowed to sell?" asked Tommy while his mind was trying to calculate what all this meant.

"I don't care, that's your problem. All I can guarantee is that you will make money because I'm giving you the best price by far. How much you make? That entirely depends on you. Deal as you see fit but don't make war where you don't need it. Keep away from Texas and LA, those fucking gang bangers are crazy. New York and New Jersey are mine."

"Deal," said Tommy stretching his hand across the table. No more was needed. That deal was signed in blood.

"So...what's good here?" Ian Carlo looked at the menu.

"I love the lamb, they cook it like you want and the flavor is incredible. Some scalloped potatoes and a wedge. That's a hell of a meal."

"Make that a double, medium rare for me. And since you're buying get a decent bottle of wine or two."

* * *

By the time Joseph Delany had compiled all the information on the sheik and downloaded the list of banks that he controlled, it was late in the day. The news of another murder in the rarified group where his father had dwelt and again chalked up to Cardinal Dupree by them most surely called to action; but what was there to do? The only reason that Mason and company knew who-done-it was because they had been into something that the cardinal found unforgivable, going with the sheik. But what proof was there, none that any law enforcement organization in the world would even consider, let alone investigate. There was no evidence, no fingerprints, no DNA, nothing. All police knew was that it had been murder by person or persons unknown. A Latino looking man had been seen leaving the premises. He looked like a third of the men in the US and about seventy percent of all men living south of the border all the way down to Chile.

Joseph Delany Sr. and Ana Meredith had died for dancing with the devil and then turning their backs on him. Dupree was not to be trifled with and they knew this all too well; and as powerful as they were The senators and the handful of congressmen who formed part of their circle were scared. How do you get rid of a Roman Catholic cardinal and who do you get to do it, thought Mason, and what were the consequences for them if they did get someone to whack the dammed priest? He had intimated that if anything happened to him every one in their group would go down with him and he had sent small samples of the information he had on each one of them. Samples that were more than enough to end any political career and they all knew there was a lot more, from sexual indiscretions to straightforward larceny and in a couple of cases, murder. Dupree had them by the balls and they knew it.

When Ana Meredith had decided to go with the sheik and dump Dupree's network the only one present of their group had been Mason and he did not have much pull with Ana. The money was hers. She was a brutal force on her own and now she was dead, murdered in her bedroom. A bedroom in what was supposedly a secure house with CCTV cameras, perimeter security, and service staff and only by luck alone the possible perpetrator had been seen by some Mexican gardeners. Mason was thinking out loud going through all this when he suggested that maybe he knew someone that could help. He would call a fixer with whom Delany had worked and was supposed to be absolutely reliable in the most difficult circumstances.

* * *

Amiable Manning was sitting in his cubicle thinking. While all the higher-ups were busy finding an ass to kiss and noise to make, he was thinking. There had to be a lead and he knew it was staring him in the face; he just had to put a finger on it, and as the commotion around him that included calls to Interpol, the FBI, and even the CIA subsided to background noise, a bit of light blinked in the back of his mind. He called the support office of the department where ten officers ground away at leads requested by the detectives and asked them to get copies of all the car rental contracts of the last 24 hours from locations around the airports, bus terminals and train stations within a perimeter of a hundred miles; he wanted copies of the driver's licenses and credit cards. He sat back and continued thinking.

* * *

Marco had been busy on the phone with Leon Goddard; he wanted to know what the position was in regards to the multimodal transport division. He was told that it was networked into every significant transporter by any means in the western world and most carriers elsewhere. They could transport anything anywhere at a competitive rate. Marco gave Leon a long list of corporations in the United States, Canada, Puerto Rico and several South American countries, also one in New Zealand and one in Australia. He told Leon that their business should be pursued at all cost. All those companies were affiliated with Meredith. Most were grain and meat exporters, cold storage manufacturers, animal feed producers, oil and coal companies, and mining enterprises and so on; all of them in need of fast efficient and economical logistics. He had been buried in business all morning and had declined a fishing trip to the flats with Patricia.

She had spent the morning working with the manager of her father's wine business. She was pleased to hear that they had secured large contracts with Costco and Global Wine in the USA and with the world's largest wine retailer in Britain, Tesco. This assured about fifty percent of the output and allowed the companies to hold strong prices on the better vintages that would be sold to smaller and more discerning retailers. Business was interrupted by a light lunch of poached salmon and avocado salad which they shared on the deck and returned to their respective offices shortly after. Marco now used the office that had been Sal's and Patricia used her own. Marco slept in the guest quarters and had insisted that Patricia take the main house. The arrangement was not what either desired but it was what their sense of propriety dictated, hard as it was to conform.

*　*　*

"Yes, Senator, we are on a secure line. I don't think even the NSA can break my scrambler, but as always discretion is advised."

"Yes, Senator, I know who you are talking about. I'm very aware of him. He casts a long shadow. What would you wish me to do in respect of this person?"

"I understand what you are saying, Senator. I have to evaluate the consequences and get back to you on this."

"No, Senator, I didn't say it can't be done. I'm saying that I must evaluate consequences much wider than those immediate to the event."

"I understand that delicate documents have to be retrieved before termination. That is one of the things I must consider carefully."

"Yes, I will get back to you as soon as possible. Expect a call before tomorrow evening, your time."

M&M hung up. Pressed a button and heard the conversation all over again. This was panic, he thought. Panic in the minds of those elected not to panic. He saw no possible advantage to act on the senator's behalf now that their pockets were not so deep and politicians cannot be trusted to return a favor. He decided that deep meditation was needed so he went to his tying desk, put a hook in the vise and began winding thread over the shank, but had not decided yet what pattern he was going to tie. He would not mind if his hands improvised while his mind was elsewhere.

*　*　*

With the help of two officers, Amiable Manning had cut the pile of interesting car rentals to nine men, all Latino in appearance and name. Five had rented at the airport, two at the train station and two at a bus terminal. He rapidly eliminated four of those because they had returned the cars before the murder, then he eliminated two more because they were noticeably short and that would have been said by the witnesses. That left him with three candidates. This was a hell of a long shot, thought Amiable, but he had little else. He asked a patrol to bring in the witnesses and presented the license photos to them. One did not know anything; he was dead scared of the police, but the younger one, a kid of barely eighteen, pointed to the dark face on the driver's license of one Joao Pernambuco, a Brazilian driver's license to be precise. The kid was absolutely sure that he was the person he saw leaving the Meredith estate that afternoon, but Amiable knew that eyewitnesses were in most cases very unreliable.

"What the hell," he thought, "at least it's something to go with."

He called Border Control and identified himself as a police officer following a murder investigation and for once got a cooperative person at the other end. An ICE officer named Maria del Carmen Hidalgo said she would get back to him on it and true to her word came back with an entry for Mr. Pernambuco, who had passed Immigration at the Atlanta Airport just two days ago. He had arrived from Santo Domingo on a Delta Airlines flight and declared a stay of ten days or less in the USA. He had been issued an entry for ninety days.

All Amiable could do at this stage was issue a POI, or person of interest BOLO, on Joao Pernambuco and see what came of it. The BOLO was sent to all car rental offices, Post Offices, law enforcement, airlines, bus companies, train operators, and hotel chains. He did so without telling his boss, who would immediately try to get approval from everyone including God himself so he could cover his ass in case it backfired. If this didn't pan out he would issue an Amber Alert on the vehicle but that did involve a lot of paperwork so for the time being he waited.

* * *

Testa was packing his bag and listening to the local news when he saw his own face looking back at him from the screen. He paid attention for the thirty seconds that the bulletin lasted and decided what to do. He went methodically through the room wiping every surface including the door inside and out. He emptied the trash taking the plastic liner with its few contents and wiped the can. He destroyed the soap and sent it down the toilet, then he went over everything again. He walked half a block to a Walgreens pharmacy and bought some hair dye, a pack of cigarettes, a can of barbecue lighter fluid, and took a couple of clips of matches from a basket in the self-pay check-out. He then took a room at another cheap motel that asked no questions. He had a watch cap and dark glasses but the truth was that the Pakistani clerk didn't even look at him. He took the thirty bucks for a two hour stay and handed over the key.

Enrico dyed his hair, took a shower wiped everything clean and made sure no hair was left in the drain or elsewhere. He destroyed this soap too and left the room leaving the key in the door after wiping it clean. He went back to the first motel and set up a fire bomb using the cigarettes, the barbecue lighter fluid and a stack of paper, including the Joao Pernambuco passport and other documents. He called a cab and when he saw it arrive he lit the cigarettes, two of them to make sure, tucked them under the matches, soaked a towel in the fluid, poured the fluid all over the carpet and the bed and went to the cab. It took about three minutes to ignite the matches that lit the papers that lit the carpet, then the bed took and finally another minute for the fire alarm to go off. By then Enrico Testa was far away. The cab left him at the Greyhound bus terminal, where he took a shuttle to the airport. There a first class ticket to Rome via Atlanta was waiting for Mr. Theodor Miles of NYC. Joao Pernambuco was no more.

* * *

First, M&M called Francisco Lujan and let him know what was going on with Senator Mason, then they added Ernie Goldman to the conversation, and finally they added Marco. They decided not to include Joe Delany because Francisco did not trust cops. After a half an hour of discussion and consideration of different alternatives they decided on a course of action.

* * *

Amiable Manning was talking to the office manager at the motel. The fire had devastated half the building and the room where it started did not even exist as it had caved into the floor below. Only just after the fire was put out did the manager think that the man in that room looked a lot like the one that the police were looking for and now all he could tell the detective was that the man definitely was the one in the photo he was being shown and that he did not have a foreign accent. He was very embarrassed to say that he hadn't asked for ID and that the man had paid for three nights in cash. What he did have was the car plates, but Manning already had those from the rental company. A day later a realtor would call the police about a car that had been abandoned at one of her properties and a point was connected to others. A neighbor who had nothing else to do remembered a man arriving in the car and then leaving on foot with a small suitcase on wheels. No description that could be of any use. A man in dark clothes was as much as she could remember. That same afternoon a girl about eighteen years old and mousey came to the precinct and asked for the detective in charge of the Brazilian man's case. Eventually she was taken to Amiable Manning and he got his first break.

14

The next morning Ian Carlo flew to Tampa from Vegas and checked in to the Hyatt and then left the building via the parking lot, where a SUV with Pete and two of his own men were waiting to take him to Sarasota. The drive is an easy one hour door to door and by 4:00 p.m. the two cousins were sitting with Patricia and a bottle of Prosecco. They spent the afternoon getting up to date with each other and what Francisco, Ernie, and Leon had for them. Joe Delany's participation in this whole deal was discussed thoroughly. Ian Carlo was very wary of the man and insisted on a need-to-know policy with the agent. They had a leisurely dinner including the bodyguards because the perimeter was closed down by Allen Security and they could relax a little. Ian Carlo had a suite at the guest house the same as Marco and they only met for breakfast at nine. They spent most of the morning by the pool discussing a plan of action that Marco and Francisco had come up with and by noon Ian Carlo was totally with the idea, plus he understood why Marco was falling for Patricia. The woman in a bathing suit was a work of art.

The suite at the Hyatt had been occupied by one of his men who promptly left for the airport and flew to Teterboro about the same time as Ian Carlo boarded a NetJet that took him to La Guardia in the company of his two bodyguards. Security at his level was expensive, but worth every penny. Now it was time to play, he thought, and relished the plan that Marco had explained to him.

* * *

"I'm almost sure it was the same man," said the little Walgreens customer service assistant. She said it in a squeaky voice at the verge of tears.

"Here, look at him again, and see if you can be sure," insisted Amiable. "Now close your eyes and try to think of the moment you saw the man...Good. Now look at the photo again," he asked the girl.

"Yes it was him, he wore a cap and sun glasses but I'm sure it was him. He had a deep tan that was not the color of his skin and I remember his ears; I always look at people's ears."

"Why?"

"Why what?"

"Why do you always look at peoples ears?"

The attendant looked down at her hands and didn't answer,

"Tell me, Dale, why do you always look at people's ears?" For some reason Amiable thought this was important.

"Because my mother always said that I had beautiful ears."

Amiable Manning understood instantly and his heart went out to this minuscule creature whose self-worth was hanging from this one feature of an otherwise unattractive whole. That was why she looked at ears...to think hers better and feel a little justification for her existence.

Amiable had no doubt. Dale had seen Ana's murderer and had the civic consciousness to take a bus half way across town to give him his only clue.

"He bought some hair dye, caramel blond. He also got a big can of barbecue lighter, cigarettes, and took some matches. Those are free," she added.

"What was he wearing?" asked Amiable Manning.

"Black cargo pants, dark grey T-shirt, and a dark jacket that was like those you take camping because they fit in a little bag. We sell them at the shop; $7.95 plus tax."

"Anything else you can remember, Dale?"

"It was about an hour before the fire, you know...the motel down the block. It was very exciting."

Amiable had one of the computer whizzes on his staff who was good with PhotoShop make a new picture of Joao Pernambuco, making his hair a caramel blond. He sent the BOLO to all the logical places and to his surprise a couple of days later a Delta flight attendant –whose husband, an Atlanta police officer, had left his computer open to the photo of the POI – was sure that she had served him on a flight to Rome. The passenger in 4B had been identified as Theodore Miles, but after landing in Rome he had disappeared. No news from Interpol, but he didn't expect any soon. Furthermore the official autopsy results came back showing that Ana Meredith had died of asphyxiation due to muscular paralysis, not from hanging, thus dissipating any doubt of murder. Blood tests showed the presence of D-Turbocurarine and Decamethonium. Both used as anesthetics, but in certain forms, deadly. Further examination found tiny titanium darts lodged in the aorta. They were being analyzed for traces of the chemicals.

* * *

Meredith shipments in their own vehicles had started suffering a series of setbacks that obstructed transactions and triggered complaints from customers and sometimes from their own subsidiaries and associates. Little things, like being detained at weigh stations for inconsistencies, hours of delay because DOT held the trucks for small deficiencies or expiration of the "oh so many!" licenses required for interstate transport, or a train failed to couple, and so on. Cranes did not work, silos did not empty, and ships missed crew members. Eventually there was a lot of pressure to move repressed cargo and that's when the sales efforts of the multimodal division of Carducci Enterprises, Scorpio Multimodal Brokers, started to pay off. Thousands of tons of cargo were booked on trucks, trains and ships to destinations within the US and the world. The efficiency achieved in short time by the head of this division promptly drained the overflow and got more contracts from the Meredith companies because managers did not want problems, they wanted action, and here is where they got it. Now Scorpio Multimodal Brokers, centrally located in Memphis, Tennessee, used their weight to maximize tonnage efficiency and, amazingly, profits were being made a year before expected.

Now with all the details of every load that Meredith was moving at his disposal, Ian Carlo ordered the plan into action. Money was smuggled into containers, drugs in boxes of goods… lots of money, lots of drugs. It was going to cost hundreds of millions of dollars but by the time they were finished, so would be Meredith. It started slowly, just enough so that Joe Delany could claim special knowledge of criminal activities by the Mafia and tell local authorities about the suspect cargo, always after it was delivered. Soon he was getting attention. Calls were coming in from local law enforcement all over the country thanking the FBI for their help and asking for more. Naturally his superiors wanted to latch onto his success and he was promptly promoted to head a task force of his own. Every day the capture of money and drugs increased and so did the problems for Meredith subsidiaries that didn't know how to deal with this. Then as luck would have it, a couple of small amounts were stashed in containers that were heading for the Middle East and when they were detained the cops couldn't believe their eyes. In one container they found fifty million dollars in hundreds and in another close to thirty million dollars, this in addition to the small stashes of a hundred grand that Ian Carlo's people had placed there. No more was needed; if there is more than ten grand being transported from one state to another or worse, out of the country, the Feds get testy.

Edward Meredith had called his friends in high places but they could do little when combined local, state, and federal authorities were forced to work together on the information received from the FBI task force. They had tried but the evidence was too damning and they had to retreat before they got tainted. All they could do was pray that all these isolated cases were not connected to Meredith and would be dealt with at local levels, but Edward lost all hope of that when he found out Joe Delany, his ex-friend, the one he had thrown to the wolves by order of Senator Mason, was the top dog of the task force. Panicked, he called Mason, who called the others now that they had a target for their discontent. The meeting did not go well. Most of the politicians, knowing that campaign money and other valuable benefits would be short on the Meredith side and possibly poisoned if the investigation went to the top, declined to assist and those that did promoted conciliation at any cost. The only rabidly stubborn one was Congressman Terry Taylor, Joe's brother-in-law, who wanted to have him whacked. He was acting like a spoiled kid who had been shown up by another kid. He got no sympathy from anyone else and not even Uncle Archie gave him the time of day. It was every man for himself moment.

"What a bunch of pussies," thought Terry. "Where I come from these things get settled out of court. I'm from Texas and no shit kicker FBI momma's boy is going to fuck up my re-election."

All his campaign money came from a couple of Meredith-managed cattle ranches and some feed factories, as well as from well-orchestrated Catholic Church campaigns that were also being jeopardized. It looked like he would be riding around in a Greyhound Bus instead of a corporate jet like he had last time. And that fucking wife of his, sitting on a prenuptial was not going to give him any of "Daddy's hard earned money," as if the son of a bitch had ever made an honest buck. No, he had to put a stop to this himself.

* * *

Edward Meredith was in a black mood. Since his mother was killed, instead of sympathy and time to grieve all he was getting was shit from all quarters. The managers of every one of the divisions were bitching about something or the other and bringing problems and not solutions…but then what solutions could there be to problems that had no apparent cause. It was just a relentless rain of shit coming down on him. It was probably Ana from hell, where she surely was, advocating for his misery. That's when he thought, I can turn this around. He called in his secretary and asked her to have the G550 ready for wheels up at short notice. Then he made one important, no, crucial phone call.

"Your Eminence," he said, "my mother who now is with the Lord made some rash decisions in her later days. Mistakes that I want to correct immediately. If Your Eminence would be kind enough to see me, I will fly forthwith to Rome."

"No, Your Eminence, I prefer to speak to you in person and in private."

"Thank you, Your Eminence; I should be there no later than noon tomorrow. I'll stay at the pied-a-terre that we keep in Via Lugari and be with you at your convenience."

"Thank you kindly, Your Eminence, and the Lord be with you too."

"Hell," he thought, hanging up, "Dupree did me a favor getting rid of my mother."

Edward smiled and thought that Mason and company could go suck eggs. It was his money that kept all their so called positions of power. Let's see how well they did without it and without an easy way to launder all their graft and the cash that their "friends" generated from trafficking everything from drugs to influence. He would see how some of these senators and congressmen would explain to their less presentable constituents that they couldn't manage their cash any more or get their usual kickbacks without getting caught, hung and quartered by the press. He called his PA, a woman named Margarita Lefebvre who handled all the "Dark Division" as his mother used to call it. He instructed her to complete all in-hand transactions but not to receive one dollar from anyone until further notice.

Within a couple of weeks half the criminal organizations in the country and thousands of politicians, police, churches, charities, NGOs, military, and corporate executives were choking on their own money, not only in the US but in several other countries as well. Margarita used the excuse that the FBI was interfering and that until that was solved no money could be received.

Naturally the FBI was bombarded by all sorts of people claiming that the persecution of innocent people by the FBI task force was not in their purview and must cease immediately. A rumor that it was the FBI planting the money and the drugs to show results took traction so complaints that civil rights were being violated were "patriotically" pursued by politicians all over... Now the big fellas at the FBI didn't know what to do. First they had hitched their wagons to the success of the task force and now they were at odds with powerful people demanding the end of that successful effort. So some brilliant assistant deputy director of something or other suggested that the best thing to do was to promote Joseph Delany Jr. out of his present position and fill that post with somebody less enthusiastic. The idea received great approval and minds were set to work. Where could they place him? What if he didn't accept? Wasn't he a friend of Senator Mason? Wasn't Congressman Terry Taylor his brother-in-law? Since no one came up with an answer, the same luminary that suggested Joe's promotion now asked, why don't we ask him where he would like to go?

* * *

"What happened?" thought the sheik. "Three weeks and not a cent has come in from these infidels." At the beginning there was a deluge of money, almost two billion dollars in less than a month and then it petered out and now nothing. "The old lady died and it looks like these others are a cadre of incompetents." The sheik was fuming because there were many people in the region that were involved in this and they had to be paid, no matter what.

* * *

Marco and Patricia had fallen into a comfortable rhythm of work and a very disturbing life together in the Sarasota house. Once Patricia had said that maybe it was a good idea if she moved back to the apartment and Marco had insisted that it was a very bad idea as there was no evidence that they were not still under the threat to their lives and that she would be better protected at the house.

Patricia had not insisted and now little by little her personal things began to appear all over the house. A picture here, a small sculpture there, much of her clothes, music that softly impregnated the household with classical notes from the greatest composers of all time, little things that made a great difference. Ian Carlo came and went a few times but in three months Marco had only gone once to New York. Francisco and Ernie had also visited; once together and another independently. Their plans were going well. Their logistics broker, Scorpio, was growing in leaps and bounds while Ian Carlo's business was flourishing under the guidance of Francisco. Tons of money that was accumulated in depots, barns, houses, containers, moving vans, and train cars started to find its way to their organizations and as demand grew, so did the rates and the profitability of the enterprise. The vacuum pipelines in two other locations were now on line and all three were working at full blast. Marijuana and cocaine prices tanked but the market of marijuana grew considerably. The law was indeed looking the other way when it came to the now ubiquitous reefer.

* * *

When Edward Meredith had made his peace with the cardinal and told Margarita to open the doors to the monies that were to be again transacted through the IOR related banks, there was less than an enthusiastic response from the field. While money did come in because the need for laundering was so great, it was less than half of what it was before. This had not been to His Eminence's pleasure and Edward had to spend more time than he could afford pursuing old relationships that he had discarded in his rage. When his mother died he thought his ass kissing days were over and yet here he was, lips puckered, looking for the proper butts. He was a multibillionaire and he had no joy. Where did he go wrong, he wondered? Not a born leader, Edward started losing power to the division heads who now took decisions that, had Ana been alive, would never have dared. Meredith as a whole had enough inertia to go ahead and the managers had been hand-picked by Ana so they knew what they were doing; but where there was no strong leadership, the pushing and shoving started to get nasty. Fortunately for Edward, the sheik was taking it out on Archibald Mason and Lord Houghton and not on him. Humphrey was feeding the sheik some money from Europe and Africa but not what had been promised. Nobody was happy.

* * *

M&M had made a killing. His alliance with Francisco Lujan had paid off marvelously and he was far from a greedy man. He had told Senator Mason that he could not accommodate him at the moment but would keep in touch if things changed. Mason had also been quiet since the problem was now with the sheik and not the cardinal.

* * *

Cardinal Dupree was sitting in his private office with Monsignor Testa discussing the events. While the termination of the Meredith witch had been a success, there was still the outstanding inconvenience of Marco Carducci.

"Are you fit for travel?" asked Dupree.

"I believe so, Your Eminence," answered Testa, who had needed far more therapy for his knee and sternum than he expected. It had only been two weeks since he had felt a hundred percent again. "Exercise and prayer," he said, "can cure anything."

"Well, you still have an outstanding job, Enrico, and the Lord's work must be done. Carducci has been the thorn in our side that he was expected to be. The Board is stronger than ever and they have expanded their presence to areas that previously were ours alone. Our influence in many parts of the world has been weakened and our Church, the one, the only Holy Roman Catholic Church, has lost millions that would have saved so many souls. This weighs heavily upon us and we must act now. It is upon me to shore up Edward Meredith, for he has proven to be less than worthy of our expectation, yet it is his organization that we need, so of him we must make a man. You must go and finish what we started. Marco Carducci and Lujan's daughter must not live to derail our duty to God. Is that clear? Will you fail us yet another time?"

"I will not fail or I will not return. With your blessing I will prepare to leave," said Testa kneeling before the cardinal.

* * *

Time was kind to Marco and so were the ministrations of Patricia that helped him through his daily exercises and reminded him of his therapy appointments. By this time he was eighty-five if not ninety percent recuperated. He still had a twinge of pain and tension when he tried to learn how to fly cast, but little by little the muscles became nimbler and the pain subsided. Patricia and Pete spent a few hours every week teaching Marco the basics of the cast but it did not come naturally to him and his mind drifted. Early one morning in a bit of frustration Patricia stood behind Marco and, reaching around him, she held his arm and guided him through the basic back and forth motions.

She told him to imagine a large clock face and that his casting arm was like a hand on the clock. "Backcast to two o'clock, stop, forward cast to eleven o'clock, stop, repeat, back and forth, back and forth, keep the line moving on flat plane and never let it droop..."

Trying to ignore her close physical presence, Marco concentrated and the line formed a tight loop above his head, straightening out on the backcast, doubling back up into a loop as he changed direction, then straightening out again on the forward cast.

"Very nicely done!" Patricia praised enthusiastically, while her breasts held against his back. His heart rate got faster, his mind was bombarded by desire. At the backcast her pubis pressed against his buttocks...it was too much.

Marco turned around, unceremoniously dropped the rod, and took Patricia into his arms, looking her straight in the eye, and without a word kissed her passionately, deeply, with a hunger he had never felt. He was not surprised when she kissed him back in the same manner. Slowly they fit well into each other's arms and held the kiss with passion propelled by their bodies and tenderness sought by their hearts; two adults who knew what they wanted and where this was going. A few minutes and an eternity later Patricia stood by the bed in absolute nakedness; her total exposure made her look even younger and the promise of Marco's dreams was fulfilled and exceeded by reality. She was a perfect Venus and he had become a worthy specimen of male as his therapy exercises and the healthy diet that Patricia had encouraged defined his muscles and his abdomen rippled with at least the beginning of a genuine six-pack.

They came together in the most natural of embraces and his penetration was answered by a deep sigh of passion, love, and relief as if she had been waiting her whole life for this instant. Their first embrace was short but deeply satisfying, both of them releasing at the same time, propelled by months of restraint and deepening desire. Marco's years of experience with women who understood the art of lovemaking had taught him much and the second time was a different matter. He concentrated on giving this woman all of himself and soon she was in a world of unbridled pleasure, to her before unknown. The gods of love and passion took over Patricia and she let him ride her like Bellerophon on Pegasus in the quest for the Chimera. After a third time at which Patricia took him from above and showed him what pelvic muscles can do to a man's staff, revealing to him a different angle to those magnificent breasts that held their own in this battle and dance. Afterwards they lay spent and totally satisfied in time suspended. Finally they showered and stumbled down for breakfast. If Matilde's smile were any wider her teeth would fall out of her mouth.

Pete, Luigi, and José were all smiles and courtesy, awkward as hell but nothing to be done about it. Marco's soul was drenched in happiness like it never had been in all his thirty-eight years of life and to his surprise his mind felt sharper as he sat before the computer and dove into a myriad of transactions, emails from overseas companies, and a load of information and questions that came in with Leon Goddard's latest report.

Patricia was feeling differently. For her it was like she had been turned off some months ago and suddenly had been powered up and came online. Shefelt like this was the natural continuation of her life and acted accordingly. She went up to her room, put on a tight tank top over a high-compression sports bra and some loose-fitting gym pants. She went down to the beach, where Luigi and José were waiting. They all put on light fight gloves and spared through a few Katas and then engaged in competition, fighting in free style. In a first match she confronted Luigi. She drifted naturally into a Krav Maga style while Luigi countered with the most traditional of the Japanese Martial Arts, Shorin Ryu. They moved rapidly, attacking and defending, standing or on the ground; both disciplines contemplated all possibilities of aggression from single to multiple attackers. As the practice became more involved they found personal expression in their moves and a bystander could see battle and dance in the same scene. Patricia won several bouts and so did Luigi, then José entered the arena and exchanged partnerships so that at all times there were two against one. This went on for about an hour and a half, at the end of which they all felt the exhilaration of the adrenaline rush that had kept them going, but Patricia was living the experience at a higher level. Her life was back.

15

For months there had not been any progress to Amiable's search for the killer of Ana Meredith. He had been under tremendous pressure for results but as time went by even that diminished and finally disappeared as he was faced with other cases, other lives terminated by violence, other acts of mayhem that called for justice, for closure. Then out of the blue a note from Maria del Carmen Hidalgo, the long forgotten ICE agent that had helped him with Joao Pernambuco, brought him back to the case. She had placed a facial recognition cookie into the system and an entry had brought up a positive. Miami International had a positive facial match to Joao Pernambuco and Theodore Miles; confidence was high. There had been no detention as the ID took place in the sequencing process, not at the moment of entry; also there was no request other than notification. There was another problem. The passport was diplomatic, issued by the Vatican to Monsignor Enrico Testa, an American citizen; it would be a very complicated call for the State Department.

By the time Amiable was trying his luck at tracing the whereabouts of the priest he had disappeared. No car rental, no continuing flights, no knowledge of him in any dioceses within the neighboring states; nothing, nowhere, nada. The error margin on the ID by the software and the diplomatic status of the individual did not warrant an all-out detention request. A BOLO as a person of interest was not authorized for interstate distribution and the FBI turned it down flat. Then he remembered that a powerful senator had been doing a lot of posturing and had his aids calling Amiable twice a day for weeks asking for updated reports until things had cooled off. He picked up the phone and left message for the senator. He would only speak to him as it was a very delicate matter about the murder of a Ms. Ana Meredith. And no, he would not speak to the senator's chief of staff, and yes, it could wait until the senator was available.

Senator Archibald Mason sat at lunch in one of the Congress private dining rooms with Terry Taylor. The junior congressman had been acting somewhat erratic because his income had tanked and the lifestyle he was forced to provide his socialite wife, "without touching Daddy's money," was taking him to the cleaners.

"If it wasn't for that creep Joseph Jr. we wouldn't be in this situation. Meredith has not answered one of my calls and with the campaign just a few weeks away I really don't know what to do."

"You know, Delany was promoted out of the taskforce," said Mason, "and pressure on the money shipments has diminished. Unfortunately leaks are still getting to the FBI, and now shipments of cash are a hit or miss proposition. We have lost a lot of clients even though they knew the risks involved. It looks like some Vegas operation has offered them better alternatives but we haven't been able to find out who. Everybody is keeping this one close to their chest."

"I think Delany is behind this," insisted Terry. "I think he set us up. His father was a dick, so what makes you think he's any better?"

Before Mason could answer, his phone vibrated and he looked at the screen. It was his chief of staff and the call was coded 911, which made him answer.

"I'll call you back in a couple of minutes. Put on the scrambler and go to the conference room."

Mason excused himself and after about five minutes he returned to the table.

"It looks like the cardinal's attack dog is back in the States," he said to Taylor. "I got a call from the detective that's in charge of Ana's murder and now he wants help to get the FBI involved in this. I have to think this one out."

* * *

Dupree and Edward Meredith had decided to meet at the Meredith winter home in Palm Beach. The cardinal was not fond of the cold and Florida had magnificent weather this time of year. The prelate was dressed casually and so was Edward. They sat in comfortable chairs on a second story balcony that looked onto the sea. The Atlantic was calm, just a few small waves rippling the blue expanse of water that reflected the cloudless sky. Edward had rationalized that the murder of his mother was a blessing and that the man sitting next to him was somehow divorced from that deed, knowing perfectly well that if it had not been by his hand, it certainly was by his will. Edward was now complaining about the difficulties of controlling his seconds-in-command. They were always contradicting him, squabbling among themselves and taking liberties that would not have been allowed before. He had tried to get hold of the reins, but he felt that things had gotten out of his hands.

"There is always something like this when the heir to a powerful leader might not have had the full support of that person. Then others think it is not their obligation to accept the full authority of the new head of the organization, be it a corporation, a nation or a church. Then it's time for the new leader to act ruthlessly or lose forever his or her domain. I for one," said the cardinal, "have seen this happen within our church more than once and only by the hand of our Lord Jesus Christ was disaster averted."

"Well, don't think I don't pray for guidance, it's just that God hasn't answered and I'm getting desperate," said Edward.

"What do you mean He hasn't answered?" asked the cardinal. "Am I not here?"

* * *

For the last couple of months Marco's life was perfect. Living in paradise with a woman that was everything he could have dreamt of and much more. His work was rewarding and he tackled it with gusto getting results that were tangible, reflected his convictions, and showed the first tendrils of the roots that would sustain his plans for the future he had laid out in his thesis so many years ago.

Meredith was checked and every move he made was countered or thwarted. Land expansion of that family was curtailed by one means or the other and now with the help of Francisco and Patricia, he was getting local politicians in most of South America to implement farming programs targeted toward neighboring communities and avoiding gas consumption and infrastructure deterioration. This promised to sustain land reforms that had so many times failed in the past. Logistics programs were implemented using free software that was provided by Scorpio and that maximized the benefits of each mile traveled and each gallon of fuel consumed. A test run of a banking program was implemented in Colombia where the group had bought a local bank and was making short-term, recyclable loans to farms that accepted the challenge and to outlets that stocked their produce. The results were very promising. Other banking institutions were carefully looking at the results and hopefully in a not too distant future the culture of these would change. It was only the beginning of the beginning but he was encouraged to act faster and in wider scope.

Patricia had, in her mind, created a continuum between her time with Sal and now her delightful life with this extraordinary man who made her completely happy. Her father and Marco got along fine. Francisco had been somewhat taken aback when Patricia, as delicately as she could, let him know of this new love in her life. Francisco and Sal had become very good friends and were closer in age so they shared more memories than he could with Marco, but the happiness that Patricia exuded and the light in her eyes melted his heart and he wholeheartedly accepted him as Patricia's partner in life.

The success Marco's suggestions for the businesses of The Board also put him in high esteem of all. There was only one thing to mar their happiness; their enemies were still at large and reasons to hate Marco and Patricia were greater as The Board grew and they lost terrain. Francisco knew who they were, but little could be done other than what they were already doing. M&M had suggested alternative actions but the timing had never been right and it was obvious that even the death of the most powerful person in that confabulation did not diminish their aggression and the one rift between the Meredith and the cardinal was naught. Their security was heightened and Allen Security was confident that they had the situation in hand, but past events where security was high, showed that it could be breached.

* * *

Ian Carlo's power and prestige in the world of organized crime had grown exponentially and his coattails had brought Tommy Lee to heights he had not dreamed. The Liguria family was now a force to be reckoned with and that made some people nervous. The gangs of Colombians, Jamaicans, Russians, Irish, and Orientals had to buy from the Liguria or one of the Lorenzana, a family from New Orleans that Ian Carlo set up so that not all the eggs were in one basket. As usual, when this took place, Tommy Lee did not protest or even comment on it. He was no dumbass and knew on which side his toast was buttered. This earned him a huge bonus by way of becoming a partner in the largest nightclub chain in the USA, Camille's Playpen. Fifty-eight highly appointed establishments offered the best in gentlemen's entertainment. The service and security of these clubs were the highest, as were the beauty and training of the girls that worked there.

On a Sunday morning Tommy Lee took his father to church as was his custom; the service was an early one and shortly before nine as father and son were leaving the church, saying goodbye to the priest, a motorcycle roared in, jumped the sidewalk and over barriers. The person in the back was sitting looking backwards and as the bike was passing by the church door where the Liguria and a few other parishioners were saying their goodbyes he opened fire with a Double Eagle M-30 submachine gun spraying bullets indiscriminately into the small crowd. Tommy's father died instantly from a bullet through his head and one that severed his aorta. Two other parishioners, a bodyguard, and the priest also received fatal wounds. There were several wounded, including a ten-year-old girl whose father was one of the dead. The only person that came out unscathed was the target of the attack, Tommy Liguria. His security detail that was across the street in SUVs reacted fast but the motorcycle turned into an alley and was impossible to catch. Later the Honda was found abandoned a few blocks away with the rider dead beside it. One of the guard's bullets got lucky or the driver of the bike did not want loose ends. The body had no ID, his clothes had no labels, the fingerprints had been burned off with acid, and his teeth were all implants. All the police had was a male of about 25 to 30 years of age, light hair dyed blue in sections and DNA samples that would take a day or two in coming back.

Before the DNA samples even reached the laboratory, Francisco's Bogotá communications center had picked up chatter about the hit. Apparently the hit men were a Namibian squad wanted by Interpol and, surprise, surprise...they were hired by the Lorenzana family in New Orleans. Within minutes M&M, Ian Carlo and Marco were on a very secure line with scramblers and encoding that maybe only the NSA could break.

"This could turn into a shitstorm and it would hurt business beyond recovery if Tommy goes to war with the Lorenzana. In hours people are going to take sides and few if any of the families will remain neutral," Ian Carlo was saying.

"I agree and it's not to anyone's advantage that Tommy learns this from us," said Marco, "but on the other hand he's a friend and we have to be loyal as he has been to us."

"I suggest we neutralize the Lorenzana before Tommy gets wind of this. Sooner or later they will try to kill him again and maybe they'll succeed. Tommy was very lucky this time but who knows next time." It was M&M talking.

"What do you mean by neutralizing?" asked Francisco.

"The head of the Lorenzana is Paolo. He's efficient and effective. That's why Ian Carlo picked him, but he's also greedy and somewhat of a psycho. He was barred from Camille's because he roughed up a couple of girls. He rides his two brothers and his old man. They don't dare disobey him from what I hear. If we get rid of Paolo and maybe the old man for Tommy's sake, we can stop this before it starts."

M&M waited to hear what the others had to say.

"Works for me," said Ian Carlo, "who will do it?"

"Same here and same question," said Marco.

"I have a team in New Orleans that is highly efficient but expensive. Francisco knows their work. We used them with Los Locos in Matamoros."

"Money is not the problem. Time is," said Francisco. "I vote we move now but it's Ian Carlo's call."

"I'm in," said Ian Carlo. "Go."

Before noon in Las Vegas and while Tommy Lee was consoling his distraught mother, the team in New Orleans had their marching orders. The same group that had deleted Los Locos was sitting in a large room a block from Bourbon Street listening to their boss; a small black woman of thirty-four was outlining their plan of action. Juliette Lefebvre was the great-, great-, great-granddaughter of the first free black man of that fair city. She was an ex-Army Ranger, combat experienced in three tours of duty with hundreds of hours in enemy territory.

"We will divide up in three groups of three. We have Intel of the probable whereabouts of the targets this evening. Target one goes to Pat O'Brian's and drinks hurricanes until he has to be taken home by his security team, who by the way are six dangerous dudes. One I know personally and he will rather kill you than shake your hand. Fortunately for us O'Brian's is a security nightmare and our target likes the piano bar which is indefensible. People go in and out constantly and sometimes after a few drinks you get a punch or two thrown. That is our opportunity.

Team One including myself will get to the bar early as patrons. Team Two will be headed by Tom, and you will be drunken newcomers, rowdy and loud. This will be up close and personal. I will terminate the target with one stiletto stab to the heart. I depend on you all to keep your cool because when he goes down we are not leaving. We will be the panicked bystanders and hysterical witnesses. The stiletto handle will be on the floor with no fingerprints or DNA on it. The blade will stay in, because we don't want blood squirting out of him; do we? In case the bodyguards turn on any of us, Team Three will terminate any of them with silenced guns. Locate yourselves close to them. Three will be inside and three outside. The ones inside are the dangerous ones. The others will have no possible way of knowing who is who in the chaos."

The termination of Paolo Lorenzana went almost as planned. The party at the bar was as usual, with lots of people in a festive mood. Unfortunately Paolo was sitting with his back to a wall surrounded by his bodyguards. Even a fight was not going to offer an opening to kill him with the knife. When Juliette was about to signal a retreat in order to implement Plan B, which required a tenth operative with a sniper rifle and the problems that that could generate, Paolo saw a leggy blonde approach the bar and shout for a hurricane.

He got up and signaled his men to stay put. He headed for the bar and crowded the blonde from behind, pushing other patrons out of the way. This generated a small scuffle with some pushing and shouting. Paolo's men moved in to cover their boss and this gave Juliette her opportunity. She crowded against the bar, where Paolo had his arm around the blonde's shoulder and was trying to grope her with his other hand, and in a lightning-fast move that was covered by her body she drove the stiletto between his ribs and into his heart. She was ready to start screaming at the top of her lungs when he dropped but…he didn't. Paolo sort of relaxed into the girl and the bar, pinning her to it, but didn't drop. He just looked drunk while talking up the poor woman who was trying to hold herself up. This gave Juliette the chance to grab a drink from the bar and move out to the patio followed by her team.

It took another two minutes for the blonde's scream to cut through the noise and the music. Then it was chaos. People were pouring out of the bar and into Bourbon Street, some shouting and some laughing not knowing what had happened. With them went all of Juliette's team, who dispersed rapidly to meet back at their place, just a couple of blocks away. Paolo's bodyguards didn't know what to do. The bar had hidden the blood and only when the girl, tired of the drunk's weight, shoved him off did he fall to the ground. It took a few more seconds for them to realize that their boss was dead and not just plastered by the hurricanes for which O'Brian's is famous. By then there was nothing they could do. The barman called 911 and within minutes the place was crawling with cops. NOPD pay a lot of attention to what happens on Bourbon Street. The investigation would produce no results, no witnesses, no evidence, and no suspects.

That evening when Nicolo Lorenzana received the news of the demise of his oldest son he collapsed and had to be taken to the Tulane Medical Center. In the ER he was admitted without his bodyguards who stayed in the waiting room and outside the Emergency Room entrance. A few minutes later a man complaining of chest pains was also admitted and placed in one of the curtained cubicles. He got up from the gurney the moment the nurses were off to see someone else and before the ER MD arrived. He walked over to the bed where Nicolo Lorenzana was connected to an IV and was being oxygenated. He stuck a small syringe into the IV and walked out of the ER and into a waiting car. Nobody even noticed him. When the MD got to Nicolo's bedside he was dead.

Early next morning, the Lorenzana family was in chaos. Their real and nominal heads were dead and there was no one to blame.

Tommy Lee, who was the obvious candidate, was facing his own losses and had not moved from his mother's side. Who then could have done this? The answer came promptly.

At 9:00 a.m. a full contingency of FBI and NOPD rounded up all the family's *capos* and soldiers, something that was easy as they all were at the family home trying to make sense of this. The two remaining brothers, Nicolo Jr. and Maurizio, were separated and taken to an interrogation room. There they were met by a team of attorneys who argued for their immediate release and obtained it without difficulty. The two brothers, in the company of their attorneys, who they didn't know but assumed were on a family retainer, left the precinct and were taken to the parking lot of the Ritz-Carlton and then to one of the better suites. The lawyers left and the two brothers looked straight at their host. In a comfortable chair, dressed to the nines, was Ian Carlo de la Rosa. He did not offer the brothers a seat. He addressed them in a low but audible voice that he used when stating unquestionable facts.

"Yesterday morning a hit upon an associate and friend of mine, Mr. Tomaso Liguria was executed by mercenaries hired for that by your brother Paolo with the approval of your father."

Maurizio started to say something but a hand raised by Ian Carlo shut him up.

"Don't even think about lying to me. I have undeniable proof and I do not stand by while a greedy bastard like Paolo, in whom I trusted, put at risk a very profitable business of which your family has gained riches and prestige. Tommy Lee doesn't even know yet that your family was involved in the attack that ultimately failed, as he is alive but his father, like yours, is dead. Your brother and your father died under an execution sanctioned at a level that you don't even know exists and it is the justice that we hand out when disloyalty and stupidity combine to jeopardize our enterprise."

"I told Paolo it was a stupid idea and this is what I got for my trouble," said Nicolo Jr. ,pointing at a black eye that was just turning yellow. "Now what?" he asked.

"It can be business as usual or you guys can choose to escalate this, but I guarantee it won't go well and you lose your participation in the best business your family has had since your grandfather came from Calabria."

"What about our people? They will want to do something, especially Jamie Packard; he was real close to Paolo."

"Let me worry about the men," said Maurizio, already taking the lead. "They have to understand this was business."

"Fair enough," said Ian Carlo. "A week from today we continue with the shipments. I don't know how much you know of how we operate but this is how it works."

Ian Carlo explained to the brothers how the operation is done, which they did know as each had been at a pick-up or two. They didn't know that they owed Ian Carlo for the last shipment. Twenty million dollars, even.

"No problem," said Maurizio. "Just say when and where and the money will be there."

"Good, then if all goes well we will not be talking again until I call for a meeting...if at all."

Ian Carlo's next stop was Las Vegas. He had a tough job there. He had to tell Tommy that the score had been settled but that he, Tommy, could do no more.

16

The Bombardier was delivered with the usual fanfare when a ticket as big as that is concluded. The proper faces of the owning corporation showed up and lapped at the free champagne and got the first and only free ride on their corporate jet.

* * *

Since it was time for the new member of The Board to meet the others, Francisco suggested that the meeting be held in Argentine Patagonia at the estancia of his friend Antonio Arquiza, far away and highly defendable. No easy approach without being seen. Major Allen concurred on the choice and saw with good eyes the many possibilities of extraction if the case should warrant it. San Martin de los Andes has a runway that accommodates large airliners and Bariloche is only a couple of hours' drive, or minutes on an airplane. Chile is also an option, with an easy flight to Puerto Mont or a drive over the mountains to several secluded destinations. The only inconvenience was the long travel for the other members of The Board that would have lengthy travel times, but that's what private jets are for and one thing was for sure, they could all afford it.

Plans had been made with sufficient time and now that the Bombardier was at hand the schedule was confirmed so Marco, Patricia, and Ernie, who came from NYC in the Bombardier, flew to Lima and picked up Francisco. They took with them only Luigi, Pete, and José; the bulk of the security group flew down a couple of days early in a NetJet 787 with full gear.

Argentina can be very accommodating to their richer citizens and Antonio Arquiza was certainly one of them. The Board owned an estancia almost as large as that of Ted Turner, who has a big chunk of Patagonia. They had bought it when undermining Meredith on that deal had been necessary. Now the land was administered by Arquiza's land manager and was being regenerated and reforested. A full water management program was in development seconded by experts from Utah, Idaho and New Mexico whose experience could match with a terrain like Patagonia.

The members of The Board arrived in Argentina via Buenos Aires and Bariloche because San Martin did not offer customs and immigration services. Only the Bombardier flew directly to San Martin, courtesy of the Argentinean government who waived these procedures. The drive from the airport to the estancia was about an hour and most of the time it was within land owned by their host or administered by him. Three checkpoints were encountered and serious looking gauchos armed with submachine guns or assault rifles inspected each vehicle with professional thoroughness. At one point Marco saw a flash from a neighboring hill and realized that snipers were also covering the approach. This meeting was not going to be interrupted. He knew that even the airspace was being carefully monitored by the military radar in San Martin and one high in the Andes that covered the frontier with Chile; remnants of a feud that still had both nations sniping at each other. By six that evening all the members of The Board had arrived and were handsomely accommodated in the ample guest quarters of the estancia while the main house had been reserved for Marco, Patricia, Francisco, and Ernie. The meeting was set for the next morning after breakfast. The evening meal was informal and some of the guests were tired and preferred a small meal delivered to their rooms. That same night anyone that didn't already know now understood that Marco and Patricia had, since their last ill-fated meeting, become a couple.

* * *

Enrico Testa had been traveling under his own name and had reserved a room at the Sarasota Ritz-Carlton for three nights. He checked in with the parish priest at St. Martha's Catholic Church and requested mass privileges that were immediately granted. He would say a daily mass at 6:00 a.m. every day while he was in the area. He declined the offer of a room at the residence as he needed privacy. He rented a Mercedes 300E because he did not want to look out of place when he did surveillance around Marco Carducci's Florida residence. As it turned out the house, which was heavily guarded, was inaccessible from land. No problem; the next morning he rented a jet ski from Siesta Rentals and approached the house from the ocean side. The second floor was shuttered which indicated no one was in residence. He would have to review his plans. His contact in NYC had confirmed that Carducci was not in residence at the Third Avenue house and the Roslyn Estate did not appear on his radar as the principal resident of that home was Ian Carlo de la Rosa and his family. Monsignor's plans then changed completely when he reported to the cardinal and was told to fly to Chicago because his services were needed there and he would be instructed upon arrival.

* * *

Amiable Manning had traced the elusive monsignor to his Vatican office and was told flatly that they did not divulge the whereabouts of Vatican personnel but that he could leave a message and be assured that it would reach Monsignor Testa. He will return your call soon, he was told. He also got copies of Joao Pernambuco's fingerprints, which did not match those registered for Enrico Testa, but today's biometrics were very accurate comparing facial features with more than one set of parameters, computer generated facial maps making the margin of error less than one in a million. The forensics lab in Chicago where the traces of D-Turbocurarine had been detected also established that it was synthesized somewhere in Eastern Europe, probably at the University of Minsk. It had been powered a thousand fold and would kill in minutes with minimum dosage.

Amiable was buried in a mountain of work but his mind always went back to the murder of Ana Meredith. He could not shake the memory of the nonagenarian hanging from the rafters, her little woolen night gown soiled and her parchment-like skin waxed in death. Unfortunately his time was limited; the department had other priorities and the case's progress was slow as a tortoise on a cold day.

* * *

Dupree had spent ten days of his precious time trying to make something of Edward Meredith, but the man's mother had extracted with poisonous criticism every ounce of self-esteem he ever possessed. Dupree needed to build him up even if it was only to show enough character to be his Pinocchio. He needed Edward to transmit and execute Dupree's orders with enough backbone so the heads of division would cooperate and follow orders. Thus His Eminence needed to set a precedent and back Edward, putting the fear of God into these unruly but very capable executives. He helped Edward determine who the leader and chief undermining agent was among the heads of divisions and others who, while not being so high up the corporate ladder, had strategic positions they were using to extort the company. Once he had established who the culprits were, cardinal Dupree summoned Enrico Testa to Chicago. Meredith would have to be seen as someone ruthless and that was not easy. The man was a pussy. There was so much at stake. The Catholic Church needed the attention of the world and if there was one thing that made people listen was their stomach. Meredith could in time, if he followed the cardinal's directives, make the world, or at least a big part of it, hungry, and only the Catholic Church would be there to feed them.

* * *

Congressman Terrence Taylor had been smoldering with indignation and political poverty since Mason had been less than supportive in obtaining funds for his re-election campaign. The senator had been trying to mend bridges with Joseph Delany Jr., whose star was rising with success after success in ever ascending posts within the FBI. Again that bastard had crossed Terry's plans. He had married that ugly little social climbing shit of his sister because Senator Joseph Delany Sr. had promised him a brilliant political career, rising from District Attorney in a Texas backwater to Congressman for that state. He had hardly tasted the good life in DC when The senator had died and he had attached himself to his intellectual killer, Archibald Mason, now to be neglected as soon as the senator had compromised him in the aftermath of the murders; all for nothing. It was time to get rid of his brother-in-law because without him Marla would have no one but him and then she would have to loosen the purse straps if she wanted to continue being invited to the party circuit at Embassy Row. He had to get rid of Delany, but how?

* * *

When Testa arrived in Chicago a message from his office awaited him; a missive that also had been received by Cardinal Dupree and which they were discussing.

"This police officer, Amiable Manning, I believe his name is, has to be looking for you in relation to Ana Meredith. I can see no other connection," said the cardinal.

"True, I have no other connection to Kansas City other than my visit to Ms. Meredith. Somehow this policeman has connected the dots. Probably my rental car; they always keep a copy of the driver's license and someone saw me leave the premises. It was a very challenging task. There were security guards and CCTV which I'm sure I eluded, but God only knows what else there might have been."

"I can only think that you have been identified using facial recognition software. When you enter a US airport you are on camera from the instant you leave the airplane and your face is systematically placed under the scrutiny of very sophisticated biometrics programs. If there is a flag for the corresponding facial map, the authorities are advised. In some cases the priority is high, like with those subject to a no-fly order or known terrorists or those on the top FBI wanted list. I don't think you fit any of the above, but obviously Mr. Manning has been advised of the match to the alias you were using."

"I was using the Pernambuco identity with corresponding fingerprints but the facial features are extremely hard to alter, specially the distance between the eyes and their location in the facial quadrant. What do you suggest we do? This could complicate things a lot."

"I think we must find out what Mr. Manning knows and who he has told about you. Let us use some of our friends in DC and I'll get back to you as soon as I know something. For the moment I suggest you rest and see if you can alter your image in some significant way."

Within minutes the cardinal was talking to a faithful collaborator in the DOJ, who immediately followed up on the request, and two hours later the cardinal had a full report on the investigation. It was clear how a hunch by the detective had set him on the right path and how luck had played an important hand in the results which were putting Testa at risk. Among other things there was a repeated request to the FBI for help but it had not progressed. Dupree waited until Testa called his suite asking for information. He invited him over to discuss it.

"Misfortune would have it that a gardener saw you leaving the Meredith home and described the vehicle to the police. The detective guessed it might be a rental and you, or rather Mr. Pernambuco, was identified by the gardener from the photo on the driver's license. Further inquiries brought forth another witness, an attendant from a pharmacy where you bought some things. Then a flight attendant, wife of a policeman, recognized you, and by your seat number the passport photo of your latest identity was obtained so that the individuals on the two IDs matched. Apparently Manning requested ICE for a biometrics tag and that brought up a flag when you came in through Miami. Lucky for you the FBI has not answered the repeated requests by Manning for help. No further progress was reported. I think you are safe for now because the request for biometric ID was limited to immigration and has not gone viral to all points. You might have been traced as far as Chicago, but not to this hotel. I suggest you make some radical changes to your appearance because there is God's work to do and mobility is essential."

"I can take care of that but I will need your help in getting the necessary elements to do so."

"No problem, tell me what you want and I'll get it to you as soon as possible. In the meantime we need to go over some tasks that have to be accomplished promptly and efficiently. Let us hope these tasks prove to be less challenging than Mr. Carducci has been so far."

The barb in the cardinal's comment did not go unnoticed by Testa, who lowered his head.

"Here is a list of three individuals who have to be neutralized in such manner that a message is sent to all their colleagues in the Meredith organization, making it clear to them that Mr. Edward Meredith is the undisputable boss. Two of them are in Chicago and one is in New Orleans. This one, Alfredo Rojas, is the head of trading operations for the Meredith organization. He manages traders all over the world and sustains commodity prices for items dear to Meredith. He needs to be terminated publicly and rather harshly. The other two must not die; but must be adjusted in such way that they never act against the will of Mr. Meredith."

"It will be done as you wish. I will need a new identity. I have a contact for this in NYC but not in Chicago. I will have to go there and return in a couple of days. In the meantime I will require a few credit cards with sufficient funds and if possible about $20,000 in cash. I will give you a name for the credit cards no later than this evening."

"We will have these for you upon your return. We will stay in Chicago for a meeting with the International Banking Association that will take place this weekend. May God be with you, my son," said the cardinal, rising from his seat. He extended his hand to Testa, who knelt before him and kissed the ring.

"And with your spirit," answered Testa.

Two days later Testa was back at the hotel; he checked in under his new identity. The Meredith organization had booked the suite in the name of Mr. Eliot Pix. The man that claimed the room was unforgettable. The whole left side of his face, from the chin to above the ear, was covered in dreadful burn scars; so was his left hand; he walked with a limp and the aid of a rather elegant ebony cane with a silver and gold handle. His left eye was covered by a patch that was held in place by a leather cord as black as the patch. The remaining brown hair was well groomed and salted with silver. His suit was a fitted Hermenegildo Zegna of impeccable cut. The dark pinstripe contrasted nicely with a white shirt and a school tie that claimed he had studied at Harvard. His bags were taken up to the suite and he followed shortly but stopped first at Dupree's suite. Cardinal Dupree did not recognize the man before him and asked politely if the gentleman had not mistaken his room or floor. It took a crooked smile and a few words before the Cardinal, astonished, let Testa in.

"I don't think your mother would recognize you," said the Cardinal by way of salutation.

"Neither will any biometrics software or fingerprint scanner. Before the day is over my identity can be confirmed in Google, the Motor Vehicle Bureau of NYC, and FGA, was a private contractor for security services in Afghanistan. Eliot Pix is a real identity of a mercenary from Dillon, Montana, who died in a suicide blast near Kabul but whose death was never recorded. He had no close family and his general description fits me to a tee. This disguise is only for travel. Mr. Eliot will never be seen by any of the sanctioned individuals or any possible witnesses. I have a couple of additional identities but they are only driver's licenses and a couple of pre-paid credit cards, and they will do in a pinch."

"You have outdone yourself, Enrico, and may it be for the greater glory of God. I have here all you requested; 20,000 in US dollars, fifties and hundreds. I've added 5,000 in Euros, ten €500 bills, just for use in an emergency. There are five credit cards in the name of Eliot Pix with funds up to $100,000, and these can be refurbished if needed. Also I have for you a small computer and a tablet. They will be necessary to read the information on this flash drive as both are encoded. You must scan your index fingerprint when you first power up each one and then no one will be able to read this except you. It contains all the information you need on each individual and the specific requirements that we need from each."

"How much time do I have for this?"

"Do this as soon as possible but without jeopardizing the mission because of haste. We need Edward Meredith acting decidedly and with authority. These sanctions will make it possible."

17

The meeting of The Board convened early in the morning. It was the first time they had met since the horrifying events in the *Toscana*, but it was also the first meeting at which tangible results could be measured of the influence of Marco Carducci on their activities.

"For the second time we meet with one board member missing. Now it is the irreparable loss of Sun E, or Sunny as we all called her." It was Airy Takahashi who was speaking. "I know we will all miss her sharp intellect and her dedication to this group and the objectives that we pursue. To this effect, today I'm honored to present to you a candidate who will in our humble opinion fulfill those duties and contribute to the goals and aspirations that we stand for: Mr. Edmund Cartwright. Mr. Cartwright has been a longtime associate and head of a board of which Sunny was chairperson; he is the owner and director of Cartwright Geological Endeavors of Perth, Australia. His mining enterprises extend the globe and comprehend an ample variety of metals, common and rare. His Canadian company is now the second largest mining enterprise in South America with operations in Colombia, Brazil, Chile, Bolivia and Peru. You have all received and, I hope, read the extensive information on Edmund which was given to you when this meeting was called. I now formally present him and move to vote."

They all voted aye with a slight hesitation from Marco, which didn't go unnoticed by Francisco, who caught Marco's eye and raised one eyebrow.

* * *

When Henri Leclerc walked into his office in the Port of New Orleans, he was very surprised and annoyed to find a man immaculately dressed in a white linen suit, canvas-and-leather shoes, and open sky blue shirt. He moved to call his secretary but the man was faster than the wind and Leclerc found himself being pushed into a seat. He was about to shout but an open-hand slap that made him see stars and left his ear ringing shut him up. All he could do was barely whisper,

"What do you want? I have money in the safe; just don't hurt me..."

"I don't want your money. I want you to listen very carefully at what I'm going to say. Mr. Meredith has given you some specific instructions about the transfer procedures from the barges to the ships, but you have chosen to do differently. So have you done with every directive you receive."

"But, his instructions were absurd...they would have cost us a lot more per ton and delayed each barge an extra four hours."

"Did you tell Mr. Meredith that?"

"Well, no. I didn't see the..."

"I know you didn't see, Mr. Leclerc," Testa interrupted the man, "that's precisely why I'm here. You might be right, but you also owe Mr. Meredith the courtesy of telling him why you consider his orders inadequate. Why did you not do that?"

"I..." Leclerc was at loss for words.

"Let me explain this to you once, and only once. Next time you see me, you will never see anybody again; not your wife, not your children and not that lovely Creole girl you visit so often. Do you understand me?"

"Yes sir, I do. Please tell Mr. Meredith that..."

"Tell him yourself. Write him a letter of apology and explain with detail your suggestions. It will be his decision but he's not stupid. And copy of your letter should be sent to these people that I have listed here."

"Yes sir, I will do that."

"Today."

"Yes sir, immediately."

The man left Leclerc's office without saying a word. Leclerc was sweating in spite of the ice cold AC that kept his office below seventy degrees but he sat down to his computer without taking off his jacket and wrote:

"Dear Mr. Meredith…" Then he corrected it and began again. "Most Respected Sir…" yes, that sounded better…Leclerc began to breathe again.

That same afternoon Testa was back in Chicago and prepared the package he needed for his second visit. Mr. Arthur Tallinn of Meredith Food industries, a holding company for chicken, beef and pork processing plants and feed manufacturers, would not be pleased. Testa wanted him very displeased so he went about acquiring the rest of what he needed for tomorrow's early visit. He got into his rented Taurus and drove to Tallinn's near north neighborhood where the house values were in the upper seven figures. He was back in his hotel by seven, had a light meal, and knelt to pray.

The following morning Arthur Tallinn got into his Mercedes Benz 600S and headed out of his driveway. When he reached the intersection of N. Orleans and West Division he had to stop at the light. When he did so he felt a pinch in his neck and passed out. He was hauled into the back seat of his car and Testa took over the driver's seat. The light changed and nobody bothered to see just what had happened. When Arthur Tallinn woke up with a headache and a metallic taste in his mouth, he was disoriented and had difficulty focusing. Testa waited patiently until the man got his wits back, and when he did he almost jumped out of his skin; the person sitting next to him in what appeared to be an abandoned warehouse was dressed totally in black and wore a black ski mask that only allowed the sight of cold eyes.

"Look at this," said Testa, passing Tallinn a manila envelope.

Tallinn was too scared to say or do anything but obey. He took the envelope, opened and looked at its contents with ever-growing alarm. In each photo he had an image of his daughter, son and wife in their daily routine; going or coming from school, at the gym, shopping and so on.

"How much do you want?" asked Tallinn, still looking at the photographs.

"Not a cent, absolutely nothing."

"Then is this a kidnapping? I can pay...my company will pay, just don't hurt us."

"I said I don't want anything from you other than your undivided attention."

Arthur didn't say a word; all he could do was look at the man who addressed him in a calm but compelling voice. His hands trembled and the photos in them began to fall to the floor of the car.

"Who do you work for?" asked Testa.

"Meredith Foods...but you know that," said Arthur.

"Wrong...try again."

"I swear to you, I work for Meredith Foods; I've been with them for eighteen years."

"Let me clarify this for you, Mr. Tallinn; you work for Mr. Edward Meredith"

"That clown? He couldn't..." Whack!

The punch hit him dead center in the solar plexus and he almost passed out. It took a minute for him to catch his breath and another two before he could speak in barely audible whisper.

"What the f..." Whack!

This time the slap came from behind and hit the back of his head so hard that it bounced off the dashboard. He lost consciousness for a few seconds and when he came to he had a new frame of mind.

"Who do you work for?"

"Mr. Meredith, Mr. Edward Meredith," said Tallinn, rubbing his forehead and looking at his hand to confirm he wasn't bleeding.

"Look at me, Mr. Tallinn. I will not repeat this. You will show respect to Mr. Meredith, you will do as he says if it makes sense, or if you think it could be improved or changed for the benefit of the company, you will explain it to him in writing and worded with the utmost respect. You will never make him the butt of your jokes at the club with your foursome of golf buddies; yes, we know about that and about your snide comments at some of the company meetings. Against my better judgment, Mr. Meredith finds that you are a capable executive and ordered me to spare your life, but it won't happen again. Am I clear, sir?"

"Crystal," mumbled Tallinn.

Testa dropped Tallinn off at a bus stop and took his car. He drove to where he had left his own car at a 7-Eleven close to the Tallinn home. There he left the Mercedes with the keys under the floormat and called Tallinn's office to let them know where it was; no use wasting a good car.

The next morning the *Chicago Tribune*, the newscast on ABC, CBS, and NBC all carried the story about the horrible murder of Alfredo Rojas, a Meredith Trading Executive director who was forcefully drowned in the commode of his private bathroom. He was found naked with his hands tied behind his back and his head in the toilette. There was a note next to the body that read, "Big turds don't flush." Fox News was more explicit and included details of the beating the man had received before he died; his testicles were crushed and most of his ribs were broken. He probably died before the water that managed to reach his lungs completed the job.

A tweet went out from Alfredo's own telephone and went viral within the company. It said, "I got what I bargained for; does anyone wish to join me?" Somehow the word got around really, really fast. Don't fuck with Edward Meredith. Tallinn and Leclerc were particularly impressed.

The next morning when Edward Meredith walked into his office he received more "Good Morning, Mr. Meredith" greetings than he had in all the time since his mother died. There was a hot cup of coffee waiting for him, a first, and twenty or more executives from different divisions wanted appointments at Mr. Meredith's soonest convenience. Would Mr. Meredith approve this, would he consider that, would he accept such? All things that were a normal part of his mother's day when she lived, but that had never, until today, been addressed to Edward. By noon the man was ten feet tall and had the cardinal been around he would have kissed his blessed ass rather than his ring.

* * *

The discussions held by The Board included the usual reports from each of the members, which were really recaps of what had been distributed in the weekly reports. The principal theme was brought to the table by Marco Carducci

"While we have been successful on many fronts, our opponents are capable people who cannot be underestimated. They have resilience and have been able to sustain land purchases in several key regions while they maintain a significant part of the asset conversion business in spite of a heavy toll on their endeavors in the US. If one thing has been achieved, it is that this activity has been divided between the Arab banks and the IOR with dissatisfaction of both parties. The Northern Europeans are dealing with Sheik Faruk Al-Enezi and the Americans are with the IOR's group of banks. A significant number of clients have sought our help and moved a lot of their cash transactions to us; this is most noticeable in the United States, where we have particularly capable logistics for the movement of cash. As you well know the low denomination policy adopted by the United States makes cash bulky. Estimate that roughly one million dollars weighs ten kilos or about twenty two pounds; so one billion dollars weighs ten tons, assuming that it's all in one hundred dollar bills. Reality establishes that it is about a third to half more when other denominations are present. For the more curious of you, it's about 400 cubic feet, which fits comfortably in a container. Double that when lower denominations, twenties and fifties are included."

Francisco noticed that Marco was sticking to generalities and telling distracting stories, rather than touching on the major issues that concerned them. He was going to ask him about this during lunch. Coincidentally the same thought had crossed Ernie's and Patricia's minds, but knowing Marco they made no comment and let him go on with the fairytales.

Marco continued. "We are moving about one billion dollars a day through Mexico and another billion through Caribbean and Adriatic destinations. We believe our opponents may be moving about the same or maybe a little less. Most of their cash originates in Canada and Europe but they are still players in the US. We cannot evaluate yet the effectiveness of Edward Meredith as head of his group or if others, maybe Senator Mason or Senator Caldwell, could take point. It's still to be seen. Our clients are being credited with their money in layered money market and commodity accounts but soon we will need to find other vessels for these transactions attaching our accounts to arbitragers that are hedging against the dollar."

Francisco also noted that the figures were intentionally off and now he suspected that Marco was onto something that he didn't know about and was being coy with the information. He and Ernie exchanged loaded glances but said nothing. When they broke for lunch there were a few minutes of personal time and Francisco, Ernie, and Patricia all converged on Marco, who was outside looking at the lunch set-up that was a work of art. A long wood-plank table was loaded down with cold cuts, salad, fruit, breads, and cheese of great variety. Jars of lemonade, ice tea, maté, herbal tea, and water were all over the place, a simple but exciting lunch.

"OK, what's up, Marco?" It was Ernie who broached the question.

Marco looked around and took out a sheet of paper and passed it to Francisco, who showed it to Ernie and Patricia. In it was a list of companies and two of them were highlighted. He addressed mostly Patricia.

"If you remember, among the things that Sal left me was a list of people and companies that he believed were opponents and of whom we should be wary? Well those that I highlighted belong, via a Tangiers holding, to our esteemed new board member Mr. Edmund Cartwright. When I saw all the documentation that Airy had sent us I knew that there was some information that resonated with me, so I opened the file from my tablet and did a search for several of the companies listed and these came up. I did not think it was enough to stop the voting but it was enough to fudge the figures a little for the time being."

In his room, Edmund Cartwright pulled out a satellite phone from his satchel, walked out to the balcony and sent a message that said "I'm in."

* * *

Joseph Delany Jr. had been promoted upwards and outwards away from the taskforce on money laundering and to a very visible and risky position. He was now head of Major Crimes, Eastern Seaboard. He was supposed to head priority investigations into crimes considered a threat to National Security as well as those that were politically charged or could be categorized as hate crimes. Any of these were high profile and Delany knew his butt was hanging out in the wind every time one such crime was adopted by the press. Among a ream of files on his desk, one caught his eye. It was labeled A. Meredith. Murder. K.C. He was very familiar with that name and also was aware that Ana Meredith had been murdered by some UNSUB a few months back. He had lost track of it among all his changes of office and reports but now he took the file and read it through. When he had finished he dialed the phone of the detective in charge of the case.

"Manning," answered a firm and hurried voice.

"Detective, this is Special Agent Joseph Delany with the Federal

Bureau of Investigations. A case you have been working on just crossed my desk and I wanted to know if there have been any further developments.

"The case being...?" inquired Amiable.

"The murder of Ana Meredith, about four months ago..."

"Well, how far updated is your file?" asked the detective.

"It ends with a search you issued on a man named Joao Pernambuco"

"Well, there was some progress after that. We used a biometrics program at immigration and we came up with two identities in addition to Joao Pernambuco, the last of which was detected entering the United States via Miami a couple of weeks ago. It corresponds to a US citizen working at the Vatican, a Monsignor Enrico Testa. But we've lost track of him and I haven't been able to get traction with the FBI to do a more robust search."

"Well Detective Manning...now you have. I need everything you have on this case as soon as possible. Once I read it I will get back to you.

Delany was running hot and cold because he immediately linked this crime with the murder of his parents. There was no possible doubt. This was the assassin that had been at his father's home when he and his mother were poisoned. Now all he had to do was catch him. He looked at the photo of Joao Pernambuco; this man had killed his father, he had killed his mother and who knew how many people more. He was the henchman for an untouchable scoundrel but he wasn't untouchable. He would face the law. He would face it in the person of Joseph Delany Jr.

* * *

Faruk Al-Enezi sat in his office overlooking the bay from the forty-fifth floor of the recently built Index sky scraper that housed his offices and apartments he used for himself, some select guests, and a few of his wives. Faruk was not a poor man. At this moment he was looking at his phone, where the short message on the screen made him content. He owned Edmund Cartwright lock, stock and barrel since the mining magnate had bet and hedged his vast fortune on biofuel ventures in Brazil and Kenya. None of the two had panned out and he was vulnerable. In came Sheik Faruk Al-Enezi and salvages the man, only to keep him on a tight leash that he yanked once in a while to keep him straight. In a recent conversation, Cartwright had mentioned that he was up as a candidate for a board of industrialists and financiers because an associate of his had perished in a yachting accident and he was to replace her. Now Cartwright was his Jack-in-the-box at The Board and he relished the possibilities it offered. He was going to treat himself to a weekend in Geneva. He called the prince and arranged for some fun and games with English girls that he loved because of their ultra-white complexion with just that touch of strawberry that made them irresistible to him. He called his PA and told him to have the plane ready for wheels up at 3:00 p.m.

Heading…Geneva.

18

Ian Carlo had been keeping an eye on Tommy Liguria since the killing of his father and then the liquidation of the two top Lorenzana in New Orleans, but Tommy had been business as usual and kept his side of the bargain in spite of the heightened volume of marijuana that came up. He had extended his market only within areas designated by Ian Carlo and had never tried to horse in on the Lorenzana or gone into California, the most tempting of markets. That did not mean that tons of the stuff wasn't going there, but it was handled by his clients and that was not his problem.

There was one particular strain of the weed that had wild demand called Sinú. It came from the Sinú River valley in Colombia and was much stronger than the legendary Colombia Gold that had reigned in the seventies and eighties. Those who practiced meditation were particularly fond of Sinú as it produced a sense of focus and purpose so highly sought by the "enlightened," as they liked to think of themselves. As predicted, the mindset of the US and other countries was changing rapidly in relation to the criminality of using and selling marijuana. The only diehards were the federal government and they were under a lot of pressure from the states that either legalized the stuff or changed their laws to be ever more lenient about it.

Mexico was no exception and the management of the logistics of the northbound bales of marijuana became easier and much less expensive as the volume kept all the greedy hands well greased. The Lorenzana side of the business had continued under the watchful eye of Ian Carlo's lieutenants and had so far run smoothly. A major development was going to take place in New Orleans. The first evacuated air pipeline from an offshore rig to a pumping station in the river port was to be inaugurated in a few days. The Lorenzana did not know of its existence and would only perceive the increased volume which they would have to spread in the southeast of the US This tube was going to be used for cocaine and not for marijuana because the technology used here was somewhat different and could only handle capsules with about ten kilos of cargo. The investment in the experiment had cost close to a billion dollars including the part that moved the liquid gas. If successful it would breakeven in a year or less.

* * *

Since Joseph Delany had moved to DC he and Terry Taylor had avoided each other at all costs, but unfortunately the wives of both had joined the same gym and become friendly. They had in common busy mates who were out or away a lot of the time and had found it easy to be in each other's company. Both were aware that their husbands had no lost love for each other and had kept the friendship limited to the gym and an occasional lunch with lots of wine... until now.

"Are you crazy, I don't want that son of a bitch in my house," shouted Terry to Marla, "he has been nothing but trouble for me."

"May I remind you that he is my brother and I can have him and Rita to dinner whenever I want without asking for your permission. You also might want to mend those bridges; Joey has done brilliantly at the FBI and Uncle Archie asked me to bring you two together, so that's that. I had lunch with Rita last week and the kids get along just fine. We don't need your petty little feuds."

"Well, I won't be here."

"Oh yes you will. Rita's father is a big donor to the party and you need the support. Don't think for a moment that you're going to use my father's hard-earned money for your campaign, so buck up and be real nice to them."

Terry was fuming. Not only was that bastard once again Washington's pretty boy, he had done it on his own. Since his father died he had fallen out of grace but with amazing luck the son of a bitch had scored a few busts and now the buzz was that he would make deputy director in no time. And that two-timing jackass Mason was trying to play tootsie with the guy when just a few months ago he wouldn't give him the time of day. Shit! He needed to do something, but for crying out loud...what? Then he remembered something; when he was DA in La Belle, Texas, he had done a kid a favor because his dad had made a big contribution to his campaign for a seat in the House. He and the young man had become kind of friends and had some good times together. Well, it was time to reacquaint with Gene Barco. He located him through Facebook and made an appointment to see him in Dallas. It was a good ol' boys reunion and they painted the town red recalling younger, wilder days. Gene was working full time with his dad who, according to rumors, was connected and ran West Texas for the Mob. After the appropriate amount of drink and getting rid of the girls that Gene had rounded up, they were having a nightcap in Terry's hotel suite when he broached the subject of his pain-in-the-ass brother-in-law.

"Hey Gene, how would you deal with a guy like that? He makes your life miserable even without trying."

"I would whack the fucker," answered the more than half drunk Gene responding off the top of his head.

"Easier said than done, I wouldn't know how to go about it."

"If you got the dough, anything is possible"

"How much are we talking about?"

"A real pro that leaves no trail, about fifty to a hundred grand... or you can go for a Mexican gangbanger and they do it for almost nothing, but they are unreliable and if they get caught they sing like birdies. Fortunately they generally get killed themselves in the process."

"I still wouldn't know who to go to," said Terry.

"You got the cash?"

* * *

M&M was on the phone with Francisco Lujan. He had just received notice that Sheik Faruk Al-Enezi was on his way to Geneva for a meeting with the prince and apparently he had told him that he now had an asset on The Board. He knew that Francisco would compensate him well for this intelligence, but most of all he was happy to stick it to Lord Humphrey Houghton who was the latest best buddy of the sheik. The Brit had purposely shunned M&M at a meeting with Senator Joseph Delany some years ago and M&M had a long memory.

* * *

"I think we have confirmation that our friend Cartwright is more than what he appears to be," said Francisco to Marco and Patricia during a break in their meetings. "I'm ninety-nine percent sure but I'll have a confirmation by tomorrow."

"We will have to tell Airy," said Patricia.

"I don't know about that. Let's sleep on it and make a decision tomorrow once we have confirmation," suggested Francisco. "It can be to our advantage to have this guy on the hook for a short time. We will have to re-convene the meeting anyway, but in the meantime some good can come of this. Just keep the conversation light. No solid figures. I'll give the others a heads-up without giving anything away. Be particularly careful not to mention our banking assets."

"I'll juggle the figures so it's believable and he won't suspect a thing," said Marco.

That evening was the closing dinner so there would be wine and other drinks if desired, but everyone was looking forward to the "house wines," which were sure to be superb. Both Arquiza and Francisco would want to have the members of The Board enjoy the best of their vintages. The meal was a typical gaucho fare with huge steaks the size of a dictionary, grilled trout, and piles of fresh greens, carrot salad, tomatoes, grilled provolone with oregano and paprika, breads and ricotta cheesecake for dessert. The wines left nothing to be desired. They were the best from Mendoza, Patagonia, and Salta.

Cartwright felt flush with success; the sheik had promised that after a year on The Board his debt would be wiped out and he would no longer be at his command. He had a bit more wine than the others, was a bit more loquacious, laughed louder and went to sleep earlier. When Cartwright was off to bed, Marco convened the others, none of whom were even a bit tipsy. He explained the situation now that confirmation had come from M&M that Cartwright was beholden to the sheik and that the figures and plans presented during the meeting were a diversion. They all agreed to postpone their departure the following day without letting Cartwright notice the changes.

The next morning, in the fog of a considerable hangover, Edmund Cartwright was chauffeured over to Bariloche from where he would depart via Cape Town to Perth. All the others, who had apparently departed also, were back at the estancia within an hour. The meeting was immediately called to order and the first point of discussion was obviously Edmund Cartwright and what to do with him. After a short debate, and a thousand excuses from Airy for having been taken in by Cartwright, it was agreed that he would be fed information that would derail the sheik's plans and damage their European opponents, particularly Humphrey. What to do about the IOR continued to be a very difficult issue and no specific ideas were put forward.

The next point was over a report Marco received from Leon Goddard that he, Ernie, and Patricia had agreed to share with the other members of The Board without saying where it was obtained. Goddard had sent an extensive investment program into a relatively new technology based on a carbon product called graphene. Apparently there was enough evidence that graphene would replace silicon in many computer functions and would be, together with gold, the mechanism by which light, instead of electricity, would power the world.

Again, the "local factor" so preached by Marco would come into play. Transporting electricity is expensive and very wasteful. If sufficient energy could be generated at venues close to the consumer the cost would be a fraction of the electricity brought from hundreds and even thousands of miles away. In a more ambitious future the "Tesla Effect" could be used to capture light, convert it to energy, and transmit it wirelessly to any point on earth from a power station in space. In the meantime hundreds of applications for graphene were being studied and developed all over the world. It was their gamble to choose the right ones to invest in.

Goddard had suggested that they create a think tank exclusively dedicated to locate, evaluate, and recommend which applications were the most commercially viable. The corporation had been created and Marco put to vote the investment of the Board and/or its members into the graphene venture. There was a general aye with particular interest from Airy, whose silicon ventures were involved already with some graphene applications as nano-capacitors, and so she was particularly enthused about the idea. The meeting went on all day, with the correct figures and the proposals that Marco presented approved without debate because the track record for the year he had been on The Board was astonishingly positive. That evening a new closing dinner took place, featuring a whole red stag, two lambs and several geese roasted on an open quincho. It had taken all day for five of Arquiza's gauchos to prepare. This feast was for The Board, all the security people, and workers at the estancia.

The next day everyone departed except for Marco and Patricia who accepted Antonio's invitation to stay at the estancia for a few days of fishing and hunting. Antonio brought waders, boots, and gear for Marco and Patricia and he took Marco apart to teach him the basics of casting for trout; a different affair from the power cast required in ocean fishing. The rods and lines were lighter, the flies minuscule by comparison, and the rhythm of the exercise in general was slower, softer, and more calm. This favored Marco's shoulder, which, even after all this time, still gave him trouble on occasion. With the light fly rod, a 3-weight with corresponding line, it was easier for him. It was an older Sage model, an RPLX, but it was the perfect weapon for the feisty browns in that stretch of the Rio Malleo.

After a couple of hours' instruction on the basics that Luigi and Pete had taught him in Sarasota, Marco was casting up to forty feet of line without difficulty. By the time they got to the river it was almost noon but the day was overcast and there was still some activity in several pools and runs. Antonio had pointed to several rising fish but walked on until they reached a small run at the end of a pool. The tail water formed a nice feed line where splashes of feeding fish could be seen. Antonio explained that when the trout splash taking the fly it's because they're eating caddis flies, trichoptera common to the Malleo more than to other rivers in the area. Antonio told Marco to cast a few times away from the feeding fish until he felt comfortable with the distance and control of the line.

When Marco was ready, Antonio told him to cast to the last trout along the feed-line so he wouldn't disturb the other fish. Marco was short on the first two casts, an error typical of neophytes. Then he overcast and "lined" the fish, which promptly skedaddled out of sight. They rested the water a few minutes and then Marco cast to the next fish up. The fly landed perfectly on the feed line but the trout put its nose right up to the offering and rejected it. Antonio decided to change the fly to a smaller one and thinner tippet to accommodate. The fly he chose was a #18 green body, elk hair caddis imitation that he covered with silicon, which he also spread onto the tippet. They repeated the exercise as before and this time the fish did not hesitate in taking the fly. Seconds later Marco was fighting the first trout he had ever caught. The fight was not long as the half pound fish, after jumping a couple of times, came quickly to the net. Soon afterwards the hatch ebbed and eventually no fish were rising. It was getting close to lunch time and they went to a spot upriver where they met with Patricia, Luigi, Pete and one of the gauchos who was guiding them. They were all smiles and pointed to a fire where several trout were spread out on sticks, roasting slowly over the embers. A cooler with white and sparkling wine invited the thirsty. A chickpea salad, bread, and provolone completed the light riverside fare.

After lunch, with sated hunger and thirst, Marco lay down on the thick aromatic grass, leaned his head on a log, and with Patricia curled up against him had the best two hours of deep, undisturbed sleep that he could ever remember. He woke up refreshed but remained still to not disturb Patricia, who was still asleep. Gazing at the breaking sky, he saw the fantastic lenticular clouds common in this part of the world. They looked like huge flying saucers hovering over the undulated landscape. As he watched, a huge bird glided onto a hill across from where they were and seconds later another two came in for landing. They were condors, Andean Condors to be precise, the largest flying birds in the world. They came to pick on the carcass of a guanaco, a relative of the camel and the llama. Herds of these herbivores can be seen all over Patagonia and constitute the main meal for all types of scavengers and of the only predator of size, the Patagonian puma. Other wildlife in the region include the huge Patagonian hare and large partridges. These are the prey of a ubiquitous little devil called zorrito, or small fox in English.

When Patricia woke up they decided to take a walk along the river and Luigi, Pete, and the gaucho went with them. Antonio had to go back to the estancia to take care of some business. Francisco was probably doing the same and would not show up until cocktails late in the day. Pete pointed out a big curve in the river that he fancied for nymph fishing. This is done with imitations of insects in their larval stage and today by proof of record, the fly of choice would be the larva of the caddis fly. This bug creates a shell for itself made of tiny stones and twigs glued around its body by a secreted natural polymer. To imitate this bug, Pete chose two small flies – just barely dressed hooks, really – covered in sparkly dubbing and weighted by a small bead where the head was supposed to be. He tied the two, one brown, one olive green, in line onto the tippet. About two feet up from the fly, just above the knot that joined the tippet to the leader he placed a small styrene ball that acted like a bobber and would indicate when there was a strike.

Patricia preferred to fish without the strike indicator and with a larger fly than those used by Marco and Luigi. They spread out along the long curve of the river and each began their quest for trout. Pete went with Marco and helped him "mend" the cast by raising the rod and doing a small flip against the current so that the fly did not drag. In a short time Marco was casting and mending correctly and was rewarded by the sudden disappearance of the strike indicator. Pete told him to simply raise the rod to set the hook, but it was too late and the fish spit the fly. After a few casts more the small bobber disappeared again and this time Marco properly set the hook and the trout raced upriver, taking line at an alarming rate and making the small Hardy reel scream with delight. Pete stayed next to Marco and coached him how to use the flex of the rod to fight the fish, how to recover line and when to put the fight on the reel. The fish was not ready to give up like the one Marco caught that morning and it took line several times. It never broke the surface and neither Pete nor Marco could guess the size. Obviously it was bigger than the earlier one. After about fifteen minutes the big fish tired and let the weight of the line and Marco's retrieval bring it to the shore a few feet downriver where Pete waited with the net. It was a beautiful brown trout, a little over twenty inches long and about three pounds. Pete taught Marco how to take the hook out without hurting the fish by using long surgical hemostats. Then he held the fish in the water with its mouth facing the current that flowed through its gills with life giving oxygen. Eventually the powerful fish that had remained calm in Pete's careful hold began to move its body and elegantly took to the river on its own, leaving behind only the memory of his valiant struggle.

Marco was hooked; far more than the fish had ever been. His whole body shook with an emotion of communion with nature that he had never felt before. The landscape, the light, the water in its crystalline rush and the infinite sky above took on a different dimension, ever so larger, ever more beautiful, and now an inseparable part of him. Pete realized the sacredness of the moment and kept silent seeing the new light in his boss' eyes.

A little later Patricia and Luigi joined Marco and Pete. They all continued fishing down river for a few hours, without hurry, enjoying the beauty that surrounded them and listening to the holiest of hymns as nature rejoiced in itself. They took turns fishing in several spots, Marco and Patricia differing most of the water to Luigi and Pete who were more than delighted to take advantage of this rare opportunity. Pete, the most capable angler of the four, landed the trophy of the day, a 28-inch rainbow trout that jumped several times out of the water in great somersaults, splashing back and throwing liquid diamonds into the waning light of the afternoon. They kept no fish, releasing every brave contender back to its home in the unforgettable waters of the Malleo.

The following day the group woke up at four in the morning for a day of hunting. On the land that belonged to Antonio, and the adjacent land that belonged to The Board, there were red stag and wild boar. Both, like the trout that populated these waters, brought from abroad by early English settlers. The red stag, very close to the American elk, was an imposing animal with proud antlers upon a large strong body. The boars were true *jabalí* – black, big-shouldered, humpbacked beasts whose character matched their countenance. Six-inch tusks stuck out the side of their snouts, promising swift death to any foe that crossed their path; but my goodness, they are delicious roasted on a spit over *quebracho* embers!

The hunters were Francisco, Patricia, and Antonio. Marco had no interest in hunting and the others came along only as guides or as part of the security detail. A paraglider was going up as a spotter and everyone left on horseback, riding up into the hills where a group of animals had been seen last week by the gauchos from the estancia. It was a two-hour ride and when they reached the location dawn was breaking into a luminescent, clear day with the Lanin Volcano as spectacular backdrop to the view. A thousand feet up above their heads the paraglider was making lazy circles no different from those made by the condors as they rode the thermals for hours waiting for a whiff of carrion that would guide them to their next meal.

The pilot called on his handheld radio to one of the gauchos and indicated that a stag and three cows were about a mile west from where they were. They followed the lead of the guide and soon he told them to stop and dismount. About a thousand yards away they could see the animals profiled against the lighted slope. Unfortunately the wind was coming out of the east and if they approached any closer the deer would surely spook and run. The shot would have to be taken from here.

Only Patricia had the vision and pulse for a shot like this, as Francisco and Antonio did not trust their older eyes or the overall steadiness needed for such a task. The guide took Patricia a couple of hundred feet away from the rest of the party, walking behind the rise so they wouldn't be seen by their quarry. They came up behind some sparse bushes and used them as camouflage. Patricia and her guide took turns with the spotting scope and estimated that the shot was about 850 yards and five degrees uphill. The wind was not a factor as it came straight from their six. Patricia was shooting a single-shot custom-made Gibbs Farquharson Style 600 North Eastern, armed with a hand-loaded 270-grain bullet with a dovetail point. She had used this same gun twice before and felt comfortable with it. The Zeiss Scope had a hunting turret and the 850 yards were just a neighborhood watch for the powerful optics. Calculating the shot with the help of the guide using a targeting scope took a few minutes because the wind speed had increased and from behind it could make the shot lower or higher depending on speed and humidity. Fortunately it was a dry day and a click down should compensate well. The shot resonated like thunder across the hills and the bullet flying at almost 3,000 fps reached its target in less than a second. The stag bolted and disappeared behind the hill.

"Tal vez la próxima vez, señorita," said the guide, "maybe next time, miss."

"Estás loco? Ese venado está muerto."

The radio crackled and the guide listened then answered something she didn't hear.

"Si, cayó al otro lado," said the guide, "yes, it fell on the other side."

Obviously the paraglider had seen the stag fall dead after a short run over the hill. The whole party went down the valley, crossed a creek and rode to where the animals had been. Then, on foot they followed the guide to where the stag had fallen. The shot had severed a major artery and the beast had lived only a couple of minutes after being struck, dropping dead at the other side of the ridge. The gauchos went to work dressing the stag, which, they estimated was 500 kilos or over a thousand pounds. The meat was for them and the household servers, the entrails and bones would feed the dogs, the skin would make a great rug in one of their homes. Antonio would only take tenderloin for the roast and a patch of belly skin for flies. The antlers would decorate the living room.

After lunch back at the estancia they all took a siesta. Later, Patricia and Marco, followed at a distance by the security people, walked along the river hand in hand, talking about everything as had become their custom. They were rarely apart and both were comfortable with this. For Marco it was the first love of his life and in Patricia's mind each day fogged the difference of her life with Sal and now with Marco. It seemed like there had been no death but a metamorphosis of one man into the other. They had two more days of this holiday without being haunted by death and they were going to make the best of it.

19

A few days earlier, Cardinal Jean Dupree and Monsignor Enrico Testa were enjoying a glass of fine port in the bar of the hotel. Dressed in civilian clothes, they conversed about the success that the necessary adjustments in the Meredith organization had produced. Edward Meredith was ecstatic with his new found authority and, guided by the cardinal, was seeing results in the actions taken. The coffers of the church in the dioceses of Kansas and other important cities were flush with cash. African missions and South American church charities were again active and fruitful. Pressure by the FBI taskforce had practically disappeared and the cash shipments to the IOR associate banks were getting there without problem.

The television above the bar was silently showing the news on a local NBC channel and suddenly Testa was looking at himself on the screen – not only his Pernambuco passport photo but that of Mr. Theodor Miles and, much to his disgust, Monsignor Enrico Testa in his latest passport portrait. To make things worse and cause the good cardinal to choke on his Portuguese libation, the talking but soundless face of FBI Special Agent Delany blabbed away in earnest with only the caption ribbon underneath the image showing what he said.

Apparently the FBI, in a joint effort with the police departments of Kansas City and Washington DC, sought this individual for suspicion of multiple murders in those two cities. Photos of Joseph Delany Sr., his wife Arlene, Congresswoman Tatiana Wells, and Ana Meredith appeared one after the other. Finally the torture was over and the anchor was talking about the Middle East with the usual car bomb carnage in some city where those Godforsaken people lived in mud within mud. As they were sitting there watching the last of the news, the cardinal's phone rang and was advised by one of his assistants that Interpol was trying to locate him in regards to Monsignor Testa.

"Merde," hissed the cardinal. "Now we are the target of this idiot Delany."

As if his taskforce had not done enough damage, Delany was handicapping his most valuable associate. Testa had to disappear. He and Enrico, who was in his wounded-soldier disguise, spoke softly in Latin with occasional French phrases, hoping that if overheard nobody would understand them and create further problems. After a few minutes they retired to the cardinal's suite and sat down to plan Testa's disappearance and whatever further actions were necessary to secure his services to the cardinal. Testa wanted to terminate Marco Carducci and Patricia Lujan before he left the US but it was a logistical nightmare and the cardinal did not want to lose his sword to some cop's lucky break.

They finally decided that Testa would fly to Bogotá, Colombia where a new passport and disguise would be available and then fly to Rio de Janeiro via Manaus on TAM. He could not fly directly to Brazil, because US citizens need a visa to enter that country but Colombians don't. Rio was famous for facial reconstruction surgery and fingerprint obliteration techniques that, combined with a few tricks, could allow Testa to work for the cardinal again. In a few months a cleric from Minas de Gerais would be transferred to Rome to serve in some obscure department and be there for the greater glory of God...and of Cardinal Dupree, of course.

* * *

The Mafia in the United States is still the bastion of an Italo-Jewish collaboration that existed since Lucky Luciano and Meyer Lansky first sat down to discuss business. While the individuals as portrayed in the film *Goodfellas* do exist and make their living administrating petty crime in assigned territories, they are far removed from the true seat of power where the lives of all Americans are affected.

With his very successful venture into pipelines, Ian Carlo de la Rosa had reached the pinnacle of that organization. He and Ernie Goldman were moving billions of dollars and making immense profits. The Liguria and the Lorenzana had also emerged above others because of their association with the Carducci empire. Naturally this did not go unnoticed by other families across the US that, while also benefiting from services offered by Ian Carlo et al, felt that they were not getting their fair share and grew uneasy. Slowly an association of sorts was formed by a Genovese offshoot from Miami, a Chicago mobster named Ted Wilkins whose mom was Italian, and two California independents who worked as intermediaries between some of the Central American gangs and families in the West and Midwest. While there was no specific issue that they could adopt as reason for war, they created and shared grievances among themselves. Finally they concentrated their dissatisfaction with the Lorenzana family because they did not want to be involved in smuggling for these individuals between Honduras and Chicago via New Orleans. They believed that the Lorenzana were the ones doing all the smuggling for Ian Carlo de la Rosa and they wanted the same services for themselves.

None of them knew of the pipelines, including Maurizio and Nicolo Lorenzana. So far the secret had been kept since no one outside the Carducci top tier knew about it. A delegation of mobsters descended on New Orleans and summoned Maurizio to a meeting. He went as requested but made sure he was well covered by choosing the location and having four of his most capable enforcers strategically located to avoid surprises. The lobby of the Hilton on St.

Charles Avenue fit the bill perfectly and the delegates kept their hands visible and their voices down. But the message they brought was not so nice. Basically it was "play ball, or else." Maurizio was becoming a good poker player and did not say anything to offend the visitors. He simply stated that he had to study the best manner in which he could accommodate them and for that he needed a day. He invited them to stay for the night at his expense and they would reconvene the following day. Immediately he called Ian Carlo and let him know what the mobster delegation wanted. Ian Carlo got on his plane and the following day when the ol' boys got to the meeting, they met with Ian Carlo de la Rosa, an army of his men, and the two Lorenzana. Without intimidating anybody...at least not overtly, Ian Carlo asked them to be specific about their requests. He underlined the word "requests," making it clear that demands wouldn't be well received.

"We need for Maurizio to help us with a small problem," said a man named Julio Rossini who hailed from Detroit.

"And that favor consists of...?" asked Ian Carlo.

"Maurizio already knows," huffed the man.

"Humor me," said Ian Carlo. "Tell me what you want."

"The same you are getting from him. We need his help to import some merchandise our associates in Honduras and Nicaragua have for us, and then help us deliver the payment."

"I'm sure Maurizio will accommodate you." Ian Carlo gave the man a figure for the services.

"That's outrageous," shouted Rossini, standing up, but when he saw that Ian Carlo's face changed slightly to less affable, he sat and listened.

"The figure I gave you, Mr. Rossini, covers Mr. Lorenzana's service and it compensates me for the service I'll forfeit in your favor; all in goodwill."

"Why should you be compensated? It's Mr. Lorenzana who will do the service."

"Well, Mr. Lorenzana and I are partners and right now he has a full plate with my merchandise so he would have to render less to me in order to accept your requests."

"I'll have to consult with others. We'll get back to Mr. Lorenzana...or should we talk to you?"

"Mr. Lorenzana will be waiting for your decision," answered Ian Carlo, subtly putting them a rung below himself.

Maurizio and Ian Carlo stayed in the lobby with all their people in place until the delegation of mobsters had cleared the hotel and gone back to theirs.

"We haven't seen the end of this," said Maurizio.

"No, we haven't," answered Ian Carlo pensively.

* * *

Marco was naturally fit. He had practiced little disciplined exercise per se, but he was very active in the sense that he walked or ran upstairs when he could and enjoyed doing calisthenics every morning since he had been in school. As he was getting into his waders, he noticed that he felt stronger, fitter if you may, than he had felt since early college, when he had done some rowing. Marco had a flat stomach and strong legs, but could use some upper body beefing up. Patricia and Luigi had been including him in their martial arts practices and he had learned some basic defense moves of Krav Maga and Okinawan Karate. He enjoyed the repetitive moves of the punch, kick, fend, advance, retreat, duck and twist practiced every day for at least an hour before doing Katas and some sparring. At his age he would never acquire the lightning-fast moves that Patricia and Luigi demonstrated, but now he felt that the average thug with fists, a stick, or a knife would not find him an easy takedown. It was a small sense of satisfaction that brought a smile to his face. Even in this area Patricia changed his life. She had even taught him how to kick some ass; talking of which, she walked into the wader room in the skimpiest of underwear and Marco, who had just wadered up, thought that he had to get out of that Gore-Tex in a hurry...before they got stuck on something.

Fifteen minutes and a shared shower that almost derailed their plans later, Marco and Patricia rushed out to meet the others for a day of fishing on the Rio Collon Cura. It was going to be a hoot because with only two to a raft there was going to be a water parade. The anglers were Marco and Patricia in one raft and Antonio with Francisco in another, each one with a guide that did the rowing. Add to that four rafts with security people, two with food and drink for all and one more with Luigi and Pete, who were on duty but brought rods just in case.

The Collon Cura is a wide river born of the confluence of the Aluminé and the Chimehuin that eventually runs into the Limay, Patagonia's largest river. On a good day huge brown trout can be caught casting streamers deep into holes and dugouts that the currents of spring create. Some of these are resident fish and some migrate down from the lakes. The river carries browns, rainbow, and *Salevinus fontinalis,* or brook trout. There is one native species called perca or perch, which looks a lot like a black bass and even has a largemouth and smallmouth variety. Some days you can catch all five species. This river, much like the Green River in Wyoming, is like a light switch: it's either on or it's off. When it's off you can't even catch a cold; but this day the Collon Cura was in the perfect mood. A partially overcast sky offered a plethora of light and shade against the banks and over the runs, riffles, and eddies, exciting the insects into hatches and the fish to feeding. Everybody caught fish for the first couple of hours. Nice-size trout were taking dries and nymphs on the bank and in dropoffs below riffles. Everyone had fun but no really big fish were taken.

Antonio, an old hand at this river, opted for a "chuck and duck" technique that sometimes produces richly. He changed to a very fast sinking line with a fifteen-foot tip; it's a tough line to cast but the 7-weight rod that he employed carried it well. He used a short 20-pound leader tied directly to the fly – a large, black woolly bugger with rubber legs and green flash-a-boo.

The cast is mechanical and repetitive. Place the fly in the deeper holes close to the bank or behind big boulders, logjams, and major obstructions, let it sink a few seconds and then strip a couple of times, let it dead drift a bit and strip again until the fly is a few feet from the boat. Repeat until successful. About an hour into this, when the fly was in a deep hole behind a boulder Antonio felt something slam the fly...KABOOOM! The rod bent deep into the butt and the fight was on. His guide, a gaucho with whom he had fished for years, turned the raft to ease his retrieve, ferrying it to the shore to maintain a smooth drift with the fighting duo. The reel, an old Hardy Perfect, worked like the perfect machine it was. The drag was precise and the clicker screamed with the excitement of each run the lunker made. Others had seen the engagement and stopped fishing to watch. Minutes went by and neither adversary gave quarter; the rod was up and its deep curve resembled the profile of a dome. The line wrote messages of defiance on the surface of the nervous waters that roofed the battle.

Finally the profile of the fish was seen by the guide, who exclaimed "la puta!" in his surprise. He edged the raft towards shore because a beach just ahead was the best place to land this fish. Antonio jumped out and walked the tired trout like a dog to a hydrant, guiding it to the large net that awaited its surrender. Everybody came to see this fish. It was all one could want in a lifetime catch. Photos were taken, girth and length were measured, and with a solemn kiss from Antonio on its wet dark back the record-size brown trout was released back into its domain. Then there was a midday meal prepared with some anticipation by the gauchos.

A shore lunch on a float is an experience that every angler deserves and it is memorable if the cooks are good. Sometimes they will fry fresh trout but mostly in Argentina you get "*asado de tira*," which are short ribs grilled on the bone to absolute perfection over embers of a hardwood fire. To accompany this there will be bread, wine, and cheese – and maybe a nap under a tree.

* * *

Ian Carlo left his Roslyn estate early because he had a rare meeting with Leon Goddard. He had included Ernie Goldman in the meeting at Marco's request and apparently it was to be a game changer. With Ian Carlo traveled eight men in two SUVs, and one more vehicle had gone ahead with another three men to scout the road and the destination. Ian Carlo liked to take a chopper to the city but today the pilot called in with a mechanical problem so he had to drive into Manhattan to Ernie's office.

As they turned to go towards the Long Island Expressway an ambulance and an EMT truck passed them at full speed with sirens and lights engaged. One Tahoe SUV with two of his bodyguards was in front and one with four was behind him, which was the usual formation, but for some reason his driver suspected something, slowed down, and radioed the trailing unit to flank them. As they turned the corner they saw the two emergency vehicles obstructing the road and the EMTs were apparently assisting a prostrated individual in the middle of the street.

"Must be a hit-and-run, boss," said one bodyguard. "I don't see any crashed vehicles."

"I don't like this," said the driver. "I'm getting us out of here."

Just as he spoke those words, the EMTs stood up and began shooting at the SUVs. All the cars were armored but soon the lead vehicle was getting riddled. They were using hardened ammunition and it was beginning to get through. The driver tried hard to maneuver the big Escalade and make a U-turn, but in the narrow street it was a three-move exercise. The man who was playing possum on the ground also got up and in his hands he had an RPG 27 anti-tank grenade launcher that could penetrate the hardened shell of the SUVs. The men in the first vehicle had been obliterated by the assault rifle fire and those of the flanking vehicle were out of the car and shooting back at the assailants. Four of his men and four of the enemy were down.

Ian Carlo was in a jam. His vehicle was sideways to the grenade shooter, who was taking aim with his scope. Ian Carlo could see the green light shine off the window. He acted on impulse and opened both doors of the Escalade as the grenade emitted its flare and shot forward. The winglets opened and stabilized the flight of the weapon straight at its target, following the reading of the guiding system that had been exactly where Ian Carlo saw it on the glass of his door. The grenade flew right through the car, burning hair off all the passengers, and obliterated a newsstand about half a block down the street, sending shredded magazines, candy, and about ten grand worth of cocaine and marijuana up in smoke. Unfortunately the vendor belonged to one of Ian Carlo's distributors.

The improbable miss disconcerted his opponents, of whom only two remained. The grenade launcher had fallen to several shots from Ian Carlo's men. Ian Carlo's driver turned the vehicle forward again and headed straight for the two assailants, who now had only handguns that were useless against the armored Escalade. One was clipped by the vehicle and landed hard with the sound of breaking bones. The other ran into an alley. Only a couple of minutes had passed since they had turned into the ambush. Now there were nine men on the ground either dead or critically wounded. The EMTs, the real ones, were on their way and sirens could be heard all over the place. As Ian Carlo's Escalade rushed into the Long Island Expressway they practically came to a stop. Traffic was heavy and the river of cars on the LIE was barely doing 25 miles per hour. The driver jumped the intersection, blasting his horn and got back on a city street. He found the parking garage of an office complex and crashed through the barrier heading for the top floor. There were no other cars and the men, including Ian Carlo, found shelter along the air conditioning units and a stairwell.

In a few seconds Ian Carlo was on the phone with Ernie Goldman and his bodyguards were on the phone to Ian Carlo's home where his wife and daughter were being picked up and taken to a heliport at the hospital. The emergency plan had been designed and planned by Allen Security and it worked smoothly. Within the hour Ian Carlo's family were in a safehouse high in a Manhattan skyscraper and Ian Carlo, who had been picked up by a chopper in the parking lot, was secure in Ernie Goldman's office, where calls were being made to assets in every police and law enforcement organization from Manhattan to Long Island. They needed to know who the perpetrators were and they needed to know the status of Ian Carlos' men. Marco and Francisco were out of range but would be reachable in the evening.

Ernie, Leon and Ian Carlo speculated about the authors of the attempt but with all the developments of the last few months, the list of possible adversaries had grown long. Within the hour reports started coming in from the field. The first was from one of Ian Carlo's men who had only been creased by a bullet, and when he came to he had assessed the situation just before the police and emergency vehicles invaded the scene. He was now hiding in a porno shop, where the owner was helping him. The other men in his team appeared to be dead. The enemies were dead except for the one that they had hit with the car, who had a badly broken leg. He said the cops were going through the dead bodies looking for ID but only Ian Carlo's people carried IDs, permits, etc. The others had nothing on them, but the cops were taking photos and probably sending them of to be identified. The same was happening with fingerprints. These and the photos would be sent electronically to CSI labs so that they could go through biometrics software and bring up the data. If that didn't work, the autopsy would likely generate lots of information by which to identify the culprits.

"Both your families are at safehouses here in town," said Ian Carlo to Ernie and Leon. "It's part of the protocol that Allen Security set up for us and it triggers automatically. I'm sure your folks have done a couple of dry runs, as my wife and kid have. I just received confirmation from the details with all our families. I think this was a business thing directed at me, but just in case we follow Allen's orders until we know it's safe. Is that clear? And Leon, I'm sorry that this is involving you, it must be difficult to understand, but it's an indispensable security measure."

"Actually, I understand. I have a setup like this that would have triggered if it was an attack on me. There isn't a corporation worth its salt that doesn't have emergency security protocols for their executives, key personnel, and their families. I know of a Utah corporation that has a cave outfitted to sustain 200 people for months. And besides, like you said, a man of my income..." Leon kept his strange sense of humor.

"All we can do is wait for information. Those responsible for this have to show their hand one way or the other. At this time I don't want to play the guessing game. We stay safe and keep our communications open."

"I'm going to call Francisco's operation in Bogotá. I know he's not there but he gave me a password in case of emergency and maybe they can help," said Ernie

"Do what you can and I'll try to get Marco on the satellite phone. He was taking a few days off with Patricia and Francisco, but he is a contact maniac and I know I'll hear from him unless he's in the boondocks and even then he might try the sat-phone."

* * *

Information was coming in from different sources, including the mayor's office. Suspected mobster or not, Ian Carlo de la Rosa was one of the largest taxpayers in the city and a generous contributor to every campaign, charity, and fundraiser that Gracie Mansion sponsored. An attempt on his life was a huge no-no. The mayor did not want a mob war on his watch and had the police commissioner working every angle to find out who the perpetrators were before Ian Carlo did and acted unilaterally on this. Even though technically the jurisdiction of this criminal event corresponded to Nassau County, it was part of Metropolitan NYC and the PC could act with jurisdiction.

The fact was that the only surviving perpetrator was being interrogated at Glen Cove General before his leg was set. Two detectives from Nassau County and two from NYC were grilling the man, who was more than willing to talk. He and the others were from Jersey and were hired by a man who said he was from Los Angeles. His name was, oh surprise!, Mr. Smith. They had received a payment of two hundred grand in advance and were promised three hundred grand more when the mission was finished. The weapons were provided by Mr. Smith; and that was the one good clue that the cops got. The guns were examined inside out by every test available and they turned out to be stolen from a National Guard Armory in Detroit, Michigan. More of those guns had been found in Detroit and Chicago, so it was easy to assume that Mr. Smith came from one of those cities. What the survivor did not mention was that the dead RPG shooter was Mr. Smith.

* * *

M&M got the news of the attack on Ian Carlo de la Rosa almost at the same time as the mayor of NYC. His network was impeccable and this kind of information was vital in his line of work. Unfortunately Francisco Lujan did not answer his call immediately and neither did Marco Carducci. He was tempted to call Ernie Goldman but decided to wait a bit more until he got more information from his sources in the NYPD.

* * *

Cardinal Dupree worried that he might be implicated by default but he had no quarrel with the Mafia. To the contrary, many families in the US and in Italy were his esteemed clients and carried huge accounts in the IOR banks. His problem was Marco Carducci because of his plans to fortify sectors of society that Dupree wanted weakened, not for any other reason. The Board was the opposing group, not the Mafia. He was thinking of how to make this known to Ian Carlo when he remembered that M&M was a neutral, or so he thought, element in their world. He called the facilitator and asked him directly to do him that favor. M&M agreed in exchange for another favor...could he use the services of the cardinal's assitant? Thus M&M found out that the nefarious priest would be out of commission for about six months.

* * *

The first thing Marco did when he returned to the estancia was to call Ian Carlo on the satellite phone because there was no cellular service there. In a few coded words Ian Carlo told Marco of the attack and asked him to call from a landline that could be scrambled from the Third Avenue house, where Ian Carlo and his family were reunited and very well guarded. Marco asked Antonio and immediately was taken to a hotel in Junín de Los Andes that was the shortest drive from the estancia. The Hotel San Jorge did have a landline and immediately directed Don Antonio's friend to a room where he could use the phone. The hotel had profited with the overflow of people that necessarily traveled with The Board members as support so they were happy to accommodate the request.

Ian Carlo answered at the second ring and told Marco to wait a few seconds while the scrambler engaged with the frequency of the line. Marco heard the buzzing and clicking that corresponded to the machine's protocol and then Ian Carlo was back on the line.

"Well, now I know how you feel and it's not what I imagined. I tell you I was scared shitless but thinking fast in spite of that. I guess Uncle Sal did rub some street sense into us."

"You've always had better sense than me in this respect. You didn't get a knife in your back."

"I just got an RPG burn half my hair off but no permanent damage."

"Any idea who did this?" asked Marco

"The list would be too long to include all possible actors, but I have my suspicion that this had to do with a meeting I had in New Orleans about a week ago."

Ian Carlo told Marco about the meeting with the delegates from Chicago, Detroit, and Miami and some other minor players. The one he suspected was a character called Ted Wilkins whose mother was related to someone in the Chicago outfit and was allowed a piece of the action in drug distribution. He was trying to make a mark and had a source in Central America for C and H but didn't have the means to bring it in, so he had been strong-arming Maurizio Lorenzana when Ian Carlo had showed up at the meeting and put a damper to his plans. Needless to say, Wilkins was pissed off.

He might think that if he got rid of Ian Carlo, then Lorenzana would work for him. Wilkins had no idea how things really worked, and for that matter nor did anyone else in organized crime or in law enforcement. The pipeline operation was a secret kept within a restricted number of people, all of whom were paid beyond the possibility of bribery and who knew that if they opened their mouth the reprisals would be equally immense.

"If you can pin this on Wilkins there is the option to talk to the boss of the Chicago outfit. They are not stupid and I don't see them authorizing a hit on you. If Wilkins acted without their approval, he's a dead man. They can put the other guys from the Midwest in order...but Miami I don't know. Those guys are too wild. You might have to touch them a little."

"That may happen, but first I like your idea of talking with the boss in Chicago if we get more solid on Wilkins. In the meantime the cops are digging up everything they can on the dead perps and I should know something soon."

"I'll cut this short and Patricia and I will fly directly to New York. Do you want us at the Roslyn place or in Manhattan?"

"Make it Manhattan. My wife and the kid are here and they can use the company. You and I can make a plan if we have enough information."

Ian Carlo thought that Marco was much more than he had expected. The man showed him respect at every turn without ever being subservient or even deferent. He treated Ian Carlo like an equal with capabilities other than his. Marco treated Ian Carlo like a friend. It was a realization that caught Ian Carlo off guard. Ian Carlo thought about that and realized that apart from Tommy Lee, who was a college friend, he had no other and now Marco popped into that scenario unannounced. He liked that. For the first time Ian Carlo thought of Patricia and Francisco as family in an extension of Marco; he hadn't felt that when Patricia was with Uncle Sal who had been so secretive about her. That was a big deal in Ian Carlo's world...a very big deal.

20

Enrico Testa had been sitting at the Dann-Carlton Hotel in Bogotá, waiting for his documentation. He had to get a real passport of a real person who could be traced back for years. Pulled documents were of no use to him; even when they were issued by the proper authorities they would never pass muster with the sophisticated software that the US had made available to most of their allies and even to some not so friendly nations like Russia and China. The war on terrorism had tightened the noose around everybody. The slightest inconsistency sent red flags all over to the three letter agencies of interested nations... all of them! So the person whom Testa would become had to have disappeared from the world without leaving a trace of his demise. He had to match age, face characteristics, medical conditions if any and little or no family. Acquiring such a person meant a lot of money and a worldwide search.

The attorney in Bogotá who handled this delicate endeavor had two choices of facilitators who could achieve this; M&M in Switzerland or Basil Pope in the Isle of Jersey. He chose Pope and transferred the initial payment of a hundred grand to his bank. It took ten days but at the end he found the perfect individual. Claude Petite was thirty-seven years old when his wife, the woman he had adored since they were children living in Monaco and going to school a few miles away in France, had committed suicide after a long bout with clinical depression. Claude had given up on life but could not find it in himself to end it all with a bullet in his head like Elisabetta had. Instead he gave up the world by entering a Carthusian Monastery in Northern Spain.

Pope had got hold of the man's original passport. His features were close to those of Enrico Testa but Petite had a swatch of white hair dead center above his forehead; otherwise they were the same height, same weight, and about the same age. He had traveled extensively; his Monaco-issued EU passport was well used and valid for five more of the ten-year issue. Careful work replaced the photo of Claude Petite with that of Enrico Testa, now with the distinctive swatch of white hair. The entry seal from Colombian Immigration Services appeared clearly on the last used page, showing that he had come in from Paris on a direct flight ten days ago.

Pope had purchased the small apartment on Avenue Grande Bretagne that Petite had last rented so that the address would be valid for the next year, as had been specified by the lawyer in Bogotá. A pile of letters and bills that had arrived after Petite had gone into the monastery that he would never again need were mailed to Bogotá so that Testa could carry a few pertinent ones in his briefcase. A photo of Petite with Elizabetta had been minimally Photo-Shopped to make it closer to Testa, close enough for some scrutiny, but not bulletproof…but it wasn't really needed; that with authentic credit cards from American Express and Visa plus a valid driver's license that were sent DHL to the attorney's office. Testa had also discovered that Bogotá had top plastic surgeons, some of which would work quietly for cash and lose any records of the modifications made. With a couple of photographs of Claude Petite, Testa went to the *clínica de reconstrucción facial*. The doctor worked with sophisticated software that superimposed the two pictures and determined that the surgery needed would be simple. The chin had to become wide and square rather than pointed and the eyes a bit larger. The left ear should rise about half a centimeter and the earlobes had to be increased. No big deal. The $25,000 fee was about right. He tossed in for free the white swatch of hair and the Botox treatment to the forehead and around the eyes. The results were very pleasing to Testa. So much so that he decided not to kill the medic just in case he needed him again.

When he wasn't working on his new identity, Testa was praying. He prayed for guidance and he prayed for understanding of his diminished circumstances. Testa knew that God sometimes answered no and that most of the time the Creator would leave it to his creation to sort things out. That was why he had given humans reason and free will. Testa had mulled over this and concluded that it had not been his mistakes, or that the cops got lucky, but that he had not completed his main mission. He had failed twice to eliminate Marco Carducci. Obviously God wanted him to be successful in that endeavor before he liberated His servant from his present problems; so he decided to go back and finish the job. This time he would be acting alone, without support from the cardinal or his minions, but he had the will of God to sustain him...and access to a lot of money in the Luxembourg account, which the cardinal had forgotten to close. Testa had only one point of reference where sooner or later he could find Carducci and finish him off: the house in Sarasota, Florida.

* * *

The dinner at the Taylors' had been a disaster. If Joe Delany had tried to be civil, if not cordial, Terry Taylor had acted like a teenage prima donna. He was snotty, disrespectful, and brash; he acted like the moron that he was. Neither Joe nor his wife understood how his sister had married this idiot or why she put up with him. In their view he didn't have a redeeming grace. Some years ago he was handsome, but he really had gone to the dogs; he was fat, balding, had poor personal hygiene, and ate like a pig. If he was re-elected, the people of the seventh congressional district of the Lone Star State needed social re-adjustment.

If Terry thought Delany hateful, the dinner had powered that hate to the tenth. He found him condescending, smartass, dressed like a college professor, and treating him like he was unworthy of Marla, as if the fucking bitch was some sort of prize. She should be kissing his ass twice a day for not having dumped her when her old man died. That night after he smacked his wife good night he made his call. He didn't have the cash but he would solve that in no time. He knew the combination to his wife's safe and took from there several jewels that had belonged to her mother. The diamond bracelet alone should be enough to pay the hit man twice his price. Once Marla no longer had big brother Joe, she would have to be real nice to him or she would really get it. He went downstairs and got drunk.

The IOR had informed Interpol and they in turn had informed Special Agent Joseph Delany that Monsignor Testa had disappeared in the jungles of Brazil, where he had gone on a penitent's pilgrimage. They would inform the police if and when the monsignor surfaced.

Delany called Amiable Manning

"That's all I have, Detective. Our face recognition software has extended the search to hotels, CCTV, and traffic cameras, as well as ATMs all over the country. All the airports, bus stations, railway stations, and ports of entry are covered, but no hits at all have been registered."

"He'll show up sooner or later. He's a professional hit man or a serial killer; either way he won't stop, we'll get him."

"From your lips to God's ears," said Delany. "That bastard works for a very sick cardinal whose name I can't give you; not yet at least."

Amiable made note of this in his case file and went back to his latest and more pressing cases.

* * *

Ian Carlo called the heads of the other New York and Jersey families and asked for a council. Since Ian Carlo had been smart enough to share the wealth and let them all enjoy the benefits of his endeavor without telling them where it was coming from, his request was immediately accepted and the location chosen was a suite at the Trump Towers that had private access from the parking lot. It had been secured without the knowledge of the operator, who thought that Sir Elton John had rented the suite. The descendants of the Bonnano, Luccese, Colombo, and Gambino were present and accounted for. A little small talk was allowed for and after everyone's favorite libation had been served and with the room cleared and checked for electronic eavesdropping for the third time, the windows equipped with small scramblers that attached with suction cups, and the elevator blocked, the meeting began. Ian Carlo went to the point. He didn't recount the attempt because every one of these men had been fully briefed by Ian Carlo and by their own sources.

"The autopsy report of one of the men that tried to kill me has identified him as Cosmo Fernandez, who we know worked directly for Ted Wilkins. He's a made-man with the Chicago outfit and Fernandez has been one of his enforcers for a few years. He's a Cuban exile who was with the Cuban Secret Service and defected to the CIA and was relocated to Chicago. Apparently he was good with an RPG, but then…"

"And what do you want us to do about this, Ian Carlo? It looks like something you could take care of yourself," said the Bonnano delegate.

"Yes and no; I think this guy acted without the approval of the outfit because Toledano is not stupid and to do something like this he would have had your approval. That, I know, is not the case. "

Ian Carlo was elegantly telling the delegates of the other four families that he had tabs on all of them.

"What I respectfully request," added Ian Carlo, "is that this commission invites Mr. Toledano to a conference and hears what he has to say."

"Okay by me," said the Genovese delegate and so did the others. The invitation was issued and accepted within the day.

* * *

Marco and Patricia arrived that same evening having stopped in Lima to drop off Francisco. They flew from Teterboro to Manhattan on a chartered chopper and the limo took them a few blocks to the Third Avenue home. They went to their room, showered changed and went down to meet with Helena, Ian Carlo's wife, and his daughter Teresa for a late dinner.

Ian Carlo and his people arrived a few minutes later and for the first time in a long time, they were all together. The conversation centered on the child's school, Marco and Patricia's vacation, and Helena's art purchases, which was a new interest in her life. Luigi and Pete stayed at a nearby hotel and took turns with other security people at the house and the perimeter...together with about ten NYPD plainclothes cops. Now it was a waiting game until Toledano from the Chicago outfit set a date for the meeting. It would be very soon; this kind of invitation did not offer room for delay.

Even though they were tired Marco and Patricia talked late into the night with Ian Carlo getting up to date with everything that had happened since they left. Some things they already knew but the days in Patagonia had made a parenthesis in regards to business.

The following morning Marco went to Carducci Enterprises and spent the whole day with Leon Goddard and Ernie Goldman, discussing the progress of key projects such as the multimodal brokerage and expansion of financial investments, including a well-layered acquisition of one of America's largest hedge funds and the venture capital firm that was rapidly taking positions with research companies that were working on practical application of graphene.

By the time he got home, Ian Carlo had received news that Toledano and a couple of his people were coming to the meeting set for tomorrow at LGA VIP Club, outside the security zone but also patrolled to infinity by NYPD, The Port Authority, ICE, DEA, FBI, and more. It was not a place where a turf war could take place. The club was secured and closed for repairs so the meeting was as private as it could get. Area scramblers were set up and cell phone jammers were placed strategically. Ian Carlo with his bodyguard showed up for the meeting five minutes before scheduled, but found that Toledano was there already with one of his lieutenants and another man. Seconds later the family's representative and two more men arrived. The meeting went straight to the point.

"Mr. Toledano, a man named Cosmo Fernandez and a group of men tried to kill me two days ago as I was leaving my home for a meeting in New York. He was an enforcer that worked for Ted Wilkins who is associated with the Chicago Outfit."

"Are you sure that it was Fernandez who attacked you?" asked Toledano

Ian Carlo passed him the autopsy results.

Toledano read it and passed to one of his men, a lawyer or an advisor.

"That's Cosmo Fernandez," said the man, returning the paper to Ian Carlo.

"The Outfit had nothing to do with this. It will be taken care of, I guarantee it," stated the Chicago boss

"That's good enough for me," said Ian Carlo.

"Likewise," said the family's delegate

"I'll keep you posted," said Toledano.

They all stood up, shook hands, and left the club. Toledano and his people were leaving for Chicago and had to go to the General Aviation terminal to their chartered Citation.

"No wonder Wilkins didn't show up. I told him to meet me before we left for NYC but the fucker didn't show and now we know why. He might be in the wind but I gave my word to New York and I'm going to whack that son of a bitch if it's the last thing I do."

Back in Chicago, Wilkins was doing his own planning and it didn't include getting whacked for trying to do the same to De la Rosa. His crew, like many in the history of the Chicago Mob, was not Italian; they were mostly Puerto Ricans and Cubans who had no particular loyalty to the Cosa Nostra and didn't give a shit about anyone above their immediate boss. Wilkins also had the loyalty of crews in Kansas City, Iowa, Wisconsin, and Minnesota who always felt that the bosses of the Chicago Outfit treated them like second-class citizens. Furthermore, some of them had been witness to Ian Carlo de la Rosa putting Wilkins in his place but still thought that they should be able to get their coke and heroine from their sources without the New York Mob getting in the middle of the deal, so while Toledano was in NYC several mobsters from those cities were on their way to enforce Wilkins and his crew.

A turf war was brewing and chatter among these individuals and Wilkins was increasing by the minute. Since brains and sophistication didn't prevail among them, little attention was paid to electronic surveillance of their calls and within minutes an eclectic cross-section of law enforcement agencies, Francisco Lujan's listening post, and M&M had received the gist of the chatter.

Francisco called Ian Carlo; Ian Carlo called Toledano who was sitting in his plane with at least an hour to go before La Guardia ground control allowed him to taxi to the active runway. Airliners were backed up about 45 minutes and his flight that had only now logged their IFR plan was not a priority. In a few words Ian Carlo de la Rosa told the Chicago Outfit boss that Ted Wilkins had associated with others and planned to hit Toledano on his way from the airport.

"I think the New York guys are pushing the envelope," said Toledano to his guys. "Maybe they have doubts about what I'll do. I don't like to be pushed, so maybe I'll give Wilkins the benefit of the doubt. Anyway how the hell would De la Rosa know about what Ted is doing if it was just happening?"

Thus were the mobster's thoughts when a call came in from a police lieutenant who was on his payroll telling him exactly the same thing. The FBI had an all-points warning on the probable conflict and details were coming in fast.

"Holy shit! Fucking New York is faster than the Feds," exclaimed Toledano as he hung up. Then his phone rang again and an informant of his from the Kansas City crew told him just about the same thing.

Toledano went to the cockpit and told the pilot to change the flight plan from Midway to Chicago Executive and decided not to tell anyone in his crew what he was doing. They would find out soon enough. When he was walking back to his seat he saw that the lawyer was texting something. He took the phone from him before the man even realized what was happening and read the text. "Toledano knows" was all it said.

* * *

Special Agent Joseph Delany and Kansas City homicide detective Amiable Manning were talking about a possible mob war in Chicago that could involve the local mobsters. Traditionally, since the days of Capone, Kansas City has been a satellite of the Chicago Mob and being prepared for a turf war that could extend to Kansas and Missouri was important information. Delany had called Amiable as a courtesy and they spent some time on various topics. Finally Amiable asked if Delany had anything else on their multi-identity suspect.

"Nothing other than what I already told you. The man was in Brazil on the way to a mission deep in the Amazon and that was the last time the IOR heard of him. I don't think they're lying because the monsignor who I spoke with sounded honestly concerned. I tried to talk with Cardinal Dupree and got nowhere with that."

"Who's that?" asked Manning.

"He's one of the executives at the Vatican Bank. He manages a lot of money for Catholic Charities...and guess who his principal benefactor was."

"Ana Meredith?"

"Bingo!"

"Then he must really be pissed off at the monsignor," said Amiable.

Delany had a hard time keeping the truth about that to himself, but getting the detective all riled up served no purpose.

"Thanks for the heads up, Joe, I'll let my captain in on this and he'll talk to the commissioner, I'm sure they'll be grateful."

"They should be grateful to you," answered Joe. Then he said goodbye and hung up.

* * *

The lawyer had pissed his pants and puked all over himself and the small cabin of the Citation smelled horrible. Toledano had punched the guy out so he would stop squealing and they had tied him up with his tie and belt and threw a couple of blankets on him to isolate the stink; not that it helped much. Then he and his lieutenant, Giorgio Calamateo, discussed the possibilities of what awaited them in Chicago.

"If the guy's smart and he knows that we know he might guess that we'll go to Executive Airport. That could catch us with our pants around our knees. I don't want to tell anybody because I don't know who we can trust."

"Anywhere we go's gotta be on the hush," said Giorgio, "but we have to get a crew together or we're really fucked."

"Any idea who we can trust?" Asked Toledano

"I'd bet my balls on Danny Castellanos but it's your call, boss."

"Call Danny when I tell you and ask him to get anybody he can trust together. We'll tell him where to meet us later. Tell him he has to be heavy."

When they were twenty minutes away from touchdown in Chicago's Executive Airport, Toledano went to the cockpit and told the pilot to change the plan to land at Gary International Airport. He called Enterprise and reserved a car in a name he used occasionally for which he carried a driver's license and a credit card. It was his Hail Mary option but he had to use it. He also made a reservation at a Marriott Hotel nearby and discussed with Giorgio what to do with the fucking lawyer.

"Let's put a bean in him and dump him at the end of the runway," proposed the right-hand man.

"Nah," said his boss, "chances are somebody will see us. How about calling a private ambulance and we can take him to the Everton place and there we can take care of him."

"OK, but let's have the ambulance take him to Lomax Clinic. They work well with us and we can keep him on ice until its smooth."

"Sounds good to me."

Giorgio did the calls and Toledano told him to get the people together at the Hampton Inn, which was right across from the Marriott, and that way he could keep tabs on what was going on before he met with his crew. When they landed the ambulance was there and it approached the airplane without raising flags among the ubiquitous police and security officers. They loaded the unconscious lawyer onto a gurney that rapidly disappeared into the ambulance, which took off with its siren whooping away.

Toledano and Giorgio walked to the FBO and waited for the Enterprise vehicle to pick them up, which just took a couple of minutes. In a few more they had their SUV and were on the way to the Marriott.

Toledano checked in as Mr. Tobias Clark and went to his room, where Giorgio met him shortly. From their window they had a clear view of the Hampton Inn and saw their men arrive and park. Nobody left the vehicles and no suspicious activity was noticed. They waited a few minutes and, satisfied that all was copacetic, Giorgio called Castellanos and told him to come over to the Marriott by himself and have the men set up a perimeter guard around the hotel. They had ten men in all that Castellanos brought with him that werem by his reckoning, trustworthy. They didn't know how many men were with Wilkins but estimated a minimum of eight plus whatever he got from outside. Now they needed a plan.

Some miles away, close to the intersection of Willow and Milwaukee Avenues, a not-too-clever ambush had been set up by Ted Wilkins. He had his men on the roof of a Burger King with an RPG and a 30 caliber machine gun with hard ammunition that could penetrate Class IV armor; more than enough to disable Toledano's car and blow him away. He was waiting for news that the plane was on the ground and that the lawyer had taken a cab in a different direction. A few minutes later he got a text from the man, "Where are you?" and he answered automatically, "Milwaukee and Willow, did you get out?" The answer was "Not yet, some delay; one hour."

Ted Wilkins received a text about forty minutes from the last one. "They're leaving." So he gave his team a heads up; the car would be there to pick up Toledano in a few minutes. He saw the SUV go by and tension grew. It would only be a couple of minutes and he would be the boss of the Chicago Outfit. He needed to see this happen so he walked out of the Burger King and located himself in a place from where he could see it all. Just a few seconds more, he thought and...it was all he ever would think again. A garrote ripped through his throat so fast and violently that he had no room for thought, just pain and then blackness from where he would not come back. Giorgio had only taken a few seconds to do the job. He dropped the body out of sight around the corner and took off the bloodied plastic poncho and the mask that covered his face and threw them in the dumpster. He walked back to the rented SUV where Toledano waited for him.

"Done," said Giorgio.

"OK, good. Now we have to deal with his men."

"That's easy. Castellanos has been watching them. When they smelled something was wrong they scattered like rats. Most of them will drift and land up in some gang. Others might come hat in hand...who knows. What we do know is that not one of them has enough brains to organize and take over that crew."

"How do we deal with the people from Kansas, Iowa, and Minnesota?"

"We don't. I'm going to give de la Rosa a call and he can decide what he wants. This shit party belongs to him; he'll decide what to do.

* * *

The house at Roslyn was sterile. No bugs, no possibility of eaves-dropping. Ian Carlo de la Rosa, king-apparent of the Carducci fami-ly of greater New York and New Jersey, met with the only people he trusted in the world: Marco Carducci, his brilliant cousin who, God knows how, was the partner and soon to be husband to the widow of their uncle Salvatore di Dio Carducci, Patricia Lujan, daughter of his friend and partner in crime, Francisco Lujan. Also present were Attorney Ernest Goldman and his oldest son Samuel, his right hand and heir to the Carducci connection. The meeting had been called by Marco and after some preliminary discussions they were joined by Leon Goddard, who was president of Carducci Enterprises, the legitimate arm of the family. The meeting went about with recounts of the most recent events, including the clean-up of the Chicago, Kansas, Detroit, and Miami mob families orchestrated by Ian Carlo and Toledano through Special Agent Joseph Delany, Jr., the undis-puted star of the FBI who, smart as he was, followed the script to the letter, arrested those who had to be arrested and let the others be. Proof beyond doubt of their nefarious deeds was in the hands of district attorneys in the respective jurisdictions. The message was loud and clear...you fuck with Ian Carlo de la Rosa and you fuck with the Feds. Oh my! Peace was restored and now there was solid business that had to be considered.

Marco gave an astonishing summary of the business that he managed for the family, not including the very successful Carducci Enterprises that would be presented by Leon Goddard. Then he dropped the bomb...

"I propose that we as a family retire from all criminal activity in the New York area."

"What have you done to this guy," Ian Carlo asked Patricia, "He lost his marbles?"

"Take it easy, I think I know where this is going," said Ernie.

"It's really a numbers game, Ian Carlo. How much of your time and how much risk do you incur by managing betting, hookers, dope and protection which compared to the figures I gave you and the ones Leon will bring, is absurdly insignificant. I know that a bushel of people take care of the day-to-day, but the string invariably leads to you. I just think it's a waste of you."

"I'm listening," said Ian Carlo, intrigued by the line of thought.

"You have two fronts that are by nature contentious to our family. Law enforcement, which sooner or later turns around and bites you, no matter how many of them are on your payroll, and then the other families. What happened to you with that nut Wilkins is just one of many that are potentially out there. Also, if we give up the local business it puts you a rung above everybody else and nothing that's indictable touches you."

"I'd love it," said Ian Carlo to everybody's surprise. They all thought that he was going to fight the idea tooth and claw but he added, "I want a life for my children away from this all this shit."

"Children?" they all asked in unison.

"Yes, Helena is pregnant with a boy!"

"Congratulations," said Marco, to the agreement of the group. "So this comes at the right time for all of us."

"All very nice, but I don't see how we give this up and not create a war within the families," doubted Ian Carlo.

"I think we can do this," said Samuel Goldman, speaking for the first time. "It has to be set up and presented like a business plan showing, in numbers, that nobody is getting more or less than anybody else. The reason we give is that Ian Carlo de la Rosa, outstanding citizen, wants to run for office and has to divest himself of all activity that could mar his image. We can lay it out as a four year campaign plan, which makes sense and gives you time to maneuver any which way you want. Whether the others think it's crazy or brilliant, it doesn't matter; they will buy it. The only way they can see someone leaving the mob alive is if he's joining a bigger mob and they're getting their pound of flesh. Your immediate subordinates have to get compensated in some way because they would expect to become heads of their own families but I don't see that happening. The structure of the New York organization has stayed stable since the beginning of last century and it's not going to change without major upheaval so think of something to make them happy."

They all watched Samuel, who until now was Ernie's shadow, walk confidently into the light, much to his father's satisfaction. They discussed the idea for a couple of hours but found nothing that could derail it; they all agreed it was a one chance deal. There could be no errors, the numbers had to be backed up with significant information, and the work on the plan had to be airtight confidential. The presentation was crucial. All the families would have to sign off on this at the same time and a bulletproof pact had to be reached. They also knew that their ace up their sleeve was the pipelines across the Mexican-American border. Everybody needed Ian Carlo for that and as long as the secret was safe, so were they.

Leon Goddard made his presentation and blew everybody away with the returns obtained for the Carducci Enterprises businesses. One company that while not being very large, had produced amazing results was the Industrial Laundry Servics headed by Matilde Torres, who not only made profits off a marginal business but was hugely creative. She decided it was a good deal to go into the uniform-rental business for the hospitality clients that they served and so went vertical, manufacturing the uniforms in owned factories in Honduras and renting them with laundry service included. The business had doubled in size and quintuplicated in profits. Goddard wanted to promote her to VP of Carducci Enterprises. Marco had some questions but Patricia thought it was a great idea and pushed Marco towards giving his okay. A poor immigrant woman was now a powerful New York executive with a seven-figure salary. The multiple franchises of McDonald's, Pizza Hut, KFC and other minor ones had developed by acquisition and the parking lots had grown by constructing over and under existing lots. The Canadian branch was successfully producing plywood and compressed wood in new, less poisonous versions, and companies in Mexico and the Caribbean were doing fine, but the greatest success was Scorpio Multimodal Brokers. The rationalization of the cargo had saved their clients hundreds of millions of dollars, not to mention the environmental impact of so much less fuel spent and savings in road and railway infrastructure. Even the Secretary of Transportation had taken notice and several universities were doing studies based on the unique method of profiling and responding to the client's needs that the Scorpio software presented. The investment in graphene was far from paying off and was a risky move, but indications so far were encouraging. Leon insisted on the benefits of going public with Carducci Enterprises but Marco and Ian Carlo still weren't convinced and postponed decisions on that issue. Otherwise all the projects presented were approved and funded. One drawback was the recently acquired hedge fund that was having management problems. An audit of the fund had raised some questions and a group of managers felt personally scrutinized. This had given the VP of Finance some headaches but he appeared to be resolving the situation; he had fired about half the top echelon of the fund and replaced them with younger, hungrier, and more dynamic people that came from lesser markets but could bring fresh bread to the table. The results would soon be seen.

The meeting finished and only Marco, Ian Carlo and Patricia stayed on.

"You do realize that if we can't pull this off we're in for a turf war that will make the twenties a picnic. There may be more than one of these families that think they're entitled to the whole she-bang and believe they can enforce it."

"I was thinking about that," said Marco, "and the solution might come from a much unexpected quarter. Maybe our friend Special Agent Joseph Delany, who owes his bright star to all the information we feed him, might serve the purpose of preempting any greedy thoughts among the families."

"Well, the Federales can really stifle any street war if they set their mind to it, especially if their interest in the matter is high," answered Ian Carlo. "I remember when John Gotti went to prison and then when he died, there was supposed to be some serious take-over efforts, but the Feds made it pretty clear that the roof would come down on everyone if there was even one shooting. As you know, Uncle Sal took off for someplace until the waters cleared and so did many others. Nothing significant happened and it was business as usual. But this is different. Our family as an organization in greater New York would disappear. Spreading out what we have built over the years is going to be difficult if not impossible. Someone is going to feel shortchanged no matter how we split it."

"Well, that's where the FBI can play a role," said Patricia. "They don't want a war and they will impede it at all cost, particularly if we keep them informed of how things are turning out. If someone dissents they can come down on them fast and hard. That will dissuade anyone from following suit. Besides, nowadays being notorious like it was with Gotti and before him is just not fashionable. You have held a low profile and even Delany accepts that they could never pin anything on you. That pretty much goes for the other gentlemen who head the families."

21

Enrico Testa looked at himself in the mirror. Who he saw reflected there was very different from who he had been a few weeks back. The tuff of white hair was the perfect touch. People could not avoid looking at it and ignoring the rest of the face. His ears, which still hurt, looked bigger, flatter against his head, and carried full earlobes that were not there before. His eyes were wider and nose thinner. The butcher had done a good job.

Testa wondered if it was enough to fool the biometrics software but he had no intention of testing it yet. He was going to the USA via Cuba and his entry to Florida would go undetected. He would be an illegal alien, he laughed. His Monaco passport was enough to get him a temporary entrance but better not tempt fate. He had transferred and converted 120,000 euros into diamonds and gold. He would carry only about $20,000 in cash. That should get him to the States and then in Miami he had a banker that could get him half a million more in dollars if necessary.

Enrico spent the day buying several airline tickets that would take him to Medellin, then to Panama and from there to Cuba. Apart from his Claude Petit identity he had bought a Colombian passport under the name Enrique Cabezas, which he found humorous as it translated to Enrico Testa. A credit and a debit card from Banco de Occidente together with a driver's license issued in Usaquen, a town adjacent to Bogotá, completed his acquired fifth or sixth persona...he had lost count. He went out and sat in a café in the 93rd Street park and enjoyed a balmy day. He was thinking how to stake out the Sarasota home of Marco Carducci without being suspected by the tight security that surrounded the house. It would be tricky, but apparently the beach or the water would be the only viable approach locations. He thought long and hard but had only a reference of the sight. He would have to do the survey personally. So until then he would just live, pray, and hope to complete his mission to God's satisfaction.

* * *

The Chicago PD had conducted a full investigation into the death of one Luis McBride, attorney-at-law and all around scumbag. He had been found beaten to death in a vacant lot close to Mercy Hospital. When they went through his computer files, apart from all the dirty deals and services rendered to the Chicago Outfit they found a most interesting folder that sent them into high gear. Apparently Mr. McBride was brokering hits for several clients all over the USA. They resolved at least ten cold cases and derailed a couple of corporate hits, but the one that really made them sit up and pay attention was a hit contracted by a code name "Washington," the target being Special Agent Joseph Delany, Jr. of the Federal Bureau of Investigation. The sum agreed upon was one hundred thousand dollars, paid in advance, and the hit man who took the job was Ted Wilkins, whose garroted bloody body had been found in the alley next to a Burger King just one day before Mr. McBride's. Could this possibly be a coincidence? Ha! Both men worked for known mobster Toledano but that would be a dead end. Nobody was gonna talk to the cops. That was for sure. Naturally a case like this disturbed the wasp nest and the place was swarming with FBI agents from the local office and from Washington. Feds are very protective of their own and strongly detest the idea of some dumbass hoodlum going after an agent. Unfortunately there were no clues as to who Washington was.

Washington, a.k.a. Congressman Terry Taylor of the great state of Texas, was blind with ire. He had paid more than double what he expected the bastard's life was worth. It took the bracelet and a string of pearls to raise the money and he knew that he had been cheated on the deal. They had to be worth at least twice that but the shyster wouldn't budge. It had been more than two weeks and that meddling creep was still alive. The Delanys had not even called to thank him for the dinner after his wife spent good money to wine and dine them. He was so distraught that he had missed two vital votes on the hill and the whip was after his ass.

So, brilliant as he was, Terry called the attorney to find out what was holding things up. The voice that answered was not the lawyer's and the man insisted on finding out who wanted to talk to him in spite of having been told it was personal. Terry hung up and called again. Same voice, same insistence on knowing who was calling.

"Damn it!" He thought it was just his luck. Now he was going to get ripped off by his friend's contact. "Well, today the office can go suck. I need to calm down and get my shit together."

Lucky for Joe Delany, because his office was occupied by at least five FBI agents, several capitol police officers, and his nervous secretary who honestly did not know where he was, Terry's call had been traced and when Delany saw who the caller was the dime dropped and he knew immediately that it was his miserable brother in law who had put out the contract on him. Terry had managed to get himself half tanked at the bar of the Marriott by the time the law descended on him. They dragged him out like a common criminal in spite of the tantrum that he put on about being a congressman of high standing, etc. etc.

When Joseph Delany showed up at the FBI operations office interrogation room the Honorable Congressman Terry Taylor was reduced to a blubbering ball of tears and snot. If there was circumstantial proof before, now it was overwhelming. Taylor talked non-stop, blaming everyone from his father-in-law down to the officers that arrested him and with a long diatribe about the shyster McBride who had accepted the jewelry and hadn't come through with killing that son of a bitch Joey who made his life impossible. All his wife did was talk about Joey, day in day out; and if that wasn't enough Joey's wife and kid and blah, blah, blah. When Terry saw Joseph Delany enter the interrogation room he would have literally tried to strangle him if it wasn't for the restraints and an officer who sat him back on his fat ass.

Joseph just looked at him and turned to leave without a word when Taylor shouted at him. "Uncle Archie'll take care of you. He said you were no better than that shithead father of yours, and others have it out for you too. I'll see you rot in hell you son of a bitch! As soon as Marla bails me out you'll see."

"Marla isn't bailing you out. She never wants to see your sorry ass again and believe me, the charges against you will not allow for bail," said Joseph calmly.

"Charges… What charges? I'm a sitting congressman, you can't touch me."

This elicited a good laugh from everybody and on that note of humor Delany left the room.

* * *

M&M was thoroughly amused at the turn of events for Francisco Lujan. His daughter was going to marry the nephew of her dead husband, who as predicted by their opponents had turned out to be a star for The Board and a pain in the ass for Dupree and company. Dupree was smart and managed to get back in the grace of Edward Meredith, who was bathing him in glory within the IOR. Money was flowing in as before, but without having to share much with the senators and congressmen that had facilitated that relationship. Dupree made sure that Edward threw them a bone once in a while just to keep them quiet. A senator on the warpath can be a real nuisance but as long as they believed more money was coming, they kept their peace. The relationship between the senators and Lord Humphrey had petered out and he was playing doctor with that ravenous Sheik Faruk who thought he had a tab on The Board but was getting fed a red herring for breakfast and a load of bull for dinner – all of it laced with enough truth to keep him going.

Brilliant, M&M thought to himself; brilliant! The crumbs he had tossed to Special Agent Joseph Delany had flourished and the man was the first candidate for Deputy Director when the job came up for grabs. It was time that Marco Carducci told Delany who his benefactor was so that in the future he could collect on his investment. He and Marco were to meet in the latter's Sarasota home and he was tantalized by the idea of a few days of fishing where some of the biggest tarpon in the world lived – the 16-pound line-class fly rod record being just over 200 pounds; and surely there were much bigger fish there that had never been caught. What a great investment it had been to cast his lot in with Francisco Lujan and not the cardinal. A "cardinal move" he smiled!

Allen Security had done a thorough re-evaluation of the security measures at the Carducci home in Sarasota and at Patricia Lujan's apartment. More CCTV cameras were added and high-tech movement, heat variation, and sound detectors of the latest technological advances surrounded the properties. The docks were covered and a large section of the beach was being monitored discreetly from the roof of the house. The Carducci would be back in a couple of days and from past experience Major Allen knew that the enemies were extremely resourceful and highly dangerous. He had the hard experience of telling the families of the guards that perished on the *Toscana* and paid high bonuses to them; not that it would in any way diminish their pain or his.

Across the water of the artificial harbor that had been home to the *Toscana*, and nested among the red and black mangroves that knitted a thick barrier to the next property, Enrico Testa, camouflaged in such a perfect manner that he was invisible even a few feet from where he perched on the nylon "hammock" that held him slightly above the tea-colored water, observed the work of the security experts with total attention to detail. He had arrived from Cuba on a vessel headed for Canada.

A small motorboat had picked him up at the border of international waters and in the dead of night brought him to the small fishing village of Chokoloskee just outside of Everglades City, once famous for its "Square Grouper" bonanza that ended with most of the male citizens doing time for contraband. True to their past some of them still dabbled in all types of smuggling and getting Testa in without notice was a piece of cake. Ten grand had changed hands and Lefty Noland delivered his care to a bus station in Naples. The reason he survived this day was that, being an old hand at contraband, and with a scar to remind him of the danger of this kind of deal, he didn't take his eyes off the guy and made him travel in the back of his pickup, not stopping to see him get off.

Testa was planning on six to eight hours of surveillance per day using a dark green kayak to travel from a nearby boat launch and paddling close to the shore and out of sight of the Carducci house. To anyone looking he was just another sea kayaker doing his thing.

The low-profile watercraft was now pulled deep inside the mangroves and didn't present a profile to anyone going by on the water. Obviously Carducci was not home but was probably going to be there in a few days because he saw the maid come in with a lot of shopping and the guards setting up outdoor furniture and opening shutters. He took careful note of all activities that involved the house. There were only a couple of frequent visitors: the supervisor of the security team and a mailman who went only to the box at the front gate. Other than that there were no pool cleaners or even a maintenance person; all that was done by one of the guards who was also a handyman of sorts.

Today he would have to take a risk. He was going to paddle around the beach front of the house because he didn't have a proper view from where he was and he didn't want to walk on the beach not knowing what kind of security, if any, was on that front. He waited until four in the afternoon, took off his camouflage, and put on a Michael Jackson Lives T-shirt and shorts. He wiped his face and put on sunblock all over it, sunglasses, and a Nike cap. As he turned to go parallel with the beach he could see the biggest front of the house, its huge windows, the terrace, and the deck around what appeared to be the pool.

The beach itself was sparsely populated. Just a couple of small groups with beach chairs, some runners, a couple of older folks walking hand in hand and a woman watching two young children play. The next people were south about a couple hundred yards and they were surf anglers with several rods set up. The distance to the house from the water was about three hundred feet and some very small dunes with sparse grass separated the two. Testa could guess that there were all sorts of perimeter sensors that were not visible but sure to be active. He could not use binoculars but he imagined there were at least two cameras scanning the beach from some-where on the roof. From all points the house seemed impenetrable, but if there is a will there is a way and he would continue his vigil until God in his wisdom decided to show it to him. For Testa the wait was a simple penance to strengthen his faith.

He was staying in a cheap motel on 441 and eating all his meals at low-end diners where he was sure no surveillance cameras were recording him. He only went once to a pawn shop to sell a one-ounce gold coin but had kept his cap and sun glasses on. The Paki-stani suspected he was in some difficulty and after haggling paid him only one thousand dollars; two thirds of its real value. What he didn't see was the ATM in the corner of the shop. It had taken his image and sent it to a database of the BB&T bank to which the ma-chine belonged. On a routine run of the footage his image generated a flag and was sent to the FBI automatically. The seventy percent match to a wanted individual did not generate a rush for the doors. It shuffled along the bureaucratic railway until it reached the office of an eager FBI agent fresh out of Quantico who looked at every-thing so that he could find a shining comet to whose tail he could adhere. The flag on this individual was placed by no less a heavenly body than Very Special Agent Joseph Delany Jr. whose exploits and success were now legendary in the agency. Toby Carson worded his message very carefully making sure that it was directed to his immediate boss but copied to Agent Delany as the originating authority. If well presented it would prompt the attention he wanted and Delany would get in touch with him directly.

*　*　*

Idhaya Bupta, the young hacker who became the IT director at Francisco Lujan's Bogotá systems and eavesdropping complex had brought two more young prodigies, a socially challenged Polish kid who set up the most inviolable protection system based on nano-mechanics and a hacker from China who could circumvent the NSA and sit on their laps without leaving but a faint trace of his visit. The Bogotá complex was set up to leach from the most aggressive diggers that exist, NSA, CIA, Chinese Security, the French and Brazilian governments. Some secondary operators also contributed; Iran, Israel and Saudi Arabia had robust systems but were not universal like the others. This complex generated information that The Board and its members requested and everything on some subjects that were permanent flags. This worked much like Google Alerts but went directly to the source rather than electronic publications. The system had been tracking the biometrics search by the FBI of the notorious Monsignor Testa and the seventy percent recognition post popped up on a screen in Bogotá. Flagged for Francisco Lujan, he had been pinged seconds after it had showed and he brought up on the screen this photo plus the other three that had been used as basis for the search. He studied them closely but could not be sure it was the same person. To the eye this individual had nothing to do with the others. The shape of the face was square, the ears different, the nose thinner, yet the machines had found seventy percent reliability that it was the same person. He decided to do a reverse check and had his people hack and run the Inter-Agency Biometrics facial recognition system that searches all the databases to match a photo. After only two hours the system had run through tens of millions of photographs and found only one more photo, and this one was only sixty two percent match reliability. The interesting thing was that it came from a camera at a 7-Eleven not two blocks from where the other one was taken: Sarasota, Florida, just off highway 441. It was too much, too soon for Francisco to be complacent about his daughter's safety. He prepared a brief and sent it to Marco and Patricia. Not satisfied with this, Francisco had his IT people do a search in all of Europe and the Middle East. An hour later he had the file on one Claude Petite, citizen and resident of the Principality of Monaco, a man in his late thirties with a distinctive white swatch of hair, widower and numismatic broker in a small scale. His life was well documented for the last ten years since he opened his coin exchange in the lobby of the Grand Hotel. The problem was that the biometrics comparative of the photo taken in Florida and the one from the official files in Monaco did not match more than fifty percent. The damned priest was back!

Delany received the full documentation on Claude Petite from Marco Carducci and was astonished that he could have outdone the most sophisticated law enforcement software, yet there it was in black, white, and full color. There was no doubt in his cop mind; Enrico Testa and the man in the ATM photo that the kid had sent to his attention were one and the same. A search of Immigration entries showed nothing for a Claude Petite from Monaco anytime in the last year, so the guy had crept into the US like the vermin he was. Further inquiries by Interpol found the real Claude Petite in a monastery a few miles from Barcelona. Delany called Amiable Manning and gave him a heads up on the priest and decided that a few days in Florida would not hurt. Funny enough, so did Manning; he hadn't seen the ocean in years and with his latest success he would be given ample leeway to pursue his suspect. Each man called their corresponding people in Sarasota; Delany called the local FBI SAC and Amiable called the Chief of Detectives at the

Sarasota PD. Both were very circumspect, or secretive in the nature of their mission. Delany did share with Marco Carducci his travel plans and they agreed to meet as soon as Delany got to Sarasota.

Marco and Patricia had one more meeting with Ian Carlo and Ernie before flying to Florida, and made them aware of Testa's return. Major Allen was briefed and his contact in the SPD let him know that a detective from Kansas City was following up on a clue to a murder related to the suspect Allen was inquiring about. They were to meet with Delany in two days and they wanted to review the security of the house and meet with Major Allen. They wanted this to come to a head. If the priest was there they would flush him out. Ian Carlo and Ernie agreed with them and suggested they take some re-enforcement from New York but both Marco and Patricia rejected the idea. Their people were enough; Luigi, Pete, Jose, and Cucho would be there, plus Allen Security's full contingent. It was time to confront the monsignor and finish this once and for all.

When Delany got to Florida, the SAC and a contingency of four agents were at the airport waiting for the VIP. They were at the door as he disembarked and took Joseph to the Ritz-Carlton where they had secured a suite for him. On the way he briefed them on the subject of his pursuit and made them aware of the extreme danger that Testa presented. Now they had an extensive background on Monsignor with details of his Special Forces and NSA activities. This guy was a force to contend with. At the FBI Sarasota office they mapped the points at which the two CCTV takes of the suspect were located and they decided on a search of all the hotels, motels, and boarding houses within a two mile radius of them.

They would use local police to extend and accelerate the search and that was how Delany found himself in the company of Amiable Manning, who was at the time coordinating a similar effort. A meeting of all interested parties of the FBI, the SPD and Amiable Manning produced a plan that was put into practice immediately. Uniformed, plainclothes, and undercover cops were deployed with photos of the suspect and divided into a grid that would visit possible locations where he could sleep, eat, or buy food. An action force including Agent Delany, Detective Manning, and local SWAT were ready to deploy on contact.

* * *

When Enrico Testa got off the bus about half a block from his motel he noticed the patrol car at the front office and decided to wait at a local café while he observed. Then two men, obviously cops, walked up to the cashier and started a conversation that Testa did not want to witness. He slipped out through the kitchen to the service alley behind the joint and walked towards a municipal parking lot about a block away. He walked along the rows of cars and tested a few that appeared to be unlocked. He was lucky on the third try. A Pontiac G5 had been left unlocked by its owner who was either a scatterbrain, in a hurry, or had grown complacent because of Sarasota's low crime. Testa needed about thirty seconds to hotwire the car and drove away from this location at the speed limit so as not to attract attention. His cover was blown. No doubt about that. They had pinpointed his location and he could not afford to go back there. Fortunately all his documents and money were with him in an impermeable fanny pack. His gold and diamonds were stashed in a locker at a local gym where he had paid for membership for a year in advance. He visited the place frequently and was satisfied it was safe. Now he needed a place to stay and plan his next move, knowing well that his target would be aware and prepared, but God's will was clear and no amount of obstacles were going to deter him. He went to a Sports Authority and bought a small tent, a sling spear gun, a lantern and a cooler, a tropical sleeping bag and a hunting knife, two cord saws and camouflaged clothes to replace those lost at the motel. He also bought a case of energy bars and about two pounds of beef jerky, pepperoni sticks, and a case of water. Then he parked the stolen car close to an Avis office and rented a vehicle with one of the IDs he had bought in Colombia.

He went to pick up his kayak and other equipment at Kayak

Haven and drove to Gulf Beach Campground, where he rented a pitch for a week. Now he was far away from the place where the cops would be looking. He went to the nearest CVS Pharmacy and bought hair bleach so that he could make all his hair white, not just the tuft. Finished with these ministrations he went to a Best Buy and bought a cheap tablet. At a Starbucks he got online and sent one email to "mercenary's online" and in ten minutes had an answer and a price. He would have three people for what he needed; a short action and retreat that would not compromise the mercs; $30,000 up front transferred to an account in Portugal.

22

M&M arrived at the second-level terminal almost at the same time as Marco and Patricia were taxiing into the hangar at Sarasota's International Airport. M&M did not fly private aircraft. He actually liked commercial and had met a lot of promising young prospects among the crews and fellow passengers. As he walked out of the concourse he saw a Latin-looking man holding up a large bag of M&Ms. He appreciated Marco's sense of humor and walked towards the man. He simply said hello and handed the man his claim ticket. In a few minutes they were on their way to meet Marco at the FBO that hangared the Bombardier. Marco was reminded instantly of Robin Williams in The Bird Cage. The similarity of physical appearance and mannerisms was uncanny. M&M was quite a character and Marco had to remind himself that he was in front of a very powerful, ruthless, and influential person. M&M shook hands with Marco and gallantly kissed Patricia's hand

"I trust you had a good trip?" asked Patricia

"Most pleasant indeed," said M&M in perfect British English. "Swiss Air does not disappoint and the hop over from Miami was just a tad inconvenient. I'm so looking forward to our meetings, and perhaps a few hours of fishing?"

"You are here at the very early part of the tarpon season in Sarasota. It peaks in June, but you can catch the first migrants that are sometimes the largest of the season, and there are snook and redfish in abundance…you'll love it."

"Oh my, I'm giddy with anticipation," chirped M&M. "I brought some flies but could I impose on you for a rod?"

This made both Patricia and Marco laugh. "There are more rods than furniture at the house. You must remember."

"Indeed I do. I just want to say that I'm so delighted that the new Mr. Carducci and you have found each other. I know Sal has to be happy, wherever he may be…he and I fished in Cuba just a month before he passed," said M&M thoughtfully. "People like us find few kindred souls in our journey."

The trip to the house was uneventful and Matilde was at the door twittering with excitement. Luigi, Pete, and Jose took in everyone's luggage and accommodated M&M in the guest house. They gave him plenty of time to rest and do his ablutions, and agreed to meet at the main house by the terrace bar at seven that evening. As soon as Marco arrived home he went to his office, checked emails, and called Special Agent Delany.

"Well, excellent timing," he said. "I'm here in Sarasota trying to track down our dodgy monsignor. We located the place where he was staying and found what must have been most of his luggage but no documents, money, or weapons. We have the place staked out but I think he made the cops and skedaddled. I also think he's still in the area. With the information at hand you could ask for police protection," offered Joseph.

"No need, but thank you anyway." They both knew that was a formality. "But I do think we should meet as soon as possible. I have someone here I'd like you to meet," answered Marco.

"Funny you should say that. I have someone I would like you to meet. He's a detective from Kansas City who was on the Meredith case and is looking for Testa also."

"Well, what about dinner tonight, here at my house. I assume you have the address," said Marco somewhat facetiously, knowing that

Delany had been the head of a taskforce that had investigated him.

"That I do," answered Joseph, "there is no one on your case right now so it shouldn't raise any eyebrows in the wrong places. I'll see you around seven?"

"Seven is fine, bring the detective," said Marco and hung up.

Marco told Patricia about the call and asked her to tell Matilde it would be them, the two policemen, and M&M for dinner. The bodyguards would take their dinner in the kitchen.

"Inside or out on the terrace?" asked Patricia.

"Let's do this inside just in case. I'll talk to Luigi about security. I want cellphone jammers and reverberation scramblers just in case somebody is listening in."

* * *

Ian Carlo, Ernie, and Samuel were deep into the details of the presentation they had prepared for the other families. Like in all other businesses, some had strengths and capabilities in one area, others in another It was important to present opportunities to each group's expertise. Ian Carlo was surprised at the detail with which everything was put together. The accounting for the Carducci darker enterprises was done overseas by different accounting firms for different rackets. Bringing it all together in a cohesive and understandable format was a titanic enterprise. Ian Carlo realized that he had found in Samuel what Sal had found in Ernie. This would be most important when Ian Carlo took the step they were planning. These things were long term and even though Ernie was vital he was getting old and sooner rather than later he would be less effective. Fortunately Samuel was there to take up the slack.

"This brings us to the most difficult part of the presentation," Ian Carlo summarized for the umpteenth time to Samuel and Ernie. "Why am I doing this? I think we let greed get the better of these people and then we ask if what we're thinking of has their approval. Respect goes a long way with these men, but greed goes a lot further. Here we feed both their demons."

"Yes, and here are the rules of the game," said Ernie, picking up from Ian Carlo. "If they approve, they get their part of your business; they all have to approve or no deal; if there is no deal, we go back to business as usual; the rules are put on the table before we present anything. Once that is clear we make our presentation and ask for their acquiescence. Then we all discuss your run for office and we show the advantages that they would have with their man in office…whichever that may be. Then very tactfully we have to address the big question. Will they still be receiving the two major services from Carducci? Will they be able to convert their assets as they have been recently? Will they be getting quality merchandise at competitive prices?"

"I gave that a lot of thought," said Ian Carlo, "and Marco came up with an idea. We explain to them that all movement is done by flash drives that can only be read on encoded laptops or tablets that have no connection to the web. If the encoding perceives external contact it automatically erases everything. New encoding is also done by flash drive on a regular basis. These drives are useless to anybody else that might get their hands on one. I can claim that it was the way I operated and that now they would be directly approached by the source, whoever they may be. The benefit to them will be obvious. It also gets me off the hook as to giving them my source. It's simple really. We are adding the New York families to Tommy Lee and Maurizio Lorenzana and taking us out of the equation as far as they are concerned."

"This can fly," said Samuel and Ernie agreed. "Now it's really a question of finding the right moment to call this meeting."

* * *

Marco and Patricia were talking just before their guests arrived. "Did you know this M&M fellow well?" asked Marco.

"Not really. He and Sal went fishing once in a while. He's a real enthusiast. He stayed here a couple of times but other than small talk I really didn't have much to say to him. I think Sal used him as a source for information and I know my father has for years. That's how Sal met M&M, through my father."

"So M&M wants to meet Delany and just by chance the man is here. What can this guy want with an FBI agent?"

"Use him, would be my guess. People like M&M do nothing if it's not for profit in some way or another. Anyway, I feel I should stay in grace with M&M; honestly he scares the crap out of me."

They went down to the terrace and found that M&M was already there with drink in hand, talking animatedly with Matilde, who shrieked with laughter at everything the man said in her native language. When he was aware of their presence he switched to English and said that Matilde was telling him about their uncomfortable romance and how totally adorable she found them in their naive ways. In Panama the brother or nephew would have moved in with the widow after a few days…whether he was married or not. After all it was the right thing to do.

Marco looked at Matilde but saw no malice in her and had to laugh along with the others. Patricia wasn't embarrassed so why should he be?

"I see you know your way around so please make yourself at home. I know you want to meet Special Agent Delany and…"

"I would very much appreciate it if you could arrange that meeting. I'll go to DC when necessary," interrupted M&M.

"There is no need for that," said Marco. "He will join us for dinner tonight."

M&M was speechless for the first time in years.

The door opened before the two men rang the bell and they were welcomed by Luigi, who was playing butler for the evening. They were escorted directly to the terrace where Marco, Patricia, and a somewhat European-looking man awaited them. Introductions were made and drinks were offered. All of those present were accustomed to wealth except for Detective Amiable Manning, who could not believe his eyes at the luxury of this place. He lived in a small, rented two-bedroom apartment in Evansville that was filled with books and his collection of blues records, tapes, and CDs. If he had known this house was built with money from activities he had fought against his entire career he might have admired it less.

Luigi came around with a tray of tiny lamb chops covered in mustard infused cornbread crumbs and fresh plums filled with brie.

"If these are the appetizers dinner must be cooked in heaven," said M&M, who with that remark caught Amiable Manning looking at him. Was he maybe a soul to search?

"I have been hoping to meet you, Special Agent Delany. We have some things to discuss."

"I wasn't aware we knew each other," said Delany, somewhat taken aback.

"Not personally, no," said M&M, "but some notes I've sent you over the last year or so have been useful, no? But don't give it a thought right now. We have time to talk about this later. Now we must enjoy this company and the fantastic meal we are being offered by our graceful hostess."

"Talking of food, Matilde is signaling me that dinner is ready. Shall we sit down? Mr. Manning at my side to the right and Marcelo at my left if you please." Patricia had caught a flash between the two.

M&M almost had a conniption; nobody had called him Marcelo in years, yet this extraordinary woman did it with such grace...so he thanked her and proceeded to his place. Amiable was dumbstruck so all he did was nod and follow suit. Marco sat next to Delany and an empty chair. The meal was supposed to be informal but everything that Patricia did had a feeling of elegance, class and exclusivity. The starter was a chilled cucumber soup with avocado chunks and cilantro. The main dish was roast beef on the bone and small pan-fried yellowtail snappers accompanied by miniature baked potatoes and a watermelon, jicama, and spinach salad with passionfruit vinaigrette. The dessert was cherimoya ice cream with blueberry sauce served on chocolate sponge cake. Coffee was served at the bar so those who wanted private conversations could go pair off.

"The notes I have sent you over the last year have been useful to you, Joseph, yes?"

"They have, Marcelo, very much so. While I can't do much about the cardinal, it stopped me from going off in a wild goose chase."

"Please call me M&M, I like the moniker, it gives me separation from the mundane. And the other information I have been sending you through Marco? It has been useful, no?"

"OK, M&M it is. You know how that has turned out. My success is in great part due to your help and Marco's. What I'd like to know is why...apart from the obvious that is."

"The obvious?"

"Yes, you may someday need me and I will owe you. And if I can I will help."

"I, dear Joseph, am like an elephant. I don't forget and I don't forgive. Your father was a client and a friend who kept me informed of certain activities of the Royal Saudi family, with whom he had special relations. I in exchange made his progress within the political body... easier. He was eliminated because of that. The people that did it were Cardinal Dupree, Archibald Mason, and your brother-in-law in the United States, and Lord Humphrey Houghton in the UK. They have been using the expansionism and ruthlessness of the Meredith family and when they in turn changed alliances they killed Ana. Now the cardinal has Edward Meredith in his pocket. But I digress...as I said, I don't forget and I don't forgive. Because of my...hmm...peculiarities, Humphreys and Mason have snubbed me in public and treated me like dirt and I will not let it stand as such."

"Yes, you made me aware of this early on. Terry Taylor is in jail. My sister is divorcing him and the jewelry he stole was found in an attorney's safety deposit box. Taylor used it to pay for a contract on my life."

"So we have Archibald Mason still at large...no?"

"He has been trying to get in touch with me and I have been avoiding him. But he is a sitting senator and there is little I can do about him."

"Here is where my small contribution may be of help; that is, information and advice. Uncle Archie, I think you called him, has a peccadillo that he keeps very close to his chest...but not close enough. He is a consummated child pornographer. He has a collection of active pornography of little girls in particular that he keeps at arm's length through his chief of staff. There is a small apartment in Rockville, Maryland, rented to a sister of the chief of staff. In it you will find this collection."

"The difficult part will be to link him to the collection once we find it," said Joseph.

"True, but he does go there once in a while. He cannot stay away. He has to be caught when he is watching this filth, red-handed you might say. Let me explain how he does it..."

* * *

Patricia and Detective Manning were doing a tour of the house. For Amiable it was like visiting paradise. He had seen the luxurious home of the Meredith, but it was dark and stuffy, full of tired old furniture and pictures of people long dead and not happy when they lived. On the other hand this house was alive with happiness; it craved the voices of joyful children, of the celebration of life. Amiable looked at every detail with the eyes of one whose life centered on detail. The more he saw the more he liked the people that lived in this place. Patricia took him through the vine cellar, which was a hoot for Amiable, whose idea of having wine was a white in the fridge and a red in the cupboard. The semi-basement where the fishing tackle was kept was completely foreign to him, as the only memory he had of the sport was once with his father on a long forgotten vacation, trying to catch bluegills in a pond. He did not envy this but felt happy that Patricia and her husband had such a place to love. It was the nature of the man; he was possessed of a natural goodness so distant from the lives of the victims for whom he sought justice and perpetrators whom he relentlessly pursued. In his thirty-three years of life, Amiable had loved only once. His heart had been captured by a boy a couple of years his senior in high school, a jock who had seduced him, used him, and dumped him unceremoniously. He had repressed it and never again allowed himself such pain, but today he could not keep his eyes off the elegant European, who, while occupied with Joseph, managed to glance at him occasionally. What he felt was as alien as the man himself, yet this was something that stirred deep within him and made him catch his eye again and again.

Marco was watching M&M talking to Joseph Delany; probably setting him up for future possibilities he thought. Elsewhere, Manning was following Patricia through the room; he could see the detective was fascinated with the house. Probably the first time to Florida, he thought. He also noticed the visual tag that Manning and M&M were playing, looking, dodging, looking again…well to each his own, he said to himself.

After a while Patricia brought Manning back to where Marco was and they started talking about the troubling man who had brought them all together. Marco told Amiable about the attacks on him and Patricia in the restaurant in Sarasota and the thin escape they had on the *Toscana*. The detective told Marco – without sparing a detail – the gruesome murder of Ana Meredith and the sequence of clues and luck that had brought him to conclude that the murderer was Monsignor Enrico Testa, in spite of the multiplicity of identities the man used. They were in that conversation when the whole group came together and the discussion about Testa continued.

"We have traced the activities of the cardinal's hit man to eight years ago when he first went to the Vatican to assist Dupree in a disciplinary arm of the Church. I can tell you that more than one unrepentant pedophile died in questionable circumstances when Testa was around," said M&M.

"Who is this cardinal?" asked Amiable with certain alarm.

"Oh, excuse me, detective, I was unaware that you did not know that Testa is a servant of a most nefarious and powerful cardinal of the Catholic Church, His Eminence Jean Dupree of the Vatican Bank."

Amiable looked to Delany for confirmation.

"He killed my parents, Amiable, for business reasons I believe. He came to their house for dinner and the monsignor that follows him around poisoned them. It was M&M here who told me about it, but it was a dog that I had for brother-in-law who confirmed it. And now he's here in Sarasota again," said Delany. "I just received a text confirming the DNA sample taken from a brush in the motel room. It's Testa alright; no doubt about it, and he's in the wind."

"We have reviewed the security measures here but there is no such thing as impregnable," said Marco. "By the way, Detective, where are you staying?"

"I'm at a Residence Inn just off 441, not far from where Testa was holed up."

"Well," said Patricia "that just won't do. If Testa knows you're after him that place is not protectable. You must stay with us. The guest quarters are ample. I'll have Jose bring your things and cancel the room."

"Oh! But I couldn't," said Amiable. "I'm here on special leave to pursue the Ana Meredith murder and the department will pick up the bill."

"It's not my place to insist," said M&M, "but I do...don't I, Patricia?"

"We all do," said Marco, "let's get Jose cracking on this. It'll only take about an hour. We can have a drink in the meantime."

M&M smiled and smiled and smiled...

"You are also welcome, Joseph," said Marco.

"Thank you, I have a suite at the Ritz-Carlton at Federal expense and it's only five minutes away. I have FBI and SPD protection there, but thank you again for the kind invitation; perhaps another time."

Drinks were served, the conversation continued, the luggage was fetched and the SPD detail deposited Special Agent Delany safely at his hotel. All the others retired to their beds. It had been a long day.

* * *

As dawn cracked inland the sun caught Testa already out of his tent and stretching his limbs on the beach for his morning run. It would be fast and short because he had a distance to paddle in order to get to his netting among the mangroves across the harbor from the Carducci home. When he got there he realized that the house was alive with activity and decided to keep paddling until he had covered the whole place from the water. The shutters were gone and he could see the maid and a man setting up a table on the terrace. Breakfast, he thought; all he had eaten was a power bar and a bottle of water. That would be his lunch also. He went back to the mangroves, pushed the kayak in as deep as it would go, and climbed on the netting and accommodated himself as best he could. He was excited. Carducci and his woman were here. They had hours to live and they didn't know it. He felt tense with anticipation like a lion hiding in the grass, stalking the gazelle that would be his meal, not missing a detail of his victim's movements, waiting patiently for the right moment.

Waiting.

23

Matilde went about her preparations for breakfast riding herd on Luigi, Pete, and now Jose. She set the table on the terrace because it was a beautiful spring day and Ms. Patricia and the patron would enjoy it. She was ever so happy to see them together. When the old patron had died she had felt terrible for her but now she was as happy and radiant as could be. Radiant, she thought…hmmm.

She set up fruit and juices, a bottle of Prosecco in case someone had a hangover, and set two French presses with coffee and decaf to which she would add boiling water when they were all seated. Her breakfast specialty, corn "arepas" with mozzarella cheese melted in and topped with sunny-side-up eggs would be prepared and served when they were all eating their fruit. If anyone ordered she could produce hot chocolate or tea in minutes. She and the men had eaten early before they had gone out to check on security. Pete had already prepared the skiff because one of the guests was going fishing, so breakfast would be served at seven-thirty this morning.

Again M&M was the first to arrive. He was dressed head to toe in Ex-Officio fishing wear. Gray pants, green shirt, breathing underwear…and Crocs. He had a tackle case with his flies, and hanging in back- a full protection fishing cap, also from Ex-Officio. The man was serious about keeping the sun from frying his skin. The next to arrive was Patricia, who went about checking that everything was to her liking. The Latin-American woman in her demanded it. Then Amiable showed up and he exchanged air kisses with Patricia, said hello to Matilde and Luigi, then went to stand next to M&M. Neither of them said a word. Marco was the last one to arrive and went directly to where M&M and Amiable Manning were standing.

"Good morning, did you have a good night?"

"Wonderful, simply wonderful," said M&M.

"Thank you, fine," said Amiable, who was flushed red!

"We had a few drinks after you all went to bed and maybe it was a bit too much for the detective here," said M&M, trying to distract from the obvious.

Breakfast was served. The arepas were a hit and M&M gobbled up two of them, had his coffee and begged off because "the fish are out there and I'm over here" and practically ran to the dock where Pete was ready with the skiff.

"Why didn't you go with him?" Marco asked Patricia.

"Oh no, he's too intense and he honestly prefers to go alone the first day to get to know his guide. M&M takes fishing more seriously than anyone I've ever met," answered Patricia.

"Agent Delany is picking me up," said Amiable, finding words with some difficulty. "We're going to…"

At that moment Joseph entered, escorted by Jose.

"I hope there is some coffee left, I ran out without a second cup," said Joseph, looking at Patricia, who smiled and indicated a chair in front of which Matilde was setting up for him. He helped himself to an arepa without shyness and poured himself a large mug of coffee and a glass of orange juice.

"I know this place is super protected, but I assume so was the *Toscana* and this maniac still managed to get to you. He killed Ana Meredith inside her own bedroom and left without any of the perimeter security people or cameras seeing him. If it wasn't by mere chance that the gardener from across the road saw him, we would never have known it was him. We also received a report on some broker that was murdered in his own toilet. It turns out he had some skin under his fingernails and the DNA report tells us it was our Monsignor Testa who was trying to flush the man down. Funny thing is, he worked for Edward Meredith. Coincidence? – I doubt it. It sounds to me that the cardinal was helping Meredith clean house after the old lady was out."

"Which makes me wonder if the son had a hand in his mother's killing," said Amiable Manning.

"My point," added Delany, "is that you can't let your guard down."

"Not for a second," answered Marco. "We have reviewed every detail with Allen Security and we can't find a flaw...naturally that doesn't mean that there isn't one, but we're doing everything foreseeable. We even have undercover "tourists" on the beach and electronic surveillance including satellite sweeps every three minutes."

"Well then, we'll be on our way. The detective and I have a new lead to follow. A partial ID showed up at the cash register of a Sports Authority. We're going over to see the tape and talk to the people there. I'll let you know what's up." Then he and Amiable left with the SPD detail.

* * *

Testa was sitting inside the mangrove canopy that had become a home away from home for him. Even the critters had become accustomed to him and a night heron fished peacefully by his feet. A big, beautiful iguana shared a power bar with him and snook swam around fearlessly. He watched the breakfast come and go and observed as one of the guests who he did not recognize went off in a fishing skiff with one of the men he had seen doing security patrols. As he sat there a plan started to form in his head. He went over and over it again, checking for faults until he was pretty sure that it would work.

* * *

The people at the Sports Authority were very cooperative and both the FBI agent and the detective from Kansas were looking at the security tape. The man with white-blond hair under a baseball cap and wraparound sunglasses had pinged the facial biometrics but as much as they looked this guy could not be positively matched to any of the photos of Enrico Testa. The man had bought a small tent, sleeping bag, lantern, batteries, water, cord saws, all-in-one fishing gear, power bars, and a sling spear. The last could be considered a weapon but was nothing out of the ordinary. He had paid in cash a total of $287.50 and never looked at the camera. On the way out he had his head down while examining his purchases and no more was seen of him.

"That didn't help much" said Delany as they left the shop with a copy of the tape and the bill.

"I'm not too sure about that," said Amiable. "If he knows we're on to him he won't go to a hotel and the things he bought means that he can be camping out somewhere. The problem is that there are hundreds of places where he could be."

"In that case I suggest we start looking from the Carducci house outwards progressively and see if we hit pay dirt. Let's go to SPD headquarters and brief them on this. They can do the legwork and we can follow up if they find anything suspicious."

* * *

Marco and Patricia spent the whole day following up on their respective businesses. Patricia was looking at the southern harvest that was just about completed while Marco was reviewing his encoded mail systems that were now on the secure servers that Francisco Lujan's organization had. All of the Carducci communications were being routed through there, which meant that the electronic digging that NSA and other interested parties were doing was hitting a very hard and permanently changing wall. Among the many routine emails, the reports from Leon, and updates from Ian Carlo, Marco found a rather cryptic and intriguing one from a Mr. John

Convers of the British Overseas Investment Bank. He asked for a meeting, in person, as soon as possible. He had signed it Chair Person and Director.

* * *

Toby Carson had been working for Special Agent Joseph Delany for a few weeks since he had wisely sent him a heads up on the subject he was searching for through the facial identification program. The only thing was that so far it was really boring. All he did was review cases that were being investigated by FBI offices all over the country and prepare hundred-word briefs for Delany. Some were interesting but most were terribly mundane and repetitive; that is, until today. Toby had been instructed by Special Agent Delany, his SAC, to join seven other agents on a special surveillance detail. He could hardly believe the target of this stakeout and the difficulty that it implied.

Since their two sons had left for college, Archibald Mason and his wife Cristina had found each other's company increasingly unbearable and as discreetly as they could, separated and then divorced. The senator maintained what appeared to be an exemplary life of dedication to duty and service to the state; but today was one of his special days. He left his office a little after five and headed for the Round Robin Bar at the Willard Hotel. There he met with a lady friend with whom he had an occasional rendezvous, which was no news to the reporters that staked out the place. When they left the bar for the elevators nobody noticed. Once inside the room the senator shed his clothes and put on a white waistjacket like those used by the room service attendants. He left the lady watching television and slipped out of the room, holding a tray and keeping his face away from the cameras. He went to the service elevator and again avoided the camera behind the mirror on the upper corner. He got off in the basement and walked out to a loading platform, covering his face as if lighting a cigarette; the old worker catches a smoke and a few minutes rest. A car came to the back and the senator got into the passenger seat. It headed west and a few blocks away the driver got out and Archie took the wheel. He headed for Maryland.

Several cars back at a discreet distance, Toby and a female agent named Betsy Blues followed the senator's car. They had almost missed him when he came out, confusing him for whom he was supposed to be, a worker taking a break, except that Toby was on his toes and insisted that the target had just gotten into the car that was leaving. Betsy was smart enough to defer to Toby and followed the Buick as it left the alley and headed west. They saw the driver get out and Archibald Mason move to the driver's seat. An oncoming car illuminated his face and the agents got their positive ID. They followed the senator to a small apartment building in Rockville just a block from the mall. They waited outside until a light went on. They checked the door for names on the third floor and only 3C had no name. They made a note of this and waited until the senator left two hours later and followed him. They observed the same routine but in reverse until finally Archibald Mason came out the front door of the Willard and headed home.

* * *

M&M came back from his fishing at about noon. The morning had been slow and only one small school of tarpon had been seen, and they had no interest in the fly. Pete had moved onto a grass flat where he picked up a few redfish and a small snook but it was not what M&M was looking for. Later that afternoon he would try again and see if the change in tide would bring better luck. He joined Marco and Patricia for lunch and treated himself to a long siesta. That Amiable, he thought as he drifted off to sleep...what an intriguing and delightful person.

Just when Delany and Manning were going out to have a bite they got a call from one of the patrol cars that were checking out the camping places. It was not a long drive and they decided to check it out first. The Gulf Beach Campground and Water Sports Rental was only a couple of miles from the Carducci home...maybe less by water. The manager had identified the photo from the Sports Authority film and took the officers to a small campsite that held the bare minimum equipment: a one person pop-up tent, a flimsy sleeping bag, some water bottles, a half-empty box of power bars, and a cheap fishing rod and reel with a box of jigs and lures. That was it. The manager said that he didn't know which car belonged to this guy as they were all parked away from the site. Most of the campers were out and probably wouldn't be back until late. He hadn't seen the man that day and had no idea where he could be.

"This guy's gotta be stalking the house from somewhere but I don't see the point. It's a fortress," said Delany.

"It has to be from the beach or the water somewhere. The front offers no view other than a solid wall and the side is that harbor where they keep their boat, and that's wide open." Manning pointed out.

"Then it has to be the beach. Who's out there?" asked Joseph.

"I don't know…it's one of your people and a policewoman from SPD."

Delany called the FBI office and got the cell for the agent on the stakeout.

"Agent Frost, this is Special Agent Delany. We have reason to think that the suspect will be using the beach or the water to check out the house. Have you seen anybody or anything even mildly suspicious?"

"No sir, the beach is practically empty; a mother with two kids, some older couples playing cards, and a few fishermen down a hundred feet from where we are."

"I want you to check out the fishermen and call me back."

"We did that already. We walked past them twice and there's nothing odd about them. Both are much younger than the suspect, kids really."

"Are there any boats around?"

"Nothing at all; we saw a couple of kayaks earlier but they kept on going and we lost them around the point north of the house.

Lots of boats go by but far out from the beach."

"OK, keep sharp; you should be replaced in an hour or so. Tell your replacements to stay on their toes."

"Yes sir."

'Not knowing what Testa is up to gives me the creeps," said Delany. "We are talking about a cold-blooded killer with the highest training our beloved country can give a man to do that job and not someone that will give up because there are some guards and a few cameras."

'I hear you," said Amiable, "but whatever he's planning, it'll be soon. Nobody can live for long on what he has here."

When Testa saw the skiff leave the house and head north he made two calls, one confirming a transfer and the other to give his hired help the go-ahead. It was just a few minutes before four in the afternoon. He would have his people ready to go around six.

Delany called Marco and gave him an update on their day, and warned him that there was going to be some action soon and that he should take Patricia and leave the house.

"Maybe that's just what he wants us to do," said Marco. "I feel safer here. I'll alert the security company and we will be attentive, but leaving is not an option."

"We should be there about seven in the evening, we have a status meeting with the SPD but that should not take long and it's about twenty minutes from your place, so expect us around that time."

"Be hungry, there will be dinner," said Marco and hung up.

24

As the skiff meandered north M&M thought about last night. He and Amiable drank a couple of bottles of excellent Malbec and talked deep into the night. The boy had opened his soul to him and M&M had found it a treasure to be harvested with care and understanding. Any consummation of his lust would have to wait until Amiable really understood who he was and what he wanted. Until then he would exercise his well-honed patience.

M&M and Pete had been searching the water, looking for the torpedo shapes of tarpon on the move or maybe tarpon rolling on the surface.

"There's a patch of nervous water at two o'clock," said Pete pointing twenty feet left of where the tide ran through a pass rushing water into deeper contours that edged the flat.

"I see it, but this angle doesn't let us see the fish, cut the engine and we can use the trolling motor and see if it's as good as you say..."

"There...see that roll?"

"Yes, got it!" said M&M getting ready.

He had 40 feet of loosely coiled line at his feet, the rod out at 90° and a 15-foot loop of line dragging along. In his left hand he had a few loops of line and the fly held lightly between his thumb and forefinger. One back cast would be enough to take the fly high in back and ready the cast. Pete angled the skiff to give M&M the best possible shot at the oncoming fish, of which they could only see their backs and occasional tailfin as they rolled towards them. Baitfish took to the air, clearing away from the string of tarpon. M&M made the needed back cast to get the line and fly airborne and the rod loaded. He made one false cast forward, then another, and landed the cockroach fly right in the path of the lead fish. The tarpon veered off and opened its huge maw to inhale the tiny fly. M&M saw the take, waited a few seconds, and then grabbed the line in his left hand and jerked it hard away from the fish in a strip strike to set the hook. He hit the fish with three more strip strikes before all hell broke loose. The line turned rigid…and a second later what erupted out of the water was a submarine heading for the sky, except that it had a huge mouth and blood-red gills that could be seen under the flapping chrome gill-covers that clacked as the fish shook its head.

Neither of the two men on the skiff could believe their eyes. This was the biggest tarpon either man had ever seen. It had to ex- ceed two hundred pounds and the 16-pound class-tippet suddenly seemed like a thread leash for a St. Bernard. It was going to take ev- ery bit of skill from both men to get this fish to the boat before one of the knots failed or the tippet itself snapped.

M&M gained on the fish with help from Pete who used the troll- ing motor expertly, and the tarpon jumped again not thirty feet from the boat. M&M bowed deeply to his flying majesty. It was even more impressive up close. Its silver flank and dark back spoke of a mature fish that had swum this migration many times and most probably lived through this experience before. M&M and the fish traded glances and continued with the battle. It was up close and personal. The fish would not run but held its ground, jumping only once more in hope of dislodging the hook that was well stuck into the corner of its lower jaw. M&M held the rod down with the tip close to the water, trying to anticipate and counter any roll that would give new air to the behemoth. Suddenly the fish changed its tactic and, peeling line from the reel at a nauseating rate, headed for deeper water. It used the current of the pass to its advantage and Pete tried to follow, poling as fast as he could and then with the trolling motor, but it was of no avail. In desperation M&M applied maximum pressure to the drag and, using the butt of his rod, put as much force to the side as he dared to see if he could turn the fish's heading.

Then...a muffled snap and the line went limp, followed almost instantly by M&M's very spirit. It was nearly too much to take. Both men stood silently, thinking of what could have been, regretting moves, recounting ifs, but the tarpon was nothing but the memory that haunts the few lucky anglers who have glimpsed the impossible dream, if only for a moment.

The afternoon dragged by at the Carducci home. Marco and Patricia had spent it working. They didn't need to pay attention to their guests and there was nothing more that could be done about the crazy priest. They knew he was coming and they were ready for him; or at least as ready as they could be. Marco thought about this. He had everything that money could buy protecting his home and their lives, yet he had the lingering thought that a determined man with no fear for his own life could breach these gates of heaven...

Delany and Manning listened to the reports of the SPD and the FBI contingencies that had worked all day on finding Testa. After locating the campsite they had combed the beach; water patrols then ran continuously up and down the adjacent miles of water from the Carducci home. There was nothing out of the ordinary. The patrols would be out until late but nothing was expected. Even a SPD helicopter had flown several overpasses around the house, the harbor, the mangroves and adjacent properties; nothing. No one had any new ideas; maybe Testa had seen it was an impossible feat and left the area.

Patricia looked at her watch and saw that it was almost six in the evening. She went to the kitchen to see if Matilde had dinner under control and, satisfied, headed to the bathroom for a shower and change of clothes for when their guests arrived. She was quite fond of the young detective. He was such a contrast of smart and naïve that made her maternal instincts subvert her cool. M&M was a character for sure and she wondered if he had returned yet from fishing. The man was very independent and made himself at home without being in the least intrusive. She liked that in a houseguest. Then there was Delany, a forceful person but not offensive. He was non-judgmental and treated everyone with respect but there was a coldness about him that spoke of repressed anger and defensiveness. She wondered who or what had wounded his soul.

Marco finished a long email to Leon on the international corporations, particularly the Canadian ones, and asked a series of questions about Scorpio Multimodal Transport Brokers since they had taken over the logistics of all of the Lujan and Carducci wine and the southern harvest promised to be a large one. Tired of working and tense with the thought of Testa, Marco felt like a swim. He changed into trunks and headed for the pool.

* * *

M&M had cast to several other schools of tarpon that swam by deep and at an increasing speed, sensing the change of tide and ignoring his efforts. With his soul still drained from the loss of the giant tarpon that had escaped him, he decided to head back to the house to clean up and change for dinner. He looked forward to that. The table at the Carducci was exceptional and the vine unsurpassable, not to mention the great company that all of these people turned out to be...well, all but Delany; he was elusive to say that least.

Pete pulled up the pole, rose, and shackled the trolling motor and cleared the deck for the run home. He started the big engine, which responded with a deep rumble, and quickly coaxed the skiff onto a plane heading south. The trip was only a twenty-minute ride but towards the end he would have to be extra careful with the low tide as he approached the point just north of the harbor. The water was calm and the sun was just above the horizon when he started south. By the time he reached the curve along the mangroves that led to the point it was beginning to get dark. The long shadows melted into dusk and then disappeared altogether when all that remained was the luminous horizon after the sunset.

When they reached the point Pete stood up to keep a better view of the pass and slowed the flatsboat to maybe five miles an hour. As the bow came back down he noticed a kayak adrift just by the point. Some idiot must have left it untethered and now it had become a hazard. Pete slowed down even more to avoid hitting it.

As he maneuvered the big skiff around the kayak an explosion of water burst from behind it and then he felt an impact on his right shoulder that sent him flying out of the boat and into the shallow water. He was disoriented but found the bottom with his feet and instinctively went for his gun only to discover that he had no use of his right arm. He felt with his left hand the place where the pain was centered and touched the spear that was imbedded in him. He tried to reach for the gun with his left hand but there was nothing in the holster. At that moment he heard the engine accelerate and the skiff depart. There was little he could do.

M&M was paralyzed with fear; he was non-violent at a personal level and was overwhelmed by the sudden and unexpected attack. In seconds Pete was no longer there and a man dressed only in trunks and a T-shirt jumped into the boat and showed M&M a knife.

"Stay still and you might live to see another day," said Testa to the terrified passenger, who only looked at him without uttering a word.

Testa took a cell phone out of a small waterproof pouch, auto-dialed a number, and said "now" into the mouthpiece and threw the phone overboard. He moved behind the center console of the skiff and inserted a plastic "key" into the emergency shut down plug vacated by Pete when he fell off. Testa started the engine and motored slowly back north until he was about 200 feet back, where he had shot Pete out of the boat with his speargun. There he shifted the engine back into idle and waited for his hired help to put up their show.

In a few minutes the calm waters in front of the Carducci home were invaded by a couple of jet skis that were jumping and doing stunts over each other's wake. They went north and suddenly turned into the harbor and headed for the dock at full speed. They did serpentines and tight circles and generated all the necessary alarms among the security detail of the house. Armed guards appeared from nowhere and waved the intruders away. The jet-skiers ignored them, knowing that the guards would not shoot at some rambunctious and probably drunk kids. They circled the harbor once more and then headed towards the beach in front of the house. The guards converged to the front that faced the beach so that they could make sure the jet skiers did not to go beyond the public area.

The FBI and SPD "beachgoers" went towards the intruders but could not interdict them as no law had been broken; the waters of the harbor were considered public, as was the beach where they were now. Suddenly a third jet ski appeared and entered the harbor at full speed. It circled the tight area twice and slowed in front of the docks. Now the guards that were up front turned their attention to this third intruder, who again turned away and circled the harbor at full speed. In the meantime the ones that had gone onto the beach returned to their jet skis and joined the third one. At the same time as this was happening the skiff returned and headed for the dock. The jet skis played around at the entrance of the harbor and the beach in front of the house, keeping the attention of the guards on them. Little attention was given to the skiff or its passengers. They saw "Pete" tie the skiff to the dock and help the houseguest out. Everything normal there, and then the jet-ski trio entered the harbor again and continued carousing without paying any attention to the guards that kept shouting and signaling them to leave. Then, as fast as they arrived, they left and headed south along the beach. Everyone kept their eyes on them until they disappeared. Nobody noticed the angler and his guide enter the guest quarters.

M&M could do nothing but follow the man's instructions; the knife at his ribs was quite eloquent in that respect. He walked ahead at a normal pace, ignoring the jet skis and the guards that were trying to shoo them away and went directly to the guest quarters. They were empty, as Manning would only arrive later.

As they crossed the threshold Testa hit M&M behind the ear with the knife wielding hand and knocked him out. He gagged and bound him with plastic ties, and then he turned on the light and went to the closet, chose a shirt, and tried on a pair of shorts. They were loose but they would do; the shoes were too small so he had to go barefoot. He searched the place for weapons but found nothing, and then he walked out of the guesthouse and nonchalantly walked towards the pool area. There he saw Marco doing laps and Matilde setting table with the help of one of the bodyguards. He waited in the shadows for his chance. He needed Marco and the woman together so he could strike once and for all. If he did not survive the guards it wouldn't matter. Everything was in God's hands after he killed the pair.

* * *

Major Allan had received the heads-up on the jet-skiers that had invaded the Carducci harbor and had immediately gone to see the CCTV cameras of the area, but by the time he saw them, they were on the way out; it looked like it was just a bunch of crazy kids getting the last blast of the day. The skiff was docking and the occupants were getting off. All was normal, he ordered the guards back to their posts and told them to keep their eyes open. He was thinking about some way to close the harbor entrance so that this did not happen again. As he walked back to his office, there was something about the incident that bothered him. Something he saw that was skewed, so he decided to go back to the operations room and see the playback on the big screen.

Marco got out of the pool, toweled himself dry, and went to his room to get ready for dinner. He heard nothing of the commotion created by the jet-skiers and had his mind on Patricia, who at this moment should be naked in the shower, a thought that brought love and lust to his heart. With new spirits he climbed the stairs a little faster, his step younger. When he got to the huge suite he saw the bathroom open and heard the shower running, still time to join Patricia was the thought. From behind him, silent as a jaguar in the night, Enrico Testa approached Marco with one of the cord saws stretched taught between his hands. He had successfully followed Marco without anyone seeing him and he would now kill him quietly and then take care of the woman in the bathroom. He knew her name was Patricia Lujan but could only think of her as "the woman."

As Testa moved his hands to wrap the improvised garrote around Marco's neck and with one swift pull cut his throat down to the bone, Patricia appeared in the doorway wrapped in a towel that she held up with one hand. The sight of her made Testa hesitate for just an instant, enough for Marco to drop like a stone, leaving Testa to catch nothing but hair on the very top of his head and just miss getting scalped by the tense wire. Testa could not take his eyes off Patricia. She had dropped the towel and in combat stance was heading towards him. Marco rolled on the floor trying to get out of reach and when Testa went for him, Patricia went for Testa. She took two steps and jumped, coiling into a ball away from where feet and hands would shoot out with lethal force. Testa was forced back away from Marco to confront the attack. He bent backwards and let Patricia fly by him but she still managed to rabbit-punch him in the sternum as she went by. The punch hit him exactly in the ribs that she had broken during their short skirmish on the *Toscana*. Roaring with pain and fury, the Sword of God moved in a windmill of punches and kicks towards Patricia, who was already back in her stance.

She blocked his punches with forearms and hands while jumping up on the bed to avoid his kick. She landed one good kick to his chin and Testa flew backwards to be halted by the wall. He used it to catapult back and punched Patricia on the upper thigh before she could defend. The impact was brutal and sent shards of pain in all directions, but the worst was the numbness that slowed her down. She had only one option. Go to ground with the man. There Krav Maga would give her an advantage. She waited for his attack, which came in the form of a high kick aimed at her head. She raised her hand and forced the foot to pass over her head, and with her open hand she went for his testicles, but there was nothing there. She grabbed the shorts and twisted, pushing herself as best she could with her good leg and sent Testa to the ground. She went to jump on him with two elbows ready when Marco fell on the man ,doing exactly the same maneuver that she had taught him.

Both of Marco's elbows hit Testa on his chest and abdomen, but the lack of expertise in this form of combat softened the impact and Testa was up before Marco could get hold of him. Testa was now in a full combat state of mind. These people were not easy to kill and he respected enemies who could hold their own; but God wanted them dead and he would not leave until his will was done. Testa knew that the real opponent here was the woman. Carducci could hold his own but wasn't really a problem; he had to deal with her first.

Testa feigned an attack at Marco and turning in the same motion sent his body flying towards Patricia, who had returned to a defensive stance when she anticipated his attack. She was ready for him but the sheer difference in mass favored the priest. They both fell to the ground, taking Patricia's dresser with them. Again Patricia kneed Testa in the balls and again found no reaction. The man had been totally castrated. She curled into a ball, knowing the two fisted attack that would come and the readiness that it would give her to counterattack the aggressor. Nothing happened. Testa was wriggling around and making horrible noises. Marco stood behind him, pulling hard on the garrote while Testa with his fingers on the wire tried to avoid being decapitated.

"Don't kill him, Marco," shouted Patricia while she roundhouse kicked the monsignor, hitting him with her heel on the left temple. The bone around the eye socket broke and the left eye popped out and hung by the optic nerve. The man was out.

It took a lot of willpower on Marco's side not to finish the job.

At that same instant the alarms went off in the house and its surroundings. Major Allen had set them off from the operations room when he saw what was amiss. On the dock, discarded on the decking, was a fly rod. Not in a million years would an experienced angler leave his gear abandoned that way, much less a guide. It meant that one or both of the people on the skiff were assailants. He hit the alarm and headed for his car. The noise brought M&M back to his senses and he realized that he was still alive. He got up using the wall as support and hopped out the door to see armed men running all over the place and then Luigi, who grabbed him and threw him back into his room, cut his bonds, and told him to stay put. He watched Luigi head up the stairs of the main house, and then nothing. The alarms were shut down and an eerie silence took over the place; only the occasional sob from Matilde punctuated the stillness.

A few seconds later Amiable Manning and Joseph Delany entered with guns in hand looking around and finding nothing. Jose came out of the staff quarters in his shorts, also holding a gun. Now there was an army of armed people looking for a target, who saw nothing, heard nothing. A few seconds later Luigi shouted that he and Marco were coming out so they wouldn't get shot by mistake. Everyone was looking at the main house as the two men half carried and half dragged another man to the terrace. They set him down on the floor and instantly were surrounded by Jose, Delany and Manning. They all watched the unconscious man and realized that they were looking at the elusive assassin that had been their quest for so long. Everyone was quiet. Suddenly Amiable Manning squatted down, grabbed the dangling eye, gave it a good yank and tossed it into a flower bed.

"That's for Ana," he said and walked to the guest quarters to see what had happened to M&M, leaving the others amazed at what just happened.

"Did you see that," asked Delany in general. "This guy of all people..."

Manning found M&M in his room, sitting on the bed rubbing the back of his head where Testa had knocked him with the knife. M&M told Amiable of the attack and he ran out to tell the others about Pete. In seconds, Luigi and Jose were running to the skiff. They took with them powerful lanterns and headed off in the direction that M&M had indicated the attack had taken place. They searched up and down the mangroves for an hour but found no trace of Pete. When they came back, disappointed and low on gas, it was Marco who told them that Pete was at Sarasota Memorial, where a couple of crab fishermen had taken him after they found him kneeling on a clam bed with the spear sticking out of his shoulder. It had been touch and go for a while but he was going to pull through. Marco had arranged for a private room and the best trauma doctor in the hospital to care for him, but the ER had done a great job and now Pete was resting in IC under the constant care of a private nurse.

25

They were all discussing the event, including Patricia, who was now dressed in T-shirt and shorts and joined them around the unconscious priest.

"He has no balls," said Patricia

"I wouldn't say that," answered Luigi, "it takes a lot of cojones to invade a property as well guarded as this one."

"I mean he has no balls...literally. As a matter of fact he has nothing there!" exclaimed Patricia.

Marco pulled the man's shorts down to find what looked like a deformed, scarred vagina between the powerful legs. Testa's sacrificial mutilation was there for all to see.

Major Allen arrived with reinforcements and left them at the perimeter while he joined the others around the Cyclops who remained unconscious. He had nothing to say. It was obvious that at some stage the man had overpowered the skiff and taken over, using it as a perfect subterfuge to invade the house. It was impossible, he thought, to make something perfectly impregnable to a decided assailant. Sooner or later a chink is found in the armor and the whole thing falls apart. It was a known truism of his trade; a hard one to swallow but true anyway.

At that moment Matilde came to them, discreetly knocked on

the door and inquired, "How many for dinner?"

Minutes later Patricia was on the phone with Francisco, Marco was on the phone with Ernie and Ian Carlo, Delany was reporting to the director of the FBI, and Manning was consoling M&M, who felt violated by the events of the day. How was it possible that he'd lost the giant tarpon?

Testa was placed in the custody of the FBI and flown directly to a special holding facility outside of Denver, Colorado, where he would be interrogated by specialists about the crimes for which he was accused. He was being held under the Title VIII Patriot Act, which did not require that he receive all the benefits of US Criminal Law and which would subject him to indefinite imprisonment without a trial. Even though Testa was a US citizen, his use of several passports of various nationalities gave the FBI time and leeway to interrogate Testa at their leisure in the hopes of having him compromise Cardinal Jean Dupree as the intellectual author of the crimes committed by him. The monsignor had been given primary care in Sarasota and then in Denver, though not much could be done for him. He would be a one eyed demon for the rest of his life.

* * *

M&M made sure that the cardinal received the news of Testa's capture and imprisonment with rich abundance of detail and relish. He also made sure that everyone in the Holy See received a full account of the monsignor's criminal activities, capture, and detainment, but without mentioning the cardinal directly as it could be counter-productive. Better to let the church bureaucracy reach their own conclusions.

Ian Carlo and Ernie decided to go with Samuel to Sarasota immediately and Francisco had told Patricia that he would be there as soon as he could arrange a flight, but she told him that the Bombardier would be on its way in an hour so that Francisco should be at the airport in about six hours. By tomorrow they would all be there. Agent Delany and Amiable Manning were on their way to their respective headquarters but M&M was invited to stay. He would be very valuable in what the Carducci were planning to do.

* * *

The following day was a write-off in regards to meetings because the police were in and out of the house all day, taking statements, and photos of the netting from where Testa had stalked the house, and of the abandoned kayak. These were the secondary details after the CSU had examined to exhaustion the main crime scene – which was the bedroom. The group stayed together but couldn't really talk about business. The meeting with the Carducci friends and family was set for noon of the following day so as to have lunch and start discussing their plans. It gave everyone a bit of down time to rest and take a swim. Marco, Patricia, and Luigi had gone to visit Pete at the hospital and found him well enough to get a full account of what had happened. They told him that Major Allen's people had found the netting in the mangroves where Testa had been hiding, probably for a couple of days. Now they had a complete picture of the resourcefulness and audacity of the priest. No wonder the cardinal held the man in such high regard. It would be a terrible loss for the elevated prelate not to have such an efficient weapon at his disposal.

* * *

His Eminence was having breakfast at his favorite café when a priest brought him the urgent dispatch with the news about the capture of Enrico Testa while attempting to kill the American businessman Marco Carducci. Interpol wanted an audience with his eminence at his earliest convenience and so did a special attaché of the US Embassy to the Vatican. Dupree did not care much about these but he knew and dreaded that His Holiness would want to see him in the course of the day. Lying to him was practically impossible. Dupree didn't really believe in God, much less in the God portrayed by the Judeo-Christian religions, but he fervently believed in the Catholic Church. He held it as the only true form of governance that could save humanity from itself by fostering a re-distribution of wealth, and he had dedicated his life to achieve that lofty goal. Now, this damn priest had gone off the rails and jeopardized everything. He had to think and maybe even pray, to whatever, in order to save something of his work. There were powerful people to whom he could reach, not all was lost. He still could save this. He finished his brioche and capucho and headed for his office at the IOR.

* * *

Within hours several high-ranking liberal politicians were ranting about Testa's human rights and a powerful law firm out of Chicago was presenting every form of relief petitions and habeas corpus to inconsequential courts, because if there has ever been an ironclad law in the US it's the Patriot Act. Testa was in the seventh circle of hell and nothing short of a presidential pardon would get him out of there. The assassination of a US senator and a high-ranking bureaucrat were acts of terrorism, period. The murders of others, while not government officials, were piled on to the charges because they were considered an overall terrorist conspiracy and carried more substantial evidence, such as testimonial witnesses and DNA results together with CSU reports from the different crime scenes. By design the attacks on Marco Carducci, including this last one at which Testa was captured, were minimized or didn't appear at all – such as the bombing of the Lear and the destruction of the *Toscana*.

While there was alarm about the vulnerability of such well-guarded places as the *Toscana* and the Sarasota house, there was also relief that the author of those attacks whose ability would be difficult to match, was out of the picture. Yet none of those present underestimated the persistence of the real enemies, the cardinal, Meredith, Humphrey Houghton, and the cadre of politicians that helped them. Francisco and Ernie were long in the battle with these people and knew that the war was yet to be won. Marco and

Patricia were new blood to the ranks and their contributions were already felt within the extended influence of The Board.

With the events of the past few months new factors appeared within the Carducci family and consequently upon The Board. The emotional alliance of Marco and Patricia, the possible extinction of the Carducci crime family from the New York organization, and the probable IPO of their legitimate operations were going to affect everything. The one thing that impacted everyone and everything and they didn't know about – but enjoyed the fruits thereof – was the existence of five pipelines that shuttled drugs to the US and cash south. These were the purview of the intimate circle of the now extended Carducci, which included Francisco and Patricia.

Those in the know were sitting together around the table in the Sarasota home of Marco Carducci and Patricia Lujan. Apart from these two there was Ian Carlo de la Rosa, Francisco Lujan, Ernie Goldman and Samuel Goldman; this last one was just to be inducted today. M&M was off fishing. The best guide in the area, Captain Brian Jill, had been contracted at a grand a day to keep the fixer busy for the next two days until he was brought in to discuss plans that did not include the pipelines. If he couldn't put M&M onto record tarpon, nobody could.

"What are the chances that these attacks are over?" asked Ernie

"The intention will still be there but the cardinal's capability of executing is highly diminished," answered Marco.

"There are always mercenaries," added Samuel.

"Yes, but the motivation that made Testa so dangerous will not be there," responded Patricia. "It is easier to defend against an army of mercenaries than against somebody like the monsignor."

"That's a historical fact," said Ian Carlo. "Lone assassins, deeply motivated, have had much more success than conspiracies or coordinated assaults by hired muscle. Ask Lincoln, Garfield, McKinley and Kennedy if you don't believe it," he added, listing the US presidents assassinated by lone, willful men.

"I'm afraid risk is part and parcel of our lives," added Francisco.

"Over time I have seen more than my fair share of violence. Since the horrendous murder of my wife by the Sendero Luminoso I have sheltered Patricia from the risks of my lifestyle, but now she has overcome my ability to do so and together with Marco they must face and defeat the challenges as they have done till now."

They were all in a reflective mood when Samuel spoke up.

"I have to ask all of you to concentrate on the challenges that the Carducci face in the near future," said Samuel. "I have some recommendations that I would like to present in regards to the decisions you have to make. First to consider is the divestment of all unlawful activities of the organization headed by Mr. de la Rosa and the conversion to public property of Carducci Enterprises. My recommendation is that the second take place first because if not, when the time comes to cede the illegal part of the business, the families that benefit from that may want to take over Carducci Enterprises as well. It's the nature of the beast and I estimate the possibilities of that outcome at a hundred percent.

"You're telling us that if we give the families what I manage, they will want us to give them what Marco manages, correct?"

"Exactly," added Ernie. "You know these people, everything is never enough. They'll split up your business and never look back, but they will go to war for what you don't offer...first against you and then each other. If the IPO has taken place, there is nothing they can do that would not bring the law down on them hard and fast."

"How long would this take?" a frustrated Marco asked.

"It's not so much the time but the way," Samuel explained. "First we have to divide the business into two groups, segregated if possible by affinity, and then these new groups, with different names, proceed to apply for the IPOs, one here in the US and the other in Canada, based on how the ownership of these has been structured. It's a big job but we have mapped it out with Leon Goddard and we think it's possible to do within six months for the US offering and eight months for the Canadian offering. The beauty of this is that we can press the sale if necessary through affiliated or friendly entities so the pre-marketing of the shares is not so onerous."

"There is a British investment banker I would like to discuss this with. When could we have some rough prospectus on the two groups?"

"Practically now. As I said we have this mapped out with Leon. Give me a week and we can give you a preliminary prospectus just for discussion purposes. Is that good for you?"

"Works for me; we should meet in New York a week from Monday. I'm flying from there to meet with the banker and this should give me an idea of what we can expect."

The group discussed the IPO and the succession of business to exhaustion, hoping to consider all the liabilities. Finally Francisco made a suggestion that made them re-think one of the plans.

"There's got to be someone in your organization who could take over your business, Ian Carlo, I don't think it's fair to your team to hand them over to other families where you don't know if they'll fit. And another thing; however this goes down, in the best perspective, your people will take a demotion. This could have repercussions."

"I know but traditionally there has never been a trade of leadership unless it's by default. That's not the case here. I'll still be around," said Ian Carlo.

"Don't you think that may be a problem in itself? Some people might think that if you're not around the deal is better sealed," asked Patricia.

"I can't say I haven't thought of this a lot, but nobody has the management capabilities or the respect of the others. This needs a natural leader and I don't see it among the *capos*, which is precisely why Sal had them there. He only trusted Marco and myself and didn't want anybody that thought strategically among the heads of the crews."

"How about Tommy Lee?" asked Marco.

By dinner time they had it hammered out. Ian Carlo would call Tommy to NYC and he, Ernie, and Samuel would sound the man out as a possible candidate. The advantage was that Tommy had proved himself time and again as a friend and a cool operator. The decision was something they could take after they drilled the man to make sure he had the mettle for a hike this big and if he had someone to take over in Vegas so as not to jeopardize the business there.

About six, M&M was back with a smile on his face; he had landed a couple of nice tarpon and it was like nothing had happened during his previous fishing expedition, which was only two days ago.

"I had a couple of good opportunities at migrating 'poons this morning and in the afternoon we went looking for resident fish inside the bay. It was fantastic. I don't know how to thank you," said M&M, who the day before had spent the whole afternoon with Pete at the hospital where they both talked about the great king that had escaped and never mentioned a word about the assailant.

"What have you heard about Pete?" he now asked, and was told that he was doing fine and expected home by the end of the week. The spear was not strong enough to break the shoulder bone but it would take time and rehabilitation to get him back in shape.

"I know what he's gonna go through," said Marco. "It's a bitch, but he'll be okay."

"I would like to invite Luigi and Jose to sit with us at dinner tonight. They both feel that they let us down," said Patricia

"That's ridiculous," said Marco, "how could it be their fault? This guy fooled an army of guards that had nothing else to do."

"Nonetheless, I think they feel really bad and I want to reassure them that they have our trust."

"A brilliant idea," interceded M&M. "I know Luigi is hurting bad. He went to the hospital yesterday and was at the edge of tears asking Pete to forgive him for not foreseeing the attack."

"Hah!" said Marco, "the only time that goombah would cry would be at his momma's funeral because he was forced to go."

"Marco!" scolded Patricia, and she went to call the two bodyguards.

Dinner started subdued. The gazpacho was eaten practically in silence. Not even Matilde said anything. It was a real icebreaker when Francisco stood up and, calling the attention of all, made an announcement:

"I would like to share with all of you some wonderful news that should distance our minds from the recent events. Earlier today I had a short conversation with Patricia and Marco and they announced to me that they are getting married."

Everyone erupted in cheers, toasts, and commentaries among themselves. Matilde was literally dancing around the table kissing everyone that could be kissed and chattering away in her Kuna dialect, which nobody understood.

"I cannot express in words how happy this makes me. We here, all present included, are a family and this union makes it evermore close."

Being included in something as momentous as this for the Carducci, M&M felt emotional and internally swore fealty to them. Something he had never done before in his whole life. As a matter of fact it was the first time anyone had called him family and he was overwhelmed.

"Including me in this intimacy has touched me deeply. Far more than you can possibly imagine. Count on me for anything at any time and I will be worthy of your trust. To our beautiful people," said M&M, raising his glass.

Maybe only Francisco knew of the significance of such declaration. The others didn't know it, but they had acquired one very powerful ally. Luigi and Jose, who had started the evening very quiet and somewhat timid, made toasts of their own and the little group, including Matilde, felt the intimacy and joy of the occasion. Nobody noticed that Patricia, who was a constant if moderate wine drinker, had only had lemonade all evening. At a moment before they had their dessert, Patricia asked Marco quietly if they could have a moment apart.

When they came back, Marco stood with his glass raised and said, "Ian Carlo, it looks like your coming son is going to have a little playmate…Patricia just told me that I'm going to be a father."

For the second time that evening everyone joined in with this momentous piece of news. Glasses were raised, toasts cheered, love expressed, and joy shared. It was, unbelievably, M&M who had tears in his eyes as he drank to the new parents. The evening went on until bodies could not hold on any longer and, for the first time in months, they all had a peaceful sleep.

26

Delany had done all the paperwork on Enrico Testa to assure himself that the culprit would spend the rest of his life in Guantanamo or another similar vacation spot at the expense of the US taxpayer. In the meantime Senator Mason had been using all his influence to have Testa charged as a common criminal and US Citizen with no other result than confirming his hand in the priest's crimes, so when people from Homeland Security started asking questions he rapidly distanced himself from the case. Now it was Delaney's turn to go after the senator. He called in Toby Carson and got the latest update on the senator's visits to his Maryland apartment. Toby came in with his partner in the stakeout, Agent Betsy Blues. Everybody liked Betsy Blues because she was always in a good mood and had a great sense of humor. She told everyone that she was the illegitimate daughter of one of the Blues Brothers but didn't know which one because her mother had shared the company of both on a one-night stand in Pocatello. The duo had been very effective and had become de facto SACs of the project while Delany was elsewhere.

"He's been there twice," said Toby.

"Twice in a row actually," added Betsy.

"He keeps to the same routine, doesn't change a thing, pretty stupid," quipped Betsy

"Don't underestimate him," answered Toby. "He made senator didn't he?"

"Money makes senators, not brains, look at the roster of the Senate and you'll see what I mean."

"Okay, so what's the status now" asked Delany.

"He's playing the perfect senator. Doesn't miss a beat, votes every time, hits the committees regularly, does the handshaking thing with all sorts of visitors and leaves work late. He goes home or to some official function and then home – Mr. Boring."

"What about a search warrant for the apartment?"

"No can do; it's in a woman's name and so far no judge wants to sign an unwarranted warrant," he smiled.

"Very funny. How about tracking Internet communications out of that apartment?"

"No hardline, not even a telephone line; he doesn't get his smut via internet. He gets it in the mail somewhere else, not here. We checked," said Betsy.

"The possibilities are so many that it's not even worth pursuing," added Toby. "We have to get him in the apartment doing his thing."

"I doubt he gets the stuff in the Senate mail. Everything is scrutinized to the umpteenth degree. No way has he got any smut delivered there."

"Well, the team has followed him twenty-four-seven and we've been attentive to any possibility but the guy is like clockwork with his routine. Except for his clandestine visits to Maryland, it's very predictable. It's even made it easy for us to go unnoticed by his protective service. Those Capitol Police agents must be going nuts. When he goes to the hotel to do his switch, he has them wait in the lobby and will not allow them to wait by the door. It must be a nightmare for them. They have CCTV on the door permanently monitored, but the only thing they see is a waiter bringing in dinner and wine, he leaves and then returns in about three hours to get the table. That's how he does the switch because he knows the cameras and the waiter has the same body build and outfit. Mason always keeps his face away from the cameras."

"Is there anything else he does for recreation? Movies, bars, anything?" asked Delany

"Sometimes after late session on one or another of the committees he serves he'll go to the Round Robin at the Willard. He goes to the smoking room, orders a cognac and lights up a cigar. The cheap bastard always steals the matches; you know the longer ones in a box for lighting cigars."

"Toby, he's been getting his smut right under your nose," said Special Agent Delany. "This is what I want you to do..."

* * *

Dupree's interview with His Holiness the Pope did not happen as soon as he expected. It wasn't until three days after the news of Testa's arrest that he was summoned to the private offices of the new pope. Dupree, in full bishop regalia with his red zucchetto and cincture, knelt before the Vicar of Christ and kissed the ring of Peter. The pope invited him to a small sitting room where privacy was assured.

"Has Your Eminence been well?" asked the Pope in perfect French.

"Yes, Your Holiness, thanks to God."

"And do you talk to him frequently, Jean?"

"I pray, Your Holiness...."

"But, do you talk to him? Do you believe he listens?"

"Holiness..." was all Dupree could say. He couldn't lie to this man. Nobody could. He was the most humble man Dupree had ever met. There was no subterfuge to him. No love of earthly power or glory, yet in a few weeks he had more influence in the world than any other pope in recent memory.

"We know you love the Church, Jean. Nobody works harder to help us sustain our missions and our duty to the poor...but do you love God?"

Dupree could not bring himself to answer.

"The Church is a glorious institution, Jean, but a man-made institution none the less and not a substitute for God. I have been very disturbed to see that the Church has become its own reason to be and we have forgotten that it is here to foster the communion of man with his creator, not to propagate its own power."

"But the Church needs the strength of worldly power and that only comes with a strong treasury, your Holiness. I think that is my calling and my strength."

"As a Jesuit we admire some Machiavellian undertones in the pursuit of our goal, which is the salvation of man's immortal soul, but we cannot cross the line of sin, Jean. It is a thin line, but it creates an infinite divide between salvation and perdition."

"I pursue no glory of my own, Holiness, only the glory and power of the Church so that it can bring humanity out of its misery and in that way we can save them. They are too hungry and sick to think of God, or salvation. First we must save their bodies in order to save their souls."

"A noble thought, Jean, but at what cost? Do we become the rulers of their hearts by ruling their stomachs? And when that happens who rules? Do we have the moral right to give or withhold according to the recipients faith? Are we to become the Taliban of Christ?"

"But Holiness, all I want is for the Church to be great again. To be what it was."

"Nothing will ever be as it was, Jean, nothing ever is. Each moment is unto itself and we are not to anchor our hopes or effort on what has been, but on what man needs to reach salvation by his own free will. Feeding the poor is a noble calling, consoling the afflicted is our duty, teaching the ignorant is our obligation. But holding mankind in ransom is not."

"Forgive me, Father, for I have sinned..."

The bulletin from the Holy See read as follows: Cardinal Jean Dupree, Prince of the Holy Roman Catholic Church and, until today, one of the governors of the Institute for Religious Organizations, has asked His Holiness for dispensation of his duties as he wishes to enter a spiritual retreat in a monastery that has not yet been announced. He has effectively retired from public life and his duties at the IOR have been distributed among several of its governors until a replacement is appointed.

The *Wall Street Journal* and the *Financial Times*, published the bulletin without much comment, the *Economist* did the same but recounted some important issues about the IOR. Sub-rosa the news was another story. A lot of very important financial leaders, like the Secretary of the Treasury and the Head of the Federal Reserve, as well as their equivalents in Great Britain, Russia, China, Japan, and Brazil took note of this and made adjustments...because the show must go on. Lord Humphrey huffed and puffed and congratulated himself on going with the sheik. The sheik did a jig...however it was done in Dubai. The one who was left out to dry was Edward Meredith, but not for too long. Lord Humphrey and the Sheik were on a G650 hot for Kansas. The Carducci group, M&M, and Francisco Lujan were relieved but preferred to wait and see, as did The Board.

M&M took advantage of the Carducci Bombardier that was flying Marco and Patricia to the Channel Islands to meet with a banker and from there went on to Geneva to meet with a very important ally, a line prince of the Saudi Crown. Things would be very momentous in the next few months and he needed the Saudis to invest in a couple of IPOs that were soon to be issued. His wild ride in Sarasota had given M&M a shot of adrenaline and an emotional makeover, but now was time for business and his mind was sharp on.

Marco and Patricia, accompanied by Luigi and Jose, got off the Bombardier in Jersey where they were met by Mr. John Convers of the British Overseas Investment Bank and a security detail sent by Allen Security, these being invisible to the banker and any other observer. It was a tough assignment in the tiny island where a duck out of place is easily noticed.

"Welcome to the island, Mr. Carducci and Ms. Lujan. I have been very keen on meeting with you and thank you for coming all this way. I would have thought we would meet in the Indies, but better, yes, much better that you're here."

"I also was set on meeting as soon as possible but circumstances did not allow it until now," said Marco

"We did hear a rumor...something about an assassination attempt by some deranged prelate or words to that effect?"

"Nothing so dramatic," said Marco dismissing the matter.

Marco and Patricia went with Convers and the bodyguards followed closely in a second car. The drive to St. Helier from the airport is an easy ten minutes along a pleasant road, but they stopped for lunch at a restaurant that was exceptionally French. Marco was surprised at the menu, but not Patricia.

"This was part of Normandy in the Middle Ages and the influence persists in two things, the cuisine and the affinity for fine wines," she said.

"And flowers," added the banker. "They have been cultivated here since time was young and we are preferred suppliers to Her Majesty as the seasons permit."

"Banks have flourished here as well," said Marco, touching on the reason of their visit.

"Yes, indeed we have," answered Convers, "there are more than a hundred banks in Jersey, most of which are foreign branches but some of us are headquartered here."

"Is there any particular reason for this?"

"The Channel Islands are ascribed directly to the Crown of England, not to the United Kingdom, and that has given us certain independence from regulators..."

"Ah, yes, the ubiquitous regulators; fortunately they seem to out-regulate themselves. For each hole they plug two new ones appear."

"Yes, but they are a tiresome lot. We might save this discussion for when we are in the safe environ of my office," said Convers nervously. "Walls here have ears."

Lunch went by with easy conversation and tidbits of the island's history, the French, the German occupation during WWII, the summer invasion of hikers and the autumn invasion of bird watchers.

Later, in the very comfortable office of the British Overseas Investment Bank, well insulated in the conference room, Convers initiated the conversation.

"We have observed," he stated, "that when you initiate certain transactions in regards to your portfolios, a significant group of investors from all over the world follow suit. The probabilities of coincidence, our analysts say, are close to zero. This makes us nervous."

"And...what can I do to assuage your worries?"

"Not much I'm afraid, but it is important that we both know where we stand with each other. Your extended influence answers for well over forty percent of our deposits and managed portfolios, so you understand my feelings of vulnerability."

"I do. And I also realize how difficult this revelation must be to you, but let me tell you something with equal candor. I have followed your comportment on a daily basis and our satisfaction with it has not been diminished in any way. We consider your bank a solid ally that we value and trust."

"Yes, but for all intents and purposes, you own us."

"Not really. We depend on your bank and a number of others that have proven solid and navigate carefully the regulated waters of the financial world for our survival and growth. If any company or private institution in the world followed the laws and regulations to the letter they would cease to exist. The financial wisdom of nations is the greatest oxymoron of all times. The one man who saved the world from economic collapse was Richard Nixon when he eliminated the gold standard for the world's currency; the US dollar. From that moment on, the value of anything is imaginary because so is currency. The value of any monetary instrument is what the market perceives it to be and in the hands of governments, imagination runs wild. We depend on less-regulated banks to keep the train on the rails and for that matter so do the financial institutions of the over-regulated markets such as the US and Great Britain...or am I wrong?"

"You scare me, Mr. Carducci," said the banker with a smile.

"Well, what I have to say might scare you a bit more, but rest assured that you and your bank have created an excellent alliance with our group."

"And what you are going to tell me is...?"

"In the last twelve months, eleven of your seventeen branches have received a little over thirteen billion dollars...in cash."

The banker almost had a heart attack.

"Don't fret, Mr. Convers; I can give you the exact figure, down to the dollar. This money was later sent to about twelve hundred different accounts all over the world and much of it stayed here under your care."

The banker kept staring at Marco without saying a word. He was waiting for the other shoe to drop. Was this man a government plant by the US or the UK? Anything was possible.

'So, it might be a tad over forty percent of your deposits, no?" said Marco setting the barb.

"What is it that you want, Mr. Carducci?" asked a very pale banker.

"We are going to increase our business with you, Mr. Convers; here is a list of three banks that I would like you to buy. We will need them in the near future and you will profit generously from these transactions. Just be aware that we all have to profit fairly."

The banker looked at the list as some color was coming back to his face.

"Two of these are a piece of cake. We can buy them outright without any problem; the third one in Malta might not be so easy."

"Why is that?" asked Patricia

"Because it belongs to the Camorra from Napoli, they have owned that bank since the thirteenth century when they were Venetian traders with a post there."

"OK, any suggestions?"

"Yes, there is a very nice opportunity to buy a bank in Cyprus that plays well with the Russians and can be bought through a shell we have in Delaware."

"Delaware as in the USA?" asked Marco.

"Yes. It's a lot easier than you think. Delaware has about a million corporations because of its tax and privacy laws. By the time the Fed catches up the property has moved, but the initial transaction is thus made simpler precisely because it's a US corporation that is buying the bank. Once the transactional protocols are set and tested we buy it from the Delaware Corporation and sell it to a Turkish or Spartan bank that we own."

"With the...ah...changes taking place at the IOR and the new efforts made by a Middle Eastern group we may see some disruption of the world's circulation of cash. At this moment some competitors of ours are working to engage a big American consortium who launders more money than we do. So we need British Overseas Investment Bank to up their game. We will need to move about eighteen billion this year. The money comes from the US, Mexico, Guatemala, Panama, Colombia, Peru, Venezuela, Brazil, and South Africa. The money arrives at each location containerized, film-wrapped, counted, weighed, and coded. The protocols upon arrival are yours. That's what your percentage is for. Use it wisely."

"Just to confirm, the percentage stays the same, ten percent and every penny comes out of the mint, shiny and clean."

"I was thinking that with such a volume..."

"We should reduce the commission?" interrupted Patricia with steel in her eyes.

"Let me make this clear, Mr. Convers, you try something like that again and your bank will cease to exist."

"Sorry, it's the banker in me..."

"OK, now that we understand each other, there will be two IPOs, one in the USA and another one in Canada. We want you to manage the Canadian IPO. We are aware that you own Wattenberg & Ilse so there should be no problem."

"What's the estimated value and how many shares are we talking about?"

"That is not yet available but in a month max you will have all the paperwork to start your analysis."

"Do you have a timeframe?"

"Within the year, eight months preferably; in a week you'll have a preliminary prospectus."

"You can count on us, Mr. Carducci."

"I know," answered Marco without a smile, "and one more thing. I will need assurance that thirty-three percent of the stock will be sold to Canadian financial institutions, funds, and private investors within the country. You can spread the rest."

"Yes sir."

Marco knew that the banker was going to play by the rules. His greed and his fear would keep him in line. Patricia caught his eye and gave him a minuscule nod. She agreed. This visit was over. The Bombardier should be landing within the hour.

"OK, Mr. Convers, our business is concluded unless you have something else to discuss…"

"No sir, madam, I think we're done. I thank you for your understanding and…"

"Forget about it…it never happened. We have about an hour to kill, how about a tour of the town?"

When the plane departed, John Convers took a deep breath. That stupid, stupid Australian had told him that Carducci was a pushover. He would keep away from Edmund Cartwright, far, far away. He could still feel Patricia's and Marco's eyes on him when he was going to propose a modest increase in the rate. It chilled his blood.

Marco's next stop was Luxembourg, then Monaco, San Merino, and then Lugano to meet with M&M. He had to repeat the exercise he had done in Jersey with these other banks that needed some re-adjustment before business got more complex. By the time they reached Lugano, Marco and Patricia had visited five countries in two days. It was exhausting but needed doing.

The approach to Lugano-Agno airport is exceptionally beautiful as you glide over the lake and into the narrow valley that cradles the runway and airport facilities, which are close to the town of Agno;

and you get a magnificent birds-eye view of it on the approach or departure. This time of year the mountains are still white but as spring approaches the white turns to blue and then the melt floods the rivers and the whole landscape acquires innumerable tones of green that contrast with the white structures of the surrounding towns. The big Bombardier was not the only private jet by far but it was the biggest. M&M was there to receive them with a mean looking security detail that made Luigi and Jose look like turtle doves. M&M was taking no chances with "family." The ride to Lugano is a short ten minutes along a narrow road surrounded by houses with gardens that compete with each other. M&M's villa overlooking the lake left Patricia breathless. It is one of the most beautiful settings in the world, even though it's getting a little bit overpopulated as Swiss from other Cantons find the Italian lifestyle of the Luganese relaxing compared to the arthritic north of the country.

"I'm overjoyed that you are here. First personally and as a businessman because the meeting I had in Geneva was momentous indeed. My people will take care of your bags and arrange the accommodation of your entourage. We reserved rooms for the air-crew close to the airport as per your instructions. I have arranged for a van with driver in case they want to come to town for dinner or something. They will never be more than ten minutes from the airport."

As he talked, M&M guided them down two short sets of stairs and into a wide living room that was totally surrounded by glass with view onto the lake. Now even Marco was short of breath at the sight. And there was yet another surprise; in a comfortable leather smoking chair, enjoying a glass of wine and dressed casually, was Amiable Manning.

27

Across the ocean Tommy Liguria was flying east to meet with Ian Carlo de la Rosa. He was wondering what the boss wanted. He always thought of Ian Carlo as the boss since he had been given a big chunk of Carducci business. He had no concerns; whatever Ian Carlo wanted it was fine with him. He had played his hand as clean as could be and Ian Carlo had reciprocated by giving him increased access to interesting markets. Ian Carlo's G550 had picked him up at the crack of dawn and he would be in New York in time for a late lunch with the boss. He had been served a nice breakfast and the flight attendant had offered him a selection of movies and music. He watched an old spaghetti western that Ian Carlo seemed to enjoy because he had a big collection of them on board and before he knew it the plane started it's descent for MacArthur where Ian Carlo's chopper would be waiting for him. Tommy had never been an extravagant guy even living in glitter town where limos and private jets were the standard. He kept it simple, took care of his family and his mom. He had developed a taste for golf but never really had the time for it. Tommy Lee put in a good ten hours a day, Saturdays included. He was a demanding boss but led by example and with his second on board, Joe Tellez, he had developed a great work ethic among his people and had acquired respect among his peers. The chopper took Tommy to a building in downtown

Manhattan where Ian Carlo was waiting for him in the company of an older man he did not know and a younger one who was a newer version of the aforementioned. He was introduced to Ernie and Samuel Goldman and they went directly to the offices of Goldman & Goldman Jr., Attorneys at Law.

* * *

Patricia was all smiles when she hugged Amiable. There was no doubt in her mind why he was here. She had caught that flash the instant these two had set eyes on each other. Naturally, Marco was far clumsier socially that Patricia and was naïve enough to ask Amiable what he was doing in Lugano. It was M&M who answered:

"A vacation; Amiable is here on vacation. He will be my guest for as long as he wishes to stay. He only arrived yesterday evening via Milano and while we have our meetings he will get a tour of the area. It is lovely, you know."

"I won't be imposing for too long," said Amiable. "I have a job to go back to. I was lucky to get a paid leave for having helped in the closure of the Meredith case. It was a political home run for my bosses and they were happy to see me off for a few days. You know how it is...politicians."

"Nonsense," said M&M. "You haven't been to Europe before and there is so much to see. Venice is only four hours away and Rome a short flight...then Paris; we must go to Paris."

Finally the dime dropped and Marco caught on. Patricia saw it in his eyes and burst out laughing, he was so clueless. Her laughter made the others look and she was not shy to explain the motive of her laughter which elicited equal merriment in M&M but face reddening embarrassment in Amiable. But he saw no malice in either Patricia or M&M so he lowered his guard and had a bit of fun at Marco's expense. Dinner was a feast among friends and local cuisine was the fare. Fresh-fried smelt from the lake, roast lamb with carrots and pearl onions in a thick wine sauce, a variety of cheeses new to all but M&M, as they were local produce. Fruit was scarce at this time of year but South African pears and grapes were served with the cheese. A chocolate soufflé so light that it could have flown off by itself closed the meal. Coffee, cognac, and Sambuca were offered but no takers. Patricia had kept to San Pellegrino all evening, much to her regret because the wines tabled were exceptional and rare.

* * *

Lunch at Goldman's office was a simple variety of sandwiches from a local deli, water, fruit juice and soda, and Snicker bars in case of a sweet tooth; it was Ian Carlo who invariably had to have dessert. The lead was taken by Samuel Goldman from the beginning and he dragged Tommy from his earliest memories to what he had for breakfast on the flight over. The meeting was being observed by two behavioral psychologists via CCTV who fed Samuel questions via earplug. It was grueling but did not faze Tommy, who kept his cool throughout the whole ordeal. What did surprise Ian Carlo was that Tommy was planning to marry his pregnant girlfriend Tatiana, whom Ian Carlo had met on Long Island what seemed a long time ago. The management of the Vegas outfit was not a problem because it came across clearly that Tellez, Tommy's lieutenant, was loyal, capable and decisive. A few years ago the fact that he wasn't fully Italian would have been a problem, but today it was considered an asset in a place like Vegas where the Mexican influence was everyday greater. The other advantage was that the system did not depend too much on local talent. The encryption of all orders and the separation of functions kept things tidy. Not even Tommy knew about the pipelines and that wouldn't change even if he took over the New York family. At the very end of the day Samuel floated the idea of Tommy taking over the New York operation and to everyone's surprise Tommy didn't jump at it. He asked a lot of questions, quite smart ones in Ernie's opinion, and said he needed the night to think about it. This gained Tommy a lot of respect with the Goldmans but Ian Carlo was a bit irked as he did not like to wait for others to decide. Ernie counseled him to patience and the meeting was set up for early next morning.

A suite at the Plaza and a good night sleep was what Tommy needed, that and four hours of solid thinking.

Morning came with a start. Tommy forgot where he was and took a second to reorient himself. New York, the Plaza Hotel, the biggest promotion of his life, the scariest promotion of his life, the craziest promotion of his life...a game-changer. He could understand why a guy like De la Rosa wanted to be governor of New York; he had all the qualifications needed. He had no scruples, all the leadership a man could want, more money than God, and a rap sheet without even a parking ticket on it. He was a practicing Catholic, with a wife and kid...soon to be two, high school football star, connected to everyone and everything...wow! And he, Tommy, had to fill the man's shoes in the toughest mafia environment in the US. Well, why not, he thought. I can do this. So he showered, got dressed like he was already the man, and headed off to breakfast in the courtyard restaurant where he would meet with Ian Carlo privately.

* * *

As Dupree approached the small town of Tiana in a van provided for his transport from Barcelona to the monastery, his mind was far away from God, Church, or prayer. He was thinking of Enrico Testa locked up in some Godforsaken jail from where escape was impossible. He did not worry about Enrico testifying against him. There was no chance of that. Jean Dupree knew the heart of that man and not one word would leave his mouth until he was in front of his leash, Cardinal Jean Dupree. When they arrived at the door of the monastery the driver got out and with a club that was standing against the frame he knocked three times. In a while, a long while, the door opened and a young friar stood there silently. The driver took Dupree's bag as far as the door, went back to his van and took off without a word, leaving a cloud of dust and smoke behind him. Dupree watched him go and followed the shrinking van until all he could see was the dust it left along the unpaved road. Dupree turned toward the door and the friar indicated for him to follow. The Cardinal was expecting the friar to carry his bag but it was left where the driver put it. Jean picked it up and followed the man down a long corridor and across an ancient courtyard where a couple of fig trees were beginning to show new sprouts. In a dark and damp corridor the friar stopped in front of the door, opened it and indicated for Dupree to enter. There was a small bed, a wash basin, a bedpan, a few boards held up by bricks and two hooks on one wall. From one hook hung a tunic of coarse material with a scapula attached by rudimentary wood buttons. On the bed was a nightgown of sorts made of raw cloth. There were no sheets, just a thick raw wool blanket. On a small table there was a clay jar and a corresponding mug for water.

The friar gave Dupree a piece of paper and left without having said one word. On the paper was written, "The world is behind you. Whoever perseveres without defiance in the cell and lets himself be taught by it tends to make his entire existence a single and continual prayer. But he may not enter into this rest without going through the test of a difficult battle. It is the austerities to which he applies himself as someone close to the Cross, or the visits of God, coming to test him like gold in the fire. Thus purified by patience, fed and strengthened by studied meditation of Scripture, introduced by the grace of the Holy Spirit in the recesses of his heart, he will thus be able to not only serve God, but adhere to him."

The words of St. Bruno, founder of the Carthusian order, did not pull strings of piety, repentance, or love of God in the stone cold heart of Jean Dupree. He was fond of meditation as an exercise in mental strength and clarity of ideas, but constant prayer? Give me a break, he thought. The paper also indicated that at vespers he would meet with Friar Domenici, the prior who would be his master for the foreseeable future until Dupree found his place in the monastery.

"You are a cardinal of the Holy Roman Catholic Church; you are a priest, ordained to be a messenger of God, those things will always be, but only between you and God. Here you are simply Father Jean and your daily mass will be said in private in the donate's chapel. Food will be brought to your cell twice a day except in days of fast for the first weeks, later you will eat with the rest of us in the refectory. Water is available at several spouts throughout the cloister. Your bed pan is to be emptied in the cloaca behind the wood shop and washed with the spout there available. You may walk around the grounds when you need air and exercise and you may choose an occupation, which may be one that fulfills our needs, woodwork, pottery, or gardening, but most of your day must be spent in the solitude of your cell seeking God's word to you. You will suffer while you incessantly talk to Him in prayer, but immeasurable joy will fill you when He answers. We will speak again in one week or before only if sickness overcomes you. Go with God and be silent."

* * *

M&M listened intently while Marco explained to him what the plans of the Carducci were for the immediate future; Ian Carlo's withdrawal from the crime families of the NY/NJ area, the IPO of the Carducci Enterprises, and the dedication to bring about the social redirection that Marco had laid out in his dissertation at Kellogg and how The Board had embraced this led by Francisco Lujan. M&M knew a lot about The Board, but not everything that Marco and Patricia were telling him. There was more to these people, much, much more than he ever imagined.

M&M also understood the nature of this organization that, like him, had a different set of moral and social rules that allowed them to exploit the corruption of the system without corrupting themselves. There was little regard for the fate of individuals but great regard for the fate of humanity. They considered the present social structure of most countries as a degeneration of democracy in which the rules had been reversed. Laws, regulations, geographical voting areas, and spin allowed the politicians and the puppet-masters that pulled their strings to choose their voters and repress anyone that would vote against them. He listened closely to Marco's thesis.

"The United States, which is supposed to be the most successful democracy in the world, has been hobbled by gerrymandering to such a degree that congressmen who are generally detested by most people are assured re-election by having manipulated voting districts to choose only the voters that are inclined in their favor. Politicians with approval of twenty percent or less are elected and re-elected time and time again. These individuals rob the country blind and what's left is misspent and squandered. And, to make sure that people are distracted by everything other than what matters they invent wars – unnecessary invasions of countries where we are not going to achieve change no matter what, gender wars to appease zealots, war on drugs to make sure there are plenty available to generate billions, war on terror so we can sell arms to anyone who wants them. Today the USA gives weapons to rebels in Syria who will use them tomorrow to kill kids we sent to another war that the dark powers invent. We use the profits from laundering their money and selling them the drugs they so desperately want, to defeat them."

"You are telling me, Marco, that what The Board wants to do is a mega judo move," replied M&M. "Use the strength of the enemy to defeat him or it as may be the case."

"Strangely put, but yes, something like that. Political corruption is not going to disappear, so why not use it to make enough money to start a social change that gives society a fair chance? People are going to use drugs no matter what, so why not make the whole process easier and avoid the carnage that the current process claims, and make a huge amount of money while we're at it?"

"And the money; does it matter?"

"How much money is needed? For some people a hundred dollars is a windfall; for others a billion is just another billion. We consider this part in very human terms. We, you, all of us like a limitless way of life, but that does not take the kind of money we are talking about. We are human and even absurd luxury has a limit. You can eat, sleep, dress, travel, see, drink, enjoy art...anything you want, but it's all tempered by what we cannot buy: time. All of the people on The Board have limitless lifestyles. It's just that their approach to that limitless lifestyle includes improving the opportunities of mankind by re-cycling the money that is salvaged and putting it to work, creating a middle class that is free of the conditions imposed by the politicians that stole their countries."

"But wouldn't that just go back to the realm of politicians via taxes, etc.?"

"Sure, but if a strong middle class emerges, higher political reasoning also emerges and the election of governments may improve, and I say may improve, which is a far lot better than what they have today which is a spiral of deterioration."

"You are talking of changing the massive inertia of social structures at levels never achieved before."

"Not true. President Truman cajoled politicians into making decisions to save the United States from falling back into depression; Eisenhower continued the work and helped construct the greatest society historically known to man. Then came all the rest and screwed it up. We as a nation abandoned our principals and plunged into living the life of others as a consolation prize for giving up our own lives. We have gone from the American Dream to the American Nightmare in fifty years. On one side you have a tiny minority that owns or controls most of the wealth and then another minority who lives off the government and causes huge costs, fueling the waste of public funds on social programs that are not needed and help no one but sate the ego of the liberal forces. Both of these extremes are terrible for this country and many others that espouse these policies...ask Greece if you don't believe me, look at Spain, Italy, Portugal, Ireland, and so many more...the world needs a strong middle-class that generates employment. Governments, ours in particular, give the middle class a lot of lip service and then turn around and give it a royal screwing."

"So what, if anything, can you do about it?"

"We, M&M, we can do a lot. We have the resources to manipulate the greater financial institutions. We manage more money than ten Goldman Sachs so we can force banks away from credit card lending and back into supporting small business, in start-up funding, and in third world micro-loans to head of household women that are entrepreneurial and need the seed money. The results are much faster than in any monetary loop and the risks are lower. Kiva lends about three million a week to hundreds if not thousands of tiny entrepreneurs with an astonishing default of less than one percent. Tell me of a credit card in the US that can offer such results. Sometimes the line between abject poverty and tax-paying middle class requires very little money to cross. We want to use the profits from the illegal money laundering and drug use to salvage a big hunk of humanity that then can turn around and save us from ourselves."

"OK, so what now. You've told me more than I think I wanted to hear…why?"

"Because Patricia, Francisco, and I want you to be our permanent advisor; you don't have to change a thing in your life. Communications are far too easy and ours are safer than most. All I need from you is loyalty and that extraordinary brain of yours."

"And my connections…you need my connections, no?"

"Yes, your ability to fix anything."

"My loyalty has been yours ever since you called me 'family'. The only question I have is who will know? You understand that part of my ability depends on neutrality?"

"Patricia, Francisco, Ernie, Ian Carlo, Samuel, and myself. Tommy Liguria might need you once in a while but that will come through Ian Carlo de la Rosa."

"I say yes. And I ask what's in it for me?"

"Anything you want."

* * *

Back in NYC, Ian Carlo and Tommy Liguria were hammering out how to handle the transition.

"I don't give a damn about the other families. They need us more than we need them and that is the only thing that counts. What does present some concern to me is how the *capos* of your organization might react. Some of them have met me, most of them know about me; but will they work for me? How much can I count on them if they do?"

"There has to be a transition period like with everything else. You have to spend time here working closely with me, then little by little the orders come from you and then I disappear for short periods, then longer ones and then we do the pass. That's when the families will know you're the man. Before that they'll think I brought you in as a consigliore. In this period we can see how the crews accommodate, if there are ruffled feathers we'll un-ruffle them or get rid of the chicken."

"How long for this transition?" asked Tommy.

"My kid is due in seven months, so call it six. I wanna be outta here in six months. How about Vegas, can you pull a fast one there?"

"No problems, since we started working together they kind of feel part of your outfit and since most are Mexicans, Tellez will be a perfect fit."

"We need Vegas working like clockwork, Tommy, no fuck-ups."

"No fuck-ups, Gucci, they have been doing this with their eyes closed for the last few months."

By the time they met with Samuel everything was agreed and the three of them sat down to do the details of the transition, including a place to live for the Ligurias, seed money, and induction into every line of business and stream of income. Of particular importance were businesses or geographical areas that touched or overlapped with other families, these were critical. But Tommy was no greenhorn, he had dealt with lots of goombah in Vegas. The first step had been taken. Ian Carlo de la Rosa was on his way out.

* * *

On a sandy inlet just outside of the city of Bergen in Norway a couple of sanitation workers made a grisly discovery; two human bodies – skeletons, actually, in tracksuits – were still attached to an airplane bench seat by their safety belts. The headless, handless and footless bodies were tentatively identified by documents carried in the belly bag of one of the victims of what appeared to be an airplane crash. Further DNA analysis confirmed that they were two young men who, with their wives, had left for an adventure of two weeks in the Caribbean and had been reported missing for over twelve months. The serial number of the seat corresponded to NCZ 995, a Lear 35 that had disappeared off the Carolina coast more than a year ago. This gave closure to four families in New Jersey who had never known what happened to their sons and daughters. The mystery of the other four passengers on the last flight of the Lear was now solved. Confident that his boss Marco Carducci wouldn't have minded, Joe Strasso had done a favor to some friends of a friend and it had cost them their lives. Obviously there would be lawsuits, but who gave a damn.

* * *

Edward Meredith couldn't believe his good luck. No sooner had the cardinal disappeared from the radar than Lord Humphrey had appeared with Sheik Faruk Al-Enezi and business was as sweet as always. The banks changed but the story was the same. He would miss the cardinal; he had been of incredible assistance in getting back the reins of the company. Ana Meredith was a distant memory and an oil painting in the boardroom. He was king and he planned to keep it that way with or without the cardinal. He had treated the Brit and the sheik with respect but had remained somewhat distant and it had worked for him. The terms of the business were good and they parted friends. The result of the first shipments of money was immaculate and his accounts and those of his clients had been credited punctually. It looked like this was going to work. His businesses grew to unexpected heights and money kept rolling in. Meredith was now one of the top five companies in the world; if they only knew...hmmm.

* * *

Way south in the central mountain range of the Colombian Andes where Bogotá is perched at almost 7,000 feet, the hackers that worked for Francisco Lujan's "call center" followed the faintest traces, tendrils really, of coded communications that spelled the journey of billions of dollars across the globe. Little by little a map was appearing and some sense was seen among the trillions of ones and zeros that flew by every second. Colombia was taking up bandwidth faster than any of its neighbors and much of that was being used by Francisco's operation. Banks of computers sucked away at the hard points in Barranquilla's Puerto Colombia cable entry, megawatts of power were used in the search, but it was well worth the effort. It had been almost a year since Francisco had seen a fray in the textile of the Meredith organization and with that single thread his people had cracked the safe. Francisco was having lunch with Guillermo de los Rios, a local entrepreneur with whom he had made friends because of his love for wine and his extensive knowledge of South American vintners. The conversation was long on a particular region in Patagonia, in the Neuquen fruit region that produced an exceptional pinot noir that this year was going to exceed all expectations. The restaurant, Ermigna Romana, had a good wine list for most patrons, but a very private and monstrously expensive one for people like Francisco and Guillermo. The choice of the day was a cabernet from high in the eastern region of the Chilean Andes – a Casa Vergara, Gran Reserva of 2007.

It was then that Francisco got the call from his office that the code had been cracked and a map of the money routes and access codes was in hand. He finished his chat with Guillermo and they walked back to their offices in Avenida Chile flanked by the ever present security that both men used and needed. When Francisco was back in his office, he immediately sat down with his little Indian hacker, who was neither little nor poor any more. The results were unequivocal. He called Ernie, Marco, and M&M. They agreed on an action date to coincide with estimated gross movement peeks and set up to wait.

* * *

Jean Dupree, failing at being penitent, felt neither generous nor repentant in the solitude of his cell within the Carthusian cloister. He was a player without a game and the lack of intellectual challenge was driving him crazy. The nocturnal babble of Gregorian chants favored by these deranged monks was equivalent to hell on earth for the cardinal. Pope or no pope he had to get out of here, he just didn't know how. The only edifice or sign of human habitat in the small valley was the monastery and the winding dirt road that snaked away into the hills. He had no way out. He was a prisoner just as Testa and maybe even Testa was better off as he was probably getting fed and had use of a proper toilette. Cleaning up his own mess was not Dupree's idea of penance, retreat, or basic hygiene.

If he had been capable of prayer his only request would have been a way out...now! As he despaired of his situation he heard the familiar rumble of the van that had bought him to this Hades. He took a small belly bag that he had managed to contraband into his cell, for all other possessions had been taken from him including his watch, clothes, shoes, ring, and gold crucifix. In the bag he kept ten gold Kruger Rand, a valid EU passport, a small bag of white diamonds, an American Express card, and a roll of ten €500 bills. Madame Dupree had not raised an idiot. He tied the belly bag under his tunic and grabbed his walking stick; the one luxury he was allowed. He walked out behind the woodshed as if heading to the woods for his exercise and followed a path that intersected the road about half a mile into the hills. There he waited until he heard an old van struggling with the rising road. When it was a hundred feet away Dupree sprang to the middle of the road and held up his hand and the walking stick with authority enough to make the van come to a halt. He approached the driver and said, "Is this enough to get me to Girona?" showing him one of the €500 notes.

The old man just signaled to his passenger side and said, "Sube."

The money changed hands and the van re-initiated its lumbering climb out of the valley. At a small outpost town that was little more than a gas station with a general store the man bought Dupree a track suit with the insignias of the Barcelona soccer team and the name Messi printed on the back, two changes of underwear, and a pair of Nike knockoffs. Jean changed in the back of the van, rolled up his tunic and put it in the plastic bag together with the sandals he was given at the monastery and threw them in the trash. With it went his alliance to the Holy Roman Catholic Church.

In Girona, Dupree bought a couple of suits, shirts, ties, shoes, underwear, a valise, and other odds and ends needed to begin his life as a private citizen and financial entrepreneur. He checked into a three-star hotel, took a long, hot shower, shaved clean the beard that he had grown out of necessity – leaving only a well-trimmed Van Dyke – and went around the corner to a salon where he got his first haircut in months. He looked at himself in the mirror and was happy to see a middle-aged man of prosperous countenance and clear eyes. He walked back to the hotel with a spring in his step and a new outlook on life. On the way he stopped at one of the international phone booths that over-populate such tourist towns. He made a call to San Marino and another one to Saint Bartholomew in the Caribbean. Using the codes he had put in place he transferred a modest amount of money to his account in Luxembourg. None of these accounts were in the privy of the IOR and would see him through a start in his new life...even if a billion euros is not what it used to be. It took three days for the prior of the monastery to discover that Cardinal Dupree had absconded. It was normal for penitents to forego food for a few days in purification fast; it was also common for them not to leave their cells for a few days, so it was only when the prior had asked to see Dupree that they discovered his absence. Word was slow to get to Rome, slower to get to the pope, and even slower for word to get back to the prior. Do nothing.

* * *

For a month Enrico Testa sat stone still and tomb quiet as the interrogators tried to get a word out of him. Neither sleep deprivation, loud noise, time disruption nor any other stress inducing method had fazed him. He had simply retired to a place in his mind where no one but God could go. When frustrated interrogators tried waterboarding him his heart rate went down instead of up and was at 45 beats when the medic stopped the procedure. He was being fed twice a day, but barely ate enough to sustain life. No one knew when he was awake or asleep as little changed from one state to the other. Thus was the situation when the transfer order arrived from the Department of Homeland Security requesting the preparation of the prisoner for transportation to Guantanamo. When the day came, Testa was shackled hand and foot to a leather belt that buckled in the back and was led out by six armed guards, two of which flanked him and held his arms. At the loading dock there was an armored vehicle with the insignias of the Department of Homeland Security and a phalanx of heavily armed guards. The prisoner was unceremoniously shoved into the back, where two other armed guards with body armor and full-face helmets awaited him. Extensive paperwork changed hands and the vehicle took off with the escort vehicles following. An hour later as the truck appeared to Enrico to be traveling along an unpaved road, it stopped and the back door opened. One of the guards got off and the driver handed the remaining guard a set of keys and he and the guard got into the escort vehicle and went off back towards where they came. The remaining guard unlocked Testa's shackles from the chain that was welded to the floor and then un-cuffed him and removed the shackles from his legs. Enrico had no idea what was going on but tensed, ready to attack if it was necessary.

"Be calm, my son," said the guard taking off the helmet. "It has been a long time..." Enrico Testa looked upon the countenance of Cardinal Jean Dupree.

28

Marco and Patricia were back in New York, staying at his old apartment that had been kept clean and updated by the management company. It was like a trip in time for Marco; this was a part of a life that he did not even recognize anymore. He was not sure Patricia was happy staying there because she made a little joke about sharing his bed with him and a dozen girls from Black Card Escort Service. He had brushed it off but made sure that nothing that might remind her of his previous life was around. They were leaving for their meeting with Leon Goddard and Samuel Goldman to see the plan for restructuring Carducci Enterprises and the preliminary prospectus for the two IPOs that would result from it.

"You don't have to go around rearranging the apartment, Marco, I know what was going on here," said Patricia with a mischievous smile. "I just hope you can offer me the same courtesies."

"You get all the courtesy you need," said Marco with a smile of his own.

"Do I?" asked Patricia.

"We can go back upstairs, you know…"

"Keep that thought for after the meetings," said Patricia as she walked ahead of him towards the waiting limo and reminding him that those curves knew how to sway.

The division of the companies was quite logical. The financial corporations, Scorpio Multimodal Brokers, the laundry, the parking, the franchises and several other smaller businesses were going to a new US entity that would go public in the fall of that year; the rest of the properties, including everything outside the US, went to the Canadian company that would go public in the early part of the following year. The estimated value of the US IPO was thirteen and a half billion dollars and the Canadian offering should bring seven billion Canadian dollars. Investment bankers were lined up for both offerings and a minimum price per share was sounded. A meeting with Ian Carlo later on would issue a confirmation and trigger this move. Now both goals of the Carducci family were on the way to being fulfilled; the businesses on both sides of the imaginary fence would cease to be in the hands of Salvatore Carducci's heirs. Ian Carlo's son would come into the world unencumbered by the shadow of lawlessness and both his children would grow up far from where their fortune was made.

* * *

When a new interrogation team that included experts from Homeland Security and a couple of consultants from Walter Reed – who were challenged with discerning the psychological nature of Testa – arrived at the secret location, they were surprised that the inmate wasn't available. It took them two hours and two calls to the director's office to finally be told that Testa had been transferred to Guantanamo the day before and another six to discover that there were no transfer orders from Homeland Security's operations director, or from anyone else for that matter. Finger-pointing reached new levels. Papers were sought, security films were scanned, viewed and reviewed until one lowly guard recognized a colleague who had left the service some months back. Once identified he was promptly located and interrogated. The man had written proof that HS personnel had called him back into service for a special transfer. He had been driving an escort van but halfway to the airport they were told to go home. He didn't know who the prisoner was, he knew they were taking him to Guantanamo and yes, he had the orders that they had received from Directorate of National Protection. This had been an inside job, no doubt about it; and until they found out who, how, and why not a word was coming out of the department.

* * *

The Piper Chieftain left Driggs, Idaho, and climbed to 23,000 feet, headed west. It flew over the Rocky Mountains in clear skies but hit bad weather just west of the range. After a few hours of tempestuous flight it landed at Bob Hope Airport in Burbank, California. It taxied to a NetJets Terminal, where the two passengers transferred to a Falcon 2000 LX. The crew confirmed that all luggage was on board and taxied with an IFR plan for the island of Oahu in the Hawaiian archipelago. Dupree and Testa spent a few nights at a small resort outside of Honolulu because Testa was getting fitted for prosthesis for his left eye. It was not a great improvement over the black eye patch, but it changed his expected appearance. Once finished with that they went to Swiss Port where they boarded a Malayan cargo vessel with a final destination of Democratic Republic of Timor Leste.

On board the freighter Enrico Testa started to exercise, awakening muscles that his confinement had numbed and reacquiring lost flexibility and speed. He found among the crew a couple of hard cases that were good martial arts practitioners and sparred with them every day until his skills accommodated his diminished eyesight and depth perception. The cardinal had explained to him that due to strife within the Church he was asked by His Holiness the Pope to start a new financial institution far away from the IOR and the greedy hands of some cardinals and lay functionaries. Testa did not question his master for a heartbeat. His was to follow God's design through the guiding hand of Jean Dupree. He had drifted from that for a short time and had lost an eye and his liberty at the hands of His enemies. No more would that happen than the sun not shine. He was obliged to call the cardinal by his first name, Jean, and that had been the hardest part of his retraining. Only after two weeks he was getting to overcome his reflexes and stopped calling the cardinal "Your Eminence." He had to pray in private and in silence because their crew was Muslim and they didn't want to offend or call attention on their devotions.

The liberation of Enrico Testa had cost Dupree a cool million dollars but it was cheap compared to having a bodyguard and servant with the capabilities of this man. His lapse in obedience would not be repeated because it had cost Enrico dearly and Dupree reminded him constantly. In Timor, Dupree had acquired a small bank that soon would reach much greater proportions, but it would need money and a strong physical incentive to get all the officials and bureaucrats on board. Thus the need for Enrico; otherwise he could rot in hell as far as the cardinal was concerned. The one thing that he didn't know was a great stroke of luck for him. The Vatican did not want to make public the AWOL cardinal, nor did the Department of Homeland Security want the other agencies to know about the major fuck-up that had let loose on the world a criminal like Testa, therefore no one was really looking for them. There was no Interpol search, no biometric scans going on, nothing. They were free but didn't know it.

* * *

Francisco Lujan and his people had been glued to the screens for weeks, waiting for the indication that it was the right time to strike. Signs that the moment was approaching had everyone on tenterhooks; numbers came and went, graphics took a life of their own, layer upon layer of information accumulated until this orchestra reached its crescendo and Francisco called Marco, gave him the status and they agreed to go ahead. It was just one small algorithm that was typed into one little keyboard that let loose the kraken. Within seconds terminals all over the world received orders, queried the sender, and received confirmations that set transfers in motion. Money flew in its electronic persona from dozens of banks to hundreds of other banks to thousands of accounts and, like a swarm of bees. landed on flowering small businesses in Africa, South America, China, the Middle East, and Australia. The loans issued were guaranteed in kind by a bank in Cyprus that belonged to a bank in Poland that belonged to a bank in Canada who co-owned it with the British Overseas Investment Bank. The money in question had left the accounts that Sheik Faruk was stewarding for the benefit of Edward Meredith, Lord Humphrey, and their associates. Eight and a half billion dollars had been spread like manure on hungry crops; all by the grace and ability of Francisco Lujan and Marco Carducci in representation of The Board.

Once the transactions were completed another algorithm invaded the bank's computers and all traces of the orders, confirmations and destinations evaporated from their memory banks. These money-laundering institutions were left holding the baby. Ufff! What a big, fat, ugly baby!

Francisco had left enough money in these accounts to cover routine payments, bank commissions, and small transfers so that the alarm would not trigger too soon. If there were big transfers, well too bad; but as it turned out it took a full week for things to get ugly. First with a couple of accounts, then with two or three more until all transfers, payments, commissions, etc. bounced from empty coffers, sending alarm up the ladder until some very powerful people got very worried and very angry. Some of these were high up in the mafias, cartels, corporations, NGOs, cover charities, political machines, bureaucrats, and churches. People who counted on the services of the banks organized by Meredith, Humphrey, and the sheik to clean their ill-gotten money found themselves short in more than funds; they had little recourse other than violence and that never gets your money back; ask your friendly neighborhood loan shark.

The banks had received the money and sent it out but had no proof as to where or to whom. This was a fatherless crisis and the banks were the unwed mothers of very nasty offspring. They couldn't say the money had not been received. The credit had been issued for every penny and confirmation of the first dispersal was in the hands of the sheik, but from there on it was a blank. The problem with the type of clients Meredith and Humphrey had was that they were not open to explanations and excuses. Where is the money? Also, the fact that the sheik, and for that matter Edward Meredith and Lord Humphrey, had proof that the banks had received the funds was of no help. They were paid a hefty sum to make it clean and available at the other side of the gauntlet. So the question they got was "Where is our money?" and unfortunately they had no answer. The only good thing, if you could call it that, was that between Meredith, Humphrey, and the sheik, together with the affected banks, they had the money to cover the loss, but it would hurt oh so much! Then the problem was how to pay it back. They couldn't use the same banks to disperse the funds and doing so from their banks could compromise them. This just got nastier by the minute.

In Nirihuau, Chile, Sonia Sotomayor had been begging the banks for a small loan to fix and convert the ancestral home of her family into a bed and breakfast for the increasing number of tourists that visited the town and its surroundings. Within one hour of Nirihuau you could see a lunar desert or a flush micro-climate valley of exceptional beauty. You could fish for trout in the river, hunt for ducks, or face very challenging sheer walls that are a rock climber's paradise. But the bank owned the only crummy hotel in town and they didn't want the competition. Yet one good day the order came from head office in Santiago: issue the loan. Sonia almost fell off the chair when the surly little branch manager told her to sign the papers and the money would be credited to her account.

The same thing was happening all over the place. In Mozambique a fisherman obtained a loan for an outboard, in Laos a woman head-of-household received a loan to buy a taxi, in Mexico a small restaurant got money to expand. The lives of hundreds of thousands of people improved overnight and a small fraction of the earth's population began the climb towards prosperity and survival. In time they would bring upwards millions to whom they could give fair and durable employment.

Marco was looking at the outcome of their move and trying to work out all the possibilities. So far he didn't see any problems or consequences that could affect him, his family, or The Board. As far as the other Board members were concerned none of this had happened because they simply didn't know.

Marco was very aware of Cartwright's betrayal and continued to feed him bull that kept the sheik misinformed and who, anyway, was otherwise engaged. Marco also realized that the money was an inconvenience for Meredith and company but not a blow; not by far. The largest consequence was the disruption of their banking system. They would have to reconstruct it from the ground up and that took time and money. The problem was that their clients, satisfied that Meredith responded, wanted – no, needed – to continue with the cleansing of the eternal river of money that came from the illicit activities of so many. If Meredith did not take the money, others would and the clients might be lost forever. If he did take the money there was nowhere to send it. This generated a lot of pressure on the pipelines because many of the people that used Meredith also used the Carducci connection so demand grew significantly and the pipelines were working almost one way all the time because it was faster to return an empty car and load it with money again than to wait for a loaded one to come, unload the marijuana and load it with money.

* * *

The sheik was listening to the group of IT experts that he had hired to cooperate with the IT experts that the banks had hired to determine how the money had vanished. They concluded correctly what had happened, they just didn't know how or who. What was certain was that the security of the electronic banking systems had been breached and that since they didn't know how it was done there was little that they could do to prevent it from happening again. The only thing that could be done was return to a manual system for the Meredith money. That way none of those banks could be breached and the money would be safe – cumbersome and slow, but ultimately safe. Now it was a question of determining who you could trust to do this process without stealing and without talking. The usual formula was applied: pay them very well and threaten them and their families to the umpteenth generation if they fail; thus started a very slow and difficult reconstruction of his network.

* * *

Weeks into their voyage, stopping at every miserable port down the southern coast of Indonesia, the freighter finally arrived at Dili in the island nation of East Timor where, for some time, Jean Dupree and Enrico Testa would make their home. Dili is the capital and main urban area where Dupree had acquired a beautiful Portuguese style home on a nice piece of land overlooking the city and its port. He had never seen it other than on the computer screen but it was time to visit it in person after such a long voyage.

A car waited for them after customs and took them to their new home. All that was needed for a comfortable life had already been delivered to the house and arranged by Antonino the butler and the rest of the staff. After the privations both had suffered in the last few months, Palmeira, as the house was called, seemed like paradise. It had an ample swimming pool, a fruit garden, and a horse stable. The house itself was an old plantation home of some Portuguese sandalwood and spice farmer, and later of one of the Australian oil executives during the exploitation of the island's resources of which Timor received little or nothing. Palmeira was a large place but in a country where most people live on less than two dollars a day. Dupree could afford a full staff and then more.

Within a few days Jean Dupree had a handle on the bank and its staff and Enrico had the measure and control of the house and garden personnel. Antonino, the butler, had been a sergeant during the independence strife with Indonesia and most of the workers had been soldiers under his command. He gravitated instantly towards Enrico, recognizing in him the officer in charge and thus, a regimental style to which everyone fell into comfortably was established at Palmeira. Morning exercises were de rigor and martial arts were taught and practiced on a daily basis. In no time Testa had himself a little army. Now he wanted weapons with which to train them.

Dupree, carefully and under the guise of an adopted name in his new role as president of the Malay-Timor Trade Bank, Senor Fortunato Bernardes, started sounding out some of the old clients he had served well through the IOR. To his delight there was positive response and though the figures were not large at the beginning, they certainly made a difference in the prestige of the small bank as it converted cash into assets through the starving economy of East Timor. It would take some time before Dupree could use his bank to buy a bigger one in a larger economy, but he was on the right track and he had the time.

* * *

Ever since Toby had busted a waiter at the Round Robin for pushing smut – but couldn't get a word out of him about his "clients" – Senator Archibald Mason had not returned to his clandestine apartment in Maryland. He had been under surveillance for a month but then Delany could not justify the expenditure nor get a warrant to search the apartment. The surveillance team only followed him once a week on Thursdays because that had been the day he went there before. Toby and Betsy were saying that it was like a standing date with them to meet at seven in front of the Marriott and see what the good senator was doing. After three or was it four months and no luck, they did not expect much tonight but lo and behold, at eight o'clock sharp they saw a car circle the hotel a couple of times and then the senator in his disguise left the hotel and got into the vehicle. As usual a few blocks away the driver got out and Senator Mason took the wheel. They followed him to the Maryland apartment and waited for him to come out again and film his return as they had filmed the sneaky exit from the hotel.

What happened next was not in the script. A van stopped in front of the apartment and an Asian woman got out the back door dragging a very young Asian girl towards the building where Senator Mason kept the apartment. Betsy perked up like a lioness on the hunt that has just picked up the scent of a wounded wildebeest. Toby followed suit and both kept their eyes on the building. The woman rang a bell and seconds later the door opened and the woman pulled the struggling girl by her coat lapels into the building. About ten minutes later the woman came out alone, boarded the van and departed. Every detail was on film.

Betsy and Toby called Joe Delany on his cell phone and gave him a detail of what had happened. They had no proof but their instincts told them what had just occurred. Delany agreed and gave them the go ahead to breach the apartment under the guise that the FBI agents believed they had witnessed a kidnapping of a minor while acting on an anonymous tip. When the door burst open and both agents entered the apartment they found the child cowering naked against the headboard of the bed while the senator in his shirt and socks showed the child his erection, which rapidly deconstructed but not before Betsy had it on her cell phone video.

Under instructions by Delany, Betsy took charge of the girl, let her dress while they waited for the return of the woman who had brought the child. The senator was cuffed and shackled on the floor exactly as he had been when they went in; naked from the waist down, his wrinkled butt getting scratched by the rough carpet and his flaccid prick next to a puddle where he had peed. Toby had spent his time tricking the stupid pedophile into a confession while still confused. He made sure the senator was Mirandized not once, but twice so that the confession would not be debased by a shyster in a $5,000 suit. When the madam showed up to get her child she was arrested, as were two men in the van.

The arrest, confession, and conviction of Senator Archibald Mason rocked the establishment and sent shockwaves through the nation. A Chinese child enslavement and prostitution ring was uncovered and a list of prominent as well as common men were arrested and convicted of a series of felony charges that assured their incarceration. Nothing much could be done about the Chinese organization, as most of it was in Shanghai and out of reach. About thirty girls of ages ten to fifteen were rescued from a house in Virginia, but only an elderly couple who were in the house was captured and charged together with the madam and her flunkies. On a happier note, Archibald's cellmate turned out to be none other than ex-Congressman Terry Taylor. Everyone thought they made a lovely couple.

* * *

Marco and Patricia were married in Sarasota in a Catholic ceremony at their home just a week before their daughter was born. Ian Carlo, his wife Helena, their daughter Teresa, and Ian Carlo Jr. were there for Marco, and Francisco gave away the very pregnant bride. M&M was there with Amiable Manning, and Leon Goddard with his wife. The Goldmans and spouses, Matilde, Luigi, Pete, and José were there, and Major Allen played the double role of guest and head of security. Joseph Delany Jr. came with his wife. He was being considered for office in his native state of Delaware and for deputy director...of the CIA.

NOT THE END

The Carducci Trilogy is like a trinity, three independent events but one integral story. Don't expect infallible heroes of mythical dimensions, here men and women have failings and strengths that guide them through a maze of improbable events and take the reader around the world in pursuit of personal and global redemption, not of an immortal soul but of the integrity of our humanity. Violence, adventure, love, lust and hate play leading roles while they inhabit a variety of individuals whom you will love, or love to hate.

BOOK TWO - THE CARDUCCI CONNECTION

A plan to kill hundreds of thousands of Americans is brewing in the Middle East, Cuba and Venezuela. The CIA doesn't know if they're confronting nations or individuals. They know it's happening, but without solid proof they cannot act. It's up to the Carducci, and a network of unconventional friends and enemies, that come together to help them stop this abomination before it sinks the United States, Colombia and other countries into chaos. Again, as in *Book One - The Carducci Convergence* good and evil are not clearly defined and only the essence of integrity, loyalty and honor may save the day. Love, intimacy and violence share the pages with a fast moving development of events. All this takes place while the original economic solution proposed by Marco Carducci in *Book One* accelerates.

BOOK THREE - THE CARDUCCI REDEMPTION

The God Machine that so many have feared makes its appearance in this fast moving thriller where the intentions of powerful individuals and organizations collide pursuing the ultimate power. The Carducci enter the fray by chance but that does not impede their total involvement in order to detain a ruthless cabal capable of destroying all we hold dear; our liberty, our nation and our right to live in the pursuit of happiness. The Carducci find redemption in the exercise of good rather than the divorce from lawlessness. Here they reach the apex of what the *Carducci Convergence* and *Carducci Connection* foresaw.

Learn where to buy print or electronic copies of all three books at:
www.carduccitrilogy.com

BONUS! SNEAK PEEK...

THE CARDUCCI CONNECTION

Book Two of the Trilogy
By Nicolas Olano

1

Red MacAlister was at the controls of an MQ-9 Reaper, the most lethal of the drones deployed by the US in Afghanistan. The silent plane flew along a mountain ridge a couple of hundred miles west of Kabul heading for a hamlet close to Dangam. The target had been illuminated by a CIA asset on the ground using a T-303 laser gun from about a half-mile away. As soon as the sensors on the drone perceived the point of heat the firing resolution program went into gear and the weapons operator sitting next to Macalister saw and heard the acquisition.

"Target acquired."

"Systems go, repeat systems go."

"Acknowledged, systems go. Deploying weapon."

Gunnery Sergeant Mary Helen Doolittle pressed the green button on the joystick and half way around the world an AGM-114 Hellfire missile ignited and shot towards land, reaching almost a thousand miles-per-hour in seconds. Through satellite imagery the CIA officer sitting in a closed operations room in Langley saw the building and the adjoining compound disappear in a bright light that momentarily blinded the sensitive camera. A minute passed and the ruins of the target became clear; only devastated rubble was left of the building and an electronic signal from the asset on location confirmed that there were no survivors and that the two vehicles in which the four men had arrived were on fire. Mission accomplished. Abu Hafs al-Najdi, also known as Abdul Ghani, a Saudi Arabian terrorist high up on the most wanted list was confirmed entering the building minutes before the missile obliterated it. His death was to be attested by local sources, but confidence was high that the man and his entourage were dead.

Insignificant to the CIA or any other three-letter-agency a young man of twenty years of age, Ramses Al Zarahni, also met his death together with the other three Saudis that were there with local insurgents in an effort to coordinate action against the US forces in the area. His presence in the house was later confirmed by a single finger found among the rubble.

A few days later Safi Al Zarahni was sitting in a domed room of her home in Riyadh, South Arabia, darkened by mourning curtains over the windows and thinking about the only thing she could think about; how to reap vengeance upon the great Satan who had deprived her of her only child. All she knew was that he was killed by a drone attack on a building near Dangam, Afghanistan where he was with close friend and mentor Abu Hafs al-Najdi. She didn't know if his body had received burial according to the precepts of the Koran or if he had fallen in the hands of the infidels, or worse in the hands of the dogs of Islam that had stooped to serve Satan. Her husband a banker who prospered greatly from his childhood friendship with three princes of the Royal Saudi Family had other wives and more male children. He mourned Ramses but he had consolation in his other boys. He was always busy with branches of his bank all over the Middle East and North Africa while she had nothing but emptiness in her soul. Even the prosperity and great wealth of her family did not assuage the pain. Ramsey was the light of her life and now that light was forever doused. As a child, her son had danced in the streets when the martyrs had downed the towers of evil and was whipped for this by a Royal guard. From that day on he had dedicated himself to the cause of Islam and the eradication of Satan's influence among the Arab world. He hoped to die a martyr, but not like a dog in the mountains of Afghanistan.

Kemal Al Zarahni was in no good mood himself. It had been hard to recuperate from the loss of nearly two billion dollars taken from several branches of his bank. Even though the Sheik Faruk had backed him up and taken about half of the loss, it was still a setback. The cash had been deposited in each branch in bricks of one hundred thousand dollars and integrated into the flow of his organization going to public and private entities as the many transactions, from travel money to auction purchases, demanded the most desired currency – the US Dollar. In trickles and rushes the money was laundered and credited accordingly to accounts all over the world. But not this time; in just hours nearly two billion dollars had disappeared leaving no trace of where it went, the records of the transactions a muddle of numbers without significance. IT engineers, hackers, programmers, you name it had tried and failed to trace the destination of the funds. The real clients had to be credited and so it had been…but the hurt was deep. He knew that the inflow of dollars would not stop, could not stop, but now he had to hire an army of clerks to do everything manually; transfers, confirmations, credits and debits, all redundant to assure security. Watchers, and watchers to watch the watchers, that was his headache and for now nothing could be done about it until the IT people could come up with a secure program…but who could trust it. Weren't they all sure that what they had before was secure? And now two billion dollars later they had no idea. Now he had a dead son and an inconsolable wife to bear with. Why would Allah burden him so?

* * *

Sheik Faruk Al-Enezi contemplated the upheaval that the loss of eight-and-a-half billion dollars had brought down on his organization. Yet he thanked Allah that Edward Meredith the President of the Meredith Conglomerate, the conduit of most of the cash he laundered, had responded with about half the loss and he, together with the banks had shouldered the rest. The clients had not lost a cent. They only suffered delays, but every penny had been eventually credited in immaculate condition to the myriad accounts of final destination. They had lost only about a third of the cashflow as the people that needed the laundering had hedged their bets and used alternative means of cleansing the money. The one good thing that had come out of this was that the rates had gone up; eventually they would recuperate their money and then some. The need for legitimizing assets was growing as the world's bureaucracy grew and with it the graft that makes it move.

* * *

Edward Meredith had always been a second fiddle to his mother. Her overpowering personality and her eternal willingness to criticize him on every count had snuffed his personality and weakened his character, but since she was murdered and with the invaluable help of her murderer Edward had grown out of his pusillanimity and headed with authority the huge enterprise that was his conglomerate of companies related to agriculture and mining with tendrils into many other ventures that required verticalization of resources...shipping, railroads, trucking, building, etc. Yet, the two greatest enterprises in which his mother had excelled had suffered hard blows. The sub-rosa land acquisition all over the third world with eyes on cornering fresh water sources for immense plantations of sugar cane, soy and palm oil, had been handicapped by leaks to the governments of those countries, and then the most profitable business, the laundering of assets for a considerable stable of politicians, bureaucrats, military contractors, mafia families, charitable organizations and drug cartels, had been brutally attacked by hackers to date unknown and eight-and-a-half billion dollars had disappeared into thin air from the banks that Sheik Faruk Al-Enezi used to launder the cash. The problem had been solved by paying up. He, Faruk and the banks took the hit and changed the way of doing business and the show went on. Oh! How he missed Cardinal Dupree, the man was a genius. With the help of that crazy Monsignor of his all the insubordination that had appeared after his mother's death vanished. One dead executive and two more scared shitless had done the trick. Nowadays it was "Yes, Mr. Meredith," "Whatever you say Sir," and so on. He was smart enough to listen to the qualified executives that his mother had placed in key positions and managed the behemoth with efficacy if not brilliance.

2

M&M sat in the living room of his villa overlooking Lake Lugano in the Ticino Canton of Switzerland where an Italian lifestyle permeated with panache the orderly land of cuckoo clocks. He was thinking about his family, a most recently acquired family, but close to his heart none the less. Marco Carducci and his lovely wife Patricia had received him into their intimate circle. A circle that few could reach; the super-private life of a group of multi-billionaires who didn't give a damn about money and yet amassed incalculable wealth in order to deflect the self-destructive spiral of economic delusion in which the world was drowning. Marco, and his cousin Ian Carlo de la Rosa, had withdrawn from the Carducci Crime Family created by their late uncle Salvatore di Dio Carducci who in his time had used his ill-gotten wealth to build an empire of legitimate businesses and, together with Patricia's father, Francisco Lujan, the world's greatest and most profitable money laundering machine ever conceived.

M&M as Marcelo Mastroianni Mascerano preferred to be called was remembering the convergence of chaotic and fortuitous events that had launched Marco and Patricia into each other's arms and brought together their immediate families and an eclectic group of allies into an economic and intellectual force that was changing the world. He counted himself among those allies. He knew perfectly well that if anyone was significant in that group it was he himself, the world's greatest fixer, who previously only served the highest bidder and in his time toppled governments, eliminated cartels, planted or recuperated incriminating evidence and plowed the way for the rise and fall of world leaders...all at a reasonable price, of course. Now money was no longer a factor in his life. There was too much of it. All he wanted if that was the case, but when you have it all, unless you are deranged, it's not significant any more. You only want to spend what you cannot buy in the best way possible...time. As he ruminated on these thoughts Amiable Manning, former homicide detective of Kansas City, Missouri, and now his live-in partner and lover walked in carrying a bottle of 1987 Chateau Cheval Blanc and two glasses.

"Welcome treats, you and that bottle," said M&M. "I was just thinking about the day we met at Marco and Patricia's home. Momentous occasion in more than one way"

"It seems like a lifetime ago and like it was yesterday," said Amiable setting the bottle and glasses on coasters. "I could have never foreseen all this that day. It's a miracle you survived that craziness."

"You know...the attack, Pete's injury, the trip to the house with that lunatic at the helm, they're all blurred, yet I remember that tarpon I lost like it was just now that it happened. That's what's crazy!"

"You've played that moment back in your mind and told me the story so many times that I kind of expect that fish to materialize out of thin air at any moment!" laughed Amiable

"Well, Cheers!" said M&M raising his glass. "Tomorrow all the Carducci's and De La Rosa' will be here so it should be a few interesting days. Marco has some new ideas that he doesn't want to discuss over the phone and we will help Ian Carlo relocate here in Lugano. It looks like he's got to be away from New York for a spell now that Tommy Liguria is the big man of the Carducci family. From what I hear, and I hear plenty, Tommy is doing everything that we told him and all the other families are happy with things as they turned out; the results are impeccable. He acquired the trust and respect of the crews, the cops, the politicians and the bureaucrats so it's smooth sailing in the foreseeable future, but time will tell..."

"I wonder if they're bringing Pete along," said Amiable. "I haven't seen him since that time. Have you heard how he's doing?"

"Yes and yes; he will be here with the Carducci and he is doing fine. He's recuperated most of his mobility in the right arm and the pain is practically gone. I also have some news for Marco and Patricia. I know they won't like it, but it's something they must know."

"Which is...?" asked Amiable.

"I'll tell you all together. It makes no sense to tell this tale twice. It will lose luster the second time around and I love to tell mystery, mysteriously!"

"Wow this wine is wonderful...I've never tasted anything like it," said Amiable enthusiastically, to the delight of M&M who enjoyed giving his partner the life he never dreamed of having when he was plodding the streets of Kansas City in search of the sad perpetrators of horrid crimes.

"It is one of the most outstanding Bordeaux wines of that year, but somewhere in the wine cellar I have a few bottles of the Cheval Blanc of 1947 that must be consumed soon or it may decay. It is arguably the best Bordeaux ever made. We must have a very good reason to celebrate for us to cork one of those."

M&M sipped the wine and looked at Amiable who was standing by the window staring out onto the lake that reflected moon and stars only faintly diminished by the distant lights of the city of Lugano. Amiable who had been a great detective in Kansas City was now a top asset to his operation and had gained respect for his attention to detail and his ability to extract the truth from a muddle of information. Amiable was not only his life partner now, he was an investigator with M&M's special services.

3

On the other side of the world sitting in a high backed rattan chair Senor Fortunato Bernardes was drinking a strong cup of exquisite Malayan coffee roasted and ground just minutes before its aromatic soul was extracted by boiling water poured into a French press and served to the master of Palmeira, the Portuguese style villa in the mountains above Dili in the island nation of Timor Leste or as the British call it "East Timor."

Don Fortunato formerly known as Cardinal Jean Dupree of the IOR, which stands for Institute for Religious Works and is better known as The Vatican Bank, observed from his comfortable seat the morning exercises that Enrico Testa did with all the personnel of the villa. No one under the age of 60 was excused; then the able-bodied and most athletic trained in martial arts of several schools, Japanese, Korean, Israeli, Brazilian and American origin, but concentrated on the Okinawa school of Go Yu Ryu which Testa favored. Soon the exercises would include weapons training with the lethal Malayan Sword at which these people were experts having used them in hand to hand combat against Indonesian forces during the revolution for independence. Then would come training in a series of firearms, light and heavy, including RPGs and mortars. Neither Testa nor Dupree could think of what their little army could be used for, but they did know that it was much better to have them than not. He listened to the raspy voice of Testa counting the moves of the first Kata...Ichi, Ni, San, Shi, Go, Roku...one, two, three, four, five, six...repetitive and rhythmic as the song of two women who sang verses of victory and strife in the background. The rasp in Testa's voice and the empty socket of his left eye were the remnants of his last encounter with Patricia and Marco Carducci.

* * *

The Bombardier 6000 approached Agno-Lugano Airport after almost nine hours of continuous flight over the Atlantic Ocean. It had departed McAllen International in Sarasota, Florida the day before at 6:00 p.m. and estimated touchdown at 8:45 a.m. local time. Aboard were Marco Carducci, his wife Patricia, their daughter Angela, Ian Carlo de la Rosa, his wife and his two children, a teenage girl, Teresa and an eight month old son, Ian Carlo Jr. They were accompanied by Marco's bodyguards Pete Morelli and Luigi de Tomaso both of whom were linked to their boss by surviving together several attacks on Marco and Patricia's lives. Patricia's long time bodyguard Jose Garcia was also along and to his capable and rapid reflexes Marco owed his life. In Lugano they would have the added security of M&M's big, scary guards. Finally there was Felicia the children's nanny who was a niece of Matilde who cooked for the Carducci at the Sarasota home. For the meetings that would take place in the next days they would be joined by Francisco Lujan, Patricia's father and by Samuel Goldman, attorney at law and full-time advisor to Marco and Ian Carlo. He would be flying in from London with Francisco.

While the copilot was having breakfast in the small crew lounge behind the cockpit Marco had taken his place; a fully ticketed pilot he was expertly handling the approach to the airport over Lake Lugano but a couple of miles out he handed the controls to the experienced pilot in command, an ex-Air Force Captain with hundreds of cross Atlantic flights under his belt. Marco still needed practice time on the big plane and he was not going to get it with his family on board. The touchdown was flawless and the Bombardier taxied to the main building. Immigration and Customs were handled with Swiss efficiency and in less than a half hour the group was meeting with M&M who in the company of Amiable Manning received them with the security entourage and several limousines for the short ride to his villa. On the way Amiable and Patricia chattered away like gossipy teenagers while M&M, Ian Carlo and Marco discussed accommodations. M&M had rented a furnished villa with a full staff less than a mile from his own so that Ian Carlo, his family, the entourage of bodyguards and Samuel Goldman could stay in comfort while Marco, Patricia, their daughter and Francisco would be his guests at La Giostra, his villa, which means the carrousel in Italian.

While travelling in a luxury private jet is definitely not taxing on the passengers, the morning was used for long showers, change to adequate clothes for the Alpine weather and dealing with a pissed off Angela who did not enjoy the different time zones. By noon Francisco and Samuel had been brought from the airport and by 1:00 p.m. everybody was at La Giostra for a family lunch. M&M was particularly proud of this moment because it was the first time he hosted a family affair in all his life. Everyone who considered him family was here. It was a memorable occasion and for such he had bought in the best chefs from Milano and Geneva to cook during their visit. An extra nanny had been hired for the time the Carducci were in house and Angela was, at last, sleeping peacefully next to Ian Carlo, Jr.. M&M was at the head of the table flanked by Patricia and Helena, Ian Carlo's wife, and at the other end sat Amiable Manning next to Teresa, Ian Carlo's daughter and Samuel Goldman. The rest, including Luigi and Pete, for whom M&M had great affection, were in between. M&M stood with glass in hand and addressed all for a toast.

"Welcome to your home in the Alps. Amiable and I have been looking forward to this day and your presence brings joy to La Giostra."

They all raised their glasses and sipped appreciatively the magnificent Bondola wine native to the region and very, very rare in a good vintage. A cream of cantrell mushrooms and chestnuts was followed by a white risotto from local grown rice that is unique to Lugano. It has a variety of local cheeses in it and the flavor is indescribable. Slow-cooked lamb shanks in romaine and sage, and a salad of wild greens completed the faire. Chocolate soufflé was by Patricia's special request. After lunch all the guests went off for a nap because no matter how comfortable the flight, the body's clock goes off keel for at least a day. Later that evening Marco and M&M discussed their plans for the next few days of meetings about the effect and results of the loans that they had made with the money "rescued" from Meredith and his cohorts and about Ian Carlo's temporary relocation. M&M told Marco two things, one, that Joseph Delany was in Switzerland and wanted to meet with them and two that there was an important matter that affected them all and that he would like to have as first thing in the morrow's agenda. It referred to their old enemy Cardinal Dupree. Marco asked for more specifics but M&M declined, alleging that it was for all to know and discuss together.

"So, can we tell Delany to meet us here?"

"Yes, but when Ian Carlo is not present. He is still reluctant about cops. Also he wants to keep his whereabouts secret from everybody but us and Tommy for the time being. Make the arrangements but let's make it a short visit, OK?"

"I think this won't be a problem. He told me he only has a few hours and has to be back in Basil."

* * *

Joseph Delany Jr. late of the FBI was getting accustomed to his new job as Deputy Director of Covert Affairs of the Central Intelligence Agency officially known as The Science and Technology Division. While in the FBI Joseph recognized the agency's compass that, while not static, had a distinguishable divide between right and wrong. The CIA is, by necessity, Machiavellian in its outlook. The

United States of America is a target of choice for the maleficence of nations, hoodlums, terrorists and fanatics; in most cases all rolled into one. The most maligned organization of our nation, the CIA is single-handedly responsible for much of the peace and liberty that we enjoy. Decades ago some bureaucrats prided in manacling the agency and one of the prices we paid was 9/11; never more. The CIA always navigates in a hostile environment. It cannot act within the US and must use every wile and trick to safeguard us from outside because our enemies play by no rules, have no mercy and are always vigilant waiting for us to drop our guard.

After some months of intensive training Joseph was dropped into the world of covert affairs by joining two field agents in the pursuit of a Swedish billionaire whose hobby of preference was to finance terrorist organizations in South America. Erik Janssen lived in Basil, Switzerland because he did not like the taxation of his native country. He was a miser who inherited a monstrously big portfolio of stocks in exchanges through Europe and America. He had doubled and then doubled again his holdings and now his annual income exceeded a billion dollars. He spent most of his time trying to avoid taxes and the rest of it giving money to organizations of "freedom fighters" such as FARC, Shining Path, ELN, Tupac Amaru and more. His money financed part of the FARC drug cartel whose product ended up in the streets of Europe and America and supported the assassination squads of Shining Path that protected the coca plantations of Peru. A real philanthropist!

Delany was handling two agents that had managed to infiltrate the circle of "friends" that the Swede received in his home. One was a young man originally from Ecuador and the other a girl of Colombian extraction. Both were posing as envoys from a small town in the border between Colombia and Ecuador and were trying to get the Swede to support their emancipation from the Colombian and US forces that sprayed their plantations with deadly chemicals. They expected Janssen to direct them to his FARC contacts and work from there to dismantle his network. After weeks of café meetings and pleas for help the Swede came through with the first act of solidarity with the two supplicants; he paid for their lodging in a small apartment in the outskirts of Basil. To that effect he had opened a bank account to which the two agents had access and covered their basic needs while Janssen thought about the best way to help them.

Sitting and waiting was not Delany's strong point, so jumping slightly outside of the CIA's resources and protocols he used the information of that bank account to get Francisco Lujan's organization to follow the money. Francisco Lujan, Carducci's twice father-in-law had the most efficient and sophisticated spyware outside of the NSA. Using the front of a "Call Center" in Bogotá, Colombia he leached information on everything from the great listeners; The NSA, MI6, The Russian Secret Service and The Brazilian Security Agency among others. He was secretly connected to the mainframes and networks of the world's financial system and to the super-secret information center of The Institute for the Works of Religion, commonly known as the Vatican Bank. With the Chinese it was hit and misses as they were as slippery as he. Following the electronic transfers that fed the account set up for Delany's agents, Francisco was able to detect and download the information from an account in San Marino that apparently sustained thirty accounts throughout Europe. Presumably these were the accounts of subversive elements from South America who were there only to solicit support from a variety of strange sources who, for even stranger reasons gave money to these criminal organizations.

Within a week Delany had in his hand a map of the financial network of South American subversion beneficiaries and benefactors. He took this information to his boss and had the common sense of giving most of the credit to the field agents and to his predecessors. Touchdown! Delany showed that he was a team player and that brought him to the attention of the DCI who had herself been a handler of agents in that part of the world and therefore received a fair share of the limelight of success. Nobody questioned Joe's source. What to do with the information was another task altogether. It was a decision that required lots of thought. The easy thing would be to shut the Swede down but that produced only a short time effect and soon the network would be up again but much more secretive and difficult to trace. No, this information had to serve a higher purpose. He had to meet with M&M and Francisco as soon as possible. He had an idea but he needed them to make it work.

* * *

Marco had a poor night; he woke up at midnight and had trouble going back to sleep but Patricia slept well after doing some yoga and meditation before going to bed. The evening meal had been light and Marco looked forward to breakfast, hot chocolate and the best bread in the world. By nine Ian Carlo and Samuel joined them and with coffee in hand they began the meeting that was immediately addressed by M&M

"We have a bit of a mystery on our hands. Apparently Cardinal Jean Dupree is unaccounted for. The official version, as you may remember is that he was in a Carthusian Monastery north of Barcelona, but sources close to the Vatican tell me that he is not there. In fact they have no idea where he is. Since there are no criminal charges, the Church closed the book on him."

"I would prefer to know where that priest is," said Patricia. "Wherever it is I can guarantee he's up to no good."

"True, but so far there has been no sign of him. But there is more to this mystery. When I was trying to track him down, I also looked for Testa." M&M paused for effect. "As far as the government of the United States is concerned Enrico Testa does not exist, has never existed and there is no record of him in the Vatican either."

"How can this possibly be?" asked Samuel Goldman who still had some vestige of innocence in him.

"I don't know, but we'll find out," Francisco said with anger in his voice. "As long as those two are unaccounted for they are a danger to Marco and Patricia."

"Believe me I tried" said M&M. "Amiable used every trick in the book and it's as if Testa had been a figment of our imagination. This afternoon when Delany gets here it will be the first thing that I'll ask him. Now that he's a big shot at the CIA he has to have access to this information."

"If that cop is coming I'm taking a powder," said Ian Carlo in a very old vernacular. "I know he's a friendly, at least while he needs us, but a cop is always a cop. Present company excluded," bowing his head towards Amiable.

"Oh, don't mind me…it's true what you say…I still get the itch sometimes," said Amiable smiling.

"OK, if there is nothing more we can do about those two right now I would like to bring you up to date on what's happened with the money we lent out. The initial figure was eight-billion-three hundred-and-thirty-five-million US dollars, and we generated close to eight-hundred-thousand small loans and kept a reserve of five-hundred-million-dollars. The first interest payments were due last month and the results are as follows. ninety eight percent of the payments were on time and complete. One percent requested justifiable extensions and we have a one percent default, mostly from Equatorial Africa because of war and natural disasters. I guarantee that these are better figures than any lending institution anywhere. The analysis group that we hired from the University of Pennsylvania at Wharton estimates that the money generated three-point-five-million jobs in the first stage, including the beneficiaries of the loans. By the time the cycle is complete there should be an excess of six-million jobs generated and a ninety eight point three percent of the capital paid back with earnings of one point six percent which in general terms is a breakeven, not considering the immense social benefit."

"Has the Board been informed?" asked Francisco.

"Not yet, I just got the figures myself. The delay was from the reports from Africa, but the checks and balances we did show that it is reliable information. One more thing; about eight percent of the loans were paid back in full by the first installment date." Marco looked at his papers and said, "The report to the Board will be ready for our next meeting. Until then I don't want this information flying around for obvious reasons."

The Board is a loose organization of very wealthy people, multi billionaires in fact, who have the common goal of increasing the middle class everywhere for the simple reason that they need the consumers for their own products and oppose those who, like Meredith, want to corner wealth to extort humanity, which was, for different reasons, the goal of the now vanished Cardinal Jean Dupree.

Samuel Goldman continued with his report. "The IPO of Scorpio Investments and Enterprises which accumulated all the US assets of the entity previously known as Carducci Enterprises has been completed successfully. A hundred percent of the offered stock was purchased at twenty eight percent higher than the original offering price and now is re-selling at thirty three percent higher. The Chairman and CEO of Scorpio is Leon Goddard and a board of directors has been appointed. Twenty-five board members in all who represent a wide spectrum of investors. The IPO of the assets in Canada and other countries will take place a month from now and we expect equally satisfying results."

"How much of that was bought by members of the Board?" asked Francisco.

"Roughly fifty two percent, but through many different entities."

"So we keep control," said Patricia

"Yes, and I expect the same will happen with the Canadian IPO," answered Samuel.

The discussion went on beyond a light working lunch and finally, before the expected arrival of Joseph Delany the issue of Ian Carlo's temporary relocation was discussed.

"Tommy is living at the Third Avenue house because it's kind of symbolic and the crews needed a point of reference and that old house is the strongest image we have of the Carducci family," said Ian Carlo. "The Roslyn Estate was sold to one of our off shore corporations and it stays as is; just that it won't be used by anybody for a few months."

"How do you like the villa where you're staying?" asked M&M.

"Oh, it's just great; plenty of room and there is great Wi-fi plus an entertainment room keeps Teresa busy. The view is beautiful and it must be stunning in summer."

"It's available for six months and you can have it longer if needed. It belongs to a watchmaker from up north and he's busy right now with a contract for Armani."

"How far are we from Milano?" asked Ian Carlo, "I know Helena will want to do some shopping and she's been talking nonstop about the art galleries, museums, churches and plazas, to which I will be dragged, no doubt."

"One hour by car will have you at Via della Spiga where some of the main designer boutiques are. I can have a limo with a special guide and translator to go with you whenever you need. That will make your life much easier and you'll enjoy the city much more."

"Thanks, I'll take you up on that. Helena will be very happy. Only one more thing, can we hire this nanny for our stay. Helena and Ian Carlo, Jr. seem to be happy with her."

"Done, I'll make all the arrangements. Do you have anything else right now?"

"Hell no man, you've done plenty."

M&M looked at his ipad and checked something. "I've coordinated for local security through my group who, by the way are associated with Allen Security and so they have a full background on you and your family and the specific needs of each of you and the villa. You can discuss these arrangements with Amiable who has become very capable in this function."

"I'll need a hangar for my plane. It should be here Monday and accommodations for a crew of six will be needed. This is something our people can arrange and I will not bother you with that."

"No problem. I'll ask Fiorella, my PA to get in touch with whomever you indicate and they can do that.

"OK, I'm going back to the villa, just don't mention that I'm here to Delany."

* * *

Joseph Delany hung up his phone after calling M&M to cancel his meeting for the time being. A much more urgent matter claimed his attention. The two undercover agents that were on the Swede's case were found dead in their small apartment. Cyanide gas had been piped in from the adjoining apartment and they died in their sleep without ever knowing what happened to them. Their passports, when clued in by the Basil Police, triggered a notice to the Langley computers and minutes later Delany had been briefed in detail.

"Who notified the Police?" asked Delany.

"The neighbor on the other side felt faint and smelled the almonds and dialed 117. We were here in minutes and when nobody answered the door we broke it open and found them as you see" said the detective in charge. "Why is the US Embassy interested in these Colombians, may I ask?"

"They were persons of interest in an ongoing investigation into money laundering," answered Joseph, asking in his mind forgiveness from the young agents for the necessary lie. Later the Colombian Embassy would discreetly transfer the bodies to a US transport so that they could be taken back to Los Angeles where their families lived. Two more anonymous Stars on that sad wall in the CIA headquarters at Langley.

"Who lives in the apartment where the poison was piped from?"

"A college professor who's in Turin doing research for a week, he left three days ago. We spoke to him and confirmed with the museum. He's been there."

"Any clue as to who could have poisoned them?"

"A student that lives in the corner apartment at the end of the hall says she saw a Latino looking man knocking on the professor's door yesterday evening. He was carrying what she thought was a bottle of oxygen. We have a description of the man, but it's too generic to be of much use. She's with a sketch artist now and we'll see what they come up with."

"Please give me a copy when they are finished, maybe we can be of some help," said Joe. "Any signs of forced entry?"

"No, he must have had a key. The lock wasn't picked."

"Can I take a look in that apartment?"

"Sure, follow me."

The apartment was the twin of the one where the agents died but in reverse. Attached to the bedroom wall was a blue Oxygen tank with a tube going through the wall at floor level. It had a timing device that was set to go off at three in the morning, a time when the agents were sure to be sleeping. The tank had emptied enough gas into the other apartment to kill a hundred people. Whoever did this wanted to be very sure the kids were dead. "Kids, that's all they were," thought Joe.

"Everything has been wiped clean. There are no prints anywhere, not even the professor's, so it's going to be difficult if not impossible to identify the killer," said the detective. "But anything we get we will copy you on. Those are the instructions from up high."

"We are grateful sir. I'll leave you to your duties now." Joe said goodbye and headed for the stairs. As he was halfway down he thought of something and returned to the crime scene.

"Excuse me detective; is your fingerprint technician still here?"

Yes, they are just packing up to go, why?"

"If you bear with me, I would like to try something." Delany, followed by Detective Hartman went back to where the tank was. He asked for a glove and carefully pulled the tube out of the wall and asked the technician to dust the part that was inside the wall. Seconds later they had a perfect set of two fingerprints, an index and a thumb. "Dumbass," thought Delany. He took a photo of the two fingerprint cards and sent them to Langley for identification. Detective Hartman did the same with his offices and machines at both sides of the Atlantic started their search for the owner of those prints.

It was too late for Delany to go down to Lugano but he did re-schedule for the next day because this meeting was even more ur-gent than before.

* * *

Next morning before it was light Delany boarded the chartered Piper Navajo that took him in less than an hour to Lugano. M&M was at the airport to meet him and a little later they were having breakfast at the fixer's villa together with Marco and Patricia.

"So that's what I know as far as last night. It's too early in Lang-ley for someone to get on those prints, so now is a waiting game. If Langley or the Swiss get a hit we will have someone to track down, otherwise it's going to be much more difficult to tap someone for these murders, though I'm sure Janssen had them killed. He must have blown their cover somehow. That makes him a more dangerous man than just a financier of terrorists; as if that wasn't bad enough."

M&M had known about Janssen for a long time but had not pegged him for a killer. The man was a weird one, but he doubted he would have someone killed when all he had to do was cut them off. Somebody else must have knocked off the agents, and he was going to find out who, or rather Amiable was going to.

"Do you have copies of the fingerprints with you Joseph? Maybe we can find something"

"Before the CIA?" asked Delany with skepticism. But he pulled out his phone and forwarded the prints to a number M&M gave him.

"We'll see" said M&M while he dialed his office; he gave the person who answered fast instructions in low voice and hung up. "Maybe we'll be lucky and the Israelis or the Saudis have some-thing. I'm also tapping the Colombian Security Service. If they don't have anything, we'll fan out to others."

Delany thought that he was right in coming to M&M. He had proved himself capable of things far beyond the reach of your aver-age secret service.

"Director Delany, the financial map that we put together for you based on the Swede's San Marino account; has it been of any use?" asked Francisco who had just joined the meeting.

"Yes and thank you; it gives a clear picture of the players and the amount of money involved...and no, because it's very difficult to decide what to do with it."

"As we thought," said Francisco looking at M&M.

"Any advice?"

"Yes, do nothing until someone makes a significant move. We looked at the transactions and believe that the money so far is just to sustain the beggars in Europe while they come up with something that the financiers are willing to back. Just keep a tab on them and wait until a substantial amount goes to one of these destinations. Then you have to act fast because something big will be coming."

"Have you checked the movements of those accounts before and after the murders of your agents?" asked Francisco

"No" I've had my mind on the Swede and I haven't checked the rest of the accounts. But that is exactly why I'm here. I need to track these people from outside the agency. I think someone blew the whistle on our agents and I need to know who."

"Let's do that right now," said Francisco, typing rapidly on his tablet.

"In the meantime," said Marco. "What have you heard of our friends Dupree and Testa?"

"As far as I know Dupree is in some hellish monastery in Spain and Testa is locked up in some Department of Justice black prison or maybe Guantanamo. Once they took over I never looked back."

"Would it surprise you Joseph that the DOJ has no record of the existence of Enrico Testa, nor does the department of State," said M&M, "and the Church has no record of Dupree in any particular location? No matter how deep we looked there is nothing. Maybe you can find something out now that you are a bigwig at the CIA."

"God all mighty M&M, if you couldn't find them, then who can? I'll try but no promises."

"Try hard," said Patricia, her face hardened in resolve. "Those guys on the loose are very bad business."

For much more on the Carducci Trilogy,
and complete information on where you can get
each of these exciting thrillers, please visit:
www.carduccitrilogy.com

And to learn about our other books please visit:
www.storyartsmedia.com